The Weird Girl

CARLA DAMRON

Produced and printed by Stillwater River Publications. All rights reserved.
Written and produced in the United States of America.
This book may not be reproduced or sold in any form without the expressed, written permission of the author and publisher.
Visit our website at www.StillwaterPress.com for more information.
First Stillwater River Publications Edition

Library of Congress Control Number: 2025909798
ISBN: 978-1-965733-79-0
12345678910
Written by Carla Damron.
Published by Stillwater River Publications, West Warwick, RI, USA.

Publisher's Cataloging-in-Publication
(Provided by Cassidy Cataloguing Services, Inc.)
Names: Damron, Carla, author.
Title: The weird girl / Carla Damron.
Description: First Stillwater River Publications edition. | West Warwick, RI, USA :
        Stillwater River Publications, [2025]
Identifiers: LCCN: 2025909798 | ISBN: 9781965733790 (paperback)
Subjects: LCSH: Women social workers--Fiction. | Foster mothers--Fiction. | Teenag-
        ers--Drug use--Fiction. | Missing persons--Fiction. | Fentanyl--Fiction. | Drug
        traffic--Fiction. | Counseling--Fiction. | Secrecy--Fiction. | LCGFT: Thrillers
        (Fiction)
Classification: LCC: PS3604.A47 W45 2025 | DDC: 813/.6--dc23

Damron continues to braid social commentary with heartbreaking storytelling. *The Weird Girl*, the second in the Georgia Thayer series, is a fast-paced, page turner that holds a mirror to the deadly fentanyl crisis gripping our country. The result is something extraordinary: a sequel that somehow manages to exceed the prequel. This is fiction writing at its finest.

—Stephen G. Eoannou, author of The Nicholas Bishop Mystery Series

In *The Weird Girl,* Damron exposes the devastation of the opioid crisis and the ravages of slipping into its grasp. In true Damron style, she skillfully weaves this multifaceted story through the lives of her characters, setting them on a collision course that will have you turning the pages until your eyes give out... Damron has created a cast of authentic, multi-dimensional characters relatable to any reader. You cannot help but invest in their struggles... *The Weird Girl* is a riveting read that will fill you with outrage and hope in equal measure. It's a must-read!

—Catherine Matthews, award-winning author of *Releasing the Reins*

A riveting tale full of unlikely heroes you'll be rooting for until you reach the very satisfying conclusion.

—Libby Klein, author of the Layla Virtue Mysteries

The Weird Girl delivers thrilling suspense and startling twists as it delves into the dark world of drug dealers, teen addicts, human traffickers, blackmailers, and corrupt politicians. It also confronts our tendency to wrongly pigeon-hole folks like heroine Georgia Thayer as damaged just because they wrestle with mental-health issues. Yet Georgia's struggles help forge her brave resolve to face down villains no matter the cost. Author Carla Damron's nuanced, rich character portraits make this novel resonate beyond its explosive headlines. *The Weird Girl*'s lesson that human frailties can yield strength packs an unforgettable punch.

—Linda Lovely, author of the HOA Mystery series

Carla Damron has done it again, delivering her killer combination of characters as real and unflinching as the opioid crisis they're embroiled in, a gripping narrative laced with surprises, and an insightful examination of pressing social issues that proves as informative as it is wildly entertaining.

Like badass social worker Georgia Thayer herself, THE WEIRD GIRL is fiction on a mission, grabbing you by the collar and daring you to just try looking away.

-Rachel Stone, Author of THE BLUE IRIS

Dedicated to all who have been touched by opioids: those in recovery, those not yet in recovery, and family members who do their best. Also dedicated to law enforcement and service providers on the frontlines of this invisible war.

Acknowledgements

I am so grateful to the wonderful people who provide guidance, support, and commiseration as I bump along on this writing journey. Sending love to: Mary Jane Reynolds, Sheila Athens, Ed Damron, Libby Klein, Susan Morris, Lynne Curry, Stephanie Thompson, Catherine Matthews, Ashley Warlick, Linda Lovely, Scott Burditt, Linda Lawson, my eagle-eye husband, Jim Hussey, and the WFWA Write-Inmates.

A special nod of gratitude goes to Major Ricky Johnson, of the Richland County Sheriff's Department, who took the time to acquaint me with the dark workings of the fentanyl trade in my town.

One

TESSA DOUGHERTY PINBALLED THROUGH THE SEA OF KIDS DANCING TO Dua Lipa, desperate for an escape. The bass jackhammered against her skull. Too many bodies pressed against her, sweaty arms flailing, bony elbows jabbing.

Any unwanted touch brought back memories best kept buried.

As she squeezed between two wasted girls from her trig class, someone shoved her into the coffee table.

"Shit." She grabbed the sofa arm to steady herself. There, on that couch, her only friend Joel lay sprawled, eyes at half-mast, a dopey grin on his face. He'd driven Tessa here, so it looked like she'd be the one getting them home.

"Dance with me!" Cooper Hawthorne, the host of this disaster of a party, grabbed her hand. His orange Clemson polo matched his hair.

"No." She jerked from his grasp.

He stepped closer, his boozy breath hot on her face. "You know, Tessa, you're not bad-looking. Might help if you did something with that hacked-off hair of yours."

"Thanks for the beauty advice." She maneuvered away from him, squeezing between sweaty dancers and finally making it to the massive dining room. Everything about this stupid party sucked. The tacky, overdone house. The insane noise. All the idiots from her new school—kids that her foster mom Georgia wanted Tessa to like, but she couldn't, because she would never, in a million years, be like them.

The giant table held gouged-out avocado dip, mangled sandwiches, and an odd assortment of cookies. At the end lay an open Altoid tin holding a dozen small blue pills, the ones Cooper Hawthorne had freely handed out to everyone. Tessa had declined, but now . . . maybe she'd just take a little. Just to take the edge off. Just so she could stand these stupid people and this stupid party. She spotted a broken pill and popped the smaller portion into her mouth. Just a taste. It had to help.

Thirty minutes later, Tessa perched on the pool's edge, shoes off, her toes rippling the cool water. A fleet of candles tucked in plastic lotuses bobbed around her, their colors shifting like liquid light: sapphire, then green, then amber. The fronds of a palmetto tree rustled behind her. South Carolina loved its palmetto trees. Tessa did, too. She loved everything just then: the water, the sky, the way the night stretched endlessly above her.

Thank you, little blue pill.

Sara Clark stepped through the sliding glass doors and halted in front of the pool. Her skin shone like moonlight, her arms ballerina-thin, her usual silver bracelet gleaming on her wrist. She had long, glossy brown hair. Ridiculously beautiful, that hair. "It's like a waterfall," Tessa thought out loud.

Sara spun around. "Huh?"

"Your hair. It's like a waterfall. It's so . . . flowy!"

"You're shit-faced," Sara said. "Kinda thought you were smarter than that." She approached the white pool house near the gate and froze. She glared at the small structure, her mouth oddly open, then pushed through the door.

Tessa's phone dinged, and panic seized her. A text from her foster mother, Georgia. *Having fun?*

Tessa stared down at the tiny keyboard. Would Georgia know Tessa was stoned from her texts? She focused every brain cell on typing: *Yeah.*

Really? If you're not, I can come get you.

Oh, hell no. She concentrated hard on punching letters: *I'm riding back with Joel. Besides, aren't you at work?*

Sadly, yes. But I'll escape if you need me. Don't do anything I wouldn't do.

Yeah, that ship had sailed. Tessa clicked off the phone and prayed Georgia didn't decide Tessa needed rescuing after all. Georgia was new to the foster parent role and tended to overdo, well, everything.

Cooper wandered out, unsteady in his steps, his freckled face flushed. He rattled the Altoid can in front of her face. "Want some?"

The blue pills inside glowed like little jewels. She wanted to pocket them all. She could stay high till high school ended. "I better not."

"Suit yourself." Cooper shrugged. "You seen Sara?"

"Pool house."

"Thanks."

Tessa watched him enter the small building and shut the door behind him. A few minutes later, or maybe longer (time had lost all meaning), the door flung open. Sara stormed out, face bright red, her jaw clenched. Behind her, Cooper yelled, "Sara? Wait. Don't be like this."

Sara's voice cracked through the air. "Screw you, Cooper. Screw you and your whole screwed-up family!"

Loud. Sara was loud. Tessa could almost see the words in bright, bold text erupting from her mouth. Sara rounded the pool, arms pumping like she was doing laps, and headed toward the gate. Tessa stood up, wobbly at first as the world tilted. She caught up with Sara just as she reached the gate. "Hey! You okay?"

"I'm fine," Sara grumbled. "I just . . . I need some air. Just gonna take a little walk."

"I'll come with you?"

"No!" Her voice held a knife edge, then she added, softer now, "No thanks. I'll be back soon."

Tessa watched her unlatch the iron gate and disappear up the driveway. She spun around, only to find Cooper there, staring. Tessa studied him, his hair and his shirt, like he'd been built of clementines.

"Probably that time of the month," Cooper said with a smirk.

Tessa dropped into a lounge chair. The high buzzed through her, but underneath, a cold weight settled. Had this blue pill experiment just tanked her one chance at a decent life?

Two

LILY GRACE DUFFY SLIPPED OUT THE FRONT DOOR OF HER FAMILY'S modest bungalow, holding the doorknob to control the click. Her parents normally slept soundly—her mother's CPAP drowning out most other sounds—but she needed to be careful. Going out at this hour (or any time after dark) was forbidden, but tonight was definitely worth the risk.

Lily Grace wore black jeans and her favorite loose blue top. She'd taken in the waist of the jeans so they fit better. Her mom insisted she wear baggy clothes, but needle and thread (and wearing oversized sweaters around her mom) took care of that. At sixteen, she wanted her curves to show.

When the text arrived, inviting her to the party, she'd hopped out of bed. She rarely got invited to things—no, make that she never got invited to anything, but Ariel, the most popular girl in tenth grade, had sent out a group text that included Lily Grace. Perhaps it was an accident. Maybe Ariel didn't mean for Lily Grace to receive the invite, but it had come, and she wouldn't miss the party, even if it meant defying her parents and sneaking out so late.

She pulled the tube of lip gloss from her pocket and swiped it across her lips. She'd hurried to dab on mascara and blush before her hasty exit, and she wore her hair in a ponytail because she'd had no time to tame her unruly curls. She hoped she looked okay.

She used the flashlight on her cell phone to navigate the sidewalks. The party was at Cooper Hawthorne's house, about half a mile away, on the outskirts of Columbia. When cars passed, she ducked behind trees, not wanting to be seen. Besides, a young girl walking alone at night might be bait for predators. Her mom always warned her about predators.

Her phone's GPS guided her down Bryson Road. She knew from Instagram that Cooper's dad had built a giant home on a few acres out there and that Cooper had a swimming pool and owned a big black Labradoodle named Bear. He'd been dating Ariel, and they made the perfect couple. Both Instagram-beautiful, with slim bodies and white teeth, they walked the halls of Dreher High School hand in hand, kissing before parting to go to class.

Maybe one day, Lily Grace would have a boyfriend like Cooper, too.

No cars came down Bryson Road, and no streetlights lit her way. Party noises thumped in the distance: pounding bass, the rumble of voices. Overhead, a pearl of a moon gleamed among a spattering of stars, and she smiled, glad to be far enough from ambient light to see constellations winking in the night sky.

Two more moons appeared, lower, dead ahead. A car weaving up the road. Its headlights shone on another figure—a girl walking toward Lily Grace. Someone from the party? Behind the girl, the car continued to approach, faster now, swerving like the driver had no control. Rap music blared from its sound system, and a voice sang off-key from its open windows.

The girl started to run. As she came closer, Lily Grace recognized her: Sara Clark, Ariel's best friend, president of the drama club. The car continued its approach, weaving, the music rumbling in the night.

And then, the horrible thump of impact, a piercing scream as the car hit Sara and sent her flying. The car skidded against gravel, slid off the road, and nearly hit Lily Grace. She hurled herself into some bushes as the car smashed into a tree.

Then all was quiet.

She lay in the shrub, dazed, assessing her own body. Her limbs moved. Her head throbbed from hitting something. There were scratches on her arms from branches. But she was alive. She wasn't sure if that could be said about Sara.

Oh God, Sara.

Lily Grace stood on shaky legs, scanning the ground around her. She'd lost her phone when she flung herself out of the car's path. Dammit. She needed to dial 911.

Her chest throbbed from hitting a rock or something. Her hands bled from landing on twigs. She had to find Sara. She'd never forget the awful sound of the car hitting her, not in a million years. It echoed inside her and soured her stomach. After a few unsteady steps, she managed to get to the road. There was no movement from the car a few dozen yards away. Sara should be nearby.

There, by the cluster of pines. Lily Grace rushed to her, falling to her knees, using the faint moonlight to scan Sara's body. It was so very broken. An arm twisted in the wrong direction. Her leg askew. Her head tilted back and her eyes closed. Blood pooling beside her. The gash on her face—God. With a trembling hand, Lily Grace felt for a heartbeat. There. Faint, but there. She had to get her help.

She heard a voice—male, upset. Someone from the car talking on the phone?

"I didn't see her. I swear," he said. "No. I haven't called the ambulance yet. I should. I should call the ambulance." And then, "Bryson Road. Just up from the house."

A pause, and then, "Hurry, Dad. Please."

Cooper's voice? It was Cooper who'd hit Sara? He staggered out of the car and doubled over, vomiting on the shoulder. Who else was inside? She inched closer, but something told her not to let herself be seen. She'd always been good at hiding.

Someone lay beside the car—brown-skinned, thin. Familiar. Joel McCants, the nice guy who sat beside her in AP English, the one who sometimes talked to her (unlike everyone else). He moaned as he pulled himself up. "What happened?"

"We had an accident." Cooper wiped the vomit from his chin and stumbled over.

"An accident? Man, my head's spinning."

"You're drunk, dude."

Cooper had not checked on Sara. How could he not? Lily Grace glared, willing him to act. He hadn't even called for an ambulance, and

6

Joel looked like he needed one. She returned to where she'd landed, desperate to find her phone and summon help, but just then, another car flew up the road and screeched to a halt. The man who emerged had thinning blond hair and a pink face. He was larger than his son and dressed in khakis and a polo shirt. He rushed to Cooper and knelt beside him. "Son? You okay?"

"Yeah. But . . . Sara."

"Where is she?" Mr. Hawthorne demanded.

"I . . . haven't found her."

She's right over there, stupid, Lily Grace wanted to yell as Cooper pointed in her direction. Lily Grace ducked behind a shrub as Cooper's dad's flashlight cast a wide beam of light into the trees. When they found her, and Mr. Hawthorne illuminated her broken body, Cooper threw up again. "Is she alive?"

"Barely."

"Oh God. We have to get help."

"Shut up," the father commanded. "Just shut up."

They returned to the road, and he finally dialed 911. Lily Grace remained crouched behind a bush, unsure what to do.

"What . . . what happened?" Joel roused himself, looking and sounding like he was about to barf, too.

Mr. Hawthorne bent over him and whispered something. Cooper stood by his car, staring at the blood across the shattered windshield. Sirens howled in the distance. Good. An ambulance.

Cooper staggered over to his dad.

"You're both drunk. Jesus," Mr. Hawthorne said.

"I know, Dad. I didn't mean—we were just . . . And Sara—"

"Shut up. Just shut up. Let me think."

The sirens grew louder. Cooper wiped tears from his reddened face. Joel let out a groan.

"Cooper. Come here," Mr. Hawthorne ordered. Cooper complied. His dad slid a hand across his shoulder and said, "You weren't driving. The other kid—what's his name?"

"Joel McCants."

"Joel was driving. He's drunk. He doesn't remember. You gave him the keys because you knew you shouldn't be behind the wheel. You didn't know he was so out of it. You tried to get him to pull over, but he refused. It was Joel who hit Sara. You got it?"

Cooper looked confused. "No, Dad, I . . ."

Mr. Hawthorne planted hands on both of his shoulders and shook him. "You were not driving! Say it to me."

"I was not driving."

"Right. That's what you tell the police. It wasn't you, it was Joel. Joel hit Sara." He pushed Cooper away. "I can't afford to have our family name attached to something like this. Not now."

The flashing lights were the most welcome sight Lily Grace had ever seen. An ambulance, an EMT truck, and two sheriff cars screeched to a halt.

At least now, someone would help Sara.

Three

I WAS WORKING IN THE EMERGENCY DEPARTMENT ON A FRIDAY evening, trying not to obsessively check my phone for messages from my foster daughter Tessa. Since becoming her atypical, poorly qualified foster mom, I had found myself overly concerned about her safety, especially after all she'd been through. And she was at a party. In the country. With boys.

Tessa had a good head on her shoulders. I trusted her not to do anything stupid—it was others I didn't trust, but that had been a long-standing issue of mine.

Medical social workers like me don't typically work nights, but our hospital administrator had added evening shifts to our routine. Note: there were only two of us for the entire three-hundred-bed hospital, so there was plenty to do after hours, especially on weekends when the ER was full of people who'd made poor decisions. Tonight's caseload included a repeat offender—Mr. I'm-not-an-alcoholic-I-just-need-to-drink—and an attempted suicide whom I had sent to psych. Maybe this nighttime social work wasn't such a bad idea.

The head nurse approached me at the ER nurses' station. "Georgia? We have a teen coming in. Hit by a car. Looks bad."

"A teen?" Not Tessa. Not Tessa. "Where did it happen?"

"Bryson Road."

Shit. That was where the party was.

"You okay?" He looked at me with concern.

"Got a name?"

9

"The victim is Sara Clark. Age sixteen."

Christ, I needed to get my shit together and not panic every time some kid was in an accident. How did biological parents handle the stress without needing medication?

"We'll need to call the family if that hasn't happened already. They're well-connected," he told me.

Well-connected didn't mean the girl would get better treatment—Columbia General prided itself on taking care of all patients equally. But Administration would likely get involved and be a pain in our butts as we took care of her.

Two ambulances pulled into the ER bays, meaning two casualties. I hung back as the gurneys entered the building and let the medical team do its thing. The girl looked terrible. Splinted leg and arm. Head stabilized, face obscured by an oxygen mask and bandages. She wasn't conscious, which was probably a good thing. I tried to remember if Tessa had ever mentioned Sara Clark.

Dr. Romano, our new ER Chief Attending, barked orders as they wheeled her into a curtained-off room. From his tone and urgent body language, I knew the girl's situation was precarious. Person vs. car never went well.

When the second gurney entered the building, the young man half-lying, half-sitting on it was fully conscious and clearly upset. "How is she? How is Sara?"

His voice sent chills through me. I recognized him: Joel, Tessa's friend. Tessa's ride to that party. I hurried to him. "Hey, hey, calm down. Let the doctor take a look at you."

"Ms. Thayer?" His brown eyes, ringed with desperation, sought mine.

"Joel? Where is Tessa?"

"She's . . . not with me. Still at the party." He closed his eyes, tears squeezing out from the corners. "Oh God. Sara."

As they wheeled him into an exam area, I used my phone to text Tessa: *Joel is here at the hospital. Where are you?*

Waiting for an Uber, came her reply. *Is Joel okay?*

I think so. He's too upset to talk. I hesitated, unsure how much to disclose, then typed: *More when I get home. Get some sleep.*

Over the next thirty minutes, I stayed on the periphery as the medical teams took care of our patients. Joel had a broken arm and had to be sedated. Apparently, he had been on some substance when the accident happened, and he'd been the one driving. Bloodwork would tell us what he had taken. Sara was more complicated. Law enforcement had contacted her parents, who were on the way. Teens from the party streamed in, begging for information about Joel and Sara. There wasn't much we could tell them. This hospital was known for its emergency response and execution. We'd do our very best, but it didn't look good.

"Georgia? Can you come in here?" Dr. Romano asked.

He was a tall, spectacled man, with thick black hair and a flat nose, like someone had deflated it. I entered the curtained area where Sara lay. As they listed her injuries, I fixed my gaze on her face—too pale, around the swollen nose and lips. The bandage had been removed from her cheek, revealing pink, open flesh that would need plastic surgery if she survived. I shook my head. I'd seen a lot of horrible things in the ER, but the damage to this kid was savage.

"What do you need?" I asked Romano.

"Let me know when the parents get here. We're about to operate."

"FYI, there were drugs at that party. You might want to check her for substances."

"Terrific," he muttered. We'd seen the ravages of drug abuse in our ER a lot. Crack. Heroin. And lately, fentanyl.

A hubbub outside the examination area pulled us out of our focus. A frantic-looking couple about my age—Sara's parents, I presumed—arrived, asking to speak with Dr. Romano. The woman was thin, dressed in jeans and a sweater, her reddish-brown hair cut short and accenting high, delicate cheekbones. The man towered over her, silver-haired, broad-shouldered, his voice booming as he demanded information. Dr. Romano escorted them to a private waiting area to fill them in. Three others also arrived—a blond-haired older man in chinos and a polo shirt with two teenage boys. The older guy spotted me and approached.

"I'm Fletcher Hawthorne. These are my boys, Holden and Cooper. How's the Clark girl?" he demanded.

"We're doing everything we can," I said evasively. They weren't family and weren't entitled to the specifics of her medical situation.

"You have to," the younger boy said with an edge of desperation. "You have to help her."

"She's a friend of yours?" I asked.

"She came to my party. This . . . this shouldn't have happened." His voice broke.

The blond one placed a hand on his shoulder. "It's okay, Coop. She'll be okay."

If only that were true. I pointed to the larger waiting area. "You're welcome to have a seat. Sara's parents are talking with the doctor right now."

I hated this part of the job but knew Dr. Romano would handle the Clarks with sensitivity. He'd be gentle and honest, yet give them a thread of hope to hold. Families always needed that.

Fletcher Hawthorne sat with his boys in the more public waiting area, texting on his cell, the boys whispering to each other.

I busied myself with paperwork, but stayed close in case I was needed. My work got interrupted when the head nurse summoned me to take a call from Dr. Richard Lockhart, the hospital administrator. We call him "The Dick" because he is one.

"Media there?" he asked.

"No, sir."

"The Clark girl is the daughter of Charles Clark. As in Clark Foods. Multi-millionaire. Big funder of the hospital."

"Okay." I was probably supposed to act impressed, but honestly, rich people annoyed me. "We're taking excellent care of Sara, but she's in pretty bad shape."

"I know." The Dick sighed. "How about law enforcement? Are they there?"

"Not yet."

"Call me if they show. And if any reporters come. This thing may blow up." He sounded oddly excited, probably picturing his own fat mug on camera.

12

"Will do. But our focus is on Sara right now."

"Of course. Keep me posted."

I clicked off, praying the media wouldn't show up.

"Georgia?"

My flutter of panic returned at that familiar voice. Tessa stood there at the entrance to the ER, holding the arm of another girl—both completely soaked, wet hair dripping water on the floor.

"What's wrong? What are you doing here?" I hurried to her.

Tessa motioned me to a corner, coaxing the girl with her. My gaze fixed on the stranger. She looked pale and unfocused, clumsy, holding Tessa's elbow as though needing help with balance.

"This is Ariel. She was at the party. Something's wrong with her. She's acting weird. As in, she just walked into the deep end of the pool with her clothes on."

"Which is why you're both soaked?" I gave Tessa a thorough look-over. Besides being drenched, she looked okay. She kept looking away from me as though embarrassed.

Ariel swayed, grabbing the wall to help support her. "I don't feel so good."

I gripped her arm as she slid down, her butt plopping onto the floor. Her pupils had constricted to pixels.

"Can I get a gurney?" I yelled. An aide saw my situation and hurried over with a stretcher. Dr. Romano motioned to a resident to help me.

As Ariel was lifted onto the mattress, her head wobbled, and she threw up a liquid bile, just missing my shoes.

"Ewww," Tessa said, eyeing the puddle on the floor.

"Ariel? Look at me. Can you tell me your last name?" I asked.

She didn't answer.

"Blackstone," Tessa said.

I gave the girl a tissue to wipe her face. She moved in jerky, uncoordinated gestures. A nurse appeared and started taking her vitals.

I pulled Tessa away. "What did she take?"

Tessa shook her head. She wore an odd expression. Shock, I supposed.

"Be honest with me. Was there cocaine at the party? Pot?"

"Pot, yes. Didn't see any coke. And . . ." She glanced over at Ariel, who looked ready to toss her cookies again.

"And?" I demanded.

"I don't know. There were so many people. I hung out outside."

Right. I'd urged Tessa to go to that damn party, and she'd had a miserable time. "You did the right thing bringing Ariel here. Want me to get you a ride home?"

"I'll get another Uber. Can I check on Joel before I leave?" she asked.

"Sure. But let's get you into scrubs first." I figured Joel could use a friend. I led her to the staff lounge and found something for her to put on, depositing her drenched clothes in a plastic bag. Then I led her to Joel, surrounded by a resident, two nurses, and a silver-haired man wearing blue chinos and a pale denim shirt: Detective Lou Michaels.

Damn. Lou looked up, and I may have spotted a hint of guilt on his face. He had three inches on me, a lean telephone pole of a man. In the past year, I'd come to know him as a stubborn, highly dedicated cop. He'd also become one of my few friends.

"Detective." I stepped close to Joel on the other side of the gurney. "Are you questioning this minor without his parents?" I'd hoped that Joel had a little time before the police questioned him about the accident. Time for his parents to arrive and support him. Time to hire a lawyer. But Lou had his stupid notepad out and was asking Joel questions when the kid looked very altered.

"I wouldn't call it questioning, exactly." Lou offered one of his wry smiles. "Nice to see you, Georgia. Tessa."

Tessa hurried to Joel and bent over him. "You okay?"

Joel shook his head. "I busted my arm and a couple of ribs. They say I have a mild concussion. And . . . and they say I ran over Sara. I don't remember anything!"

The desperation in his voice touched my heart. I knew this kid. He was sweet. Kind. Not someone to get in trouble. Not someone to do something like this, except he had, thanks to whatever drugs or alcohol he'd consumed. I turned to the detective. "Lou? You're done here. At least until his parents get here."

He didn't look happy, nor did he look surprised. I cocked my head toward the door, and he exited. I wondered what other information he'd gotten from Joel. Would it count as a confession? Did this gentle, intelligent teen just kiss his promising future goodbye?

"What happened, Joel?" I asked. "Why were you in that car?"

His headshake was languid. He was a handsome kid—his skin a soft brown, eyes wide and puppyish, in that half-boy, half-man phase of adolescence. Smart, too, tutoring Tessa in trigonometry because her foster mom had the math skills of a toaster. I hated to think of him in this trouble.

"Cooper wanted to run up to the store for more sodas. I think more people showed up than he thought would. He asked me to tag along."

"But you drove?"

"I can't remember . . . So much is missing. I remember Cooper telling me to come with him, then . . . then it's a blur. I remember sitting by the car and waiting for Cooper's dad to show, my arm killing me. And my head." He looked over at the open curtain. "Then Sara lying by the road." His voice quaked. Tears welled in his eyes.

Tessa gave me a beseeching "Georgia, fix this" look, but I had no idea how to help.

"I wish I hadn't gone to that stupid party. And I talked you into coming, too. I'm sorry, Tessa."

"You're apologizing to me? When you're the one lying in a hospital bed?" She gave him a playful smack that elicited a brief grin. I was happy to see it.

"Joel, what kind of drugs were at the party? Did you take any?"

He winced.

"It's best that you tell me," I insisted.

"Pills. Blue ones. Don't know what they were."

Stupid. So stupid. All kids that age were, I supposed, but crap. I glanced over at Tessa. She looked okay. Scared, but okay.

"Are your parents on their way?" I asked Joel.

He nodded.

"Don't say anything to the police until they arrive. And make sure the nurses page me. I want to talk with them."

15

Four

FLETCHER HAWTHORNE SAT WITH HIS BOYS IN THE HOSPITAL WAITING room and considered his situation. The Clark girl looked bad. Real bad. If she died—Christ. No way he could let Cooper take responsibility for what had happened. He couldn't have the Hawthorne name attached to an event like that. It carried too much weight—opened too many doors. One teenage mistake would not shatter everything he'd built.

New voices echoed down the sterile hallway—Sara's parents. Fletcher should go have a word with them, but he didn't want to leave Cooper. He was a live wire, ready to spark. He might grab the closest police officer and confess everything. Fletcher's job right then was to be a father.

Other kids from the party began to show, gathering in anxious bevies, pestering hospital staff for news of their friends. A few anxious parents joined them, needing reassurance that it wasn't their child who'd been hurt. Fletcher didn't want to talk with any of them. The party had been at his house. The car that hit Sara—his. He was in no mood for some panicked mom to lodge accusations his way, even if they were deserved.

The social worker woman with long dark hair and stupid hippie shoes talked to another teen outside the door. Then she turned and stared at him, a pinched frown on her face. Holden noticed and shot him a questioning look. Fletcher shrugged.

When she came into the waiting area and marched right up to him, he stood, shoulders back. "Can I help you?" He kept his tone cordial, yet

16

commanding. He was the county solicitor, a member of the Hawthorne family, for Chrissake. He knew how to handle people like her.

"Interesting party you hosted tonight. We have another of your guests in the ER. She nearly drowned in your pool because she was stoned on who knows what. I'm just wondering what kind of supervision you and your wife gave this little shindig that brought us three casualties?"

"Excuse me?" He drew himself up, using his bulk like armor. Most people wilted under his shadow. She didn't.

"I'm asking because my kid was there. Tessa. I trusted that she was going somewhere safe, but clearly, I was mistaken." The woman stared him straight in the eye. Few dared to do that.

"Tessa?" Cooper looked up at the name. "Did she fall into the pool? Is she okay?"

"She's fine. It's Ariel who's getting checked out." The woman stooped in front of Cooper. "It would be very helpful if we knew what she'd taken. The little blue pills people took. What was in them?"

"Drugs? I don't allow drugs in my house." Fletcher almost lost it. His voice echoed.

Cooper's eyes darted to Holden, then down—a gesture Fletcher knew. Holden's wide-eyed innocence looked rehearsed.

"Cooper? Tell me what Ariel took," the social worker demanded.

"I don't know."

The woman shook her head. "Whatever it is, it's strong. Dangerous. I'll need to let law enforcement know."

Ice flooded Fletcher's veins. He couldn't have law enforcement searching his house. The headlines could crush his candidacy for state attorney general just as the campaign had entered its crucial last months.

He moved closer to the woman, letting his mass overshadow her. "No need. I'll tell them. I'll escort them there myself." He turned to his sons. "We need to have a come-to-Jesus discussion real soon."

Cooper looked appropriately horrified. Holden had the same perplexed expression he'd worn most of the evening. Who had brought drugs to that damn party?

"Detective Lou Michaels is here. I'd suggest you talk to him," the woman said. He detested her arrogance, but kept his expression neutral.

"Lead the way, Miss—"

"Thayer. I'm Georgia Thayer."

He'd make it a point to remember that name.

Five

LILY GRACE DUFFY ROLLED OVER AND PUNCHED THE PILLOW. SHE hadn't slept at all. After the ambulances took Sara and Joel away, she searched for her missing phone but never found it. She'd have to come up with a lie, and of course, Mama would be furious. Lily Grace deserved that fury.

Under the pillow, her hand gripped the bracelet. She'd found it beside the dark stain where Sara had lain and picked it up, recognizing it immediately: Sara's bracelet. Sara wore the silver bangle all the time. She'd want it back when she got better.

If she got better.

Lily Grace had stuck it in her pocket and walked home, avoiding streetlights, hiding from cars as they passed. Sneaking into the house had brought a flood of anxiety—if Mama or Dad caught her, she'd be on restriction until she turned sixty. Which she also deserved.

The clock read 7 a.m.—time for her to get up, fix the coffee, and start on breakfast. She'd rather bury herself in the sheets. All she could think about was the image of Sara lying on the ground. Broken, busted Sara.

And Cooper's father. Had he really blamed the accident on Joel? Was Joel okay? Was Sara alive? These questions played over and over in her mind. She should have talked to the police when they arrived, but then her parents would have found out what she'd done. Should she go to the police now? Was there some way she could tell them and not get grounded for the rest of her life?

She pulled back the covers and slid her feet to the floor. She always kept her bedroom neat: clothes tucked in the drawers of the heavy dresser she'd inherited from Grandma. Schoolwork stacked on the same desk she'd had since third grade—the Sharpie drawings of a dog still marring the desktop. The narrow bookcase with every Gallagher Girls mystery in the correct order. The arrangement of the room comforted her when so much else in her life was chaos. Like the chaos right outside the door.

She opened the door and stumbled down the hall to the kitchen, ignoring the boxes stacked by her parents' bedroom, the collected newspapers needing recycling, and the rack of clothes that no longer fit in Mama's closet. In the galley kitchen, she went to work on the dishes left in the sink, then tackled the clutter on the Formica countertops: groceries that hadn't been put away, empty cereal boxes, and an empty can of tuna that reeked. Why couldn't Mama bother to throw it away? No. She shouldn't think like that. Mama couldn't throw away anything. Dad said she couldn't help herself, and Lily Grace had to be sensitive about the issue.

Which was why she hated going into their bedroom. She wasn't allowed to clean in there. Couldn't touch the collection of shoe boxes, magazines, catalogs, and unopened packages from QVC. When Mama took food to bed, Dad would sneak the plates out when she fell asleep, but he never washed them. That was left for Lily Grace.

She heard movement. Mama emerged from her bedroom, wearing the pink fluffy robe that no longer fit across her middle. Mama's body was fluffy, too, which caused her to move slowly, shuffling up the hall, turning sideways to fit through the door. She reached Lily Grace and kissed her on the side of her head. "Good morning, love," she said, like she always did.

"Good morning. What do you want for breakfast?"

"Coffee. Toast. More coffee." She squeezed by the small table and dropped into the oversized armchair Dad had moved by the window. Lily Grace poured her coffee—cream with extra sugar—and handed it to her mother before working on the toast.

"Is Dad up yet?" Lily Grace asked.

"Up and gone. Had to go to the church to help with the charity drive." She offered a little shrug. Her brown hair, threaded with dull silver, hung too long and needed washing. Showers were hard for her, and Lily Grace always helped her climb into the tub so she wouldn't fall. As she got bigger, her balance worsened.

Mama used to go to church more often than Dad, helping with breakfasts for the homeless and Bible study. But not anymore. Now, she rarely left the house, and Dad did the church duties required of their family.

"What are you up to today?" Mama asked her.

The bread popped up from the toaster. Lily Grace put it on a plate with a jar of orange marmalade. "Bless your heart," Mama said in thanks.

"If it's okay with you, I thought I might ride my bike over to Tessa's house. We have a paper due on Monday, and I need her help." The lie tasted wrong, but what choice did she have? Maybe Tessa could advise her about going to the police without getting into trouble.

Mama grabbed her hand. "Just don't be gone too long. When your dad gets home, we need to have some family time. Maybe work on a puzzle or something?"

"That sounds like fun. We have that thousand-piece one you got for Christmas."

"Oh no, honey. I'm not that ambitious. But we'll find something. Can you get me more cream?" She held up her coffee mug.

Lily Grace obliged her but wished the half-and-half were skim milk, like the doctor had suggested. Mama would never lose weight if she didn't alter her eating habits, but that conversation always hit a brick wall.

"I'd better get dressed. I'll be back soon, Mama."

Six

TESSA AWOKE TO SOMEONE TAKING A DRILL TO HER FRONTAL CORTEX. At least, that's how she felt. She lay in bed and did a recap of last night's events. Sara's accident. Joel in the hospital. Ariel's tumble into the pool. There were gaps, too, which Tessa attributed to the little blue joy pill she'd stupidly taken.

Did Georgia figure out that Tessa had taken something, too? No, she'd been mostly sober when she got to the hospital with Ariel. The unexpected dip in the water had helped. She'd stayed on the periphery while Georgia helped Ariel. Georgia didn't have a clue that Tessa had been high. At least, Tessa hoped that was the case.

She threw on a robe and stumbled into the kitchen, where Georgia sat gripping a cup of coffee.

"Hey," Tessa muttered.

"Hey. You doing okay?" Georgia looked her up and down, assessing.

Sometimes, it was like Georgia could look right through her. "A little draggy, but it was a late night."

"Yes, it was." Georgia wore a peasant top over jeans. Odd that she was dressed this early on a Saturday.

"You hear from the hospital yet? Any news on Sara?"

"She's alive. That's what matters. Will need more surgery soon."

Tessa nodded. That Sara was alive was a miracle, but in her experience, miracles never lasted long.

Georgia stood and approached the coffeepot for a refill. "What do you want for breakfast?"

"Cereal's fine. I'll get it." Tessa grabbed the granola from the pantry and milk from the refrigerator while Georgia sipped her usual morning meal. Tessa often commented that she had more caffeine than blood running in her veins. Well, that and the medicines she took every day to keep her mental health stable. Georgia still heard voices, but not very often, and they didn't control her. Besides that and a few interesting quirks—like her plastic slinky collection (seriously—who over age six owns thirty plastic slinkies?)—she was one of the sanest people Tessa knew.

Tessa took a seat on a stool beside the kitchen island. She liked this room, though it was in desperate need of renovation. The wooden cabinets had been painted a half dozen times. The linoleum countertops looked nothing like the fancy granite ones she saw on home improvement shows, and the wooden floor could use refinishing, but she loved the wide windows that let in so much sunlight. Tessa was half-done with her cereal when a knock pounded on the back door.

Georgia looked surprised as she opened it. "Lou?"

"Hey, George. Sorry to bother you on a Saturday. Can I come in?"

Georgia stepped back, motioning him inside. He eyed Tessa and said, "Good morning."

Tessa waved her spoon at him. She didn't mind Detective Lou Michaels. He was one of only two men she trusted. The other, Elias Jasper, Georgia's best friend, owned the restaurant where Tessa worked. She'd be leaving soon for the lunch shift.

"Any developments from last night?" Georgia asked Lou.

"We went to the Hawthorne house. As expected, no sign of drugs. Someone probably flushed them." He helped himself to a seat at the table.

Without asking, Georgia poured him some coffee.

"Thanks. Much needed." He turned to Tessa. "Can I ask you questions about last night?"

She swallowed. "I guess."

He looked at Georgia for permission. She nodded.

"Did you see anyone take drugs there?" He leaned forward, watching her closely.

Shit. She didn't want to lie. But she sure as shit wasn't telling them the truth. "Someone was smoking pot in the side garden. But I don't think Ariel was with them."

"What about other drugs? Pills? Gummies?"

She put down her spoon. There'd been too many people at that gathering. The noise and the people and the familiar feeling that she'd never, ever belong anywhere had suffocated her. And there was the Altoid tin, the answer to all her problems. "I'm . . . not sure. There was a lot of chaos. And noise. And little pills that some people took. I mean, I went outside and kind of stayed there." This wasn't a lie, but a half-truth. She felt Georgia's eyes on her.

"Describe the pills."

"Blue. Small." Tiny bullets that took away all her anxiety.

"Anything else you remember?" Lou asked.

"Yeah. An argument. Or something. Sara got mad at Cooper and yelled at him."

Lou's eyes widened. "You know what about?"

She shook her head. "Sara stormed off. I tried to stop her, but she wanted to take a walk. Alone. God, I wished I'd gone with her."

"I'm glad you didn't! You could have been hit by that car, too," Georgia said.

Lou nodded at this, and it made Tessa feel a warmth inside that had only appeared when she moved in with Georgia.

Tessa looked at Lou. "How much trouble is Joel in?"

Lou gave Georgia a long, sober look that told her everything she needed to know. Damn. Joel had been stupid, sure, but he didn't deserve to have his whole life messed up like this.

"His parents have a good lawyer, but this is a high-profile case. Sara Clark's family is rich and powerful. They want justice for their kid."

He pushed the coffee away. "If you think of anything else, give me a call. We need to sort this all out soon because Fletcher Hawthorne is pushing his weight around. My boss woke me up with a five-minute lecture this morning on closing the case ASAP."

"You'd think Hawthorne would be more interested in justice," Georgia commented.

"What he's interested in is the upcoming attorney general election. He's protecting his brand." Lou stood, casting a look at Tessa. "You up to date on your trig homework?"

"Mostly. Could use some help, though."

He smiled. "Our usual time next week?"

"Thanks."

"I better get to the station. Gonna be a long weekend."

After Lou left, Georgia took a call from the hospital, so Tessa cleaned up the kitchen and changed into her work clothes: black pants, black top, and black Converse tennis shoes. She ran a brush through her choppy blonde hair—choppy because she'd cut it herself a few months ago, and it looked like she'd used a hacksaw—and dabbed on a little makeup. She'd likely have a busy shift at the bistro, and her boss Elias deserved her looking her best, such as it was.

***

Tessa's lunch shift at the bistro spiraled into three chaotic hours. Every table full. Grumbles from patrons queued for tables. The chef in a mood. Elias, Jasper's Bistro's owner/manager, running from mini-crisis to mini-crisis: avocado shortage, a no-show waiter, the patron who wrote something obscene on his check (Elias tossed him out the door). But Tessa persevered. She kept her practiced smile on, corrected a mistaken order, helped a pre-teen girl choose between chicken tenders and pumpkin soup, and marveled at her growing tip stash.

The bistro was in a converted brick bungalow close to the hospital. Elias had kept the charm of the old home—the wide-planked heart pine floors, the rippled glass in the wide windows, and the brick fireplace. He'd added a large sun porch that fit an additional dozen tables and a patio for outside seating. The kitchen expansion had been the most expensive venture, according to Georgia, with its gleaming stainless steel prep tables, massive gas stove, and minivan-sized fridge.

Elias loaded Tessa's tray with iced tea glasses. She loved how he always smelled—a bakery-warm, spicy scent from a heart-driven chef. He was Georgia's best friend and had become Tessa's surrogate uncle. Black, gay, bipolar, recovering drug addict—and one of the best people she'd ever known.

"I'm gonna buy you roller skates." Elias added a tiny bowl of lemon wedges to her tray.

"I want blue ones. With lights. Size eight."

"Lights?"

She grinned as she pictured the damage she could do to his place if she attempted skates.

"Purple lights. Like toddlers have on sneakers."

The chef placed a loaf of French bread in front of him, which Elias would use for bruschetta. "How'd you do on the trig exam?"

"C plus. But I didn't flunk."

He frowned. "I should hire you a better tutor."

"No. I should have studied more." It didn't help that she saw absolutely no reason to learn trigonometry. She could not imagine any future where she'd use it, but she never wanted to disappoint Elias, who, along with Joel and Lou Michaels, did everything he could to help her claw her way through that class.

Elias pointed to the tray. "Take that to table eight. We'll have the entrées for table four in a few." He hurried back to the kitchen as Tessa took drinks to a rowdy family near the window. The preschooler gripped the plastic tumbler Tessa handed him, while his older sister added three lemon wedges to hers. The mother explained that the entire family was vegan. Her "Is the tofu curry prepared separately from any meat product?" question made Tessa want to suggest that there was fresh grass outside if the woman cared to graze, but that would make Elias unhappy. After extensive negotiations about the use of additives and gluten in every dish, the parents ordered the most boring tofu entrées on the menu.

Tessa craved a cheeseburger.

She was entering the order on the computer when the hostess approached her. "You got a visitor."

"What?" She never had visitors, except when Georgia slipped in through the kitchen, waiting for a spare moment. There'd be no "free moments" today.

"Some girl. She's sitting by the front door. I told her you were crazy busy. She said she'd wait."

Tessa peered through the kitchen window. Crap. It was that weird girl from school—Lily Grace, the one who always said the wrong thing. The one who wore clothes fifteen years out of date. The one jerks like Cooper dubbed "Lily Gross." What was she doing here? Tessa scanned all her tables—she had no time to talk to anybody, but Lily Grace sat there, waiting.

"Tell Elias I'll just be a second," she said to the hostess and hurried over to the cramped entrance.

Lily Grace looked frantic. "I'm really sorry to bother you at work. I stopped by your house, and your mom said you were here. I had to talk to someone, and I knew you could help. I . . . I need some advice."

"About?" Tessa noticed the vegan mom guiding her daughter to the ladies' room.

"About . . . I saw something. A crime, I think. Only I was out at night, and I'm not supposed to leave the house after dark, so if my parents find out, I'm in big trouble."

Jesus. Was Lily Grace twelve years old? Tessa glanced over at the hostess, who waved frantically toward one of Tessa's tables. "Look, I have to get back to work . . ."

"If I'm going to report it, who should I talk to? Will they tell my parents? Do I just walk into the police station?" Lily Grace asked.

"Is it something serious? Or is it shoplifting or something lame like that?"

With Lily Grace, who actually said a blessing over cafeteria lunch, it could be anything. She might feel compelled to report jaywalking.

"Serious. Violent kind of serious." Her lip quivered as though the memory upset her.

"Okay, okay. Take it easy." Tessa wanted to hear more, but one of the other waitstaff pointed at the vegan table and mouthed in desperation, "Help!"

"I have to go. Listen, if you saw something bad, go to the police station and ask for Detective Lou Michaels. He can help you. Or he'll know someone who can. He's a friend. Tell him I sent you."

The hostess approached, scowling. "I just carried the entrées to table four. Can you please check on table six?"

Tessa winced. "Got it."

Lily Grace nodded. "It's okay. I'll find Detective Michaels. Thanks, Tessa. Sorry I bothered you."

Tessa felt torn. It sounded like Lily Grace had seen something pretty bad, but she needed this job, and right then, the job needed her. "You have my number, right? Call me later!"

Tessa returned to table six, checked the orders on table four, dealt with the vegans, and wondered what in the world Lily Grace had witnessed.

Seven

LILY GRACE WISHED TESSA HADN'T BEEN IN SUCH A HURRY, BUT SHE could only blame herself. Of course, Tessa had a job. Tessa didn't have parents who were so overprotective she was hardly allowed to go anywhere but to school and church. Parents whom Lily Grace disobeyed last night—the worst night of her entire life.

She climbed back on her bike and pedaled away from the bistro. The closest police substation was only a mile away. She'd go there and ask for Detective Lou Michaels, then head home in time for lunch with her mom.

As she rode up Devine Street, she mentally practiced what she'd say. Could she report what had happened last night anonymously? Or make up a name?

She pulled up to the front of the police substation closest to her house—a cement block building with a few windows painted the same beige as the school's cafeteria. Two officers exited through double glass doors as she locked her bike to a rack. She took in a breath for courage and entered the building. The small waiting area, with its lines of plastic chairs, smelled stale, like her church's basement. She approached a plexiglass window where an officer looked bored. "I'd like to speak to Detective Lou Michaels."

He looked up from a monitor. Behind him, two other officers clicked computer keyboards. A phone rang too many times before someone answered it.

"Detective Michaels works downtown. Something I can help you with?" the man answered.

She didn't know what to do. The man looked nice—shortish, with a pink bald head and a friendly smile like that man in insurance commercials. "I . . . I'm not sure."

"Do you need to report something? A missing dog? Cat in the tree?"

Okay, he was making fun of her now.

"Nothing like that. I . . . can I get a message to Detective Michaels? I was told to ask for him."

"Okay." He grabbed a notepad. "What's the message?"

"I witnessed a crime. A bad one. I need to tell him about it."

He lowered his pen, his face sobering. "What kind of crime?"

"Somebody got hurt. Bad. I need to tell the detective."

"No, you need to tell me. I'll make sure to relay the information." The bald man sounded insistent.

She didn't know what to do. Part of her wanted to run from the building, but the bigger part knew she had to do something—for Sara. For Joel.

"Well?" He tapped the pen.

"I . . . I wasn't supposed to leave my house last night, but I did. I tried to go to Cooper Hawthorne's party. And—"

"How about we take this to an interview room?"

He motioned another officer over to his desk and led her to a small cubicle with a metal table and two chairs. They didn't sit. He stood close to her, and she could see how one of his front teeth had a big chip. He smelled like too much aftershave.

"Okay. You mentioned Cooper Hawthorne? Fletcher Hawthorne's boy?"

"Yeah, only I didn't get to the party because I saw Sara walking up the road, and then the car came up, and the driver must not have seen her, and . . . he hit her." The accident replayed vividly in her mind as clearly as if it had happened again, right there in that small space.

"You did the right thing coming here. We're about to make an arrest in that case."

"Who are you arresting? Because Joel McCants wasn't the driver."

"Excuse me?"

"Cooper Hawthorne drove the car. His dad convinced him to blame it on Joel because Joel was out of it. But Joel wasn't driving. Cooper was." There. She'd said it. She'd done the right thing, and maybe it would get her in trouble, but it was worth it.

"What's your name?"

"Do I have to tell you?"

"Yes, you do." He spoke sternly, like her dad did when he was mad about something.

"I'm Lily Grace Duffy."

"And I'm Lt. Matt Palmer." He asked for her address and phone number, and she gave it to him. She'd have to tell her parents now. No way they wouldn't find out. She'd lose bike privileges for life.

The officer came around the desk to stand next to her. "Lily Grace, you did the right thing coming here. This is a very delicate situation, so I need you to do me a favor. Keep this under wraps until Detective Michaels gets in touch with you. Got it?"

"Not even my parents?"

"Not yet. Wait till you hear from him or me, okay?"

She nodded. She wanted to do the right thing. "Here's my phone number. I'll be waiting for a call."

Eight

FLETCHER TOOK HIS TIME IN THE SHOWER, AS HE ALWAYS DID. HE'D laughed when Vivian insisted on the seventeen shower heads—four down each corner and the big square one above—but showers had become a self-care ritual. Private spa time for Old Fletcher, which he needed after last night—after the debacle at his son's party.

He stepped out of the steamy, marble-walled shower, dried himself off, and slipped on a robe before tiptoeing back into the bedroom where Vivian still slept. She could sleep all day if he let her, but that wasn't healthy. He glanced at the clock: nine-thirty.

Slipping the sheet back, he nudged her shoulder. "Viv? Time to get up."

She didn't budge.

"Vivian!" He spoke louder, giving her a little jostle. "Wake up."

She didn't move. She lay there, cocooned in sheets, her head half off the pillow, frighteningly still. He drew a breath, trying not to think of the last time she wouldn't wake, fearful that maybe . . . He bent over, his ear to her lips, and heard her breathe.

He exhaled. Now, his alarm was replaced by anger. Had she done it again? He shook her harder, pulled her forward, her head lolling to the side.

"Wake up!" he commanded.

"Fletch . . ." she grumbled.

"Wake up, dammit!" He leaned her against the padded headboard, hands gripping her shoulders, ready to scream louder. Her eyes blinked open.

"I thought you were . . ." He didn't say dead. Couldn't say it. "Too stoned to wake up this time."

She pushed his hands away. "Can I . . . have . . . water?"

He opened the bedroom door and bellowed, "Marta! Bring her water and some toast!" Then he paced to the window, tossing back the curtains to let in the sunlight.

"Fletch!" she growled, tossing an arm over her eyes.

"The day's half over." He watched as she slowly pulled herself together, pushing the sheets away, glaring at him for the intrusion into her drugged sleep.

A few minutes later, Marta arrived, carrying a silver tray, which she placed beside groggy Vivian. "Here's water, toast, and coffee with cream and sweetener—just the way you like it." Marta wore her usual pale gray dress and white apron. Her black hair was pulled back in a bun, and she wore minimal makeup. He didn't know her age. She looked mid-thirties but often behaved like someone in their sixties: polite, no-nonsense, and loyal—his favorite qualities in any employee.

"You're too good to me, Marta." Vivian lifted the water glass and slurped.

"Mr. Hawthorne, are you ready for breakfast?" Marta spoke with great patience. It had to be hard for her, never knowing who would eat when. She'd been with the family for seven years, having taken care of Vivian when she was at her worst—which happened far too often. He prayed no reporter ever learned of Vivian's little problem.

"I'll be down in a few. Just yogurt and a bagel for me. Is the boy up?"

"Cooper is still asleep. I saw your note about letting him sleep in."

"Yeah. He had a bad night. Let's just let him sleep."

"Very well. I'll be back in a while to help Ms. Vivian get dressed." She gave Vivian an indulgent smile and left them.

"Feeling better?" Fletcher asked.

"Still waking up." Vivian pushed her blonde hair behind an ear. It needed brushing, and she needed a shower. "That was some commotion last night."

He wanted no reminders. He turned to look out the window. The pool glimmered blue below them. The patio chairs, which had been a chaotic mess last night, had been repositioned in their proper places, probably by the gardening crew. The door to the pool house hung open. He flashed on last night, when he'd hurried from the accident back to the house—how Holden had insisted on driving his own car to the hospital but had gone to the pool house to collect the Yeti cooler first. Fletcher had been annoyed then, but now was curious. What was so important about the cooler?

"What's going to happen now?" Vivian asked. "Are we in trouble?"

He spun around to look at her. She'd moved her feet off the bed, her hands braced against the mattress. Standing had always been hard for her since the back injury. How different she was now from ten years ago when she'd won state tennis tournaments and ribboned in regional dressage competitions. Athletic, smart, beautiful—yet somehow, she'd chosen him.

Fletcher moved closer, laying a hand on her shoulder. "I don't know. We didn't do anything wrong, but I don't need the media attention." This had haunted him last night when he tried to get to sleep. He had to protect the Hawthorne name—his most prized legacy.

"But our boys are all right. That's what matters."

"Yes. That's what matters." He worried about Cooper. The kid had been a frantic wreck last night, threatening to tell the police the truth without even considering what that would do to the family. Fletcher had given him one of Vivian's Valiums to settle him down.

"Help me stand. I need to pee," Vivian said.

Fletcher lifted her from the bed—she weighed so little these days—and steadied her. Vivian winced, and it hurt his heart. Pain was much too big a part of her life.

"Are you doing okay?"

"How do I answer that? I'm never okay? Or rather, I'm fine, don't worry about me? We'll go with that one. I'm fine." She clutched his arm, and he guided her toward the bathroom. After three steps, she pulled away, patted his hand, and took the rest of the journey by herself.

Fletcher took a sip of her coffee. He needed to strategize, to get in control of the situation: his son, the drugs in his house, the accident. He could feel his whole future—his whole life—slipping away. He would NOT let that happen.

Thirty minutes later, Fletcher sat at the polished desk in his home library—an immense room with heavy oak shelves and leather furniture. Vivian had insisted on adding framed "artwork" from the boys: a portrait from Holden, drawn when he was six, of the family, which included a dog that Holden had given six legs; from Cooper, a landscape—or something—drawn in purple crayon, completed when he was in kindergarten. His boys had brought them so much joy. And stress. And heartache. Before marriage, Fletcher had never thought of himself as father material, but once they were born, fathering flowed in his blood. He marveled at how different they were. Holden: confident, logical, a little arrogant, in his second year of law school, destined to join the family practice. Cooper: creative and hyper-emotional. "He's got an artist's eye and temperament," Vivian liked to say, to which Fletcher would answer, "Which means he'll never make any money." Cooper had caused them the most worry, beginning with his premature birth. That probably made them overprotective, especially Vivian. Both boys had been spoiled, but Cooper? They'd overindulged him. He could come off as entitled—a brat, at times—but he'd outgrow that. He'd better.

Marta tapped on the door and entered, carrying his newspapers. "Late today," she said.

He fumbled through the *NY Times* and *The Wall Street Journal* to get to the local paper.

"There's nothing about the accident," Marta said. "I already checked."

"Good." He exhaled. "But that won't last long."

"Cooper is up. I made his favorite breakfast, but he won't eat."

"Just give him some space, but he's not to leave the house."

"Yes, sir," she replied with a sad smile and left him.

35

The cell phone that suddenly rang wasn't his usual one, and he had to rummage in the desk drawer to unearth it: the flip phone few knew existed. He closed the door before answering, "Who is this?"

"Matt Palmer."

Matt Palmer—the cop who'd once been busted for cocaine. Fletcher remembered taking one look at him in the courtroom and feeling sorry for him. People make mistakes. Lives didn't need to be ruined. He negotiated with the judge, who dismissed the charges and expunged the arrest, which left Palmer owing Fletcher a few favors. It was always handy to have a cop in your pocket. "What's going on?"

Palmer told him something he'd hoped to never hear: "A girl came to the station. She was a witness to the accident last night. Claims she saw Cooper behind the wheel."

Crap. So much for damage control.

"I have her contact info. Want it?" Matt asked.

"Definitely." Fletcher wrote down her name, address, and phone number, unsure what he'd do with it. "Thanks, Matt. Can you keep this under wraps?"

"I can contain it here, but you know how this kind of information spreads."

"She's just confused. We'll have a talk with her," Fletcher said evasively. "I'll be in touch."

He hung up, leaned back in his chair, and closed his eyes. Jesus. A witness. Cooper could kiss his future down the drain, and Fletcher—well, this could damage his reputation beyond repair. All because some dumb kid couldn't keep her mouth shut? No. That kid would not be a problem. He'd do whatever he had to make sure of it.

Nine

"Is this Ms. Georgia Thayer?" an officious woman said when I answered my cell phone. I didn't recognize the number, but the ID flashed "Department of Social Services," which meant it had to be about Tessa.

"Yes, this is Georgia." A wave of anxiety hit me, as if I'd been caught speeding, but I'd done nothing wrong. Guilt always came too easily.

"My name is Lana Montgomery. I'm the new case manager assigned to Tessa."

Case manager. Not a social worker like me. She likely had a degree in English literature or art history because social services often went for the cheap hires—a long-standing issue of mine. "How can I help you?" I said.

"I need to do a home visit in the next week or so."

"Good. Let's get that scheduled."

A pause, then she said, "I prefer to do them unannounced. But I need to make sure I have your correct contact info." She read what she had from the file, which was, of course, correct.

"Why unannounced? We're both pretty busy. You may not catch me at home." My anxiety amped up. Was she hoping to catch me off guard in my own home? Hoping to catch me doing a line of coke or hosting a rave? People in authority often brought out my paranoia.

"I'll text when I'm on the way, then. You can let me know if you're available. In the meantime, how is Tessa doing?"

"She's great. Doing well in school. She's very smart. And she's mostly keeping all her therapy appointments." And she was, mostly. Tessa had been through so much. Held captive by traffickers. Forced to sell her body in ways I never wanted to think about. With the help of a few friends, I'd gotten her out of that life. Detective Lou Michaels had captured the men who held her. And Tessa was doing all that she could to recover from the trauma. But we both knew the wound ran deep.

"Good to know. And you?" she asked.

"Me? What about me?"

"I understand you're in therapy as well? I just want to make sure that keeping Tessa isn't too much for you."

Did her tone change? Did I hear a hint of accusation? Did she think my seeing Lenore, my sainted therapist of three years, made me unqualified to be a foster parent? This had been my fear since Tessa came to me. It had taken special permissions—letters from Clancy, my boss, a head nurse, and even Detective Lou Michaels, assuring the powers-that-be that I was the logical foster mom for Tessa, given her history. Our shared trauma history, in a way.

"I am in therapy. That's going quite well, too. I highly recommend therapy, Lana. A job like yours has to be stressful."

"I'll take that under advisement." Another shift in her attitude. Defensive now. "I understand you work at the hospital. So after five will be the best time to see you?"

"My hours fluctuate. But when you come, I'll do my best to be there."

"Thank you. I'll be in touch."

We hung up, and I did a mental postmortem of the call. What if she decided I was too unstable to remain Tessa's foster mom? The idea panicked me because I'd gotten so attached to that kid, and I was doing my best, even though I often felt lost. The thought of losing her, of her being placed with someone who didn't understand what she'd been through . . .

She's where she belongs, the Counselor said.

"Shit," I whispered. I hadn't heard from any of my voices in months. I have a catalog of them, though their numbers have diminished. Their recent silence had me hopeful that they were gone for good.

Stop catastrophizing, the Counselor whispered. She's female, gentle. Often right, but sometimes very wrong. *Tessa is yours.*

I wanted that to be true. I'd find a way to keep her as long as she wanted to be with me. If that meant sucking up to Lana Montgomery, that was exactly what I'd do.

She might not be yours. The Advisor's voice—male. Mansplaining. *Not if that woman figures you out.*

Shit. I had to keep that from happening.

Ten

THREE KNOCKS (TWO FAST, A PAUSE, THEN THE THIRD) ON THE EXTER-
nal door to Fletcher Hawthorne's home office signaled an arrival. Marcus Landry didn't wait to be asked in, but opened the door, sauntered to
Fletcher's desk, and took a seat in the leather chair across from him.
Marcus treated everywhere like he owned it.

Marcus was younger than Fletcher. Shorter, too—probably five-ten,
with dark hair styled in waves and a sculpted goatee he tended to stroke
with affection. His clothes came from New York, his shoes from Italy,
but most of his wallet lay in offshore accounts.

Fletcher longed to be free of this deadly man.

"I hear you had a little problem here last night," Marcus said.

The incident hadn't made the news; yet, Marcus knew because Marcus knew everything.

"That terrible accident. I hear a girl was hurt?" Marcus continued.

Fletcher picked up a fountain pen and dangled it between his fingers—a nervous habit. Marcus always slithered under his skin.

"And drugs were involved," Marcus added with a quirk of his eyebrows.

Shit. There it was. He should have known. "Did you have anything
to do with that, Marcus?" Fletcher asked.

"The last thing I want is you in legal trouble." He strode over to a
shelf and removed a book: *Constitutional Law*, a six-pound tome.
"You've been ignoring my calls and texts."

40

"I've been busy. You know—running for office. Something you insisted on." Fletcher often wondered why. Marcus had come to him ten months before with a spiral-bound notebook of campaign notes from a hired consultant—the plan for Fletcher to win the South Carolina attorney general seat. He'd never considered such a thing, but Marcus wouldn't take no for an answer. Fletcher had no choice but to comply, and now the campaign was in full swing.

"My idea, yes. But you've seemed to grow fond of it. All that power. Seductive, isn't it?"

It was, damn it. The notion that he'd win a statewide seat. Show his family that Fletcher was the best of all of them. And remind South Carolina itself how the Hawthorne name carried weight. Power. Importance. But being in Marcus's pocket meant Marcus would pull the strings—and Fletcher loathed being a marionette.

"How is that lovely wife of yours? I'd love to tell her hello. Vivian is much on my mind lately."

Marcus was never one to pull his punches, and Fletcher felt this one right in the solar plexus. His wife, Vivian, started them on this path. The fall down the concrete steps that broke her back. The pain attacking like a relentless dragon. Her surgeon gave her OxyContin to help—until he wouldn't refill it. Fletcher had been desperate to help her when the doctors wouldn't.

A woman on their cleaning staff knew someone. She introduced them to one of Marcus's men, who gave Vivian a dozen pills. Vivian slept through the night for the first time in months. The following morning, she'd come down the stairs unassisted, sat at the breakfast table, and sipped coffee with the family like she used to do. Fletcher nearly wept with relief.

He didn't know then, but now he knew all too well that he'd let the devil into his house.

"Why were you ignoring my calls?" Marcus asked. "After all I've done for you, you don't get to ignore me."

"I wasn't ignoring you. This campaign you launched keeps me very busy. And we need to keep our distance, don't you think? The last thing we need is for anyone to connect me to you."

"True. And you'd love to be rid of me." Marcus's smile was reptilian. "Which reminds me. I have something for you." Marcus reached into his pocket for a manila envelope, which he tossed to Fletcher.

"What's this?"

"Security. A reminder that you don't get to decide the nature of our relationship. Go ahead. Open it."

Fletcher slit the flap and retrieved a small stack of photos. The first took his breath. The second had him quaking—a face he ached to see, but a sight that always brought a familiar shame that punched him in the stomach. How did Marcus get these? Had Fletcher been followed to Florida? It had been four years, but God, the wound still burned. And Marcus knew. Dear God, Marcus knew.

"Yours to keep. In case you get nostalgic. I have other copies." Marcus grinned again.

Fletcher shoved the photos in a drawer and slammed it shut, forcing his hand to still. He cleared his throat. "Why is this election important to you? Warren Chappel's a good attorney general." Fletcher had known Warren since law school. He was smart. Not afraid to take on the state's most challenging criminals. Did he have Marcus on his radar?

"I find him to be a problem," Marcus said.

"Is there . . . a particular threat?" The idea churned ambivalence in him. Seeing Marcus go to prison would feel like Christmas—he'd no longer be a threat. But Marcus would fight dirty. He'd take Fletcher down with him.

"Mr. Chappel is a problem. That's all you need to know. Your job is to take care of him."

"I'm doing my best. But it's an uphill battle. Chappel's leading in the polls. He's the incumbent. The party loyalists love him."

And Fletcher? He had sons who flirted with trouble, an addicted wife, and, after last night, a potential scandal nipping at his heels.

Marcus let out a sigh. "So. Your son Cooper. He's in trouble because of the accident?"

"Cooper wasn't driving."

"His car. His inebriation. A very injured girl from a well-connected family. Drugs offered in your home to a group of teens. It won't reflect well on you."

No, it wouldn't. Fletcher needed the whole thing to blow over. Needed the police to arrest that Joel kid and plead out some kind of under-the-radar deal, and for that Sara kid to be okay, and for the news to stay focused elsewhere.

But then came the call from Officer Matt Palmer.

Marcus stood. "Anything else we need to discuss?"

He lifted a hand to stop Marcus from leaving.

"What?" Marcus asked.

"I do need your help. It's about the accident. I think I have a job for your guy, Saul."

Marcus smiled, white teeth gleaming like a shark's. "It's nice to know you still need me."

Fletcher closed his eyes and felt himself being pulled underwater.

Eleven

SAUL LIVED SIMPLY. A TWO-ROOM APARTMENT OVER ONE OF MARCUS'S warehouses outside of town, furnished with a Murphy bed, a bookcase, a scuffed-up table, and a high-end espresso machine in the galley kitchen. The rest of the space held workout equipment. He drove an old car—several, actually, but he only kept one at the apartment. His phones were all burners, replaced monthly. He operated in cash and favors, keeping his world small. He wished he could be invisible. His boss, Marcus Landry, said he was.

He finished his workout: five miles on the treadmill, followed by forty-five minutes on free weights and the punching bag, then showered. He kept his head shaven because he saw no use for hair. It was bothersome, and nobody ever looked at his head when they could glare at his face. The two deep scars like red, crooked canyons: one down his left cheekbone to below his chin, the other a grisly slash across his neck. Everyone always gawked, but he was used to it. In fact, he used it—part of his job was intimidation, and damned if he didn't look the part.

Someone pounded on his door. No doubt who it was—only Marcus knew he lived here. He pulled on sweatpants and a T-shirt to let his boss inside.

"Got an assignment for you," Marcus said by way of greeting. He only came up to Saul's shoulders, yet still managed to command the room. "Fletcher Hawthorne's boy has gotten himself into a bit of trouble."

"Which one?" Both Hawthorne kids were entitled shits as far as Saul was concerned, but their dad was important to Marcus, which made him important to Saul.

"Cooper. He had a party at his house last night. Got high. Ran over a girl."

"Kill her?"

"Not dead yet, but she doesn't look good. Just found out there was a witness. We need her to disappear."

Saul dropped into a chair and took down notes. "Details?"

Marcus handed him a slip of paper and a picture. "Here. Name's Lily Grace Duffy. Sixteen years old."

Crap. A kid. Saul hated hurting a kid. He looked at the photo. An average-looking girl—brown hair. A nose too big for her face. Bushy eyebrows. She looked like one of his sister's friends back in Nicaragua. He'd seen none of his family in three years—for their protection—but sent them money every week.

"I'm surprised you're not using The Shadows for this." Questioning Marcus came with risks. But The Shadows had always been his preferred hitmen—two well-trained assassins who moved like ghosts. They scared the hell out of Saul.

"I have them working out of town. You can handle this one for me." Marcus paced the short length of Saul's apartment. It really belonged to Marcus—just like he owned the warehouse downstairs, the three out-buildings, and the two acres of land surrounding the complex. He spun around and glared at Saul. "I need Fletcher Hawthorne to win that elec-tion, so I need his kids to be pure as snow. We can't afford for this Lily Grace Duffy to open her mouth—now or ever."

"I understand."

"Take care of her, then." After Marcus left, Saul didn't dress in his usual black jeans, black T-shirt, and black jacket. Instead, he chose kha-kis and a polo, hoping he'd be less noticeable in the light of day. Time to meet Ms. Lily Grace Duffy.

Fifteen minutes later, he parked his car under an oak tree one house down from the small bungalow where the girl lived. No car waited in the driveway. Dandelions populated a front lawn that needed cutting, and the siding on the gray house could use a coat of paint. He slipped on some shades and stepped out of the car.

Invisible. It was his superpower. He tucked his hands in the pockets of his jacket and hurried around the house, peering in windows to assess, and saw clutter. Dear God, the clutter—stacks, mounds, piles. How could anyone live like this? Saul liked things clean. Simple. Sparse.

He shifted to another window—the kitchen. Under a painting of Jesus rested an armchair where a large woman slept. Large as in gargantuan, with puddles of fat drooping over the cushions, her face pillowed by flesh. Could she even move on those blubbery legs?

He moved on. One last window that looked into a bedroom, only this one didn't match the rest of the house because it was neat. Spartan. A poster of Billie Eilish over the bed told him this was the girl's room. Lily Grace.

He checked the backyard, then jogged back to his car, where he'd wait. He needed to catch the girl before she walked into her house. Parents could not be a part of their interaction.

He remained in the old Land Rover, and twenty minutes later, a teenage girl rolled up on her bicycle, dismounting in front of the mailbox. She wore jeans and a frumpy blue sweater, her brown hair fraying from its ponytail. She had a childlike softness—not fat, exactly. Doughy soft, as if puberty hadn't finished with her yet. He glanced at the window. Her father hadn't come home, but Mom was still inside. Could she be watching? No, probably still in the back of the house, sitting in that chair that barely contained her. Now was his chance.

He climbed out, pocketing the keys. "Lily Grace Duffy?"

She closed the mailbox, empty-handed. "That's me. Are you Detective Michaels? They said you'd call me."

Nothing about him looked like the police. But he faked a smile and said, "Uh, yeah. That's me."

"Good." She hurried over to him. "Can we get away from the house? I don't want my mom to see you."

This couldn't get any better. "My car's over there under that tree. Why don't we take a ride?"

"Sure." She glanced back at the house, then followed him to the car, arms swinging like a little kid. "I've never reported a crime until today. Tessa said you were the best person to talk to. She said I could trust you."

When he unlocked the car, she climbed right inside. Way too trusting, this kid.

Saul glanced around the vehicle, making sure nobody watched them. The vigilance was second nature to him. It kept him alive. No cars. No pedestrians. Perfect. He started the Rover (which looked nothing like a police car).

"How long have you been a police detective?" the girl asked.

"Uh. Ten years."

"Do you like it? I bet it's exciting! Have you solved many crimes?"

"A few." He remembered the information he'd received said she was sixteen, but she acted so much younger.

"This crime won't be hard to solve. I'm a witness. I know exactly who ran over Sara Clark. I hope she's okay. Do you know if she is? I mean, she had a lot of injuries, but the ambulance came, and she was still alive." The words came out of her mouth like water from a fountain. He had an aunt who talked like that back in Nicaragua. Once she got going, you couldn't shut her up.

"I don't know her condition," he said.

"It was Cooper Hawthorne who hit Sara. Not Joel McCants."

He hadn't decided where to take her. Somewhere away from town, obviously. His Luger waited in the trunk. Maybe he'd take her to the country and leave her body in the woods—somewhere isolated, somewhere that he could bury her with no one noticing. She deserved to be properly buried.

She chattered on. "Cooper Hawthorne can be mean. He has been to me. But I never thought he'd do something like this. Not that he meant to. He was swerving all over the road. And she had on dark clothes. She was kind of weaving, too. Maybe they were both drunk. Do you think they were drunk?"

"Could be." He'd want it to be painless. She was just a kid.

"He should not have been behind the wheel in that condition. He should know better. But Cooper's cocky like that. And he can be a jerk, too."

"A jerk?"

"Oh, yeah." She described several tricks he'd played on her, and they were cruel. Tripping her when she hurried to her desk. Pretending a boy was interested in her only to set up a public humiliation in the cafeteria. The Hawthorne kid wasn't just a jerk, but a bully. Fit right in with what Saul knew about the Hawthorne family. Marcus said so many disparaging things about Fletcher Hawthorne, but having him in his pocket proved profitable. And what benefited Marcus benefited Saul.

"He really put a clown in the chair?" Saul clarified.

"Yes. I thought I was having lunch with Kyle, but it was a big dopey clown doll instead. And everybody was watching. And laughing. And . . . and I didn't want to cry, but it was so awful. I felt like such an idiot."

Saul thought about his little sister, Fatima. Before they knew why she was different, kids picked on her. She didn't catch on to the social cues the counselor had told them, which made her perfect prey for schoolyard bullies.

He glanced over at Lily Grace. She looked a little like Fatima, too. Same mousy brown hair. Same wide-eyed expression. Same odd innocence that made her poorly equipped to navigate this awful world, but more articulate, clearly smarter, than his sister.

His cell phone chimed. Marcus. "Yeah," he said.

"You take care of our little problem?"

"Still in progress. I'll call when I'm done." He ended the call before Marcus pressed harder.

Lily Grace looked out the window. "What a pretty day. I love fall, don't you? All the pretty colors."

This was something Fatima might say. An image flashed in his mind: someone raising a gun to Fatima's head, the alarm and fear that would fill her eyes. But it wasn't Fatima who sat next to him. It was Lily Grace, and she had to go.

"Very pretty," Saul said and headed toward the state park.

Twelve

THE NA MEETING CLOSED WITH ANOTHER RECITATION OF THE SERENITY Prayer. Rus recited the words he knew in his heart and soul, words that had kept him alive. As usual, he watched for anyone who might recognize him from his past. He'd changed so much, though. Leaner. More grizzled. Shaggy hair and a beard that hid who he used to be.

He stood from the metal folding chair, clutching a half cup of cold coffee, scanning the dozen faces around him for the umpteenth time, hoping to spot his friend.

Tanner wasn't there.

Rus said a few goodbyes before slipping out quickly from the small AME church. Tanner liked this meeting, yet he hadn't come. He was only a few months into recovery, and daily meetings kept him going. They kept Rus going, too, and he'd been clean for over a year.

He had to find his friend. He prayed that Tanner's absence didn't mean what he feared. Folks in early recovery often crashed and burned.

The air hung heavy with moist heat as Rus checked Tanner's usual haunts: under the Gervais Street bridge. The Riverfront Park. The parking garage near the Capitol. But he found no sign of Tanner or his motorcycle. Rus trudged up North Main, getting more anxious with each step. He wasn't Tanner's sponsor, but he felt responsible for the kid. He was so young. Had only been on the streets for a few months. Rus had taken him under his wing, teaching him how to stay safe. What soup kitchens were good and which to avoid because they preached too much or served stale crackers. And, finally, the agonizing steps of quitting drugs. Walking that path with Tanner had brought back awful memories:

49

the years Rus lost to the needle and pills. The countless times a bad deal left him bloody and unconscious. That midnight on the beach when he died.

Only to be born again.

There. Movement behind the old Trestle building. Rus edged closer, catching a glimpse of a man running from the gravel parking lot. Not Tanner, too big to be Tanner, but suspicious. Rus lost sight of him in the shadows, so he hurried to the rear of the brick structure. Years on the streets had taught him to be wary. Vigilant. His internal radar had him on high alert. He spotted a strange hump at the very rear of the lot. Rus held his breath, his vigilance edged with fear. As he grew closer, the lump took shape. Human shape. Lanky. Lean. Familiar.

"Oh shit, oh shit, oh shit." Rus took flight, charging to the shape and rolling him over to check for breathing.

Tanner had the look Rus had seen too often. Flour-white skin. Blue-tinged lips. Vomit smeared across his cheek. Hardly detectable heartbeat.

Rus had a single dose of Narcan in his pocket and, with a shaking hand, pulled it out. He tilted Tanner's head back, inserted it in Tanner's nose, then pressed the plunger. No response. He needed a second dose, but Rus only had the one. Shit.

Rus had no phone, but Tanner did. He fumbled in the pocket, found the cell, and dialed 911. Waiting was the hardest. He kept a hand on Tanner's chest, grateful for each shallow rise and fall, but terrified when the pace slowed.

"Come on, Tanner, hang on," he whispered.

Finally, the blessed sound of sirens. He hurried to the street to flag them down. The two EMTs rushed over, and within a few minutes, they'd ripped off Tanner's jacket, administered a second dose of Narcan, and attached electrodes. The two EMTs bore grim expressions as they worked, communicated with the hospital, and then loaded Tanner into the ambulance.

"Can I go with him?" Rus asked.

"No room," one replied.

Shit. It was a good five miles to the hospital, and on foot, that would take a while. He gripped Tanner's jacket, felt the pocket, and found the keys to his motorcycle, which was parked right beside the building. "I'll get myself there. Please take care of him."

He'd only driven a motorcycle once, though he'd ridden behind Tanner countless times. It took five tries to start it, and he did a few practice laps of the parking area, twice stalling when he tried to stop. Soon, he felt competent enough to drive it and opted to stay on the back roads in case he spun out.

Rus made it to the hospital a few minutes after the ambulance, but nobody would tell him anything. "We need to talk to family," the clerk said, but Tanner had none, not really. Rus was the closest thing to family Tanner would claim.

The clerk didn't believe him.

He took a seat at the rear of the waiting area. His foot bounced up and down as though possessed. His worry for Tanner amplified with each passing minute.

Maybe he'd be okay. Maybe he'd learn from this, that there'd be no more setbacks. No more relapses. Tanner would find his way to the happiness he absolutely deserved.

Somehow, Rus couldn't make himself believe it.

Thirteen

HOLY HELL. I HAD NEVER BEEN TO WAR. BUT THAT NIGHT—AND morning—our emergency department felt like a battlefield. We had the usual car crashes and falling-off-the-ladder accidents. Sports-related fractures. Those we could manage. But it was the string of overdoses that stretched us beyond our capacity.

The ones not sent down to the morgue became Trauma One-level emergencies: resuscitation, intubation, and other drastic measures to save lives.

All from opioids.

"Georgia!" Dr. Romano yelled for me from bay four. He rarely yelled; this level of chaos changed all of us.

"What can I do?" I asked as I pushed through the curtains.

I froze. The patients they were tending couldn't be older than twenty: too-pale skin, dark hair cut short. Lips tinged a scary shade of blue.

"This kid went into arrhythmia. We need to intubate, but all the respiratory therapists are at max capacity. Nursing called the temp service, but they say they can't send anyone. You had luck with them the last time."

A nurse arrived with an injection and inserted it into the boy's IV.

"We've done four doses of Narcan," Romano said to me. "Not looking good."

"Shit," I whispered. I tried not to imagine his parents, his siblings, his friends mourning his loss. But Romano wasn't giving up, so I left him to it.

Scurrying away from the bay, I reached the nurse's station, where I glanced at the clock—8 a.m. I didn't know why Dr. Romano thought I'd have any luck getting a respiratory therapist. The only time I'd had success with the temp agency, it had cost me my tickets to Hamilton. I dialed the number.

"Like I told your clerk, we don't have anyone available," the snotty receptionist said in response to my request.

"I understand that, but this is an emergency." I explained in excruciating detail what we'd faced over the last twelve hours. "We've got everyone working, and the ODs keep arriving. We're doing all we can to keep people alive."

A hesitation, then, "I'm sorry, but we simply don't have enough. You're not the only hospital in crisis."

An ambulance wailed as it pulled up, bedraggled ER techs hurrying out to greet it.

I summoned the little patience I had left. "Listen, I get it. But I also know you have a list. You can make some calls. We'll pay overtime. We'll pay a bonus if they'll cover the rest of the weekend." I shouldn't make promises I have no authority to keep, desperate times and all.

"I don't think—"

"You're not trying. Call your RTs. Extend our offer. Give them my cell number if they're interested." I used my don't-f*-with-me voice. All social workers have one.

Dr. Romano appeared, waving what looked like tickets in his hand. "Fifty-yard line, Carolina-Clemson game."

"Bless you!" I snagged them as I relayed the offer over the phone. "Fifty-yard line, Cassandra. Next month. Get us help, and they are yours."

A pause, then, "I'll see what I can do." I gave her my cell number and crossed my fingers that it would ring soon.

A nursing tech approached, looking as frazzled as we all felt. "Somebody's asking for you in the waiting room."

"Who is it?"

"Wouldn't tell me his name. Been there all night. Came in with that kid Romano's trying to save. His name's Rus. Not Russ, mind you, but

Rus. He was very specific about the single s. And about not having a last name." She shrugged.

"I'll be right there."

The clerk pointed to a young man sitting in a crowded row of seats, wearing a black hoodie and dirty jeans. His brown hair hung long and unkempt. A thick, scraggly beard drooped from his ruddy face. He looked up at me and smiled, missing one of his top teeth. "I bet you don't remember me."

I almost didn't. Rus. Everything about him looked different except those sad, expressive eyes. How long had it been since I'd seen him? Was it three years ago when he'd taken a corrupted dose of black tar heroin? A few weeks later, he'd been beaten by a dealer for failing to pay. I spent some tough hours with Rus, trying to get him on the right track. And then he disappeared.

"How could I forget? Good to see you, Rus." *Good to see him alive*, I almost said. The life he'd lived had left its scars.

"Remember when I got the crap beaten out of me? You were nice. Kind. I try to remember the kind ones."

"I do remember that."

I motioned for him to join me in an interview cubicle. "What's going on?"

"I brought in a friend. A kid I know from the streets. He OD'ed. I found him on North Main. Gave him Narcan, but . . ."

I glanced over at the door to our treatment bays. How many over-doses would we get today? "They're doing all they can."

"Thanks. I kept asking, but nobody would tell me a damn thing. Said I'm not family. Well, he doesn't have family. Not anymore. Tanner's just a kid. Kicked out of his parents' home. Got into some trouble with heroin, but now there's this new shit out there. It's killing our people." He looked at me with sad eyes. Eyes much older than he was.

"Fentanyl. We're seeing way too much of it." I leaned forward. "How about you, Rus? You clean?"

"Damn right. Been that way for over a year. Going to meetings and everything."

"Well, I'm glad to hear that." I was, too. I've known too many Ruses who didn't make it.

"You helped back then. Told me I was killing myself. Talked to me like I might be worth saving." He shrugged. "I left town for a while. Got my shit together. It wasn't easy."

I was sure it wasn't. "What brought you back to Columbia?"

"That's a long story." He looked away, evading me.

"Where are you staying?"

"A trailer off Decker. It's small and old and crappy, but it's home."

"You said you go to meetings? Where?"

"Lots of places. Just went to that downtown AME church on N. Main. I took Tanner with me over the last few weeks. But he didn't show today, and this new fentanyl shit hit the streets." He lifted a hand and dropped it. His nails were dirty and bitten to the quick. He glanced over at the door. "Would you go check on Tanner? They won't tell me a damn thing. It's been hours. I'm scared—"

I nodded. "Wait here. I'll see what I can find out."

Dr. Romano met me outside the treatment bay, and the news wasn't good. Beyond him, I saw a sheet pulled over the patient's body. "Went into arrhythmia. We tried everything, but the poor kid was in terrible shape."

"Oh, no."

"We need to contact her family."

"Her? I was asking about the street kid, Tanner."

"She may identify as male, but her body is female. Trans, I guess."

Rus had said Tanner was kicked out of his home. This had to be why. So many trans kids ended up on the streets.

Romano sighed. "There wasn't much we could do to help him. The version of fentanyl we're seeing—Christ, Georgia. It's a weapon of mass destruction."

"That's an apt description." I glanced over at the body. What a waste. A needless, tragic waste. "I'll see what I can find out about him."

Rus took the news as I suspected he would. Stoic. Wordless. Adding this loss to the long list that came with being an addict. His own brittle recovery had to make the pain worse. "If it helps, we doubt Tanner experienced much pain." I theorized this because Tanner never regained consciousness. I imagined him quietly sailing away on an ocean to forever.

"It does," he whispered. "At least maybe the end was peaceful."

"You mentioned that he'd been kicked out of his home. We need to reach his parents. Any idea about his birth identity?"

Rus gave me a long, assessing look before reaching into the pocket of a jacket for a wallet. "This is his. I think there's a motorcycle license in it."

"Thank you."

"I have to get going, unless there's something else you need from me."

I gripped the worn leather, imagining Tanner's hand holding it. Facing the belongings of the deceased always made me sad. "One more thing—anything you can tell me about the new fentanyl? Any idea where it's coming from?"

He didn't answer.

"Rus, we have to get that crap off the streets."

"You're right. I don't know who's selling it, but if I find out anything, I'll let you know."

"Stay safe. And keep going to meetings." I handed him my card and walked him to the ER entrance. He looked back toward where he'd left his friend—a young man he'd never see again—before pushing through the glass doors.

I took Tanner's wallet to my closet of an office and sat at my cluttered desk. It felt intrusive to go through his things, but I had a job to do. I found Tanner's old driver's license. His name had been Teresa Holcomb. He'd been seventeen years old two years ago, living in Greer, South Carolina—a small town, pretty conservative in nature. He had four dollars, three Dollar Tree receipts, and a photograph tucked in a pocket.

The photo was of a family: middle-aged parents, I guessed, and three kids. I matched the picture with the face on his license and saw he was the oldest of the children, with long auburn hair and a serious expression. His two siblings—a boy and a girl—looked to be under ten.

Would this family grieve Teresa/Tanner? They would, I decided. It might be much harder for them, given what had happened. Grief was far more complicated when the relationship was a troubled one.

In another fold, I found a tattered scrap of notebook paper and pulled it out. A note, written in a child's scrawl: *Don't be sad. I love you, T.*

Had one of Tanner's siblings written it? I hoped it brought him comfort.

I let out a deflating sigh at the tragedy of it all. This young life ended. This family about to receive the awful news. Why?

I closed the wallet, clicked on the computer, and googled the family name and address. Once I had the phone number, I dialed, quietly praying that Tanner had found the peace he had never found while alive.

Fourteen

TESSA COULD NOT CARE LESS ABOUT THE FRENCH REVOLUTION. IT didn't help that her teacher, Mr. McAfferty, spoke in a monotone drone that could lull anyone to sleep. And that the classroom was hot and smelled of boy sweat and disinfectant. She looked at the other students. Three girls scrolling on their phones. Two guys with heads resting on their desktops, eyes closed. One guy drawing pictures in his notebook.

And two empty chairs: Joel's usual seat beside Tessa's. And the one in the back, where Lily Grace always sat. Lily Grace was supposed to call her Saturday night after her strange visit to the bistro, but she hadn't. Tessa had texted her yesterday, but got no response. Was her absence related to the supposed "crime" she needed to report? Or was she home avoiding classes like this that bored them to death?

Tessa eyed the wall clock: twenty minutes to go.

She raised her hand and requested a pass to go to the restroom, mouthing "period" when Mr. McAfferty shot her a skeptical look. That worked every time. She grabbed the pass and hurried to the bathroom.

She gripped the chipped porcelain sink and splashed water on her face. How was she going to survive three years of this? Maybe she could find a way to graduate early—get away from these people. No, she wasn't that smart. And what would she do after? She lacked the funds for college and had no clue what her "career" might be. No, she had to serve her time in this mind-numbing hellhole called high school.

Her phone vibrated in her pocket: a text from her little brother, Brandon. *Hey*, it said.

Everything okay? she texted back. Brandon was seven, living a good life with his adoptive family in Pennsylvania. She missed him with a physical ache.

Recess. I'm boooooored.

I get that. Nobody playing baseball? She hadn't seen him play since T-ball, when he was a four-foot-tall terror who hit like a mini-Hank Aaron but then forgot which way to run.

No time, Brandon answered.

How's your team doing?

Coach benched me yesterday.

Ah. There it was. The reason Brandon had reached out.

That sucks, lil bro. But I'm sure it's just temporary.

Mom says we can practice later.

She closed her eyes. He had that now: Mom. Dad. Home. And Tessa wanted it more than anything for him. They'd endured foster care together—five or six homes until Tessa fell into the trap set by the traffickers. That awful life made so much worse by the separation from her baby brother. And once she clawed her way out of that bleak world, she'd learned Brandon had a new family. She was happy for him; she was.

But it hurt, deep down, that he might not need her anymore.

One day, I'm gonna come up for a game, she texted.

Please, Tessa? PLEEEEASE? Bell. Gotta go.

Tessa clicked off. She'd been saving most of her earnings from the bistro in hopes that Georgia would let her go visit Brandon. Maybe she could invite herself there for Thanksgiving.

Maybe.

She winced when the bathroom door opened. The last thing she wanted was company.

"Hey. I told Mr. McAfferty that I had something you needed." Ariel approached, holding a tampon.

"Don't really . . ."

"I know. But it got me out of there." Ariel leaned against the other sink. She wore a teal peasant top that brought out her hazel eyes. Her long blonde hair had blue tips, as though it had been dipped in paint. "Have you seen Cooper today?"

"No."

"Me neither. And he's not answering my texts."

Tessa didn't care if she ever saw Cooper Hawthorne again. It was his stupid party that got Sara hurt and landed Joel in terrible trouble.

"I wanted to thank you for helping me the other night." Ariel sounded contrite. "Though I don't remember much about what happened."

"You walked right into the deep end of the swimming pool. You don't remember?" Tessa recalled quite clearly: Ariel circling the pool, her arms moving in a dance to music only she could hear. An odd smile on her face tilted to the sky. A turn. A step. A splash.

"I remember being wet. And the hospital. And my parents putting me on restriction until I'm thirty."

"You were pretty stoned."

"Weren't you?" Ariel laughed.

"Yeah, I was." And it had felt so damn good. She'd not felt that relaxed, that joyful since forever. Everything made her laugh—the water in the pool, the sparkling stars, the music—everything.

She'd kill to feel that way again.

"Which reminds me." Ariel dug into her giant hobo bag and pulled out a small Mentos container. "I have to get rid of these. That's why I was looking for Cooper. I'm under house arrest. My parents are the Gestapo. If they catch me with these . . ." She opened the container and spilled out a dozen pills.

Small, blue, happy pills like the one Tessa took at the party.

"Can I give them to you? I know you like them. Everybody does." Ariel's grin had an edge of mischief.

Tessa considered it. The pills might be her remedy for high school. She wouldn't take them every day, just when things got really, really bad. She could hide them in a shoe in her closet—Georgia would never find them because she was big about respecting privacy.

"Please?" Ariel said. "I don't want to flush them. It would be a waste."

Tessa knew she shouldn't, but she reached out her hand.

Ariel smacked the tin into her palm. "Thanks. And enjoy, Tessa. You deserve it."

Fifteen

FLETCHER AWAKENED TO A TEXT FROM MARCUS CITING POLL NUMBERS
that weren't good. "You'd better put together a plan to change this,"
Marcus had said.

Always a threat when dealing with that man. Fletcher hated feeling
like a puppet, especially with a criminal like Marcus pulling the strings.

He sat on the bed, watching Vivian sleep. He remembered her from
the early days of their marriage: so damned beautiful. Her wavy blonde
hair framing a gorgeous magazine-model face. Those green eyes that always held a hint of mischief. That body for which he had thirsted from
the moment they'd first met. So much had changed.

Slipping the sheet back, he nudged her shoulder. "Viv? Time to get
up."

Her eyes blinked open to stare at him.

"There's my girl. How are you feeling?" He helped her pull herself
up, propping pillows behind her.

"Like shit."

He sat beside her on the bed. "I know you're having a tough time.
But I have a favor to ask. A huge one."

She reached for his hand. "What?"

"Can we stop with the narcotics for a while? At least until the election is over?"

She stiffened.

"I don't want you in pain, but maybe we can stick with the muscle
relaxers and the NSAIDs. Or, at least, maybe you can cut back on the
pain pills. Please, babe."

"Cut back? What do you have in mind?"

"You know how to gauge your pain level. When it's horrific, you do what you have to do. But when we have a social event, I'd like you to be, well, clear-headed."

She looked at him, her eyes narrowing. "Have I become a liability to you, Fletch?"

"No. Never." But she had. Worrying about her took so much time and energy. She was why Marcus had anchored himself in Fletcher's life.

"I think I have, and I'm sorry. I know you want to win this election, God help you. And I'll do what I can to help you get there." She braided her fingers through his.

"You will?"

"I'll cut back on the pills. It can't be sudden—I'll go through withdrawal, and nobody wants that. But I'll make sure I'm clear-eyed when you have events. But you, Fletch—you have to limit my time at them. No long nights. I put in an appearance, I smile, and I try to look my best, but when I need to rest, you make excuses for me. That has to be the deal."

He nodded. "Agreed. Thank you, my love. As always, you're the best."

"Hardly the best, but I'm trying. Now, have Marta bring me something to eat. I need to get on with my day."

He bent over and kissed her, wishing he felt the heat he once did. Wishing she aroused him like she had in those early days before the boy. That beautiful, beautiful boy.

Before everything changed forever.

***

Ten minutes later, Fletcher sat across from his son at the breakfast table, sipping his coffee. Cooper had dressed for school, disrupting Fletcher's plan to keep him home another day. He'd even considered hiring a tutor and homeschooling the kid, just to make sure he didn't blab to another student or a teacher about what he'd done.

Cooper toyed with his breakfast: eggs that Marta had scrambled with cheddar cheese and red pepper flakes—just the way he liked them—and wheat toast, while Fletcher ate his sausage and eggs over-easy.

"Son, you're not ready to go to school."

Cooper rolled his eyes.

Fletcher stabbed a link of sausage. He wished Vivian would come downstairs. She always handled their grumpy teenager better than he did.

"I hear Sara made it through surgery. That's a good sign."

Cooper lowered his fork. Glared. That lock of hair flopping down over his eyes because he refused to go to the barber Fletcher used.

Fletcher continued. "You understand that you can't talk about what happened. Not to anyone."

Cooper grabbed his glass of juice and slurped.

"Tell me you understand. A lot is at stake here."

"I get it. You're dying to be attorney general. You can't have any family scandal disrupt those plans. Like always, it's all about you."

God, the insolence of this kid. Sometimes, he wanted to reach over and shake him.

"It's not just about me." He sliced the sausage, grease oozing out.

Cooper eyed him from under those ridiculous bangs. "It isn't?"

"It's about all of us, but mostly, it's about you. Suppose you confess to hitting Sara. You were stoned on whatever it was you took, and that compounds the problem. You get arrested. If Sara doesn't make it, you're charged with vehicular manslaughter. That carries a sentence of twenty-five years. How do you think you'd fare serving twenty-five years in prison?"

Cooper opened his mouth, then closed it, saying nothing. He looked like a guppy.

"Of course, we'll get you excellent representation, but you're still looking at prison time. If Sara doesn't die—and we're all praying for that—you're still charged with a felony. You could get up to ten years for it. The best-case scenario would be a huge fine, sixty days or so inside, then probation. But you still have a felony on your record. What kind of future does that buy you, Coop? Have you thought about it?" Fletcher took a bite of egg, feeling a little victorious.

"Jesus," Cooper said.

"Don't think He can help you with this."

"Isn't Joel facing the same . . . thing?" Cooper asked.

"Joel doesn't have as much to lose as you do."

Cooper dropped his fork, his expression contorting into a look of defiance. "Why do you say that? Because he's Black?"

Fletcher laughed. "I don't care about that. But here's your situation. When I become attorney general, my firm will continue. Hawthorne-Watkins is a highly successful practice. Holden's going to make partner, and you'll follow in his footsteps. In just a few years, you'll be a named partner in South Carolina's most prestigious law firm. How many kids your age have that to look forward to? Does Joel McCants? I doubt it. His father's a middle-school teacher, for God's sake."

Cooper finished his toast and pushed the plate away. "What if I don't want to be a lawyer?"

"What?"

"What if I want to go into . . . insurance? Or engineering? Or get famous on YouTube? What if I have no interest in law?"

Fletcher knew this would happen; it was just a matter of time. Holden had rebelled, too. He'd kept talking about majoring in English or US history, for God's sake. But he finally figured it out. Their heritage couldn't be ignored.

"No interest in the law, huh? Well, you'd be going against three previous generations of lawyers. Hell, you'd be rebelling against your own DNA. I can't force you to become a lawyer. But I'll be very surprised if you don't." Fletcher wiped his mouth and folded the cloth napkin beside his plate. "Holden has the personality for litigation. But you—you have the rational brain for it. The raw intelligence. The ability to reason through an argument and convince others to take your side. You're a natural, Coop. It's why I'm so proud of you."

Cooper blinked at him, taking it in. Fletcher offered a soft smile, hoping it looked convincing. He may have stretched the truth, but the kid needed to understand—his future had been mapped out for him. A gift he needed to protect.

"You really think so, Dad?"

"I know so. But we have to get through this little problem. You have one job: keep your mouth shut. Leave the rest to me."

"Okay."

"Good." Fletcher wished he felt more relieved. Cooper was a good kid, but impulsive. What if guilt prompted him to tell one friend who told another? The secret would take flight. No, his son understood the seriousness of this and the consequences. Fletcher needed to make sure the other obstacle didn't disrupt his plan: the witness. Marcus had better have taken care of that little problem.

Sixteen

DR. ROMANO PAGED ME BEFORE I GOT TO THE HOSPITAL FOR ANOTHER unscheduled shift. "Sara Clark survived the night. Her mother is here. She could use a friendly face. Can you drop in and see her?"

"Of course."

"Dick Lockhart keeps reminding me about Mr. Clark and his importance to the hospital. Apparently, he runs a food company that made him filthy rich, so he's a big donor. Not sure what that has to do with me and my work, but Dick seems to think it's crucial."

Richard "The Dick" Lockhart was all about appearances. VIP admissions always got him excited, and an excited Dick Lockhart meant a micromanaging Dick Lockhart. We were in for a rough few days.

"One more thing," Romano said. "We got Sara's bloodwork results. She had fentanyl in her system—a new compound mixed with xylazine, a veterinary sedative. The same thing was found in Ariel Blackstone's results. And Joel McCants's."

"Jesus."

"It's bad, Georgia. That stuff is toxic and highly addictive. If this spreads in our schools, we may be looking at multiple fatalities. I'd like to think this is an isolated incident, but we both know better."

"That we do."

I took in a deep, cleansing breath as I opened the door to the small, private room in our surgery suite—the one off-limits to most people. VIP wasn't written on the door, but it may as well have been. A coffee pod machine and an array of snacks had been set up beside a glass carafe of lemon water.

I hated the waiting rooms in our hospital. They were tastefully decorated: muted colors, fake flowers in pastel-tinted plastic vases, and pretend-leather cushions in chairs and sofas that sag from overuse. Over the speaker system, decent songs were massacred in ambient music. All those efforts to soothe people didn't work because the emotions that filled these rooms took up all the space. All the oxygen. Every time I walked in, I absorbed the sadness, anxiety, panic, and desperation sloughing off the people as they waited.

Waiting in waiting rooms—for news that might well change their lives.

It's the job. You absorb everybody's pain. This time, it was the Advisor's voice sounding strident in my head. He's less gentle than the Counselor, but generally benign. Still, I didn't need the voices back. Not now. Not with Lana Montgomery snooping into my mental health. I gave myself a mental shake and entered.

Mrs. Clark wore an expression I'd seen far too many times. Blotchy red face, swollen eyelids, and sunken posture as though she might disappear into the cushions. I wondered how many years she'd aged in the twelve hours since her daughter had arrived here. I approached her quietly, not wanting to disturb her. She reminded me of Sara: same brown hair, though blonde highlights threaded through hers, and the same small nose and pointed chin.

"Mrs. Clark? I'm Georgia Thayer, the social worker. Mind if I sit?"

She shook her head, offering a tight smile.

I took the chair across from hers. "Are you alone?"

"For now. My husband should be here soon. As soon as he finishes something at his office."

"Any other family we can call for you? Or friends?" I knew how important it was for loved ones to have support in times like these.

"I don't want anyone else here." She glanced down at the ring on her finger: a wide, diamond-encrusted wedding band topped with a solitaire the size of a dime. "Just Charles."

"I understand."

Mrs. Clark didn't seem to hear me. I wondered what she was processing. Shock and grief could alter one's reality. We sat in silence for a few moments, then she blurted out, "I should never have let her go to that party."

"Were you worried something would happen?"

"I should have been. Sara is a good girl. I trust her not to do anything stupid. But other kids—kids like Cooper Hawthorne . . ." She spoke the name like it tasted foul in her mouth.

"What about Cooper?"

"I don't care for that family. They act as if the rules don't apply to them."

"I understand it was Cooper's car that hit Sara." But he hadn't been the one driving, according to reports. Joel had been behind the wheel.

"That boy's never far from trouble." More acid in her tone, but then a sigh emerged. It sounded so very sad. "They told me Sara took fentanyl. At first, I thought it had to be a mistake. Sara would never—but then I realized someone drugged her."

"Drugged her?"

"Against her will. Slipped it in her soda or something. Kids do that kind of thing."

I wondered how many times I'd had this conversation with parents and loved ones. Naive people convinced their child/husband/wife would never get involved in something like drugs. They were usually wrong, but denial was a powerful force.

"I can tell what you're thinking. That I don't really know my daughter. That kids take drugs all the time, and their parents are too stupid or clueless to realize they're in trouble. But that's not the case here. I know Sara."

"You've talked to her about drugs?"

"I didn't have to. We've lived the horror of it." She looked at me, her eyes as dark as coal. "I lost my son."

The way she spoke these words, the bleak solemnity in them, took me aback. "I'm so sorry."

"He died four years and two months ago, but honestly, we lost him years before that. At fourteen, he started with pot. Then cocaine. Then heroin and who knows what else. When he was seventeen, we forced him into rehab. He ran away. We hired detectives to find him. Tried another rehab place. And another. He was so good at escaping. Too smart for his own good, really. The last time we tracked him down, he was somewhere in Myrtle Beach. The investigators said he didn't want to be found. He was smart. Cunning, they said."

"Once you get caught up in that lifestyle, it takes hold of you."

Her eyes softened. "Yes. That's a good way to put it. It held on tight and wouldn't let go. Or rather, he wouldn't let go. Until the only way to escape was to take his own life."

I could feel the pain of a wound still fresh. I supposed that losing a child would always feel that way. "I'm so sorry. That's terrible. For him. For you and your family."

She smoothed a hand across her lap. "Alcoholism runs in my husband's family. Charles's father and brothers. Charles used to drink, too. Not all day—he never drank at work. But he'd come home to his vodka before he came home to me. I spent years ignoring it, and then I couldn't ignore it anymore. His drinking hurt my family. Damaged it. Max and Charles . . . there was a lot of tension there, and Charles's drinking didn't help."

No, drinking never did, I wanted to say.

"Max and Charles fought. A lot. And Sara would get so upset. She worshipped her older brother. Then, one summer, Max got so much worse. He argued about everything. He got into drugs and . . . and that life took him away from us. Sara took it hard. Never got over what happened to him. So, when I say Sara would never take drugs, you can believe it."

I considered this. Maybe Mrs. Clark was right—Sara's drug use was unintentional. Maybe someone did drug her, and that was why she left the party—she started to feel the effects, and it scared her. Maybe she was trying to find help. I prayed that one day she'd be able to answer these questions.

"Max's death nearly destroyed my marriage. We separated. I wouldn't let Sara watch someone else she loved succumb to addiction. Charles finally got it. He's been sober for almost four years now. Sees a private addiction therapist. He says his sobriety is to honor Max."

"I'm glad to hear it."

"Do you have kids?" she asked me.

"Yes. Well, sort of. I'm a foster mom to a girl about Sara's age."

"What's her name?"

"Tessa."

"Tessa?" She cocked her head at me. "Sara talks about a Tessa in her class. Says she doesn't take bull from people."

"That sounds like my kid." I shouldn't say "my kid." Tessa wasn't mine. I didn't give birth to her or have much of a legal right outside of guardianship. But she felt so thoroughly mine that it slipped out.

I looked up at the clock. Sara had been in surgery for an hour. There should be an update soon. But even if she survived the surgery, her recovery was precarious. I hoped Mrs. Clark could handle it if she got bad news.

A man entered the room, red-eyed and whiskered, a frantic expression on his face. "Margaret?"

Mrs. Clark stood and ran to him. As he folded her in his arms, I made my quiet exit, giving these worried parents privacy.

Seventeen

SWEAT DRIPPED FROM SAUL'S CHIN AND MADE HIS T-SHIRT STICK TO his chest as he bench-pressed two hundred and twenty pounds. Being as fit as possible had always been a requirement for his job, but he'd have kept his body in this kind of shape no matter what. He had to push himself, testing his limits, stretching the boundaries of his strength and tolerance, because vulnerability was not an option. Not in this life he'd landed in. Not in this job that had tried to kill him more than once. Not with a boss like Marcus, who paid well, but who would exterminate Saul in a blink if he ever felt betrayed.

He hated that Marcus owned his soul. It started back in New York, when Saul agreed to run a load of drugs for the Crips, only to have them stolen before he could make the delivery. That led to a death notice on Saul's head and four gang members giving him the worst beating he'd ever experienced. He still bore the scars to prove it. Marcus interceded and saved him, took him somewhere safe to recover, and even paid for the missing drugs. But the rescue came at a cost. He was now three years into paying the debt.

Marcus demanded complete, unfaltering loyalty. It wasn't a bad life, given what he'd come from. He had a place to live and made good money to send to his family. But Saul found that some of his "assignments" tested his moral compass. And yesterday, the compass cracked.

He dreaded the call from Marcus but knew it was coming, even before his cell phone chimed. Everything about this assignment made his stomach roil. He wished he could leave Marcus, leave town, and start a new life somewhere else. He'd reinvented himself before; he could do it again. But not before cleaning up his mess.

71

He grabbed a towel to wipe sweat from his face before answering. "Yeah," he said into the phone.

"Hawthorne called me this morning, wanting to know if we'd taken care of his little problem."

"It's taken care of."

"Excellent. Anything I need to follow up on?" Marcus had a special cleanup crew. It said a lot about the man that he did—workers who knew how to dispose of a body without leaving a trace.

"No need." Saul hoped his boss didn't push any harder.

"Good, then. Your payment will be wired to you in a few minutes."

"Thanks." Saul hung up before Marcus could press him or give him another assignment. He slipped his hands into boxing gloves and attacked his punching bag, showing no mercy. He pictured Marcus's face and pounded. His father's smirk as he punched harder. The punk who bullied his little sister: three cross punches that would have neutralized any live opponent.

Boxing was his therapy.

After ten more minutes, he removed the gloves, downed a pint of water, and hit the shower, trying to sort out what he'd fix for lunch. He should have stopped at the grocery store last night, but circumstances didn't allow for that. He'd make do with what was in the kitchen and hit the supermarket later.

As he climbed out of the shower, he caught a glimpse of his reflection in the mirror. He rarely looked at himself because of the ugliness there. "The body keeps the score," a book had once told him, and he knew it to be true. He was well-muscled and strong but marked: scars on his forearm and chest from a knife fight and the permanently bent fingers on his left hand from his father's twisted version of discipline. And, of course, his face, with the jagged scars from when his head had gone through a plate-glass window.

When Fatima was little, she'd run a finger down the jagged red caverns. "Like crayons," she had told him with a smile.

"Crayons?" He'd laughed.

"Red is my favorite," she had added, and he'd hugged her so tightly. What he wouldn't do to protect that innocence.

The Weird Girl

She was the reason for the problem he had now. The problem locked in the janitor's storeroom downstairs, probably hungry for lunch.

Eighteen

LILY GRACE DIDN'T KNOW WHAT TIME IT WAS. THROUGH THE SMALL, eye-height window, she could see gray clouds through the telephone wires, which meant daytime, but it could be morning or afternoon. She'd awoken from a nap shivering, the chill from the cement floor bleeding through the foam pad and musty blankets she'd slept on.

The room had little in the way of furnishings: a small, scarred desk, two rickety wooden chairs, a locked cabinet, and metal shelving that held paint cans and tarps. There was also a small bathroom with a dirty sink and toilet.

She missed her mama. And Daddy—he must have been so worried by now.

Why was she here? Detective Lou Michaels had brought her here. She remembered being in his big car that smelled like motor oil and driving through the outskirts of town—not toward the police station, but she hadn't said anything. She hadn't questioned him about where they were going or why.

And then he'd driven down a remote road, passing several warehouses and a garage, parking behind a large, cement-brick building. He'd been rude to her, not answering questions, taking her to this small room, and telling her he'd be back. "It's for your safety," he'd said before locking the door.

Everything was so confusing. She'd finally fallen asleep on an old blanket on the concrete floor, only to wake up in this cold, nasty room, hungry.

A noise sounded outside the metal door. Lily Grace cowered in the corner, wishing there was somewhere to hide, as the knob twisted. Lou Michaels stepped into the room.

She grabbed a blanket from the floor and wrapped herself in it. His face made her feel cold.

"You sleep okay?" he asked.

"It's chilly here."

"Sorry about that." He placed a small tray on the old wooden desk. "I made you a sandwich. And here's some milk."

"Why am I here?"

"That's not important. Eat."

She stood, her legs a little wobbly, and stumbled to the desk. The sandwich was peanut butter and banana, which she'd never eaten before, but she was so hungry she took three fast bites. Not bad.

"I'll be going to the store. What do you like to eat?"

"How long are you going to keep me here?"

"As long as it takes. Do you like sandwich meat? You're not a vegetarian, are you?"

She shook her head. She wasn't picky about food. She couldn't be, not in her family.

"What about clothes?"

Lily Grace took a long slurp of milk. Why did he ask about clothes? It made her think she'd be here forever. "I need to go home. My parents must be terrified."

He stalked the small room, checking the shelves, tugging on the lock that secured the cabinet. What was in there?

"Your parents know you are safe and that you're in police custody for now."

"They do?" This was a huge relief. She hated to cause her mama any worry. She worried so easily over the tiniest things.

"They send their love. But they want you to be safe."

She nibbled at a bit of the sandwich. "Am I in some kind of danger?"

He spun around to face her. "Not here, you're not. This is what we call a safe house. We use this room to protect witnesses."

"Oh. Because I saw the accident."

"Exactly."

"I heard Mr. Hawthorne tell Cooper to say that Joel was driving. Joel definitely was not driving. Why would he want Cooper to lie?"

"To keep him out of trouble. To keep the family from negative exposure. Mr. Hawthorne is a powerful man, Lily Grace. He can hurt you. You need to sit tight until it's safe for you to go home."

"I hope that's soon," she said.

He leaned against the narrow counter and crossed his arms. He was so big. The T-shirt stretched over his torso. Arm muscles bulged below the sleeves. His haggard face was hard to look at—the scars terrified her. "You'll be here for a few days. So clothes—what should I get?"

"Can't you just go to my house and get some?" she asked.

He cocked his head to the side. "I could, but that might bring attention to your parents. We don't want to do that, do we?"

It sounded like her parents might be in danger. She couldn't let that happen. "No. I wear a size thirteen in tops. Maybe a sweatshirt would be good. And can you get me a heater? And . . ." She hesitated, unsure how far to push. "Maybe a bed? I mean, if I have to be here longer."

"A bed?" He huffed out a laugh. "Sorry, princess. The police department has limited funding."

"Oh. Sorry. I didn't mean to be rude." She didn't like him calling her "princess." Daddy used to call her that, and it was nice, a compliment. With the detective, it sounded entitled and selfish. To show she wasn't like that, she took another bite of the sandwich and smiled as though it was the best-tasting peanut butter she'd ever had. "Thanks for the food."

He paced the small room, checking the sink, the cabinets, and the window. While Lily Grace hated the small space, she'd try to make the best of it. She didn't want to be a bother.

"I'll go to the store later. What else do you need?"

"A toothbrush? Soap? Shampoo?" She could have added a dozen more things to the list, but she didn't want to be a "princess" again. "Am I going to go to school? If I am, I'll need my books."

"You'll be taking a vacation from school. But don't worry. The teachers will catch you up when we let you go." He approached the door. "One more thing. This room is attached to a warehouse. You may hear noise. Sometimes, workers bring in merchandise. Do not let them know you're here. We don't know who we can trust, so let's play it safe, okay?"

"I understand."

"I'll be back later. Get some rest." He exited the room, keys clattering against the door as he locked her in.

Lily Grace sat on the floor, picturing her mom and her dad, praying they were okay and not missing her as much as she missed them.

Nineteen

RUS RODE TANNER'S MOTORCYCLE TO THE RIVER. HE PARKED AT THE edge of the woods and followed the trail that led to an encampment—a dozen tents and lean-tos that formed a tiny village. He'd lived there once, in the before-life.

Because it was a great place to score drugs.

A small, Hispanic-looking girl argued with a tall, bottle-blonde wearing heels and a torn, low-cut dress. Two men busied themselves with attaching a tarp to a tent. A woman had a small campfire going, a small pan perched precariously on top, probably heating water for coffee, like Rus used to do when he'd pitched a tent nearby.

He approached quietly, hands in pockets, doing his best to look non-threatening. This wasn't a community that welcomed just anyone.

"Don't know why you're here, but I ain't got nothing to offer," the older woman said. She had shoulder-length silver hair and wore a ragged skirt with a red cardigan.

"It's okay. I don't want anything from you, except maybe some information."

She poured some instant coffee granules into the pot. "Don't got that either."

Rus took a step closer. "I'm here about a friend of mine. Guy named Tanner."

She looked up, rheumy eyes narrowing. "You a cop?"

He laughed. "I'm about as far from being a cop as possible."

She stirred her brew, then poured it into a chipped mug. "Tanner's been here a few times."

"When did you see him last?"

She sipped. "Not sure that's any of your business."

Rus pulled a concrete block closer to the small fire. "Tanner is—was—a good friend of mine. He died."

She lowered the cup. "How?"

"Overdose."

"Oh God."

"Yeah," Rus agreed.

"Want some coffee?"

"No, thanks." He thought back to when he'd lived here, if you could call it living. He'd slept in a half-rotten tent, eaten food stolen from dumpsters behind restaurants, and scored drugs whenever he could from whichever dealer would supply him. God, that life.

"Tanner was here a few days ago. Bad timing, I guess, because that Oriental man came with his stuff. He always has bad stuff. That's what I told Tanner and anybody else who'd listen, but the Oriental don't charge much, so . . ."

"Tanner scored off him?" Rus asked, his jaw tight.

"Everybody scored off him that day. Little blue magic pills."

"You?" Rus asked.

She shook her head. "Not my cup of tea."

"The 'Oriental' guy—can you describe him?"

She shrugged. "Little guy—not much taller than me. And he laughed a lot. A big, annoying laugh."

"Catch a name?"

"Can't remember, except that it didn't fit. You see an Oriental, you expect him to be Huang or Tae or Moon or something. He had a white name. Bruce, maybe? No, that's not it."

Rus nodded. He knew. "Boris?"

"Yeah, that was it. You know him?"

"Know of him." And everything Rus knew was bad. Boris dealt all over town. Word on the streets was that he had connections to some huge crime operation.

She pointed to the arguing women. "He was looking for her, the tiny Mexican one. She always causes trouble around here. She buys from him but don't pay with money, if you know what I mean."

He did know—all too well. It was easy to sell your body for a score. "You saw Boris with Tanner?"

She nodded. "The Mexican wasn't here. Guess he wanted to get rid of some product. He'll cut you a good deal the first time, practically give it away. But the second time—and there's always a second time—the price goes up. Way up."

"You have any idea where I can find Boris?"

"I don't. But she might." She nodded to the fighting women.

The Mexican raised her voice. The blonde made a dismissive gesture and teetered away on heels too tall for safe walking. Both looked like they'd had rough nights on the street. Rus nodded at the old woman and approached the Hispanic-looking girl. She couldn't have been older than twenty.

"Hey," he said.

Her dark eyes scanned him up and down. Her black hair, streaked with purple, needed washing. A scab crossed her upper lip. "Fifty bucks. You don't look like you have it." The Mexican accent was strong.

"I'm looking for someone and thought you could help," Rus said.

"I doubt it."

"His name's Boris. I'm told you know him?" He caught a flicker in her eyes, which then narrowed with suspicion.

"You a cop?"

Rus laughed. "God, no. I was hoping . . . well, Boris has something I need."

She looked at her chipped fingernails. Sad remnants of purple nail polish lined the cuticles. "How badly you need it?"

Shit. She wanted money. He had about fifteen bucks to last him for the week, but he pulled out a five. "What's your name?"

"Why do you care?"

"Wanna know who I'm paying."

"Dulce." She pronounced it Dool-chay.

"I'm Rus." He handed her the five. "This is all I can spare."

She looked skeptical as she tucked the bill into her bra. "Boris is smart. Very smart. He makes his own product, has a lab outside of town."

Boris had actually made the drugs that killed Tanner?

"Where is this lab?"

"He won't say where. Big secret."

"He comes here sometimes. Where else does he go?"

She shrugged. "He gets around. A few bars in Five Points. The river near the zoo. I can tell him you're looking for him."

"Don't bother. I'll find him." Rus would. Because he had to.

Twenty

TESSA SAT IN HER USUAL SPOT—THE BACK OF THE CAFETERIA, AT THE end of a sea of tables, tuning out the clamor of voices echoing in the immense room. She had unwrapped the pesto chicken focaccia, a specialty of Jasper's Bistro, packed for her by Elias when she finished her shift yesterday. He'd also sent spinach lasagna for her dinner, muttering, "I gotta put meat on your bones. God only knows what Georgia is feeding you," and Tessa had laughed. Georgia didn't have much time for cooking. Or housekeeping. Or laundry. When the social services worker came for home visits—a requirement of the foster care system—they'd both do whirlwind house cleaning that meant crap stuffed in closets and bouts of hysterical laughter: "If she opens this door, and it all crashes on her head, where do we hide the body?"

Tessa had microwaved the focaccia to melt the cheese, the fragrance attracting more attention than she wanted. She had hurried back to her table and had just taken her first bite when someone sat across from her. It was Ariel.

"Hey." Tessa wiped her mouth with a napkin. Aside from Joel, no one ever sat with her, and she hadn't seen or heard from him since the hospital. This left her deeply worried. And sometimes Lily Grace would join her at Tessa's table. Lily Grace, the weird girl who hadn't shown up for school.

"Hope it's okay if I sit here." Ariel didn't wait for an answer before plopping her book bag on the table. She wore a pale green gauzy top and jeans torn at the knees. Her blonde hair hung in long waves that framed her pale, perfect face. Ariel wore just a little makeup—dabs of pink blush

82

and lipstick. She didn't need more because she was disgustingly gorgeous.

"No problem." Tessa wondered if she had pesto sauce on her chin. Elias's food, while delicious, could be messy.

"Cooper's still not here. I'm getting worried." Ariel opened a small, insulated lunch bag and pulled out a bag of veggies, hummus, and a fruit cup. That kind of meal would leave Tessa hungry ten minutes later.

"Why worried?"

She shrugged. "I talked to him last night, but just for a few minutes. He sounded different. All knotted up. I think his dad came into the room because he hurried to end the call. I think he's mad at me."

"Mad? Why would Cooper be mad?"

"If I remember right, we had a fight that night. He wanted me to ride to the store with him, and I didn't want to go. I think I was feeling a little dizzy and thought I might get carsick."

"That seems like a stupid thing to still be mad about. Especially considering what happened." Tessa could picture it, though. Cooper Hawthorne could be that immature. And controlling. "Have you heard anything about Sara?"

"My mom's talking to her mom today. She promised to text me if there was any news." Ariel's tone sobered.

"Y'all have been friends for a long time?"

"Since kindergarten. Same kickball teams in elementary school. Same dance classes and piano recitals. We've been through everything together."

Tessa envied that kind of friendship. She had nobody from her past, except a younger brother who lived five states away with his new family. She tried to imagine having a best friend for so many years, how she'd feel if something happened to that friend. She'd probably be a lot more upset than Ariel was.

"Sara and Cooper had an argument at the party," Tessa said. "Any idea what that was about?"

"They did? I remember Sara was in a bad mood. It happens." She snagged a carrot stick from the bag and swirled it in the hummus. "Do you think the police know about her and Joel?"

"Huh?"

"Sara and Joel. They used to date. You didn't know that?"

Tessa shook her head.

"It lasted just a few months. I think Sara was too intense for Joel. I kinda hope the police don't find out about it."

"I don't think we can keep it from them."

But damn it, this might get Joel in even more trouble. Why hadn't he told Tessa they'd dated?

"Was it an ugly breakup?"

"Most of Sara's are. She has a flair for the dramatic. But Joel's such a nice guy. He didn't hold anything against her. No way he'd hurt Sara on purpose."

Tessa believed that, but would the police?

The crackle of the cafeteria speaker made Tessa glance at the clock. Not time for class, so there had to be some kind of announcement coming. A few seconds later, the voice of Mr. Worley, the principal, resounded through the noisy room.

"Tessa Dougherty, report to my office. Now."

"Well, shit." Ariel leaned toward her. "What did you do?"

"Nothing!" Tessa had kept a very low profile. She hadn't skipped class. She hadn't failed anything. Why did the principal want her?

She stood, collected her half-eaten lunch, and headed to the door, all eyes fixed on her.

Mr. Worley was a small, big-eared man with a bad comb-over. What really annoyed Tessa were his teeth. Tiny little things, too tiny for his mouth, like he'd never lost his baby teeth. Whenever in the room with him, she fixated on the oddness of his mouth, even as it said to her, "I didn't mean to frighten you. You're not in trouble or anything."

If she wasn't in trouble, why was there a police officer in the room?

"Then why am I here?"

Mr. Worley continued. "The police are hoping you might have some information. A student—Lily Grace Duffy—is missing."

"Missing?" Fire alarm clangs went off in Tessa's head. She knew what "missing" could mean.

The officer, a female with short-cropped black hair and close-set, hawkish eyes, said, "Her mother contacted the station yesterday. Lily Grace hasn't been home since Saturday. Mrs. Duffy, Lily Grace's mom, thinks you may know something. She says you're Lily Grace's best friend. She told us that Lily Grace left home around 11:30 a.m. and headed to your house to study. Did you see her?"

Tessa struggled to take it all in. Best friend? She hardly knew the girl. And they hadn't studied on Saturday, though Lily Grace had come by the restaurant that afternoon. And Tessa had hurried her away.

Now she was missing.

"We didn't study. I had to work. She came by, though, and I told her to go to the police." Tessa directed this to the officer.

"Why?" the female officer asked.

"She said she'd witnessed a crime. She didn't want to get in trouble, but she said it was something serious. I told her to report it to Detective Lou Michaels. He's a friend of mine. Well, not mine, my mom's really. Or my foster mom." Tessa was babbling and felt like an idiot.

"Detective Michaels," the officer repeated, writing it down.

"So she's been missing . . . forty-eight hours?"

The mental alarm bells rang again—two full days. So much could happen in that short time, Tessa knew too well. Lily Grace was whisked away, ensnared by traffickers, forced to service men and . . .

She spoke directly to the officer. "Call Detective Michaels. Now."

Mr. Worley scowled. "Excuse me, Tessa. I don't think—"

Principal Tiny Teeth didn't know what Tessa knew. She had to talk to Lou. She used a softer tone and said, "Please get in touch with him. He can help."

The officer used her radio to contact the station, which routed her to Detective Michaels. "We're questioning a young woman, Tessa Dougherty, about a missing person. Says she's asked to talk with you."

"At the high school?"

"Yes, sir."

"I can be there in ten minutes."

85

The officer shot Mr. Worley a strange look, as though surprised by Lou's response. Tessa didn't care. She peppered the officer with questions: Nobody saw Lily Grace after she left home? No. Did she get to the police station as Tessa instructed her? No reports of that. Anyone suspicious in the neighborhood? Not that she knew. Signs of foul play?

"You watch too much *Law and Order*."

When Lou arrived, he spoke privately with the officer, then asked for time alone with Tessa. The principal begrudgingly lent them his office.

"Sorry about your friend." Lou sat across from her.

"We're not that close. I couldn't believe that her mother said I was her best friend."

Lou pulled out his notepad. "What's she like?"

What to say to that? "She's kind of weird. Always tries too hard. People make fun of her—I wish they didn't, but they do."

"Who does she hang out with?"

Tessa shook her head. "Nobody. She walks home with me sometimes, but I never really see her with anyone else." Tessa didn't say she tried to avoid those encounters. Just the other day, she'd spotted Lily Grace standing under the live oak tree beside the cafeteria. Tessa always walked that way and knew Lily Grace was probably waiting for her, so she'd circled the block to avoid her. To avoid the awkward conversation, the probable mention of "the Lord" and invasive questions about Tessa's life. If only Tessa hadn't done that. If only she'd taken the time to know Lily Grace a little better, maybe there was something she could have done.

Lou asked, "Was Lily Grace at that party? The one at Cooper Hawthorne's house?"

"I didn't see her there. And I sure couldn't see Cooper inviting her."

"Why do you say that?"

"He doesn't like her. Not that I know him well—I don't. But honestly, he's a jerk. He's been mean to Lily Grace."

This seemed to pique Lou's interest. "Like how?"

"Like putting a note on her desk pretending to be a secret admirer. Inviting her to sit at a certain table at lunch, and when she shows up, there's a clown doll sitting across from her. That kind of shit." Saying it aloud made Tessa realize how Lily Grace had been bullied. While Tessa hadn't joined in, she also hadn't done anything to help. "They treat her like she's in special classes or something, and she's not. She's odd, but she's not stupid."

Lou wrote something down.

"Cooper is an entitled asshole, Lou," she said. "I shouldn't have gone to that party."

"Why did you go?"

"Georgia keeps talking about how important it is that I make friends. That I have a 'normal' high school experience. But I'm pretty sure there's no such thing. Or if 'normal' does exist, I'm not interested in it."

This made him smile. "I hear you. And I'm pretty sure Georgia would understand."

"She just . . . worries. A lot. Too much." Tessa didn't want to be a bother to her foster mom. Didn't want to cause her any concern. Georgia had plenty on her plate as it was.

"Sometimes worrying is how we show love."

Tessa smiled. "Have you been reading Hallmark cards?"

"Fair point." Lou laughed, then glanced at the clock. "Tell me about your interaction with Lily Grace on Saturday."

Tessa told him everything she remembered: Lily Grace's panic about having witnessed a crime and Tessa giving her Lou's name. Lou asked for a description of Lily's clothes, and Tessa told him to the best of her memory: jeans, a red sweater, and *very* white gym shoes.

"She didn't go to the police station?" Tessa asked.

He shook his head.

"What's happened to her?" Her mind was filled with possible scenarios. It was just a few years ago that Tessa had met a boy at the ball field. Thought he'd become her boyfriend when he showered her with gifts. Agreed to run away with him to escape foster care, only to land in a worse hell than anyone could imagine. Had the same thing happened to Lily Grace? She wouldn't last a week. She didn't have the survival skills that Tessa had.

"You're worried that she's fallen into the hands of traffickers. And that is one possibility. But it's not the only one. You don't have to think the worst," Lou said.

"Kind of my nature." Tessa looked at Lou and saw kindness in his eyes. "I haven't been a very good friend to her. If I had—"

"Don't go there, Tessa. This is not your fault."

"Isn't it? Maybe I could have protected her."

He offered a sad smile. "It's funny, because that's how I feel about you. I should have gotten you away from Jefe sooner. We should have busted up his depraved enterprise and rescued all of you, but we didn't look hard enough at what he was doing."

"It's okay. Georgia found me, and she figured out how to save us." Tessa would never forget it—how lucky she was that Georgia was so stubborn and brave.

"How about we make a deal, then?" Lou said. "No guilt allowed. Instead, we move forward. I do whatever I can to find Lily Grace. You do whatever you have to do to pass trigonometry. Deal?"

"Deal. But find her, Lou. You have to."

Twenty-One

"LOU SAID WE SHOULD BE OVER ABOUT SIX," I SAID TO TESSA. THE invitation from Lou Michaels inviting us to his house for dinner took me by surprise, but I never turned down an offer for a meal that I didn't have to cook. Or burn.

Tessa emerged from her bedroom with her laptop tucked under her arm. "I think I'd better stay home and study. Spanish test tomorrow."

"Maybe we should just cancel then."

"No!" She hurried to say. "He's gone through all that trouble. You go. I'll be here, buried in Español. Is that what you're wearing?"

I glanced down at my outfit. The black pants and the slightly wrinkled button-down top that I'd had on at work. Nobody had barfed on me, and I'd eaten a burger at lunch without dripping ketchup down my front. "What's wrong with it?"

She looked me up and down. "It's fine, but maybe the gray tailored top would be better? It goes great with that lapis necklace we bought last month. And the silver earrings—the hammered ones."

"Uhm. Okay." Her eager expression surprised me. I indulged her, changing into the outfit she suggested. And laughed when she insisted I try a little blush and swipe on some mascara "to bring out my eyes."

Truthfully, I should probably care more about my appearance. Now that I had a teen in my home, I needed to model pride in my appearance. So I even smeared on some lipstick before standing in front of her for inspection.

"Beautiful," she said.

I almost answered with a snarky, "Yeah, right," but that would defeat my purpose. Instead, I said, "Thanks. You're an excellent fashion consultant." I told her to study hard and text me if she wanted me to bring home leftovers.

Fifteen minutes later, I found myself standing on Lou's narrow porch beside blue rockers and a planter overflowing with luscious red geraniums. It was like walking up to a magazine cover. I pressed the doorbell.

He smiled when he opened the door. I remembered when he rarely did that—always starched and rigid, the consummate professional. All that changed when we brought down the trafficking operation together— if there was ever a bonding experience, that was it.

"Hey! Come on in." He wore dark jeans and a cotton shirt that brought out his amazing pale blue eyes. He held the door, and I stepped inside. Of course, his place was immaculate. Blue sofa with perfectly aligned accent pillows. A coffee table with absolutely no clutter. A mantel over the fireplace held a few photographs and an odd pottery thing that must have weighed twenty pounds.

"No Tessa?"

"She's home cramming for a test."

"That's too bad. Want something to drink?" he asked. "I have your favorite chardonnay."

"Can't say no to that."

He disappeared into the kitchen, and I meandered around the living room. The photos were of an older couple—a white-haired woman with sparkling eyes that matched his and a man with dark hair streaked with silver. They had to be Lou's parents.

The odd pottery piece, though—blue and green, with two asymmetrical handles—where had it come from?

"Admiring my project?" he asked from behind me.

"Yours? As in, you made it?"

He smiled. "A pottery class last summer. Someone said I needed to, and I quote, 'loosen up. Get in touch with my creative side.'"

"Yeah, that sounds like me." I took the glass from him.

"And since I respect that person, I took a pottery class. That's my vase. It doesn't hold water. The sides are about an inch thick. It weighs more than I do. And the handles, well, they migrated without my permission—but I think it's probably worth a fortune."

"At least," I laughed. I liked seeing this humorous side of Detective Lou Michaels.

"Lasagna just came out of the oven. Not Elias's caliber, but it's an old family recipe."

"It smells wonderful." I sat on his sofa, and he moved beside me. It was at that moment, as I sipped wine, smelled the pasta, and listened to the jazz playing softly from his retro record player, that it occurred to me: was this a date?

That was a problem. I didn't date, not after that disastrous six months with reporter Ben Reeder, Lou's best friend. Not that I wasn't interested in men—they interested me plenty. It was just that I was too damaged to sustain a relationship. It wasn't fair to a potential partner that I brought so much baggage.

Tessa. She'd purposely stayed home so I'd be alone with Lou. She wanted this to be a date. I'd need to have a conversation with that young woman when I got home.

"Sorry Tessa couldn't be here. I know she's worried about her friend, Lily Grace. Wish I had news for her." He shook his head. "We tend to think missing teens are runaways, but this doesn't have that feel. Her bike was found in the yard. What we know about her family life—they're odd, but I didn't sense any big conflict there that would lead to her running."

"Tessa's scared she's with traffickers."

He took another sip. "We've got a team on this. We'll find her."

I believed him. I had to.

"Do you know her parents?" he asked.

"Never met them."

"That's too bad. They could use a friendly face."

"What do you mean?" I asked.

"They seem to have a lot of church support. People praying and all. But they're an odd duo. The mother, especially. She's, well, large. Very large. And very emotional. I suspect they've spent years being overprotective of Lily Grace, and then this happens. She can't make sense of it. And I hear a lot of guilt, but that's not uncommon with terrified parents."

"Would it help if I went to see them?" I asked.

"It might. Your call." He put down the beer. "I need to check our dinner."

When he hurried to the kitchen, I decided to follow. I'd never been in that room and froze in the doorway. Marble countertops gleamed. Teal cabinets stretched to the ceiling. The stove looked like something from a chef's show, and the refrigerator stood the size of a phone booth (I was old enough—barely—to remember phone booths).

"Holy shit," I said.

"What?" He spun around to look at me, and I gestured at the kitchen showroom that he'd kidnapped and installed in his house.

"Had it redone last year. This house has been one reno project after another."

"I painted my bathroom five years ago. That's as far as I got."

He laughed. "Your home has character."

"Which is a way of saying it's old and needs a major overhaul, but thanks." I glanced around again. Glass front cabinets showed nice crystal goblets. The pantry held cereal and canned goods perfectly aligned. "I'll cut a deal with you. You let me trade homes for an afternoon, and I promise to never cook for you."

He pulled a salad from the refrigerator and stared at me. "Why for an afternoon?"

I took a sip of wine. "Okay. Here's the deal." I went on to tell him about the call from Ms. Lana Montgomery, the not-a-social-worker who'd been assigned to Tessa's case, and her tone during our conversation about a home visit. "She'd love this place, Lou. She sounds like someone who's all about control."

He lifted a finger. "One, I think you just said I was controlling, but we'll let that slide for now. Two, your home is fine. You're taking excellent care of Tessa, and that Montgomery woman is going to see that."

I wished that was true. "She asked about Lenore, my therapist. And my overall mental health. I don't think she believes a mental patient should have responsibility for a minor."

His eyes softened. "Oh, George. You're so much more than a so-called 'mental patient.' But you need to believe it before you can convince her that it's true."

"Easier said than done." I studied the glass of wine. I'd only let myself have the one glass—a deal I'd made with my therapist because of the medicine I was on, but the conversation had me wanting more.

Lou served our plates. "Okay, here's what I know. You work one of the most stressful jobs there are—I think it's worse than being a police officer. And you do it brilliantly. Last year, you doggedly tracked down the traffickers who held Tessa. You risked your life to free her and the others. Nothing about any of that sounds like a mental patient."

"I hear voices."

"Yes. And when was the last time?"

Dare you to tell him the truth, the Advisor said.

"It's been a while," I lied. I always keep some of my crazy to myself.

He smiled. He had this half-impish grin; it kind of transformed his whole face. "See? Tell that to stupid Ms. Montgomery. And if she really gives you flak, then I'll talk to her, and Elias will, and Clancy, and . . ."

I could picture it, too. My whole army coming to my rescue. "I appreciate the offer, but this is a battle I'm fighting on my own."

"As long as you fight, George. That girl needs you."

I almost said, *And I need her*.

He took two calls during our delicious meal. One was an update on the search for Lily Grace (no news, he told me). The other had a different tone—Lou frowning, answering in curt responses. When he hung up, I asked, "Everything okay?"

"Fletcher Hawthorne. Pressing me about the case against Joel McCants."

"Asshole. Joel is just a kid."

"Hawthorne's like that. He abuses his power as the county solicitor. Some cases, he'll micromanage the assigned detectives to death. Others, he gives minimal attention. We had a huge drug bust last spring—pretty sure it was tied to a national cartel—and Hawthorne assigned it to a junior attorney hardly out of law school. Defense tore him to shreds. Guy walked."

"That's terrible." And it seemed idiotic. Hawthorne should want dealers like that off our streets.

"And since he's been running for attorney general? He's become a tyrant—especially with any case that's getting media attention."

"What will happen if he wins?"

Lou cleared our plates. "He'd be out of my hair, which is good for me. But I don't see him benefiting South Carolina. He's more about benefiting himself."

That was what I thought, too. "Guess I'll be campaigning for the other guy."

"You and me, both. Ready for dessert?"

I shook my head and stood. "This has been great, but I'm full. And I need to get home to Tessa."

Did I see a flicker of disappointment in his eyes? Damn. I shouldn't have worn the tailored top and lapis necklace. I shouldn't have come at all. Lou was a wonderful, kind man. He deserved someone much more "stable" than me.

"This has been fun, Lou. I really appreciate it."

He walked me to the door. I gave him a hug, tilting my face away to avoid any chance of a kiss and feeling like a complete ass.

Well, you sure screwed that one up, the Advisor said.

Twenty-Two

THERE SHE WAS, JUST AS RUS HAD EXPECTED. STANDING BEHIND Columbia's tackiest honky-tonk, the Garnet Rooster, a place frequented by truckers, motorcycle gangs, and rednecks ready to blow paychecks on beer and pool. And women like Dulce.

Dulce (Dool-chay) didn't go inside, though. She stood near the gravel parking area under a tree, waiting.

Rus had a good idea who she was expecting.

He parked Tanner's motorcycle beside the building, away from any lights, and kept an eye on her. It didn't take long. A jeep rumbled into the lot and parked near Dulce. The man who climbed out—small, dark-haired, and Asian—hurried over to her and gave her a big, sloppy kiss. He had to be Boris, the guy she mentioned at the homeless encampment. The dealer responsible for killing Tanner.

Dulce pushed him back. A whispered conversation resulted in her taking his hand and leading him into the woods. Rus didn't follow. He didn't want to see what happened next. He knew.

How well he knew.

He'd been a little older than Dulce when he lived on the streets and had to hustle for every dime and every fix. He learned to let the high lift him out of his body, so he didn't care what was done to it. That blissful numbness was how he survived—until he stopped surviving.

Part of him wanted to warn the girl, to yell at Dulce that the life she had chosen would kill her, but he knew it wouldn't matter. His voice would never be heard over the scream of her addiction.

Thirty minutes later, the two reemerged, Dulce straightening her skirt, Boris smiling and muttering something to her. He gave her a peck on the cheek, slipped her a small baggie, and returned to his jeep.

Rus started the motorcycle and followed Boris out of the parking lot, keeping his distance but not letting him out of his view. They drove down Shop Road into the warehouse district, and Boris took a rutted dirt road that led to a squat building surrounded by a welded wire fence. It looked like the kind of place that would store equipment. Boris climbed out of the car, unlocked the padlocked gate, drove closer to the building, and hurried inside.

Rus waited a few moments before approaching. He parked behind the structure and circled it, surveilling it. When he found a small window, he peered inside. Boris was putting on what looked like a hazmat suit and a face mask. He switched on the overhead fluorescent lights. Christ. The place looked like a small pill factory: bricks of a powdery substance, bottles of chemicals, big orange buckets, and a Bunsen burner. On the wall hung several other hazmat suits and a shelf with gloves and boxes marked N94. In the center of the room, two large metal tables held burners, small stashes of supplies, and a large metal device with wheels like a sewing machine.

Rus watched, mesmerized, as Boris got to work. He used his cell phone to play music—some Asian-sounding hip-hop, booming through external speakers. He moved manically, hurrying from one box to another, half dancing to the annoying music as he meticulously measured out ingredients—small amounts of a light gray powder, more of a paler one, and a few drops of what looked like an oily liquid. Once mixed, the substance was loaded into the metal machine. When he turned it on, the wheels turned, the machine rumbled, and a few minutes later, tiny blue disks spilled out. Pills.

This was Boris's fentanyl lab.

The sound of another car approaching jolted Rus. He hurried to hide himself behind a tree. The vehicle turned out to be a high-end Lexus SUV, obsidian black, driven by a massive man with a shaved head and a nasty-looking scar across his face. From the backseat, another man emerged: smaller, goateed, dressed in beige pants and a vivid white shirt.

He smelled like money. Both men entered the building, the large man holding the door for the other. Rus doubted they worked for Boris. More likely, it was the other way around.

A few minutes later, the men reemerged, the large one carrying a box—probably a supply of freshly made fentanyl tablets. When they drove away, Rus returned to his motorcycle and sped off.

He had a plan.

It was long after dark when he returned. The trip wasn't easy—he had a backpack filled with what he needed: wire cutters, two sloshing cans, rags, and a lighter.

The wire cutters sliced through the gate lock. No cars waited within the fenced-in area. No lights shone in the building. Rus used a flashlight to approach.

A chunk of concrete took care of the window, leaving an opening large enough for Rus to climb through. He hit the lights, taking in the components of the lab. He approached the pill press: a dozen pills rested on a tray attached. Freshly made fentanyl. The dragon.

The impulse hit him like a tsunami. Grab a pill. Press it under the tongue—quicker response that way. Close his eyes, let the delicious bliss come. Numb himself to Tanner's death and all the other losses that bore down on him.

God, how he needed that escape.

Dammit. DAMMIT. Rus retrieved the lighter. Opened the cans of lighter fluid he'd brought. He splashed fluid everywhere, scattered the rags, and added newspapers that had been stacked for packing across all surfaces.

He returned to the window and lit the flame. A small flicker swelled, spread its fingers, and danced up to the ceiling. Rus crawled out, hurrying away, then spinning back around to watch. Smoke bloomed out. The fire swallowed the walls, the roof, and in mere minutes, tendrils of flame stretched to the sky. A strong smell erupted, and Rus realized it might be toxic. He ran, climbed on the motorcycle, and sped away.

Twenty-Three

"YOU DON'T HAVE TO GO IF YOU DON'T WANT TO," GEORGIA SAID TO Tessa.

"I don't want to. Neither do you. But we both probably should." She climbed into Georgia's Civic. They could walk, really. It was only a few blocks away.

"Then hold this." Georgia handed her a mac and cheese she'd picked up from their favorite deli—a gift for Lily Grace's parents. This was what Southerners did, Georgia had explained. "In times of crisis, bring a casserole."

"Can you tell me anything about how Sara's doing? Without breaking your stupid confidentiality laws?"

"She's holding her own," Georgia said. "She's in the ICU, and she'll be there for the foreseeable future, but she survived the first surgery."

"First?"

"More to come. But that will wait until she's stronger."

Tessa felt relief. Every hour Sara was still alive seemed like excellent news. A miracle, even. Would they get another miracle with Lily Grace?

Georgia shot her a side-eye. "Lou said you were feeling a little guilty about what happened to Lily Grace."

"Lou has a big mouth."

She smiled. "He's worried about you. And about your trig test on Friday, which you need to study for, by the way."

"I wish I'd spent more time with Lily Grace on Saturday. I could be a better friend."

"How so?"

98

It was hard to tell her the rest. How she didn't love spending time with Lily Grace, because she was weird and said weird things. How she'd actually avoided walking home with her. Tessa, who had so few friends anyway, had rejected the one person who always reached out to her.

"You can't like everyone," Georgia said. "Just because she liked you doesn't mean you have to become her bestie."

"I could have been nicer to her. Maybe if I had . . ."

"You're giving yourself a lot of power. I doubt there's anything in the world you could have done to protect Lily Grace that wouldn't have put you in danger."

Tessa turned to look out the window. Night was falling, draining the colors from the trees, muting the sky to a dull gray. Maybe Georgia was right. Maybe what happened to Lily Grace wasn't Tessa's fault.

If only she could believe it.

Ten minutes later, they sat across from Lily Grace's parents and Tessa did all she could not to stare. And there was much to stare at. The God-awful clutter in the cramped living room: boxes and stacks of newspapers, bookshelves bulging with random things, and unopened packages strewn across the coffee table. They'd removed a box of cereal and two plates to make room to sit on the smelly, orange-upholstered sofa.

Tessa wanted to stare at Lily Grace's mother, too. She was so immense, almost manatee-shaped. Even her face—her dark eyes hidden in pillows of fat, a neck that bulged below the chin. How uncomfortable her life must have been. And the father was odd, too: a small, rail-thin man with ashen skin dressed in an outdated suit.

"We're so sorry about Lily Grace." Georgia spoke kindly, as though everything about the room and the couple was perfectly normal. "I can't imagine how hard this is for you."

Mrs. Duffy nodded, tears squeezing out of those tiny little eyes. "Lily Grace is my angel. I've never been apart from her for this long."

Her tiny husband reached over and squeezed her hand.

"Hopefully, she'll be home soon." Georgia sounded like she meant it, that she thought Lily Grace would be okay, when they both knew that was a long shot.

The fat woman turned to Tessa. "People don't understand my girl. It's just . . . we've sheltered her. And she has a unique way of seeing the world. She's still an innocent, you know? Others don't understand that. They think she isn't smart, but she is."

"I know she is," Tessa said. "She aced our history test when everyone else got a B or less."

"She talks about you all the time. About how nice you are. And smart. Lily Grace is a very sensitive girl, and she doesn't make friends easily. But she really likes you."

The guilt came like a spike in Tessa's gut. "Lily Gross," Cooper often called her, and Tessa had said nothing. Georgia patted her leg.

"Y'all don't have any idea where she might have gone after she left Tessa on Saturday?" Georgia asked.

Mrs. Duffy looked at her husband, who shook his head. "The only places she's allowed to go are school and church. I let her go see Tessa because it had to do with homework, but we're very careful with Lily Grace."

"Have you reached out to the church? To see if she came by there?"

The skinny father spoke. "I called the pastor. The altar guild was there all afternoon, and she didn't come by."

"And you can't think of other friends who may have seen her?"

Mrs. Duffy shook her head.

"Excuse me," Tessa interrupted. "Could I use your bathroom?"

"Of course." Lily Grace's mom told her it was at the end of the hall.

Tessa caught Georgia's perplexed expression as she stood. Georgia was probably picturing how the bathroom might look, given the state of the living area, but Tessa wasn't really headed there. She wanted to see Lily Grace's bedroom. She slipped down the hall, passing a large bedroom that was even more cluttered than the living room, and spotted a second open door. A peek inside told her it had to be where Lily Grace slept.

This room was immaculate. On the purple-ruffled bedspread, a rainbow array of pillows rested against the headboard. Posters of Billie Eilish covered the walls. Her desk held a lamp, their math book, and several notebooks. Tessa glanced behind her before stepping inside.

A chest at the foot of the bed held a stuffed sloth and a floppy-eared dog, and Tessa smiled. It fit Lily Grace. She moved to the closet: clothes in perfect order. Shoes paired and lined up beneath the tops.

She felt a surge of empathy for Lily Grace. Living in the chaos of her house, yet keeping this room a pristine sanctuary. Having parents that were so . . . odd . . . yet Lily Grace didn't seem ashamed of them, often talking of her mom and dad like she lived in a Beaver Cleaver family.

She sat on the bed and considered what was missing. Where was her computer? The police probably took it, hoping it would provide information about what had happened. Her phone? Probably with Lily Grace. For everyone their age, the phone had become an appendage. Tessa smoothed the pillow to the right of her hand, noting the softness of the cream-yellow sheets. Her gaze traveled the room, resting on the slick surface of the dresser.

There. Something silver. A bracelet, maybe? She'd never seen Lily Grace wear jewelry of any kind, but maybe she saved it for dressing up. Or church.

Tessa lifted the silver cuff, noting how dented it was. A design had been etched into it: a semicolon. Tessa had seen it many times before. Had seen it the night of Cooper's party.

On Sara's wrist.

"Tessa? You okay?" Georgia's voice rang out.

"Coming!" She gripped the bracelet, hurried to the bathroom (which was disgusting), and flushed the toilet. When she returned to the room, she gripped her stomach and explained, "I think I better get home."

"Oh. Okay." Georgia stood. "You okay?"

"Cramps," she lied.

"Gotcha." Georgia turned back to the parents. "Please let us know if there's anything we can do."

The father stood. The mother offered a sad smile. "Thank you for coming. I'll be sure to tell Lily Grace when she comes home."

"Please do," Tessa said and prayed Lily Grace would live to get the message.

Twenty-Four

I NEARLY CRASHED INTO THE CAR AHEAD OF ME. TESSA HAD SNEAKED into Lily Grace's bedroom? Had found a bracelet that belonged to Sara Clark? Was this proof that Lily Grace had gone to the Hawthorne party that fateful night?

I felt a mixture of excitement and dread, which made me pull over and park. "Number one. You should have told me you were doing that. Or asked Lily Grace's parents for permission!"

Tessa handed me the bracelet.

"You took it from Lily Grace's room? Dammit, Tessa. We don't steal things. And why didn't you tell her parents that you were taking it?"

Tessa didn't look the least bit guilty.

"You're not a sleuth, Tessa. You're a kid. You need to leave the policing to Lou and his colleagues."

She turned to look at me. "Exactly. Why didn't they notice the bracelet when they searched her room?"

I shrugged. "Probably thought it was Lily Grace's. And you're sure it's Sara's?"

"She wears it all the time. I've always wondered about the semicolon. Must mean something."

I turned the bracelet over. Examining the inside, where words had been etched in cursive, I read: "*Never forget. Your story isn't over yet.*"

"What does that even mean?"

I thought about Sara's mom and what she'd told me about Sara's older brother, who died by suicide—facts I couldn't share with Tessa because of confidentiality. But I could speak in generalities.

"A semicolon is a symbol in the suicide prevention world. A period is final. It's the end. But a semicolon means that even if you're having a terrible day, even if you feel like ending it, your story isn't done. Hold on, and things will get better. Or something like that."

"That's pretty cool," Tessa answered.

I noticed something in one of the dents and held it closer to my car's dome light. "Shit."

"What?"

"We better call Lou. I think I see Sara's blood on this."

Ten minutes later, Lou met us at our house. He wore a blue polo shirt that made his eyes look absolutely stunning, but I didn't comment. He took the bracelet with a gloved hand and slid it into an evidence bag.

"Our prints are all over it," Tessa commented. She'd clearly been watching too many *Law and Order* reruns. "I'm sure I didn't see Lily Grace at the party. But Sara was wearing that."

He held the bagged bracelet up to the light. "I do see the traces of blood you mentioned."

"So maybe Lily Grace saw Sara after the accident? Or even witnessed it?" I said.

He nodded. "And took this when she found it."

"That was the crime she wanted to report," Tessa said. "She saw the car hit Sara. But what I want to know is—was Joel really driving?"

Lou shot me a warning look. We were thinking the same thing. "That's for the police to figure out, Tessa. Let Lou do his job."

Twenty-Five

FLETCHER SAT IN HIS HOME OFFICE AND CHECKED THE SPREADSHEET where his campaign assistant tracked donations. Checks kept coming. Online contributions closed in on half a million. His ad campaign would click into high gear soon—TV commercials, radio spots. Promotions on Facebook and Twitter and whatever else the PR firm suggested. A family photo shoot was scheduled for Friday, and he worried if Vivian would be up to the challenge. She'd done as she'd promised—cut back on the narcotics, sticking with muscle relaxers and anti-inflammatories, but that adjustment came at a huge price. He could see it behind her eyes.

Even as thin as she'd become, she could be eye-popping gorgeous, and if they bribed their boys to put on suits, they could look GQ handsome. Especially Holden—he'd been getting regular haircuts that definitely weren't done by a traditional barber. Cooper teased that Holden had spent over a hundred on his last appointment. How he could afford it, Fletcher didn't know—he hadn't raised Holden's allowance and monitored the credit cards like a vigilant hawk. But Holden had always been resourceful. He'd probably scored some easy job at the frat house. Holden always found a way.

Cooper was another matter. The guilt was eating at him, despite Fletcher's efforts to explain why he had to stick to the story. Fletcher couldn't let the truth about the accident surface. That kind of scandal would kill his chances of winning. Even the presence of drugs in his house could do it, but so far, it hadn't made it into the press. Thank God for small favors. Or rather, large ones, since he'd reminded the editor of the local newspaper about his buried domestic disturbance charge from three years before.

He looked out his office window at the pool glimmering in the sunlight. The sight always filled him with a jumble of emotions. Awe at the simple beauty of the water. Happy memories of time splashing with his sons. And it was in that place, in that spectacular water one glorious afternoon, that he met the person who completely upended his life.

Fletcher had always been a man with robust appetites. He loved a good steak, a well-aged bourbon. He loved feasting his eyes on a beautiful sunset or indulging in prime seats at the symphony. But one appetite outshined all the others. And caused him the greatest shame.

His unquenchable love for the boy.

It wasn't that he didn't love his wife. He adored Vivian. She was gorgeous and smart and gave him two sons. When she'd been healthy, having her beside him made him sit up taller, stand prouder. Even now, there was nothing he wouldn't do for her, especially if it would restore her to health.

But the boy.

The memory of the first moment Fletcher saw him burned in his heart. He'd come to spend the day with Holden, the two kids roughhousing in the pool, Fletcher sipping his drink in the lounge chair, watching. His attraction surprised him. He'd been with men before—always so careful, driving to Florida to the private gay club where nobody knew him. The young bucks there could be so magnetic. So accommodating. He'd spend the weekend, get his needs met, and then return home to his most excellent life.

Compartmentalizing was the key.

But that day, it all went to hell. He'd sipped and sunned and kept his eyes on the teens, ostensibly to assure their safety. Holden got bored and crawled out of the pool, planting himself on another lounger and drifting off to sleep. But the boy kept going. He climbed the ladder, mounted the diving board, and executed the most gorgeous dive Fletcher had ever seen. And then he swam, his body silvery in the water, as lithe and supple as a dolphin.

Fletcher drank too much.

When the boy came out of the water and asked for something to drink, Fletcher guided him to the pool house and offered him a coke.

"Got something to put in it?" The boy had an adorable, mischievous smile.

Fletcher shouldn't have. At fifteen, the kid was too young to drink, but Fletcher was tipsy and mesmerized, so he poured himself more bourbon and added a splash in the red plastic tumbler he handed to the kid.

"Sit with me for a minute," Fletcher said.

The boy dropped down beside him on the chaise, under the ceiling fan that offered a much-needed breeze.

Fletcher sipped his drink. The boy did the same. Up close, his pale, damp skin shimmered, and Fletcher ached to touch it. Nobody was watching.

The boy leaned back. "I like it here. It's peaceful."

"Yes, it is." Fletcher felt heat rise inside him and wanted the bourbon to cool it. He shouldn't be here alone with the boy. It was wrong, but he couldn't make himself leave. "You're amazing in the pool. You should be on the swim team."

"Really?" The boy gave him an incredulous look.

"You're a natural." He watched the words sink in—a kid desperate for approval. Fletcher offered him the most fatherly grin he could muster.

"Thanks." The kid actually looked sheepish. "Can I have more?" He held up his empty tumbler.

Fletcher almost dropped it as he returned to the bar and refilled the soda—another splash of bourbon for each of them. Out the window, he could see Holden sound asleep. Cooper had gone to a friend's. Vivian napped in their room.

It was just him and the boy. He returned to the chaise and sat a little closer, testing. The boy took the drink, smiling a dopey smile that stirred something in Fletcher he rarely felt.

Fletcher took another slurp of bourbon. For courage? For restraint? He asked questions: What do you love to study? How many brothers and sisters? Any hobbies? What's your favorite football team? As the boy answered, his words slurred, his blue eyes so beautiful, and Fletcher soaked it all in. He wanted to absorb everything about him.

Later, he regretted what he did. Regretted touching him, even though he'd only gripped the pale, soft thigh. He wished the boy had fought him, had said no, he would have pulled away, wouldn't he have? But the boy went right along with it. It was only Holden's calling out his name, asking where they were, that stopped them that day.

The boy remained in Fletcher's thoughts, stirred him awake when he was asleep. Aroused his body and his heart. He'd ask Holden about him: "How's your friend? The one who visited Saturday?" and Holden would shrug as though the boy was of no consequence. Oh, if only that were true for Fletcher. But no, Fletcher had to see him again, and that led to his downfall.

His recollection was interrupted by a knock at the door. He shook himself free of the thoughts as Marcus arrived, dressed in a linen suit and smelling of too much expensive aftershave. He helped himself to a bourbon before sitting across from Fletcher.

"Your little problem is taken care of," Marcus said.

Fletcher exhaled. "Thank God. I want no details."

"Don't want your pretty white hands to get dirty, do you?" A smirk flashed over his glass.

"*I want you out of my life!*" Fletcher wanted to scream, but that was no longer an option. "No way to trace it back to me?"

"Of course not. Saul handled everything. There is nobody more discreet."

"Good. That's good."

"And now I need a favor from you," Marcus said.

There it was. The real reason for Marcus's visit. Fletcher stood, moved around the desk, and poured himself a drink.

"Your family still owns property on the Savannah River, no?"

"We've had it for two hundred years," Fletcher spoke with pride. One of his ancestors had built a plantation on a large expanse of land close to where the Savannah reached the Atlantic Ocean. He built a dock and opened it to traders, who received supplies from ships on the ocean and transported them upriver to Georgia. The Hawthorne fortune originated from his forward-thinking enterprise. Of course, their sixty slaves had helped them profit, but that was how the world worked back then.

Marcus said, "Good. We had an issue with our lab and are relocating. I have a load of supplies coming in by ship, and I need an inconspicuous way to bring it in."

"What happened to the lab?"

"A bit of arson. Not your concern, Fletcher."

Arson. Someone took on Marcus? Fletcher admired—and pitied—the idiot who wasn't long for this world.

"My shipment arrives at 8 p.m. on Thursday evening. A shrimp boat will greet the vessel and move the goods to your country estate. They'll unload it on one of my trucks. The whole operation will only take a half hour."

"One day isn't much notice," Fletcher said.

"Is anyone at your estate now?"

"The caretaker. A maid checks in daily."

Marcus smiled. "And they both deserve a day off, don't you think?"

It wouldn't be hard to arrange. Both workers had been with the family for twenty years and followed directions without question. "Isn't this risky? Especially given my campaign? If the police find out you transported drugs onto my property—I'm done."

"The police won't be involved." The glare Marcus sent him could slice through metal. "None of this is your concern. We only need your dock for twenty minutes. So no more questions."

"A half hour and your men are gone," Fletcher clarified. "And any sign of trouble and all plans are canceled."

Marcus nodded. "Of course. I can't afford exposure any more than you can. But don't worry. Everything's been taken care of."

Did Marcus have connections with the Coast Guard, too? The extent of his reach could be terrifying.

"I'll text you on the encrypted phone when they are on the way. A second message will let you know it's done," Marcus added.

Fletcher reached into a drawer and pulled out the special phone. Marcus used codes like "the lasagna is ready" or "stop at store for Pinot" when sending messages, but Fletcher always understood them. Evil genius, that Marcus.

Marcus finished his drink and stood. "I appreciate your assistance."

"Like I have a choice."

Another shark smile. "Ah. I almost forgot. A present for that lovely bride of yours." Marcus reached into his pocket and pulled out a pill bottle. "I do hope her back is feeling better."

Shit. The pills that ruined her. And kept her alive. When Marcus slapped them into his hand and crushed his fingers around them, Fletcher felt a wave of nausea.

"They will help with her suffering," Marcus said.

And just like that, he was back in bed with a crocodile.

Twenty-Six

RUS AWOKE FROM A TURBULENT NAP AND PULLED HIMSELF UP FROM the lumpy futon that served as his bed. The old trailer had a strange light in the late afternoon—rays from the sun poking through narrow windows and shining on dust mites and clutter.

He really should clean.

He let out a cough, the fumes from the fire still irritating his lungs. He needed to be more careful next time.

Rus closed his eyes, remembering. Entering the lab, ready to destroy it. Seeing the fentanyl pills on the metal tray. Wanting. Aching. Hungry to take one, slide it under his tongue, and feel the sweet release he'd denied himself for the past year.

Thirteen months of sobriety almost obliterated in a second.

He hated to think it could be so fragile.

How long would Boris be out of operation? And who were the two men who visited the lab? The smaller one, with the sculpted goatee—he looked connected. And in charge. Rus needed to find out who he was.

But more than anything, he needed a meeting.

He took a quick shower, letting the steam fill his lungs and hacking up more gunk from the fire. He threw on some jeans and a T-shirt, locked up the old trailer, and mounted Tanner's motorcycle.

The Saturday evening meeting took place in a community center in an older neighborhood downtown. He'd attended a dozen times or so, always recognizing the familiar faces of recovery. He entered the cement block room, headed for the coffeepot, grabbed two cookies to go with his much-needed caffeine, and found a seat.

Chairs filled. The leader, a thin Black man with a ready smile who always spoke freely of his addiction and bipolar disorder, stepped to the podium. The Serenity Prayer meant more to Rus that day than it had in a while.

A woman he'd seen a time or two had a share: she'd reunited with her husband. She spoke of how love had sustained her in her weakest moments, how the promise of this reconnection had held her together through detox and rehab.

Rus didn't have that kind of faith in love. It was a complex, tainted thing in his life. His parents had loved him, he thought, until he came to realize their love was conditional. As long as he was a good son. As long as he didn't embarrass them. As long as he fit the script they'd written for him. He tried for a while, but it became impossible. He had other dreams. Other interests. His father's disappointment sliced like a knife.

But there was the other. The one who seemed to adore him, who hung on his every word. Who complimented everything about him. Who made him feel special and cherished. Who touched him with such gentleness . . . and then didn't. Who gave him his first drink and then his first pill. How feeling love became being used. That "love" coiled around his addiction like a snake.

Rus shook his head, wanting to shake out the dark memories. Dwelling on them was a bleak path. A counselor in rehab had wanted to explore that time, saying it was the "trauma" that led to his addiction, but Rus saw no point in probing. What was done was done.

To him.

Another addict in the group shared that he'd almost slipped. Run into some old "friends" willing to share, but he'd turned them down. Rus almost commented that he'd had a similar crisis, that he'd been within a few feet of the pills that could undo him. It was too easy, really. A tiny blue disk that hardly cost anything, slip it in your mouth, let everything melt away. No pain. No sadness. No awful memories.

But he'd resisted. That was something to be proud of.

"Rus?" The leader spoke his name. "You have something to share?"

"No. I mean, it's been a rough few days. Tanner and all. But I'm managing." He cleared his throat and looked around at the people watching him. So many miles on those faces, even the young ones. It startled him, sometimes, to think what those outside of this world didn't know. The toll addiction could take on a body and mind. The wounds it could cause to the spirit. No, it was the wounds that *led* to addiction; at least, it was for him. He cleared his throat. "Do you ever get mad? Think about how unfair it is that we have to live like this when others"—he gestured toward the window—"have no clue what we're going through?"

Heads nodded.

A plump woman said, "The blessed non-addicts."

"They don't know how lucky they are," an older dude added.

Silence descended on the room. Then the older guy added, "I wouldn't wish this on any of them."

The group leader returned to the podium, holding a sheet of paper. "I've been asked to share this information from our friends at the Drug and Alcohol Commission. They're reporting a shipment of fentanyl that's hit the street. Comes in bright pills—mostly blue so far. Hospitals are reporting an influx of overdoses from as little as a single dose. Whoever's making this shit is making it lethal. Y'all are in recovery. I don't worry that you're gonna use. But our friends out there—we need to get the word out. Let's not lose anyone else to this monster."

Anyone else like Tanner. Rus thought about the lab. About Boris. About the goateed man and his associate.

He had more work to do.

Twenty-Seven

SAUL KNOCKED ON THE DOOR BEFORE UNLOCKING IT, NOT WANTING TO find the kid asleep or, worse, undressed.

"Come in!" she yelled out in that weird sing-songy voice she had.

He struggled with the keys and the packages but managed to enter the small janitor's room, where he dropped the bags. "Supplies."

The girl hurried over and began rummaging through the sacks. A fleece blanket. Two sweatshirts and a pair of jeans. Pajamas that he'd taken a wild guess at for size. Toothbrush, toothpaste, deodorant, and soap. New towels and washcloths. Underwear that embarrassed him to purchase.

"Thank you," she said.

"One more." He reached inside the last bag and pulled out a small space heater. "This should help with the chill."

"You got it!" She clapped her hands as though a gift from Santa had miraculously appeared.

He shrugged. "Don't want you catching a cold while you're in police custody." It was absurd that she still thought he was the police—that Detective Michaels she kept mentioning. The kid was either stupid or incredibly naive.

She found an outlet and plugged in the heater, which made a quiet whirring noise as it sprung to life. She sat cross-legged in front of it, rubbing her hands together as though sitting by a campfire.

Saul took a seat and fiddled with the two books he'd bought: a Harry Potter and what looked like a romance, both afterthoughts as he checked out. The kid had to be bored here. How long would he be saddled with

113

her? It was his own damn fault. If he'd done what he was hired to do, the Lily Grace problem wouldn't exist.

He was an idiot.

The girl stood, stretched, and moved to the other chair, watching him. "Can I ask you something?"

He shrugged. She could ask whatever she wanted. What he was willing to tell her—a different story.

"How did you get that scar? It looks like it must have hurt so bad."

He cocked his head at her, expecting to see the usual revulsion, but her eyes softened, her face full of sympathy.

"It did. Hurt like a mother. My head went through a windshield." A lie told too many times.

"That could have killed you! You could have severed an artery. Or the glass could have cut into your brain. How terrible!"

"It was." It was also kind of a lie. The injury had happened in New York soon after he'd arrived in the US. He'd been hired to pick up a shipment of heroin, but some gang members decided to intercept it—his face being the casualty when four men smashed his head through a storefront.

He'd never forget the sounds. An explosion of breaking glass, his pulse loud in his ear, the shouts from the men stealing the merchandise. Then after, a strange stillness. His head half in the window, ice crystals of glass glistening under display lights. Where had the men gone? Had he lost consciousness? He dared not move, those peaks of jagged glass encircling him.

Blood pooled. He felt no pain, but a chill climbed through his body. He gripped the sill, desperate to keep steady. One wrong move and the glass could end him.

Or maybe he'd already reached the end. How much could a man bleed without dying? He thought of home, his mother and sister. The future he wanted for them, but could not provide. If he died then, what would happen to them?

Someone yelled out. A man approached. "Oh God. What happened to you? Don't move. Someone call an ambulance!"

Saul couldn't see him. Blood filled his eyes from all the cuts. Staying awake felt impossible, but succumbing to the pull toward unconsciousness would kill him. Finally, the EMTs arrived and, with great care, extricated him from the window.

He remembered the wail of the siren as they wove through traffic. The gurney jostled as they made turns. The pinch of the needle from the IV.

Saul had no insurance, so no plastic surgeon worked on his gashes. A resident and an intern patched him up, his face railroad-tracked with Frankenstein stitches. Comments about how lucky he was that his carotid hadn't been severed. Lucky? How was having his face slammed through a window by gangbangers lucky?

Saul didn't tell Lily Grace all this. He made up a story about chasing bad guys and getting hit by a car, his face colliding with the windshield.

"It must have been an old car. No safety glass." She was smarter than he realized.

"It was," he replied. "An old Buick."

Lily Grace looked at him thoughtfully. "You're a hero then. It must have hurt something terrible."

"It did. But they gave me medicine."

"Do people stare at you?"

The question might have annoyed him, but her eyes were filled with such genuine concern that he simply answered, "All the time."

"That's rude. The scars don't look that bad. They give your face character."

"And I don't look like a cop, do I? Helps with undercover work." He remembered leaving the hospital, still numb from the medication. Snow had begun to fall in plump, fluffy flakes. He had nowhere to go. The man who hired him would be wanting the heroin that Saul no longer had. Soon, he'd be a dead man if he stuck around. Suddenly, a man appeared at his side—the same one who'd found him sliced open and called for help. His savior. "Come with me," the man said, and Saul did.

"Did you have other injuries?" Lily Grace asked.

"Huh?"

"From the accident."

"Not too bad. Busted my arm. Cracked a few ribs. Coulda been worse."

"Coulda been better, too," she replied with a smile.

It made him laugh. How long had it been since he'd done that?

She looked at the books he'd brought her. "My mom won't let me read Harry Potter. Because they have magic in them."

Oh Christ. She was critiquing the reading material?

"But I read the first one, anyway. It was at the school library. I put a different dust jacket on it so she wouldn't know."

"Clever."

"I felt a little guilty, but the books aren't bad. They aren't evil. I wished she understood that."

Saul pictured the morbidly obese woman overflowing the easy chair that he'd seen through the window. How small her world had to be.

His phone rang. Marcus.

"Yeah," he said, pressing a finger against his lips to silence the girl.

"We've had some trouble. Somebody destroyed Boris's lab."

Saul knew—and disliked—Boris. Marcus had brought him in from California to get the SC operation off the ground. "He okay?"

"He wasn't there, but the place is burned beyond repair. A few hundred thou in merchandise lost."

"What's the plan?"

"We're relocating. And I have two assignments for you," Marcus said. "One: I want the person who did this. I want him brought to me so I can deal with him."

"Any idea who he is?"

"A camera caught a motorcycle speeding away. We checked the plates. The bike belongs to a Theresa Holcomb."

Odd that it was a woman. "Okay. I'll take care of her."

"She's deceased, as it turns out. But someone's using her vehicle. He's our culprit. Find him."

Saul nodded.

"Second: I need you to pick up some supplies on Thursday. Will text you the address."

"And take them where?"

116

"To the warehouse below your apartment. I'll be using that space for the foreseeable future."

Crap. Marcus had only used the warehouse for the storage of antiques—the legal trade that hid his less lawful ones.

"It'll work for the lab, and your living above it makes it even more secure. I doubt whoever targeted the other location knows about the warehouse, but I'll want you to keep a close lookout."

Marcus continued. "The shipment you're to pick up is coming by boat. I'll text you the details."

"Okay. I'll take care of it." He clicked off and looked at the girl. If Marcus brought workers into the warehouse, where would he put Lily Grace?

Twenty-Eight

I SIGNED OUT FOR LUNCH, LEAVING A NOTE FOR CLANCY THAT IT might be a long one, and headed to my favorite dining spot. The bistro was only a few blocks away, so I parked and entered through the side door, prepared to take my usual seat at the bar.

"Georgia? Over here! Join me." Ben Reeder, former (long time ago) boyfriend and reporter for the local newspaper, sat at a table by a window. Against my better judgment, I took a seat across from him.

"You look like shit, George," Ben said, ever the charmer.

"Rough day. After a rougher night." I sized him up. "You look pretty good, considering." Considering that eight short months ago, he'd nearly been killed trying to help me catch the traffickers. The men who assaulted him left his leg a mangled mess, and he still walked with a slight limp, which he claimed made him look "even sexier."

"I'm fine. And look—Elias even lets me eat here now." Ben grinned, his whitish-gray mustache curling.

His shrimp alfredo looked delicious, but my stomach needed something light after my hellacious day. Elias caught my eye from behind the bar and winked at me. He was my brother in every way that mattered, and I always felt better when in his orbit.

A waiter hurried to our table, and I ordered soup and tea.

"So, why the rough day?" Ben leaned closer, studying my face.

"ER is exploding. Fentanyl."

"Shit, man," Ben said. "That's some nasty stuff."

"We're seeing kids OD. One after the other. It's hard to keep up. Had to call in extra respiratory therapists. Med staff is feeling the strain. It's so hard to see so many senseless deaths." I swallowed. This wasn't the best lunchtime conversation, but Ben had asked.

Ben pulled out his notepad. I grabbed his hand. "This isn't for the paper."

"Why not? The public needs to know. It's like there's a secret war happening on our streets. Don't you want people better educated about it?" Ben's blue eyes sparked with intensity. He could get like that when he was on a story.

"You should talk to Lou. The police are up to their eyeballs trying to find out who's dealing. Maybe the police will let you do a story."

"They'll send me to their public information nitwit who won't tell me shit," he grumbled.

Same thing with the hospital. I'd love to get on TV and tell the world about the war we were fighting, but it would get me into trouble with administration (something I excelled at).

My lentil soup arrived, with a generous portion of Elias's special cornbread that I hadn't ordered. I grinned at my friend behind the bar.

"I'm getting sick and tired of these stories that belong on the front page, but I'm not allowed to write. I swear it's going to give me an ulcer," Ben griped.

"Stories?" I asked.

"The fentanyl. And what happened to the Clark girl—Sara. A kid from one of the wealthiest, most powerful families in the Midlands gets run over while leaving the party at the home of our solicitor and nearly dies. Still might, from what I hear. It's got everything—tragedy, political intrigue, given that Hawthorne is up for the attorney general seat. And I wrote a fantastic article about it, too, only to have it squashed by the publisher."

I raised my brows at that.

"What?" Ben demanded.

"One, you don't usually cave. Two, why doesn't the publisher want to cover it?"

"Come on, George. Politics. Fletcher Hawthorne probably called in a favor."

119

"He seems like just that kind of asshole," I replied, remembering the solicitor's smug, jowly face.

Ben laughed. "Man, he got under your craw."

"He's everything I loathe. Self-entitled. Smug. Camera-ready smile that churns my stomach."

Ben opened his wallet and threw a twenty on the table. "I have to get back to work. If I'm lucky, maybe they'll let me cover the street repairs downtown. If that's not too controversial."

As he limped away, I took a bite of cornbread and pondered Fletcher Hawthorne's power. What must it have been like to control the press? What did it take? Money? Favors? Blackmail?

I finished my meal, paid the tab, and stood to leave just as Lou Michaels came into the restaurant.

Shit. He moved to the takeout corner. I thought about scooting out before he noticed me, but that wasn't the right thing. So, I approached.

"Hey, Lou."

He was with someone unfamiliar: tawny-skinned, angular, with bushy brows and soft brown eyes.

"Hey." Lou barely made eye contact. "It's actually good that I ran into you."

I looked at the other man, expecting introductions. "Everything okay?"

"That's a loaded question. Sorry. This is Jackson Purdy. A colleague of mine."

I shook his hand—smooth, long-fingered, like a musician.

Lou went on. "There was an arrest last night of a young woman. The arresting officer found me this morning and told me the suspect—a shop-lifter—was asking for me. So I went to holding to see who it was. It was Dulce, George."

Dulce. Oh no. I'd met her last year when, in my attempt to find my sister's killer, I uncovered a human trafficking ring. Tessa was known as "Kitten" then, a victim of a greedy predator who sold women for sex. While Tessa worked hard to recover from her trauma, Dulce chose a different path. She lived in a shelter for trafficking survivors, but the last I heard, she'd refused therapy sessions, ignored rules, and created turmoil for the other women living there. I knew this because I volunteered there.

"Can I see Dulce?" I asked.

"I was hoping you would. Here's the thing. She was high when they arrested her. An opioid of some kind. Didn't need Narcan, but they kept her in the infirmary overnight."

Traffickers used drugs to control the women. Dulce had used. Often. If she was using the fentanyl we were seeing on the streets, she might not live to see thirty.

"I'll go see her today."

"I'll leave a pass for you at the jail."

"Thanks." I pushed past them for the door, relieved that we could at least talk. But it sure felt like our friendship wasn't what it used to be.

Because, once again, I'd screwed up something good.

Twenty-Nine

LILY GRACE KEPT BUSY. WHEN SHE OPENED THE DOOR TO THE NARROW closet off the room, she found all kinds of cleaning supplies and went to work. She swept and mopped the floor and attacked the window with Windex until the glass sparkled. She dusted, then cleaned every surface, removing layers of grime and dirt. She rearranged the furniture, moving the "bed" away from the drafty door and shifting the small table closer to the light. The small space slowly became more pleasant. Not nice, exactly, but not as scary.

That done, she pulled the wooden chair closer to the window and started reading the Harry Potter book, becoming so engrossed in it that she had no idea how much time had gone by. When the sun dropped low and the light diminished, she closed Harry and smiled. She could be like him, she decided. This little room was like his dwelling under the stairwell. If only she had a pet owl to bring her messages of an imminent escape.

No, she shouldn't think like that. Lily Grace was here under police protection. And Detective Lou Michaels looked like a great protector. One day—hopefully soon—he'd tell her it was safe, and she could return home to her parents. Mama would be so happy to see her. Daddy would kiss the top of her head and call her "baby," and they'd eat her favorite meal from KFC. They'd tell her how proud they were that Lily Grace had helped the police bring down a criminal.

Which was part of the problem. Was her captivity all because Cooper Hawthorne hit Sara and lied about it? Cooper was just a kid like her—granted, a kid from a very important family, but still—maybe she'd get brave enough to ask Detective Michaels for more information. Maybe. He had a way about him that made him seem closed off, like the way Daddy could be sometimes when Mama asked him about his job. Some things you just didn't discuss.

Thoughts of her parents filled her with sadness and worry. Mama counted on Lily Grace to help her throughout the day. She fixed her breakfast. Helped her get dressed. Went to the store on her bicycle for supper fixings. Was Daddy doing all that now? Did he remember to make sure she took her pills? Had he washed and changed the linens like Lily Grace did?

She heard a noise. It sounded like a truck outside the window. She peered out, spotting a large black SUV rumbling past. It parked a few dozen yards away, and two men climbed out. One was the detective.

She backed away from the window, not wanting to be seen. The men talked outside, saying something about equipment and preparation tables. A door squeaked open, something knocked against something else, then a door slammed shut. Next came scraping sounds, like furniture being arranged. Was someone moving in? What else was in this building? All she'd ever seen was her small room.

Voices carried, but she couldn't make out any words. After a long while, the voices grew silent, and footsteps sounded outside her door. The lock clicked, and Lou Michaels entered.

"Hey," she said.

He paced the room, taking in the changes. "You've been hard at work, I see."

"Just straightening up a bit. Hope that's okay."

"Of course it is."

She remained in her chair, watching him as he moved to peer out the window. He said, "I need to tell you something. We're not alone anymore. This room is attached to a warehouse that was mostly abandoned. But not anymore. There will be some people working out of it. Bad people, I'm afraid. So we don't want them to know you're here."

"Bad people?" She didn't like the sound of that.

"You don't need to worry. As long as you're quiet, they'll never know you're here. And we have them under police surveillance. We will keep you safe."

She felt relieved to hear this. Detective Lou Michaels seemed strong. Confident. He'd lived a hard life and wore the scars to show it. She trusted him. "I'll be quiet. But I have a question. Well, two, actually."

He spun around to stare at her. "What?"

She cleared her throat, suddenly reticent. "I was just wondering when I can see my mom and dad. I miss them. And I know they miss me."

"We've been over this. It's only been a few days—and they know you are safe. They miss you, too—of course they do. But we give them regular reports that you're fine. They're very proud of you for helping the police."

"Well, maybe you can take my picture and show it to them? With your phone, I mean. So they'll know I'm okay."

He looked uncertain, then shrugged. "That's not a bad idea." He pulled a cell phone from his pocket. She stood by the window, smiled, and extended a hand with her pinkie, index finger, and thumb extended. The ASL sign for "I love you."

"Got it," he said.

"I have one more question. It's about . . . why I'm here. I saw Cooper running over Sara Clark, but I don't understand why that means I have to be in hiding? Cooper's family is rich, but his father is a prosecutor, right? So, what am I hiding from? And why?" She held his gaze, trying to be brave in the face of that scar, those dark, hooded eyes.

"Christ. I can't tell you that."

"Why not? I mean, if I have to hide here, I deserve to know why." Her little bit of courage slowly seeped away. She tried not to show it.

He slid the chair back and sat. "Okay. You want to know the truth? Well then, get ready. Because you might not like it."

"Tell me."

"Cooper Hawthorne's father isn't who everyone thinks he is. Sure, he's rich. Well-connected. Well-known in the legal world. But he's also a crook. He'll do anything to protect his son. He doesn't want the truth to come out about the accident, which makes you a threat to him."

"A threat?"

"He's running for an important state office. Any scandal will kill his chances."

"But he didn't hit Sara. It was Cooper."

He shook his head. "Dear God, you are naive. His son's actions reflect on him. Plus, Fletcher orchestrated the cover-up. He's in too deep, and he knows it. He also knows people who are criminals. Ruthless criminals. People who will take care of problems like Lily Grace Duffy. You are nothing more than a mosquito to them. They'll squash you without giving it a second thought."

Her mouth dropped open. She never imagined someone would want to hurt her the way he described. "I . . . had no idea."

"Well. Now you do. This is why you're here and why you can't go see your parents—if you did, you'd only endanger them. It's why you have to stay very quiet. I can keep you safe, but only if you play by my rules."

She nodded. "I will. I'll do whatever you say."

"Good." He stood. "Now I'm going to go buy us something for supper. It's late, so it'll probably have to be a burger."

"I'll eat whatever you bring. And . . . thank you, Detective Michaels. For telling me the truth. And keeping me and my family safe." She watched as he left, heard the lock click, and even tested the door to make sure it was secured.

Thirty

I FINISHED THE LAST OF MY PROGRESS NOTES AND SIGNED OUT FOR THE day. Time to go see Dulce. I hadn't been to the jail in a very long time. Fifteen years ago, I'd bailed out Elias after a nightmare night that involved crack, mania, and a violent a-hole boyfriend. Before that, it had been my mother. Also mentally ill, she'd never been good at impulse control, which led to throwing a beer bottle at a cop outside of Dunkin Donuts. She lived in an assisted living place now, where they kept close tabs on her. I visited once a week. I'd yet to take Tessa to meet her because, well, Mom tended to be an acquired taste.

I entered the detention area with its concrete block walls and scarred linoleum floors, passing a dozen people waiting in hard plastic chairs for their time with incarcerated loved ones. The clerk staffing the front desk checked out my hospital ID badge, scanned his list of approved visitors, and directed me to an interview room.

They brought in Dulce. She wore an orange jumpsuit five sizes too large for her. Her black hair, streaked in blue, needed washing and a trim. Thick eye makeup, her trademark, left streaks down her tan skin. She looked like she'd lost weight, too—and at about a hundred pounds, she didn't have any to lose.

"What do you want?" she demanded.

"To check on you," I answered, my voice even. Dulce liked to get a rise out of me. Or anyone, but I wouldn't comply.

Of all the women trying to recover from their experience in the trafficking brothel, I worried most about Dulce. The others seemed to be thriving in the shelter. The woman they called "Onyx" had a job at a local boutique. Mei-Mei claimed a new identity: Minh. She worked at an Asian fusion restaurant. But Dulce kept her brothel name and refused therapy. She turned down job possibilities. Refused to follow the shelter rules. And now she'd landed in jail for shoplifting. I wasn't sure what would get through to her.

"Why do you care? I'm not your girl. I'm not sweet, innocent Kitten," she muttered.

"She's not Kitten anymore. She's Tessa. You know that. And we'd love to call you by your real name, too."

"Dulce. That's who I am now." She smacked a hand against the metal table. Her blue-tipped fingernails were broken and ragged.

"Dulce, who used to work in a brothel. Dulce, who stole something from a store. Dulce, who's now in jail. That's who you want to be?" I asked again, keeping my voice even.

"It's who I am. I'm not pretending to be some little innocent princess."

This was another dig against Tessa. I didn't understand what my kid had done to deserve her resentment, but Dulce tended to resent everything and everyone. "So, tell me what happened. How did you get arrested?"

She gave me a pre-teen eye roll. While she was just a little over twenty, she was still very much a child. "I needed some nail polish. Didn't have the cash."

"Seriously? You got yourself in this mess over a five-buck bottle of polish?"

"And eye shadow. And lipstick. And not the five-dollar stuff. I deserve the best. They caught me in Ulta."

"Have you shoplifted before?"

"A few times. I'm pretty good at it." Pride flickered in her eyes.

"Not that good." I gestured at the room, at her jumpsuit. She scowled. "So. What's the plan? They set bail yet?"

"This morning. But it's a lot." She sounded like she was bragging.

"Define a lot."

"I need a thousand to get out."

"That's hefty for a shoplifting charge." I didn't have that kind of money to spare.

"I may have resisted arrest." Smug now. I was used to her tricks. She could act as tough as a serial killer, but she was basically a kid playing pretend. Maybe I could find a way to raise her bail, but I'd check with the shelter staff first. They might already have a plan in place that I didn't want to mess up.

I leaned forward, studying her mascara-streaked face. "You've lost weight."

"So?"

"I know they feed you well at the shelter. Are you feeling okay? What's going on?"

She looked away from me. "I'm fine."

"I'd like to believe that. Have you had a physical lately?"

"They took me to a doctor when I first arrived. Checking for STDs. Other bloodwork. I'm fine."

"Good." I didn't believe it. She was far from fine and heading down a dangerous path. I prayed it was reversible. "They said that you were high when they picked you up."

"So?" She bobbed up a shoulder.

"You were on opioids."

She pursed her lips. "Why is that your business?"

I leaned forward, pinning her with my gaze. "Because I'm a hospital social worker, and I'm worried about you. The stuff on the streets now, Dulce—it's dangerous. Very dangerous."

A knock on the door interrupted us. A police officer told me my time was up, and another moved to escort Dulce back to her cell. As she stood, she approached the door, but hesitated. "How did you even know I was here?"

"Detective Michaels. You have people who care about what happens to you, Dulce. Don't forget that."

I watched her leave, her shoulders pushed back, her head held high. Dulce, the tough girl. That persona might save her life in jail, but I wasn't sure how well it worked in life, especially given the road she seemed to be taking.

Thirty-One

TESSA WASN'T SURE ABOUT THIS WHOLE THERAPY THING. SHE'D
started with a woman named Lenore, who was Georgia's therapist, but
Lenore said Tessa needed a specialist. Morgan Holmes did something
called "trauma therapy," and while she seemed nice enough, she asked
Tessa a lot of questions Tessa didn't like answering. Some things didn't
need to be remembered.

Morgan's office was in a restored Victorian house. Tessa liked the
shiny wooden floors and the rippled windows looking out on Park Street.
The furniture, in shades of blue and gray, was a little too matchy-matchy,
probably because Tessa had grown used to Georgia's chaotic decorating
style—with most of the furniture purchased from thrift stores and the
Facebook marketplace.

Her appointment was at four, but Morgan often ran late, which annoyed Tessa. She didn't let it show, though. Morgan was probably working hard to help a patient who needed her more than Tessa did. If she
were honest, Tessa wasn't sure she needed therapy at all.

"Tessa? Sorry, I'm running a little over." Her therapist greeted her
from the doorway that led to a hall. She wore a batik dress with a cotton
sweater and clunky shoes, her hair cut short, with teal blue streaks that
Tessa admired. A diamond gleamed on her left hand. Morgan had admit-
ted to being engaged, but offered few other details about her life.

They entered her office, a large space with tall, wide windows and a
thick Oriental rug. Tessa sat in a yellow armchair, and Morgan took her
usual spot in a leather one. The first minutes of therapy always made

Tessa nervous. What should she say? How much would she have to dis-close? And Morgan had a way of looking at her—looking through her—that made her feel almost naked.

"How are you, Tessa?"

"Good. I'm not depressed. I'm still hating trig, but I don't think that means I'm crazy or anything."

Morgan smiled. "No, I think that makes you pretty normal. Other than that, how's school?"

"Fine." Uh oh. She wasn't supposed to say "fine." Fine was an eva-sive word, according to Morgan.

Morgan raised her thick, well-sculpted brows.

"I mean, classes are going okay. I'm not doing that great in the friend department. Though I did go to a party."

"A party?" Morgan perked up.

"Yeah. That didn't go so well." Tessa told her the rest: Joel hitting Sara with the car. Drugged Ariel's spill into the pool. "I took her to the emergency room. That was my fun high school party experience." She didn't mention her own adventures with the tiny blue pills. While she knew everything she said here was supposed to be "confidential," she didn't trust that caseworker Lana Montgomery, who might demand Tessa's therapy records.

Morgan winced. "That's terrible. Is Sara okay? Ariel?"

"Sara's still in bad shape. Ariel was back at school. My friend Joel's in a shitload of trouble."

"Your friend Joel," Morgan repeated. "That's the first time I've heard you identify anyone at the school as a 'friend.'"

That was because Tessa couldn't connect with most of the idiots who sat around her in class. The girls with their selfie obsession. The boys eyeing the girls in a way that made Tessa want to punch them. The entire scene was ugly, really, but she didn't say that.

"Joel is nice. Very smart. Funny. But I haven't seen him since the accident. Not sure when he'll come back to school. Or if he will at all."

What if he didn't? What if her only friend didn't come back to school?

"Tessa? Your expression changed. What's bothering you?"

That was a loaded question. "Nothing. Just worried about Joel. And Lily Grace." Tessa told Morgan about the weird girl who was missing and who might very well be dead and how it was all her fault.

Morgan watched her, head cocked a little to the side as though Tessa had become a confusing painting. "You feel responsible for her. Even though she didn't tell you what she'd witnessed. And you told her to go to the police, which in my mind was the exact right thing to say."

"I feel responsible because Lily Grace is . . . different. She doesn't really have any friends. I'm the one she came to. Me." Why didn't people get that? Georgia had the same response, as though Tessa had no reason to be guilty, though Tessa did. And it ate away at her.

"I think she came to you because you are kind. And approachable."

Tessa almost laughed. Nobody at school would ever describe her as "approachable."

Morgan continued. "You felt that same level of responsibility toward the women at the Orchid Estate, didn't you? That's why you helped Georgia get everyone free."

"They were trapped like I was. We all needed to get out of there." She was used to Morgan bringing up the brothel, which she seemed to do whenever she got the chance.

"But you were only a kid. Still are."

"I don't feel like one."

"What do you mean?" Morgan asked.

"I mean, I feel old sometimes. Like I've lived longer than others my age." Tessa looked toward the window. Gray, ominous clouds hung low in the sky.

"Oh, Tessa. I guess you have, in a way." Morgan sounded sympathetic now. Sad even.

Her tone made Tessa feel sad, too. She didn't like feeling sorry for herself. It accomplished nothing.

"Georgia wants me to be happy." Tessa kept her voice low. "She wants me to like school. To make friends. To have a social life. And I try—I really try. But . . ." She let out a sigh that came from a buried place deep inside her.

"But it's hard?"

"It's impossible. I'm not like anyone I know. I can't make myself give a shit about what people are wearing or who's trending on TikTok. I just want to . . ." She had no idea how to finish that sentence.

Morgan leaned forward, looking expectant. "What, Tessa?"

"I want to forget what happened to me. To not feel so damaged. I want to be able to visit my brother in Pennsylvania and not feel like I'm pretending to be someone I'm not."

Morgan hesitated, then said, "That's a lot to unpack. First of all, you aren't damaged. If anything, you've proved that a thousand times over. You've been brave and strong and resilient, and anyone who knows you should be proud of it."

Tessa tried not to squirm. Morgan sounded sincere, but Tessa knew the truth.

Morgan continued. "This is the first time you've mentioned Brandon to me."

Tessa didn't like talking about Brandon or how much she missed him. "I've only seen him one time since . . ."

"Since you escaped?"

"Since Georgia helped me get free." Free. That was a word she could grasp, could hold over her head like a trophy.

"Would you like to see him again?"

"I plan to, if his family says it's okay." She pictured Brandon: His brown hair cut short and spiky. Those dimples he'd had since birth. His hand gripping hers when they'd walked to the park to get away from whatever foster home they'd been thrust into.

Tears came, unbidden. She nodded her response, because words seemed impossible.

"You miss him," Morgan whispered.

She nodded again.

"Of all that was taken from you when the traffickers stole your life, this is the hardest, isn't it?" Morgan pressed a tissue into her hand.

Stupid tears that wouldn't stop. Morgan lingered close but didn't touch her, which Tessa appreciated. Touches from other people could make her jump out of her skin.

"I'm not the sister he knew. I want to be, but I'm not." She wiped her face with the tissue.

"No, you've changed. So has he. But you're someone he'd be proud to know."

"Proud? I don't want him to *ever* know what happened to me. Or that there are people who are so . . . awful. Cruel. That whole world I lived in—I want him safe from it."

"I understand," Morgan said. "You want to protect him. But maybe that doesn't have to mean being protected from you and what you went through. How old is Brandon now?"

"Seven. Going on eighteen, according to his mother."

"His adoptive mother, right? Not the mother you shared." Morgan always said things like this to probe. Tessa found it annoying.

"No. Not the mom who kept picking asshole men. The mom who cared more about doing crack than feeding us. Not that mother." The anger leaking out felt more comfortable than the tears had. Anger could be empowering.

Morgan nodded slowly, thoughtfully. "She let you down in so many ways."

"If she'd gotten her shit together and pulled us out of foster care, I wouldn't have met Drew. I wouldn't have been taken away from Brandon and forced to . . . to screw all those men. I might even be normal, not—" She almost said, *not the damaged mess she was now*, but Morgan would confront her if she said something like that.

Morgan finished the sentence. "Not the brave girl who survived being kept hostage? Not the courageous kid who helped bring down an elaborate human trafficking operation? Not the teenage girl who helped free twenty other victims? Not all those things?"

"You don't get it." It was maddening, really. She came here every week trying to explain herself to a therapist who put twinkle lights and rose petals on everything.

"You have a hard time believing those things about yourself, but they are all true."

"I screwed men. Dozens of them. Maybe a hundred. That was who I was." Her voice evaporated like mist. She never talked about that time, but it never left her awareness. A black hole in her heart.

"Dozens of men, maybe a hundred, violated and assaulted you," Morgan replied.

Tessa shot her a glare.

"You don't like it when I say things like that, but I want you to hear it. You are not responsible for what happened to you during that part of your life. Each time Jefe sold you to a man, he was arranging for you to be assaulted. The trauma of all that—it's very real, even if you don't want to believe it. Have you had any recent triggers?"

It was all Tessa could do not to roll her eyes. Words like "trigger" were fancy therapy words that annoyed the shit out of her. The truth was bad memories of that time churned up at the strangest, most random times. History class when a guy handed her a book and his watch reminded her of a particularly nasty buyer she'd serviced at the trailer. The smell of the aftershave Mr. Tabor, the assistant principal, wore, so like the odor left on her sheets one horrible night. And every time she saw orchids was a grim reminder of the horrors at the Orchid Estate.

Would she be haunted like this forever? Crap. That thought terrified her.

"Tessa?"

"I'm good. No triggers recently."

The lie always came too easy.

Thirty-Two

I SAT ACROSS FROM MY COLLEAGUE, CLANCY, FROWNING AT THE GREEN
mushy substance she'd identified as "lunch": a kale smoothie that would
likely leave green specks in her teeth, like she'd grazed on the lawn. Her
pre-diabetes diagnosis had come as a shock that she took very seriously.
She'd lost almost sixty pounds, and it was evident in the new angles and
lines on her face. Just a year ago, she'd have scarfed down a double
cheeseburger and a Snickers bar for her meal.

"I. Am. In. Hell," she growled over the smoothie.

"Yes, you are. But I'm proud of you."

"Last night, I did thirty minutes on the treadmill at the gym. Thirty
minutes! And it was a fast walk, not a stroll. But some big Neanderthal
guy was lifting weights across from me. Grunting. Flexing. Marveling at
his own pecs like a narcissistic prick. Think I'll bring a squirt gun next
time. You know, to cool him off and all."

"He's gonna love you." I could picture it. Clancy firing off rounds at
all the gym rats who annoyed her. She'd made similar threats about the
Hospital Quality Assurance committee.

"How's the kid? Sara Clark?" she asked.

"She's still alive, which is a miracle. More surgery this week. Hope
she doesn't get any infections. They're keeping her in an induced coma.
If I had her injuries, I'd crave unconsciousness, too."

"I feel for her parents."

"The mother is here most of the time. We put a cot in her room." But
not the father. He stopped by but never stayed long. Some people couldn't
handle hospitals, leaving all the hard vigilance to those who could.

135

"Richard called a special meeting tomorrow about the influx of fentanyl overdoses. Wants to review treatment protocols."

"I hope that includes funding more respiratory therapists. We're running ragged down in the ED."

She shook her head. "You know Richard and his purse strings. Romano needs to bring a strong case for more funding."

"I'll tell him." It was maddening, really, when money mattered more than saving lives. We were constantly trying to finesse with insurance companies to cover medical procedures or approve necessary but expensive medications for our sickest patients. I had little patience for an industry that seemed to care more about profits than helping people.

A knock interrupted us. Clancy opened the door to find Detective Lou Michaels standing there. He wore a trim gray suit and blue oxford that brought out his eyes. Sometimes, I wished I hadn't noticed those eyes.

"Uh oh," Clancy said. "It's the fuzz. Probably here to arrest me for late progress notes."

"Only you would use the word 'fuzz,'" Lou commented. "But I'm here about something else."

"What's up, Lou?" I asked.

"Two things. One, Dulce got bailed out by shelter staff. Thought you'd want to know. Second I need a favor. You'll probably turn me down, but . . . well, here goes. Have you had any burn victims come to your ED lately? Or anyone suffering with smoke inhalation?"

Clancy arched her brows. "Let me see—you want us to give you confidential patient information? Without a court order? That's a hard no."

He shot me a beseeching look.

"Why do you want to know?" I asked him.

He leaned against the doorjamb. "Here's the thing. I'm investigating a fire that happened just north of town last night. A fire in a warehouse. We found drug-making residue in the remains of the building. Our lab identified remnants of fentanyl."

"So somebody burned down a fentanyl operation? Good," I said.

"No argument there. But the fire was intentional. Accelerants were used. So we have an arsonist who targeted an illegal drug lab."

"Was anyone hurt?" Clancy asked.

"Not that we know of. But the fire was massive and got out of hand quickly. So, our arsonist may have been injured. Which is why I'm here."

"This arsonist might be my hero," I said.

Lou shook his head. "Could be a vigilante trying to put an end to a bad drug operation. Or it could be another supplier wanting to eliminate competition. We won't know until we arrest him."

I looked at Clancy, who shrugged. No way we'd give out confidential information, but I could tell him one thing. "I worked late last night. It was quiet. There weren't any burn victims treated here."

He looked disappointed. "Okay. Good to know. Thanks."

"Lou, was the fentanyl residue they found . . . is it the same stuff that's on the streets right now?"

"According to our lab, it's the same compound. But don't get your hopes up. Just because one operation was destroyed won't keep them from starting up again. There's too much money to be made, and it's too easy to manufacture." He eyed each of us. "If I can find out who burned the lab, then I can find out who ran the operation, which takes me one step closer to shutting them down. So if someone comes to your ER with suspicious burns, I'd appreciate a call."

We didn't answer. Disclosing patient information wasn't an option, but if someone came in with burn injuries, maybe there'd be something I could tell Lou.

Maybe.

"Walk me out?" Lou asked me.

I nodded and followed him into the hallway. I hoped he wouldn't talk about our "date." I'd disappointed him, but he didn't know what I'd spared him. He walked close to me, his hands casually tucked in his pockets. He smelled a little citrusy.

I wished I didn't like breathing him in.

"I've got another lead to follow from that lab fire. Hoping it produces something because whoever's dealing this fentanyl is slippery as shit."

"Wow. You cussed. It must be bad."

"It's frustrating." He shot me some side-eye. "Hey. I wanted to ask you about the other night."

I stiffened.

"I really had fun. It would have been great having Tessa there, but some one-on-one time with you was . . . especially nice."

"I had fun, too." I hoped I sounded evasive. I felt like hiding in an empty hospital room.

He halted. "Look. I know you had a tough breakup with Ben Reeder, because he can be a real ass. He doesn't mean to be. It just . . . happens."

I huffed out a laugh. Ben and I had a few good months before his fling with the journalism intern. Like many men, he was governed by the "brain" between his legs. He had few long-term relationships, except with Lou, his best friend.

"And maybe that left you a little gun-shy," Lou continued. "But here's the thing. I like you. And I'd like to see more of you."

Shit. I backed up, my butt hitting the wall. I was *not* ready for this conversation.

He doesn't realize how screwed up you are, the Advisor said.

He's a nice man, the Counselor countered.

"Hey. No pressure, George. You look panicked." He took a step back. "I thought maybe you felt . . . I guess I got that wrong."

He turned to move away from me.

God. I'd really messed this up. "Wait."

He hesitated.

"It's not that I don't like you. I do. I mean, you've been so great over the past months with Tessa and all."

"She's a great kid," he said tightly.

"But I can't . . . I don't want to mess things up. I mean, we're great friends and all." I wasn't saying it well. I felt flustered and embarrassed and horrified.

He deserves better than you, the Advisor said.

"It's okay, George. I get it." And with that, he turned and walked away.

I slid down the wall until my butt collided with the floor. Lou was a great guy. Smart. Sexy, in a nerdy way. And I'd just blown it with him.

He might never realize that I'd done him a huge favor.

Thirty-Three

TESSA HURRIED TO RUN A COMB THROUGH HER UNEVEN, CHAOTIC HAIR. MAYBE she should take Georgia up on her offer to see a real hair stylist. Maybe something could be done to salvage her disastrous self-cut, and maybe Tessa was ready for that step. Maybe.

And maybe she was ready for the hard—seriously hard—conversation with Georgia about the fentanyl she took. Georgia would be disappointed at best. Or mad. Worst would be for her to decide she was done, that Tessa was too much for her. That thought scared the bejesus out of Tessa. It would only prove that the wicked caseworker Lana Montgomery was right.

She glanced at the clock: it was time to start the Zoom call she'd been anxiously awaiting all week. She entered the address on her computer. A moment later, a familiar face appeared. "Hey, squirt!" she said to her little brother, Brandon.

Their last contact had been a phone call, but on video, she could see how he'd changed in just a few weeks. He had blond hair (darkening now) and vivid green eyes. Ears, which used to poke out, looked more normal as he grew, but when he flashed his dimpled grin, she spotted a missing upper tooth. "You lost another one!"

"Yep. And the so-called 'tooth fairy' left me ten bucks!"

"So-called?" Tessa laughed.

"I caught them, Tess. Caught Mom sneaking the cash under my pillow."

Mom. It was good, really, that he was so accepted into that family. Had he completely erased his life before them? Much needed to be erased—their lousy, horrible parents. Foster homes that cared about money more than children. But would Tessa be erased, too?

"What are you going to do with the money?"

139

"Hold on." She heard Brandon move and the creak of a door shutting. "I'm back. Look, I have fifty dollars saved up. Would that be enough for you to come see me?"

Warmth spread inside her. She'd not been erased, after all.

"You don't need to save money for that. I've been saving. Georgia said I could go visit again, if it's okay with your new . . . mom."

"When? Next weekend?"

She laughed at his excitement. "I have to work, but maybe later in the month?"

"Our little league team plays in a tournament. Maybe you could come watch?"

"I would love that. But I'll need to ask your mom first." She was getting better at the "mom" idea. Brandon deserved a real family. To feel like he was loved. That he belonged. It had taken seven years for him to get it.

They chatted for another half hour. Brandon still hated math ("It's in our genes, I'm afraid"), but loved reading. He might get to sing in the school holiday assembly. His new dad bought him a bike, but it still had training wheels, which, apparently, was more embarrassing than showing up to school naked.

She told him about life with Georgia, about how much fun it was working for Elias. She didn't tell him about therapy, or the party, or the missing Lily Grace. Thoughts of taking that stupid pill filled her with shame. When he was older, could she confide things like that in him? Or would she always want to protect him from the hard truths?

"I gotta go," Brandon said. "Time for practice."

"Okay. Great talking to you, squirt."

"Don't call me that!" He laughed. "I love you, Tessa."

"Love you more, squirt," she whispered, and they ended the call.

Twenty minutes later, Tessa arrived at Joel McCants's house. She'd been there before, mostly to cram for tests. He lived with his parents in a two-story brick house close to the VA hospital where Joel's mom worked. Tessa took the bus to the hospital stop and walked the rest of the way, curious about what she'd find when she arrived.

She hadn't seen Joel since that awful night in the hospital. She couldn't imagine how he felt, knowing he'd been the one to hit Sara. She hadn't told him she was coming to visit. Why bother, when he hadn't answered any of her calls or texts? She'd learned from Ariel, who seemed to know everything about everybody, that Joel wasn't in jail and was being "homeschooled" now by his mom. He must have hated it. Joel liked people, and he liked classes. Always the first to raise his hand, always the last to leave because he'd have one more question to ask the teachers.

When she got to his house, she saw that the shades had all been pulled. The garage door that always gaped open remained shut. The home looked abandoned. Tessa climbed the steps and rang the bell, listening for the familiar three-note chime to resonate in the house. No response, so she rang again.

Footfalls sounded inside. The door inched open, a chain preventing entry. Half a face peered out at her. Joel.

"Hey," she said. "Can I come in?"

"I'm . . . not supposed to see anyone. The lawyer and my parents were adamant."

"Only you would use the word 'adamant' in a sentence. And I'm not 'anyone.' I'm your friend and I need to see you're okay."

He stared.

"Come on, Joel. I rode the bus to get here. At least let me in and get me a coke."

He shuffled back, fumbled with the chain lock, and opened the door.

She tried not to gawk at his appearance. The usually immaculate guy she often teased for ironing a crease in his chinos wore torn sweatpants and a stained T-shirt. His short-cropped hair had not seen a comb that day, and his eyes sagged as though he needed sleep. A fluorescent green cast covered his lower left arm.

Without saying a word, Tessa stepped close and slid her arms around him. She didn't even mean to. She wasn't a hugger. And theirs wasn't a romantic relationship, but she cared about him, and he looked so gutted it happened before she could stop herself.

"Thanks," he whispered as she pulled away.

"I've missed you. School sucks on a good day, and without you there—"

"God, I'd give anything to be in Mrs. Watson's history lecture right now."

She laughed. "Then you clearly aren't well." She followed him through the living room—over-furnished with brown leather chairs and a matching sofa that looked perfect for napping. The kitchen, which Joel's mom had renovated last year, had white, thinly veined marble countertops. The island stood large enough for a double sink and wine rack. Unlike Georgia's house, every surface here remained uncluttered, gleaming under modern pendulum lights. Joel moved efficiently to the stainless steel fridge and pulled out a soda for Tessa.

They moved to the banquette under the picture window. Tessa loved how the McCants' backyard stayed lush, even though it was fall, with bright purple cabbage and blooming mums surrounding the patio. Joel's home reminded her of the home improvement shows she used to watch at one of her foster homes.

She absorbed every room on the screen, imagining. Pretending one day she'd live in a house like that. Like Joel's.

She looked at her friend. He wore a tortured expression, and it hurt to see it. "Are you eating okay?" she asked.

"Not much of an appetite."

"Are you getting your schoolwork done? We have a history test on Friday."

He shook his head. "Can't concentrate. Hard to care about the economic implications of the dust bowl when Sara could be dying and it's my fault."

She hated his desolate tone. It seemed so unlike her always joking friend, the boy with the wide smile and ridiculously infectious laugh. "Are you remembering the accident yet?"

He wiped his face. "No. I get flashes, but I don't remember driving or hitting Sara. I remember sitting on the ground after. Cooper's dad asking if I was alright and mumbling something else that's . . . hard to remember. And being real nauseous. And my arm hurting like a mother. The next thing I remember is the hospital."

She pushed the seltzer away and leaned closer, wanting his full attention. "Joel. I didn't know you and Sara used to date. Ariel told me."

He didn't say anything.

"Why didn't you mention it?"

He shrugged. "Because there wasn't much to tell. It was . . . last spring? I liked her. A lot. But she could be intense. One day, I had some Delta-8 CBD gummies and thought we'd take them and go see the new X-Men movie, you know? The special effects are insane when you're high. But Sara flipped. Acted like I was trying to shoot her up with heroin or something. Like I said, intense."

"That's why you broke up?"

"Let's say it started the process. She didn't like being around drugs at all. Or alcohol. She didn't want me drinking a beer if we were going to a party or something. I got tired of the rules. She got tired of my rebelling against them." He shrugged.

"She does sound rigid."

"Ya think? But she's a good person. Really good. Anyway. We decided to call it off. But it wasn't like a big scene. I don't think either of us left it mad or devastated. Just a little sad that a nice thing was over."

"Do the police know you dated her?" Tessa asked.

He blinked. "I didn't think . . . oh shit. I should tell them, right? Only it makes me look more guilty. Like after all this time, I ran over Sara because we broke up." His voice rose, panic inching in.

"They'll understand if you explain it. They might not if you keep it from them."

"Shit. I'll tell them. Sara and I parted as friends. Even the night of the party . . . she asked me for a favor. It was no big deal—actually, it was kind of weird—but I had no problem helping her out."

"What favor?" Tessa asked.

He rubbed his nose. "I was sitting in the den on that giant sofa. She came up behind me and said she needed help with something. Then she took my hand. I went with her upstairs—she was making a point of being very quiet, which I thought was odd. Then she went into Cooper's room. She said he had borrowed her notes for a history test and hadn't given them back. She wanted to look for them. My job was to stand guard so she wouldn't get caught. Cooper is slack about taking notes. Sara is meticulous. We had a history test coming up. No big deal, right?"

Tessa shrugged.

"Anyway, she came out a few minutes later, empty-handed. I said maybe she should ask him again for them. She answered, 'Oh, I'll get them. Don't worry,' and hurried down the stairs. The next time I saw her . . . she was lying on the road."

Tessa leaned closer to make sure she had his full attention. "Joel. Are you sure you were the one driving that night?"

He blinked, as though stunned by the question. "Why would you ask that?"

"Because . . . Cooper. He doesn't seem like the type to hand the keys over to anyone. He's always been so damn proud of that stupid car."

"If he thought he was too high to drive, he'd want me to. I can't believe I was stupid enough to agree." He shook his head. "I hadn't had anything to drink, not even a beer. But he gave me a pill. It must have kicked in."

"Lots of people took one, me included. Georgia says they were fentanyl."

"That's what they told me at the hospital. I wouldn't have taken one if I'd known. I swear." He looked at her, eyes wide, desperate to be believed.

She smiled, relieved. "Then it wasn't your fault. Even if you were driving, you'd been drugged. That has to help your case."

"The lawyer says I have to prove I didn't know what I'd taken. And I was the one who put it in my mouth and swallowed. And anyway, what does it matter? Sara's still . . ." He dropped his head into his hands.

"Sara is fighting. She's not giving up, and we shouldn't give up on her." Tessa wanted to erase his pain, but she knew it was impossible.

They were interrupted by the chime from Joel's doorbell. "You're popular today."

He shrugged, and Tessa followed him into the entry hall. When he opened the door, a red Tesla sped out of the driveway. On the stoop stood Cooper Hawthorne.

"What are you doing here? I'm not supposed to have company."

Cooper, dressed in a worn denim jacket and chinos, pointed at Tessa. "She's here. Come on, Joel. Holden just dropped me off. He'll be back in a few. We need to talk." He eyed Tessa again.

"Want me to leave?" she asked Joel.

"No. Stay."

Cooper frowned. He didn't look good—his hair needing a wash. Skin paler than she'd ever seen it.

"Come into the kitchen."

Cooper sat at the table, his hands knotted in front of him. "How's the arm, Joel?"

Joel shrugged. "Hurts. Not as bad as when I busted my nose playing soccer."

"I remember that one. You talk to your lawyer lately?"

"Mom's taking me to his office at four."

"Look. Dad's the solicitor. He says that if you plead guilty, he can make sure nothing real bad happens to you." Cooper spoke with the same cocky confidence that always annoyed Tessa.

"Isn't that, like, a conflict of interest?" Tessa asked. "He's your dad."

Cooper's grin reeked of smugness. "Trust me. He'll take care of you, Joel."

"So what? Joel gets a few years in prison?" Tessa challenged.

Cooper's smile dissolved. "Maybe just probation."

"And he has a record that ruins his life. Seems pretty unfair, considering."

Joel watched the two like they were lobbing tennis balls, his face a blank mask.

Tessa pushed further. "I keep hoping Joel remembers exactly what happened. I mean, his memory is sketchy, but that can change over time. How about you, Cooper? What do you remember about what happened?"

Joel shot her a confused look.

Cooper muttered, "Uh . . . it's a little blurry. I remember weaving on the road. And swerving. The sound of the impact when we . . . when Joel hit her."

"Oh God." Joel covered his face.

Tessa hated the pain she heard in his voice.

Cooper said, "Look. I'm sorry about the pills. I wish I'd never had a party. All we can do now is . . . damage control." His voice quavered.

What a strange phrase, like something he'd heard his father say. What would Fletcher Hawthorne do to control the damage?

"Joel, there's something else you need to know. Lily Grace has disappeared." She told him the rest, her gaze fixed on Cooper to gauge his response.

"She probably ran away," Cooper said. "She's a screwed-up girl from a screwed-up family. Who wouldn't want to escape that?"

"I don't know about that. She's not rich like you, Cooper. Doesn't live in a mansion. But her family loves her, and she wouldn't just leave them," Tessa said.

"What do you think happened?" Joel asked.

"I don't know exactly. But I do know this. She came to your party, Cooper. And something happened that night that upset her. Some kind of crime. I wonder what?"

Cooper glared. "She wasn't invited. No way I'd want—"

"Not by you, maybe. But she came. And the next day, she disappeared. Can't help but wonder if there's a connection."

"You don't know what you're talking about." Cooper sounded odd. Not angry. Not defensive. Maybe a little defeated.

"I have another question, Cooper. That night—when I was by the pool. You and Sara had a fight, remember? You followed her into the pool house, and y'all started yelling. What was that about?"

Joel stared at him, perplexed.

"You know Sara. So damn intense." He looked at Joel and shrugged. "She was mad about the pills. About everybody getting high."

"Crap," Joel whispered.

"But she was high, too," Tessa commented.

Cooper shrugged. "I thought . . . I thought it would help her chill. God knows she needed to."

"So you roofied her?" Tessa's voice boomed.

"I just gave her a little in her soda. Not even a whole pill." He didn't look apologetic, and it pissed Tessa off.

A horn sounded.

Joel stood and went to the window. "Holden's here. That's one helluva car he's driving."

"I have to go." Cooper stood. "Joel—it's going to be okay. Trust that."

"I wish I could," Joel whispered.

Thirty-Four

SAUL RARELY SPENT TIME IN MARCUS'S MORE OFFICIAL "OFFICE," BUT
Marcus had purchased a new, high-tech lock for the warehouse-turned-
fentanyl-lab below where Saul lived. Saul had been summoned to collect
it, and, of course, he obeyed.

Marcus's office was opulent as shit. Imported Turkish rug. Heavy
burled walnut desk probably imported from England or France. Bookshelves displaying what looked like rare books, which Marcus probably
never read. This office was a mask, and Marcus wore it well.

"The new lock is here." Marcus pointed to a box on his desk. "If you
have trouble installing it, let me know. Any leads on the person who destroyed my lab?"

Saul shook his head. He had so little to go on. He'd reviewed the
camera footage of the retreating motorcycle: an average-sized guy in a
dark jacket driving away. He wasn't sure where to start.

"Find him." Marcus's dark eyes blazed. "I also need you to make a
drop-off for me. Another campaign donation for Fletcher Hawthorne."

Saul steeled his face. The idea of a twat like Hawthorne in the attorney general seat disgusted him, but it made sense that Marcus would
want him elected. Nice to have a plant in the state's highest judicial seat.
Certain court cases might fall off the docket if Marcus asked.

Marcus handed him a sealed envelope, which Saul pocketed. "Anything else?" Saul asked.

A knock on the door interrupted them. The blonde woman who
served as Marcus's receptionist stepped inside. "Excuse me, sir, but
there's a police detective here to see you."

Marcus's brown eyes flared. "Me?"

"Well, not you by name. He asked to speak to the owner."

Marcus turned to Saul. "You'd better stick around while I see what this is about."

Saul took his usual stance beside the door, his hand gripping the revolver hidden in his jacket. The receptionist ushered in a tall, dark-haired man dressed in a suit. He entered cautiously, eyeing the room like a predator until his gaze fixed on Saul.

"How can I help you, detective?" Marcus asked from his chair.

"Sorry to bother you, sir. Can I ask your name?" the detective asked.

"Marcus Landry. And you?"

"I'm Detective Lou Michaels."

Saul nearly dropped his weapon. This was the real Lou Michaels? The man he'd been impersonating since he'd met Lily Grace?

"What do you want, Detective Michaels?" Marcus asked. "A donation to the Law Enforcement Brotherhood Association?"

Michaels didn't seem to appreciate this comment. He reached into his pocket and pulled out a plastic bag. "There was a fire in the warehouse district north of town. Arson. The place was pretty much incinerated."

Something flashed in Marcus's eyes as he glanced at Saul. "I sure hope nobody was hurt."

"Not that we know of."

"Good. But I'm not sure why that brings you to my doorstep." Marcus swiveled his chair, as though bored.

"Because of this." He tossed the plastic bag on Marcus's desk. "See, this burned building was a lab where illegal fentanyl was being made. The question for me is, who owned it? Who's been manufacturing and distributing fentanyl in my town?"

Saul tightened his grip on the gun.

Marcus lifted the plastic sack and studied what looked like a burned slip of paper inside. "This is a packing slip."

"Yep. And the address is this one right here. Your office. Where you're sitting behind a fancy desk. Now, why do you think that is?"

Crap. Marcus only allowed legal supplies to get sent here, and any identifying information should have been shredded and burned. That moron Boris.

Marcus dropped the slip. "I'm an importer, Detective Michaels. I ship merchandise all over the country."

"What do you import?"

"Mostly antiques and antiquities. I just sent some spectacular enameled ginger jars, circa Ming dynasty, to California."

"Yeah, well, we didn't find any evidence of antiquities. I'm wondering what was brought to the lab. From this address."

"Absolutely nothing." Marcus laughed. "We stack used boxes outside the building. People are always taking them. Look, detective—I understand you're trying to solve this crime. But you're looking up the wrong tree. I'm a legitimate businessman who's brought a great deal of revenue into our fine city. If you have doubts about that, perhaps you should talk to the police chief. Walt and I play golf regularly."

Lou Michaels blinked.

Good. Marcus had hit a nerve.

Marcus handed the plastic sack back to the detective. "I wish you luck, detective. The drug problem in our town is very bad for business. I'm grateful you're trying to get a handle on it."

Michaels turned and began to exit, hesitating when he reached Saul. "You don't say much, do you?"

Saul shook his head. "Didn't have much to say. Have a great day, detective."

Saul closed the door behind him and turned to face Marcus.

"Think Detective Michaels is gonna be a problem?"

Saul nodded.

"Damn that Boris. Nothing should have this address on it. NOTHING!" Marcus boomed.

"Agreed. You want me to look into the detective?"

Marcus sighed. "I'll take care of it. I've got a meeting with The Shadows soon."

"They're back in town?" Saul knew little about the two mysterious men who worked for Marcus. He'd only seen them once: Large. Muscular. Worked together like a single unit. And apparently, expert marksmen.

"Yes. Guess I have an assignment for them."

Thirty-Five

I HAD AN APPOINTMENT WITH LENORE, MY THERAPIST, THAT AFTER-
noon, and the timing couldn't be better. After the last week, my nerves
were beyond frayed. I definitely needed a tune-up. I arrived at Lenore's
right on time, and she greeted me in the waiting room. I've been seeing
Lenore for six years, the last in a series of shrinks and counselors. Her
ability to see through my crap and her willingness to let me manage my
symptoms without over-drugging me was key. She kept me stable.
Mostly.

Lenore wore a blue denim skirt, flowered cotton top, and a turquoise
and silver chunky necklace. Her blondish brown curls fell below her
shoulders. She'd lost the baby weight quickly—she always did—though
child number three was only three months old.

"Georgia! Do you need coffee?"

"I may be over-caffeinated already. So no."

I followed her back to the office. It was one of my favorite rooms on
the planet: wide, ripply glassed windows with stained glass art. Creamy
yellow walls holding abstract paintings in teals and golds. Comfy over-
stuffed furniture with pillows for hugging. Or pounding. Or throwing—
I'd done it all.

Lenore sat in her usual chair as I took mine, one that rocked a little.
She watched me expectantly. We no longer wasted time on small talk.

"There's a lot going on," I began, and I told her all of it: the fentanyl
overdoses that kept coming. The kid from the party who still might die.
The disappearance of Lily Grace.

"That is a lot," she reflected. "How are you handling it all?"

I blinked. Swallowed. Then stammered out, "I'd hoped they were gone. The voices, I mean. But they're here."

"Now?"

"It's just been a few times."

Okay, more than a few times. I wasn't even sure why I wasn't telling her the truth.

"Which ones?" she asked.

"The Counselor. The Advisor."

"But not the General?" She leaned forward, her gaze intent. The General always worried her, but not as much as he worried me. When he spoke, he filled my brain, seeking control of me and sometimes succeeding. But not in a very long time.

"No. He's been quiet."

Lenore's voice softened. "And Peyton? Are you hearing from your sister?"

I had lost my sister last summer. I almost died trying to solve her murder, but I didn't, and the horrible man responsible for her death was rotting in prison. During that crazy, dangerous time, two amazing things happened: Tessa came into my life, and Peyton joined the chorus of voices—only hers makes me very, very happy. It was as if a piece of my sister remained inside me.

"Not yet." I missed her.

"Tell me about your control," Lenore said.

"Of the voices? I don't control them. You know that."

"Of your actions." Her tone remained soft, but I heard the concern behind it.

"They aren't in command. They're annoying. I mean, the Counselor can be kind of comforting, but she's distracting. The Advisor's been irritating, but I'm managing. It's nothing to worry about."

Lenore leaned back, watching me. Assessing. She worried about command hallucinations because they were dangerous, but fortunately, I hadn't had them in a very long time.

"I mean it. I don't need more meds, if that's what you're thinking."

Balancing my medication—an antidepressant paired with a very small dose of anti-psychotics—had always been a tricky thing. I didn't tolerate the side effects well. I'd stop taking the pills if they affected my ability to do my job or enjoy my life, and Lenore knew that.

After a moment, I sensed a change in her strategy. "I suspect they are back because of all the stress you're under."

I nodded. "Dealing with the fentanyl overdoses has been . . . intense."

"I'm sure. But that's not all that's going on. You have Tessa."

"Tessa? She's not stress. I mean, she's a seriously low-maintenance kid."

I'd marveled at how self-sufficient she was. She managed her own breakfast. Took care of her own laundry, doing mine sometimes, too.

"Is she? One of the first things you told me was how scared you were when the girl from the party arrived at the hospital—you feared it might be Tessa."

"I guess I do worry about her." I did tend to panic that something might happen to this kid. After all she'd been through, I wanted her safe and happy more than anything else.

"Parenting is a difficult job. Even with an 'easy' child. And Tessa has been through so much."

"True. But I'm handling it."

"Of course you are. You're an amazing woman. You're strong and brave. But . . . the strain of worrying over Tessa may be what's exacerbating the voices."

I felt a flush of panic. Was Lenore implying that I couldn't manage having Tessa in my care? That I should release her to regular foster care?

"It's not that bad. I can handle it."

Lenore's face softened. "I can tell that you really care about her."

I nodded. Tears emerged. Why was I crying?

She smiled sympathetically. "It's okay, George. Caring is part of the package when you're a mother."

"I'm not a mother. I'm just a poorly qualified foster parent." I swiped my cheek. I hated feeling this out of control.

"Tell me what's prompting those tears."

I cleared my throat. "I don't know. Maybe—you connected my voices with the stress of caring for Tessa, and it scared me that you were implying I couldn't handle it. Lana Montgomery—she's Tessa's new caseworker—implied the same thing. I'm scared that she's going to take Tessa away from me."

"Oh, Georgia. You really love her, don't you?"

I sat straighter, gathering myself. "I guess I do. And I can handle having her. I need you to believe that because social services may talk to you. Please, Lenore. Don't tell them I'm hearing the voices again."

"I'm more concerned with your mental health, Georgia. That has to be my focus."

"She's a part of it. I was doing great until this week. Having her at my house keeps me on a schedule—something you've always harped about. I eat regular meals—mostly—and keep normal-ish work hours. Tessa is good for my mental health. You can tell Lana Montgomery that if she calls you."

Lenore crossed her arms, looking decidedly unhappy. "This is a problem. I can't have you looking at me as the mental health police. I need you to be honest here. Vulnerable here. This has to be a safe space."

I'd put her in an awkward position six months earlier. The social services caseworker we had then wanted proof of my mental health stability before they placed Tessa with me. Lenore had refused until I begged her to reassure them that I could manage life with a teenager.

"Georgia. Look at me."

I complied.

"If social services contact me, I'll tell them that the release you signed has expired, which is true. What happens in here stays in here. But—and this is the most important thing—I need you to always be honest with me."

"I am. I have to be." I let out a sigh.

"Good. Now, let's get back to the voices."

***

I drove home exhausted. I felt nurtured, but also all scooped out and ready to plant myself on the sofa for a binge session of *Ted Lasso* reruns. But when I pulled into my drive, a woman was standing on my front porch. She wore a black dress with red splotches all over it, like a sadistic

Rorschach test. Her black hair angled perfectly to brush her jawline. She gripped a leather portfolio, her pointed nails painted a flawless match for the red in her dress.

"Ms. Thayer? I'm Lana Montgomery."

Shit. I did not need social services on my doorstep just then. I climbed out of the Civic and reluctantly approached. "Ms. Montgomery."

"You can call me Lana. Is Tessa home? I need to meet with her for check-in."

Double shit. "Did you text that you were coming? I thought you agreed to do that."

"I had another visit in the area and thought I'd try my luck. But I rang the bell, and nobody answered."

"Then she must not be home yet. That's why it's a good idea to text." My teeth clenched.

Lana studied me. "And you don't know where she is?"

"Not every second of the day. She's not seven, Lana. She's sixteen."

"But given her history . . ."

Crap. Was I a terrible foster mother? I pulled out my phone and checked my texts. "Ah. She stopped at Joel's house."

"So she's with a boy."

I didn't like her tone. "She's with her study partner."

I texted Tessa: *Lana is here. When will you be home?*

Taking bus now. Thirty minutes, came her reply.

"She's on her way home. Want to come inside?"

Lana nodded and followed me in. I desperately wished I'd known she was coming. My house wasn't the chaotic mess it was before Tessa—that kid liked to keep things neat—but I'd left a coffee cup on the table and newspapers strewn hither and yon. Fenway, my black beast of a cat, greeted us with annoyed yowls as though he hadn't been fed since Christmas. I hurried to the kitchen and threw kibbles in his bowl in an act of self-defense.

When I returned to the living room, Lana had moved to the fireplace, where family photos of my late sister and little niece Lindsay paraded across the mantel.

Don't let her get to you, the Counselor whispered.

Don't let her figure you out, the Advisor added.

God, how I wished my voices came with an off switch.

Lana studied the picture of me and my sister Peyton. My deceased sister and best friend. "I read about your sister," Lana said. "A brave woman. I'm sorry she's passed."

"Me, too." I pointed to a chair, and she sat.

"Tell me how Tessa has been doing."

"She's great. A terrific kid. Grades are fine, except trig, but we're working on that. She has friends. Keeps her therapy appointments." I rattled on, unsure what I should be reporting.

"Sounds almost too good to be true."

I didn't like her tone. "I'm very proud of her."

She opened the portfolio and jotted down a few notes before looking up at me. "And you, Georgia. How are you doing?"

"Good. I mean, work's insane. But I'm managing." I swallowed, thinking of my session with Lenore.

Don't let her know about us, the Counselor cautioned.

"I was more interested in your mental health. I have to admit that when I was assigned this case, I was surprised to read about your history. Your . . . condition."

Intrusive, the Advisor barked. *Thinks you're going to screw this up.*

"I just saw my therapist. I never miss an appointment. Or at least, I rarely do. You don't need to worry about my mental health." I kept my gaze steady, needing her to believe.

"Your . . . psychosis . . . is under control?" Her dark eyes pierced into me like bullets.

"Of course. I take my medication as prescribed." The teeth clenching amped up. My jaw throbbed.

She pressed harder. "No voices now?"

Shit. If I told her the truth, she might decide I was too unstable to keep Tessa. If I lied, I'd be . . . well, lying to a caseworker. Never a good strategy. I chose option three: side-stepping. "Like I said, I'm fine. Which is a miracle, given what we're dealing with at work."

"You work at Columbia General, right? A hospital social worker? That has to be very stressful." She eyed me closer, assessing.

"Yes. Very stressful. But I'm part of a great team."

"And you must work long hours."

"Sometimes. What's your point?"

She smoothed a hand over the leather portfolio. "I don't mean to make you defensive, but surely you understand that a girl who's been through what Tessa has needs . . . stability. Consistency. How are you able to offer that given your . . . situation?"

I clenched so tightly that I thought I might break a tooth. "My situation is this: I take very good care of Tessa. I understand her in a way that other foster parents can't—I saw what she dealt with firsthand. I know what she needs now, and I do my darndest to give it to her." My temper flared. Not smart.

"Do you?"

"Absolutely. She is a trauma survivor. What she needs is . . ." Love. That was the word that should have ended that sentence, but somehow speaking it felt wrong. Lana might decide I was over-involved. Or worse, lacking boundaries. I was, after all, just a temporary foster parent. "Safety," I said instead. "Emotional and physical safety. And she has that with me."

"Safety," Lana repeated, watching me. "Is there a reason that you're concerned about her safety?"

I nodded. "Definitely. She's got the trial coming up. Jefe was a crime lord—what if he has connections that come after her before she testifies?" This fear nagged at me, despite Lou's promises that the FBI would keep a close watch on any potential threats.

"That's a valid concern."

"And that's not all. For example, I make sure she knows all about the new danger on our streets—a particularly lethal fentanyl analog. Do the other kids on your caseload know about it? Do they know how prevalent and dangerous that drug is? How deadly?" I was babbling now. She had me off my game.

Lana shot me a perplexed look.

"You haven't heard about it? You should have. We've had more overdoses than I can count—many of them kids. Y'all need to train your foster parents to be vigilant with their children. Given what happened at the Cooper Hawthorne party, we're very worried the dealers are gonna target a younger group."

Lana suddenly lost a bit of her composure. "I . . . we hadn't heard about that."

"Well, that's not good. I'm happy to talk with your staff about it if that will help." I threw her a sympathetic smile.

"I just might. Well." She stood, closing her portfolio. "It's getting late. Please let Tessa know I'll be back soon. I know you say she's doing fine, but I need to see for myself. With the trial coming up, there's going to be a lot of pressure on that girl."

"I know."

I didn't want to think about it, though. I didn't want to picture Tessa on the witness stand, testifying against the man who held her captive, sold her body over and over, and then tried to kill her—a man with very powerful friends and enemies. I'd do anything to spare her that pain.

"Do we have a trial date yet?" Lana asked.

"No. I'll let you know when we do."

Thirty-Six

I HAD FINISHED A PRICKLY DISCHARGE SUMMARY—MY LAST TASK FOR the day—when my cell phone buzzed: Tessa.

"What's up?"

"He was supposed to be here a half hour ago," she said in a hurry.

"Who was?"

"Lou! He was going to help me with my trig worksheet. He's never late, or if he is, he texts me."

"Maybe he's tied up with work."

"Then he'd have texted! He's anal about messaging if he's gonna be five minutes late. But not today. I've even tried calling him and he's not answering." She sounded exasperated.

"Are you sure he was coming today?"

"Yes!"

It wasn't like Lou not to show. Unless . . . Lou had been hurt when our "date" ended abruptly. When I'd disappointed him by fleeing. Even at Elias's restaurant, he'd acted weird, and I'd worried our relationship was damaged beyond repair. Still—had he ditched Tessa because of me? Oh, hell no. Not acceptable.

"I'm about to leave work. I'll swing by his house to see if he's there."

"If it's not too much trouble. I don't know whether to be mad or . . . worried."

No shit. "I'll call soon," I answered.

I signed off the computer, left a note for Clancy, and locked up my office.

158

The drive to Lou's only took ten minutes, but I had myself worked into a lather by the time I got to his street. How dare he stand up my kid? How could he be so petty? She counted on him. I counted on him. How dare he let us down?

His Crown Victoria was in the drive. I climbed out of my Civic and booked it up to the front door. I rang the bell—twice. He didn't answer.

I rang it again. When that didn't work, I banged on the door.

"Lou? Lou!" I yelled.

Still no response. I could get even louder. Disturb the whole damn neighborhood until he opened the door. But something gave me pause.

Something's very wrong, the Counselor said.

I turned and looked at his car. Exhaust wafted up from the tailpipe. The car was running? I inched toward it, my nerves prickling. Was someone sitting in the driver's seat? Shit. Another step, and I froze when my foot crunched on glass fragments. Safety glass. My gaze shot up to the car.

The back window had been shattered.

Call the police, the Counselor warned.

Fear clawed its way up my throat as I inched closer. I could see him now, slumped over the steering wheel.

Lou.

"No, no, no, no . . ." I jerked open the car door, ignoring the red streaks on the window, fixating on his odd posture, the strange angle of his chin against the wheel. The flow of blood dribbling from the back of his head.

Somebody had shot Lou.

I felt for a pulse. There, but slow and weak. I fumbled for my phone and dialed 911, fighting hysteria as I relayed the details.

I had to do what I could. I pulled off my cotton scarf and pressed it against the wound. Head wounds always bled a lot—I knew that from the ER. Could be superficial.

Or Lou could have a bullet lodged in his brain that would kill him.

I kept the scarf in place and touched his face with my other hand, terrified by the coolness of his flesh.

"Lou? Lou! It's George. I'm getting you help. You need to hang in there."

No answer.

Keep talking to him. This was Peyton's voice. The one I longed for— my sister.

"You've got Tessa all worried. She's got a trig exam next week, you know."

I hoped for a flicker of response. I hoped for the sound of sirens. All I could do was keep talking, keep monitoring his pulse and breath, and toss up ragged prayers to a deity I sometimes believed in.

"Lou? Please." Tears erupted. Stupid tears. "Please."

Listen, Peyton whispered.

Finally. Finally. Sirens. I pressed my lips against his cheek and whispered, "Help's here."

***

Waiting. God, I hated it. Dr. Romano had met us at the ER entrance with a full trauma team at the ready. Police swarmed the place—which was always the case when one of their own had taken a hit.

Clancy sat beside me in the small staff lounge. I gripped my phone, so desperate for a message from Romano that I nearly stopped breathing.

"He's strong," Clancy said. "And stubborn."

The door burst open, and Tessa stormed in. "How is he?"

I stood and approached, wanting to hug her, but touch was difficult for that kid. "Come sit down. How did you get here? I said I'd call when I had more info."

"Uber. I couldn't stand being home by myself." She looked at me, her eyes filled with tears.

"Okay, okay. Have a seat. Here's what we know. The good news is it's a grazing wound, meaning the bullet didn't penetrate his brain."

"And the bad news?"

Tessa, ever the pessimist.

I gripped her hand. "The bullet nicked his skull. Apparently, there's some . . . splintering, and it's caused bleeding inside his head. But look, he's getting incredible care. They have him in an induced coma to take care of the intracranial bleeding. Right now, all we can do is wait."

"And trust Lou Michaels to not let a stupid bullet keep him down," Clancy added. "Seriously, Tessa. Lou is far too badass to let this get him."

That brought a tiny flicker of a smile. She turned to me. "You found him. That had to be awful."

I nodded, remembering. The shattered window. Lou slumped over the steering wheel. The blood. So much blood. "It was awful, but I'm very glad you called me so I got to him and could get him help."

"Who would do this?" Clancy asked. "Who would shoot him?"

"That's what I want to know." Ben Reeder's voice boomed from the doorway. He limped over to me, his lined face red with panic. I gave him the same update I'd given Tessa and Clancy. He peppered me with questions—a good reporter wanting details and a close friend scared to death like we were.

I looked at the three of them, unsure how much to disclose. "I've been eavesdropping on the police in the waiting area. They found the bullet lodged in the visor of his car. It's something unusual. They mentioned a Russian assault rifle. They seem to think it was a professional hit."

"Jesus," Ben muttered.

"But he's safe now. Very safe—there'll be police all over this place until they find his shooter."

A professional hit. Why? What was Lou investigating that warranted that kind of attack? The fentanyl problem? The missing girl, Lily Grace?

I thought about how mad I was, driving over there, convinced he'd stood up Tessa out of resentment toward me. Lou would never do that. I should have known better. I would apologize when he woke up.

"He likes you," Tessa said.

"Huh?"

"He really likes you, and you know it, but you pretend like you don't. And I think you like him, too."

Clancy cleared her throat.

Ben chuckled.

"It's complicated," I stammered.

"Why? Y'all like each other and . . . and you won't let anything happen, and that doesn't make sense. He's a good guy, Georgia." Tessa leaned closer, staring to make her point.

"He is," Clancy agreed. "And Tessa's right. It doesn't make sense."

I glanced at Ben, expecting some snarky response given our disastrous dating history, but his expression was soft and a little sad. "Y'all would be good together. Lou's not one to take dating lightly. If he's in, he's all in."

Before I could come up with some brilliant, avoidant response, the door opened, and Dr. Romano entered. "Coffee," he grumbled.

Clancy stood to pour it for him, not something she ever did. "Sit. You look like you're ready to collapse." She guided him to a chair.

He guzzled the coffee. "Here's the latest. Detective Michaels is stable. The intracranial bleeding has significantly reduced. His vitals are strong."

"Good." I exhaled, squeezing Tessa's hand.

"What about brain damage?" Clancy asked.

"We won't know about any deficits until he's conscious again, but we need him heavily sedated a bit longer. Y'all should go home. I'll call if anything happens, Georgia. I promise."

"You need to get some sleep," I said.

"I will, but not quite yet. Somebody gave the damn police captain my cell number, and I think I'll experience some serious police harassment if I let anything happen to their detective." He winked at me. "But I'm more afraid of you."

"You should be," I replied.

Thirty-Seven

RUS HAD GOTTEN USED TO THE MOTORCYCLE. HE MISSED RIDING DOUBLE, clinging to the back of his friend. But Tanner was gone now. The grief had come in another wave, knocking him down, threatening to keep him submerged, but Rus did what he'd learned to do. He stood back up. Dragged himself out of the water.

And climbed on the cycle that was now his.

He'd come to love the feel of riding. The gravity-defying magic of leaning into a turn. The vibration of the road as the tires ate miles of asphalt. The rush of air into his nostrils. The smells—burning leaves. Gasoline. Exhaust from the bus ahead of him. The rumble of the country road leading him to JD's Roost.

Rus parked and entered the local saloon near the river. He scanned the crowd. This was a place where he felt comfortable. All the patrons as ragtag as him. The stickiness of the floor. The odor of old beer. The scattered, scarred tables with small bowls of peanuts. He approached the bar and ordered a club soda. Some of his friends from the meetings couldn't frequent places like this—too much temptation—but for Rus, alcohol had never been the demon.

He spotted a small, young-looking Hispanic woman in the corner, sipping a Modelo light. Her black hair had blue streaks that were fading to green. Her nails, gripping the bottle, were chipped and dirty. Her makeup had smeared, dark streaks from her thick mascara flecked on her cheeks. He remembered her from the homeless encampment. Dulce.

She glanced at him, smiled, and approached. "Hello, handsome."

He sipped his soda, ignoring how she sidled up close. How she needed a bath.

"You help me out? I give you the best time you ever had," she whispered.

"Help you out how?" Rus didn't need to ask. Her hand on his thigh told him everything.

"I just need a fix. Twenty should do it."

He removed her hand, gripping it. Wishing he could pull her from this place. From this life that was swallowing her whole. "Dulce, you are a lovely girl. I'd like you to stay that way."

She snatched her hand back. "What do you mean by that?"

He smiled. "I mean, you're on a bad path. It's hard to quit, I know. I've been there."

Her laugh had an ugly edge. "So? You gonna be my savior? Screw you."

"Hey, settle down. I'm not trying to be your savior. I don't believe in that shit, anyway. But I've been where you are, and it's . . . dangerous. Especially now."

She pressed the bottle against her lips and guzzled the remaining beer.

"Dulce." Rus spoke quietly. "There's some new stuff on the streets. Blues. It's killing people. Don't be one of its victims."

She smacked the bottle against the counter. The front door jingled open, and a man entered. A familiar man. The Asian from Marco's lab. Boris.

Shit.

Dulce spotted him, too. She smacked Rus on the shoulder and said, "You buy my beer, savior man," and sashayed away from him.

She walked over to Boris, touched his lips with a finger, and she took his hand. The two of them exited without saying a word.

Rus slapped a ten on the counter. He followed them out the back door, but no further. Damn that Dulce, sleeping with the devil. Like last time, it didn't take long. Dulce satisfying her dealer. Her dealer returning to the bar, a stupid smile plastered on his stupid face. He ordered a beer and sipped it, his gaze surveying the crowd, probably looking for other marks. Rus remained at a table in the corner, drinking club soda and watching.

The big man entered the bar—the one with the shaved head and nasty scar. The Asian man tossed a bill on the table and left with him.

Rus hurried outside just as the two men opened the back of a black SUV. Another car pulled into the lot, parking right beside them: a very red Tesla. Out of place for a scummy dive like JD's. The driver popped the trunk before climbing out.

Rus's breath caught. Six foot two. Reddish blond hair. Freckles— familiar freckles Rus knew so well all those years ago.

Holden Hawthorne.

What was he doing here? He said something to the big guy. The Asian—Boris—laughed.

Rus inched closer, positioning himself behind a dented pickup with oversized tires. He couldn't take his eyes off Holden, memories flashing from all those years before: Boy Scouts. Spelling Bee rivalry. Long rounds of Grand Theft Auto. First beer venture. Happy memories until they weren't.

They weren't at all.

"You got our money?" the bald guy asked.

"Right here." Holden handed him an envelope. The bald guy opened it, thumbed through the bills, and pocketed it, apparently satisfied. Boris pulled out a box and said, "Like we discussed, this is only half of your order. I'll have the rest for you tomorrow. Will leave it in our usual spot."

Holden climbed into the Tesla and sped off. Rus retrieved his motorcycle and waited for the SUV to leave the lot. He followed, keeping his distance, but not letting it out of sight. He wondered about Holden. Clearly, Rus had just witnessed a drug deal—was Holden a user or a dealer? The size of the box made Rus think he was the latter. Stupid, stupid Holden.

The SUV headed to the warehouse district. They pulled into a gravel drive that led to a large area encircled by wire fencing. A coil of menacing-looking barbed wire stretched above it. The bald man exited the car, unlocked a gate, and then drove through, parking outside a two-story cement block structure. Rus parked in a copse of trees outside the gate, climbed off the motorcycle, and circled behind the building.

The two men entered through a door. Inside, Rus could see tables, boxes, and hazmat suits. So. It looked like Boris had set up another lab. He was already in business distributing that poison.

Already back to killing people.

Shouts erupted inside, then the voices settled down. About ten minutes later, both men came outside, the crazed Asian carrying two boxes. Easy guess as to what was inside. The large man pulled out his car keys, and they both climbed into his jeep. Rus waited for them to drive a hundred yards before mounting his motorcycle to follow.

The jeep pulled onto I-26 and wound through traffic. Not speeding, but driving aggressively. Rus kept his distance. They exited onto Huger Street and took it all the way down to Blossom, traveling a few miles, then turning onto a road that made Rus's stomach clench. Again, he kept his bike far back from the jeep, but once he figured out where the large man was headed, he didn't need to follow. He could drive there blindfolded.

They pulled into the long, winding driveway, and Rus parked on the street. He slipped through the open iron gate and tucked himself in the trees that formed the perimeter of the property.

The Fletcher Hawthorne property.

The jeep didn't pull right up to the house, but parked a small distance away. The Asian climbed out, carrying the small box, while the large man kept the engine running. Rus hurried through the trees, knowing what he'd see, but he had to be sure. Yes. They followed the same pattern each time.

The Asian guy slid inside the pool house, then exited without the box. Soon, someone else would come. They would collect the box.

After the Asian man returned to the jeep, the two drove away. Rus hurried to his bike, trying to decide whether he should follow or wait here for the distributor. He opted for the former.

They made two more stops, the large man remaining in the car for both as envelopes got handed to the other victims. The third stop surprised Rus: a fancy café in the Vista downtown. The jeep parked on the street, and both men joined a third seated at an outside table, the Asian taking a seat. The large man stood like a bodyguard. Rus parked in a narrow alley and walked up as close as he could. The seated man flagged down a waitress, ordered wine, and pulled out a vape pen. Mist from it evaporated in the haze of the streetlight.

The man had an elegance about him. Clearly wealthy, he wore beige linen pants and an open-collared blue shirt. His hair and sculpted goatee were the color of onyx.

"Sit down, Saul. You look like a goon standing over us."

The large man, Saul, took a seat, but his gaze flitted around, wary.

"Boris, are we any closer to knowing who . . . disrupted . . . my operation in Lexington County?" the man asked the Asian.

Air rushed into Rus's lungs. Could this be him? The man he'd been looking for?

"Our people are trying. It is not easy with everything destroyed like it was," Boris said.

Rus smiled. Yes. Destroyed. Obliterated. Thanks to Rus.

The Asian, Boris, gave the man an update. No leads on who destroyed the lab. The new one up and running seamlessly. Profits at an all-time high. A new addition to the operation—a younger "distributor"—doing an "excellent job" in targeting a young customer base.

The goateed man raised his glass, nodded, and took a large swallow. The large man, Saul, said nothing.

This was definitely him. The head of the dragon, sitting ten feet away. But he had no name. Had no idea where he operated, apart from the second lab he'd opened.

The goateed man waved the two other men away as though batting at gnats. Saul stood, checked the surroundings, then headed to the jeep. Boris was slow to follow, but soon, they both drove away. The goateed man motioned for the check. When he paid by credit card, Rus smiled. The man left his receipt on the table and sauntered away.

Rus moved fast as a python, dashing to the table and snatching up the receipt.

At last, he had a name: Marcus Landry.

Thirty-Eight

NO CHANGE. THAT WAS THE NEWS FROM THE MEDICAL STAFF TAKING care of Lou. I remained with him for as long as I could, but when more tests were ordered, they wheeled him away.

Guess it was time for me to do my pesky job. Ten minutes later, I stood outside Sara Clark's room, steeling myself to go inside. It was always hard to see injured children, and this girl staying alive was nothing short of a miracle. When she was stable enough, another surgery awaited her, then possibly a third. I prayed she had the strength—and luck— needed to survive them all.

Her mother sat beside her, gripping her hand. She rarely left the hospital. Mr. Clark came and went, a busy man tending to his job or maybe avoiding the pain of being here. Different people handled tragedies in different ways.

Footsteps pounded up behind me. "Oh. It's you," a man's voice said.

I turned to find Fletcher Hawthorne huffing up beside me, his son, Cooper, dawdling behind him. Fletcher wore what looked like a tailored suit, gray, with a red tie that made him look like he'd stepped from a law practice commercial. Cooper wore a brown hoodie that seemed to swallow him, his head downcast as though he found his Converse sneakers fascinating.

I wasn't sure what to call his father. Mr. Hawthorne? Mr. Solicitor? I went with the former.

"Can I have an update on Sara?" he demanded.

"I'm sorry. HIPAA won't allow me to disclose much, but Mrs. Clark may want to talk with you." I pointed at her through the window.

He rapped on the door, then let himself inside. Cooper lingered outside the room with me.

"Cooper? You may not remember me. I'm Georgia Thayer. Tessa's foster mom."

When he looked up at me, his expression was a mixture of sadness and fear. He must have been closer to Sara than I realized.

"You okay?"

"I'm good. It's Sara I'm worried about."

"She's been quite a fighter."

"You think she'll . . . survive this?" He sounded childlike, but something else leaked into his question. Anxiety? Or guilt? He'd been in the car with Joel when he ran over Sara.

"Of course, that's what we all hope. Tessa tells me you haven't been back to school yet."

"Dad said I wasn't ready. This"—he gestured to the room that held Sara—"has been a fucking mess."

I wasn't used to a kid speaking to me that way. Well, except in the ER, where stoned kids said all kinds of things.

"Have you seen my brother?" Cooper asked. "Holden was going to meet us here."

I shook my head.

"We have to go get pictures made. For Dad's campaign."

I looked down at his jeans and hoodie. He looked far less camera-ready than his dad.

"I have a suit in the car," he clarified.

"What's it like, having your dad in a big campaign? Do you have to do interviews? Appear on TV?"

He shrugged. "So far, it hasn't been bad. Holden's more involved than I am. I was surprised Dad wanted to run—he likes being a solicitor. I guess this is the next step."

It didn't sound like those words were his. More likely, they had been put inside him. "Still, the public exposure has to be weird, right?"

His eyes flickered. "Dad says we're all under a microscope. But sometimes I feel like one of those ants under a magnifying glass."

"You mean . . . the ones that get burned up by the sun?" The image surprised me.

His laugh had a sarcastic edge. "Something like that."

"The accident? Is that what has you under the magnifying glass?"

A half-shrug. "I wasn't driving. But it was my car. And my party."

Yes, it had been his party. As far as I was concerned, his parents bore the brunt of responsibility for what had happened at their home.

"I have to ask—do you have any idea how the fentanyl got there? We're seeing a lot of overdoses and want to help the police get a handle on the drug distribution."

He looked away. "It could have been anyone who was there, I guess. Nobody thought it would hurt someone. They probably thought it would be fun. A little buzz."

And incredibly irresponsible. "Is that how it felt to you? A little buzz?"

"Sort of. We were high—both of us. I mean Joel and me. We shouldn't have been driving, but it wasn't like being drunk. We didn't feel . . . out of control."

"Cooper?" a voice interrupted us.

I turned to find his older brother, Holden, approaching. Holden was a few inches taller than Cooper, making him over six feet, with reddish blond hair and vivid blue eyes. A lady killer on campus, I suspected.

Cooper's smile held a hint of relief. "Dad's talking to Sara's mother."

"And who are you talking to?" Holden eyed me curiously.

"Tessa's foster mom. She works here. Georgia—"

"Thayer," I finished. "I'm a social worker. How are you doing, Holden?"

He looked through the window. "We'll all be doing better when she gets well." He turned to his brother. "What time's the photographer?"

"In an hour."

Holden looked at his watch. "I have a study session at six. Need to be done by then."

"You're in law school, right?" Georgia asked.

"Second year." He spoke with pride—or maybe arrogance—reminiscent of his father's.

"Dad's already got his office picked out in the family law practice. A big one with windows. And lots of family baggage," Cooper said with a smirk.

"Yours is waiting, too." Holden nudged his shoulder.

I'd judged these kids as entitled and spoiled, but listening to them made me realize the burden of family prestige. The weight of family money. Not something I'd ever had to contend with.

Fletcher emerged from the room with Mrs. Clark, who looked beyond exhausted. Her brown hair hung limp to her shoulders. Whatever makeup she'd applied that morning had been washed away, probably by her tears. The lids over her dark eyes were swollen like small pink balloons.

"Mrs. Clark? How are you doing?" I asked.

"Better. Sara squeezed my hand this morning. That's something, right? She must have heard me talking to her. Must have processed it was me, right?"

I smiled, wanting to reassure her, but knowing it could have been a random reflex. "Hope is very important at this stage. You're not giving up on her, and she knows it."

Mrs. Clark turned to the boys. "You can see her if you want. But just for a minute. Don't be alarmed by all the machines and things. They're helping her get stronger."

Cooper's eyes widened in absolute terror. Holden eyed his dad, who gave him an insistent nod, then he guided his brother into the room.

"Again, Margaret. If there's anything we can do," Fletcher said to Mrs. Clark.

"Thank you." She folded her arms across her chest as though they held all her parts in.

"The police are still investigating the accident. The McCants kid feels terrible, but he'll have to face the music for what he did. It's so damn tragic," Fletcher said with a shake of his head.

"Tragic? What do you know about 'tragic?'" Mrs. Clark's words held a bite.

Fletcher stiffened.

"Sorry, Fletcher. I'm just . . . tired. Beyond tired."

"Running on fumes," I said, hoping to defuse the sudden tension. "Why don't you go home, take a break? I'll make sure the hospital contacts you if there's any change."

She shook her head. "I can't leave. I've tried, but . . . I simply can't." Her shrug was oddly apologetic.

As she slipped back through the door to Sara's room, Fletcher turned to me, his pale eyes scanning my face. I kept my expression neutral, though I wondered why he was scrutinizing me. "Ms. Thayer, right? You're a social worker?"

"Yes, sir."

"I didn't appreciate the tone you took with me the night of the accident. But I didn't say anything to your superiors. Just thought you should know."

Oh Christ. He wanted gratitude. He wanted his ass kissed. I was not in the mood.

"Do you have any idea how the drugs got to your party?" I stepped a little closer.

"I do not. They weren't there when the police arrived. Whoever brought them probably panicked and got rid of them."

"If you know anything about where they came from, or your boys know, please tell the police. The fentanyl that's on the streets is more dangerous than anything we've seen in years. We've had too many fatalities and expect even more."

"I know that. I'll do whatever I can to help, Ms. Thayer." The boys stepped out of the room. He motioned that they needed to leave. I waved at the boys as they exited. Holden looking regal and confident, Cooper looking like he wanted to hide away from the world. I felt a little sorry for that kid.

I glanced at my watch. Lou was probably back in his room.

I'd return to him.

Return to the waiting.

Thirty-Nine

"YOU LOOK BEAUTIFUL," FLETCHER SAID TO VIVIAN. SHE DID. STUNNING, actually. A silk blue dress that shimmied down her lean (too lean) frame. Tan legs in tall heels. Blonde highlights in luscious waves down to her shoulders. She'd always been an artist with the makeup, too: just enough to accentuate her high cheekbones, to emphasize her full lips. To hide how pale she'd become.

"Cooper? Straighten your tie," she commanded.

Their son complied like he always did when his mother used that tone.

The photographer's van rumbled up their driveway. They'd chosen the rear garden for the pictures. Gumpo azaleas still in bloom. Freshly planted pansies tilting yellow and purple faces toward the sun. The pinkish green leaves of a perfectly manicured loropetalum behind the flowers.

Fletcher reached for Vivian's hand. "How are you feeling, hon?"

"Muscle spasms. Cramping. Same old." She spoke with a fatigue born of chronic pain.

"I'm so proud of you. I know how hard it is when you need to take something."

"No, I don't think you do." She said it matter-of-factly, with no trace of anger.

"You're probably right. I promise this won't take long."

"It better not." Her forced smile held not a trace of warmth.

As the photographer set up her tripod, Fletcher caught a glimpse of something—or someone—in the shrubs. A flash of brown. Was it hair? He hurried over to see if maybe . . . but nobody was there.

This wasn't the first time Fletcher thought he spotted the boy. It wasn't possible—the boy had been gone for four years—but he'd catch a glimpse of curly brown hair or a sweet smile or a blue sweatshirt like the one he wore all the time, and the longing—the gut-wrenching longing—returned. Four years gone now, but still . . .

Not all memories of him were happy ones. There had been that Fourth of July picnic when the boy came with his family. Fletcher recalled a dozen boisterous teens in the pool. Letting Holden and Cooper work the grill, while Marta and Vivian kept glasses filled and the food table well-stocked. Fletcher went to the pool house for more cups, and as he was rummaging through the cabinets, he heard the door open. When he turned, the boy stood there.

"Hey." The boy smiled, holding up a cup.

"Well, hello." Fletcher had to gather himself because an electrical current charged through him. Why did the kid affect him so much?

"I was wondering if you had something else to drink." The boy wiggled his eyebrows. Fletcher knew what he wanted, knew he shouldn't oblige him, not with his parents lounging just a few feet away, but he couldn't refuse.

"Just a little." He grabbed his hidden bottle of bourbon and added a splash to the kid's drink.

"Mmmm." He took a sip before plopping down on the chaise, the same one where the two of them sat before.

Fletcher couldn't stop himself from joining him. "Having fun?"

The boy shook the glass at him. "Not yet, but I will soon."

Fletcher pictured him relaxing. All stretched out, his beautiful tan legs dangling. He could offer more bourbon. He could offer something stronger.

No. No, no, no. His parents were here. Other guests. The risk was too great.

"More?" the boy asked.

"Sorry."

The boy leaned closer, laying his head against Fletcher's shoulder, pressing his nose against his neck, and every ounce of Fletcher's resistance evaporated. He turned, knowing it was wrong. So very, very wrong. And then . . .

A noise startled them, and he jumped up. Had someone peeked through the door? God. Who could it have been? A parent? That could well be the end of him. What a fool he was. He hurriedly stood, moving away from the boy, grabbed the cups, and started to leave.

"Don't tell anyone I gave you that drink!" he commanded.

"I won't." The boy sounded disappointed, but it was nothing like the loss Fletcher had felt right then. He might have lost everything.

Fletcher remembered returning to his lounge chair, his face hot and dotted with sweat, doing all he could not to look at the boy, expecting the worst. But nobody said anything. Not one word. Had it just been his imagination?

He tried to be careful from then on, but he couldn't stay away. Sometimes, he blamed Vivian. If only she could satisfy Fletcher—but since the fall, intimacy was too painful, and what was Fletcher to do? He was a man with needs. When the boy came another afternoon, Fletcher gave him his cell phone number. They'd meet at a state park, or sometimes, when the boy could get away, Fletcher would drive him to the river house. Soon, alcohol wasn't enough for the kid. He found some of Vivian's pills in a medicine cabinet and helped himself, later wanting more. The balance in their relationship shifted somehow—the boy demanding drugs, Fletcher having no choice but to oblige him.

He wanted him to be as happy as he felt when they were together. If it took drugs for that to happen, so be it.

"Fletcher! You look completely lost in thought," Vivian chastised him.

"Sorry. I thought I heard an animal in the bushes."

"Chasing ghosts again," Vivian said.

The photographer took over thirty shots—the whole family, the boys, the couple holding hands like young lovers. Vivian's smile waned. Her face reddened. Holden approached and whispered something to her.

She nodded. He disappeared, only to return with a glass of water and a pill.

Fletcher glared at his son. They'd agreed Vivian wouldn't take the heavy stuff until the photographer left, yet Holden had gone behind his back and done exactly the opposite. The photographer approached. "Everything okay, sir?"

Fletcher plastered on his politician's smile. "Everything's grand. Let's finish up. I have a thousand things to attend to."

"Of course, sir." A few dozen more shots, and Vivian's smile widened.

Maybe the photographer would be gone before Vivian's words began to slur, her eyes drooping on the edges.

Before the addiction grabbed her once again.

Forty

TESSA CARRIED HER LUNCH OUTSIDE. ELIAS HAD PACKED HER A BRIE AND apple on a sourdough panini with a fat brownie and dropped it off the night before when he came to see Georgia. The dude could COOK, and she didn't want to eat in the cafeteria where the other kids would gawk in envy.

She loved Elias. He'd become her "foster uncle" the same way Georgia was her foster mother. And Lou Michaels? What was he? Another sorta uncle. Georgia said he was still stable, but Tessa could hear the worry in her voice. But Lou was tough. Really tough. Tessa had to believe he'd be okay.

She found an unoccupied bench under a live oak tree and tore open the paper bag so that it could serve as a lunch tray. The sandwich smelled like heaven. Damn, he'd even snuck in a little bacon, which Elias called "the perfect food."

If Joel were here, she'd share it with him. Or Sara.

"Hey!" Ariel rounded the bench, holding a lunch sack of her own. She wore a short, ruffled skirt and vintage wedge sandals. Her navy-tipped blonde hair hung in loose waves. Eye makeup had been applied with a heavy hand, but Ariel made it work. "Can I join you?"

"Sure." Tessa popped a slab of bacon into her mouth, wondering if Ariel was vegan. She looked the type.

"That looks divine." Ariel pointed to Tessa's sandwich.

"It is. Want a bite?" Tessa hoped she didn't.

"Nah. I'm dieting."

Of course, Ariel was dieting. She weighed ninety-eight pounds, but so many girls never thought they were skinny enough. Ariel opened her

177

bag and pulled out a glass bowl containing salad. She dumped some vinegar-smelling dressing into the greens and stirred with a fork she'd brought.

It made Tessa enjoy the bacon even more. "Did Cooper come to school today?"

Ariel shrugged. "I guess."

"You've seen him?"

Ariel pierced a cherry tomato. "I saw him in the hall."

"You guys okay?" Tessa asked tentatively.

"No. He's changed. Changing. The accident has made him morose."

Good riddance, Tessa almost said. "I've been piecing together what happened the night of Cooper's party."

"That's a blur to me, girl."

"Yeah, I get that." Tessa remembered Ariel that night—beautiful, lithe, and so very stoned that she thought she could walk on water. "A couple of things happened that are odd. The night of the party—Sara and Cooper had an argument. And there was something else. Sara went into Cooper's room. She had Joel guard the door so Cooper wouldn't catch her. Said she was looking for some notes, but I wonder if she was doing something else."

Ariel dropped her fork. "She was in his room?"

"According to Joel."

A breeze picked up, stirring the leaves at their feet. Ariel lifted her face as though savoring it. "Do you remember a few weeks ago when an ambulance showed up at the school?"

"Yeah. Never knew why."

"It happened in our art class. Me, Sara, Cooper, and Joel all take the same course. There's another girl, Jana. She was the reason for the ambulance."

"What happened?"

"She collapsed over her acrylic pour project. Hit the floor. The teacher called the nurse. It was a lot of drama. The nurse did CPR, the teacher called 911—really, really scary shit. EMTs had that stuff that they squirt up your nose—what's it called?"

"Narcan."

"Yeah. That revived her, thank God. The nurse said something about a fentanyl overdose. Sara flipped. She stormed over to Cooper and accused him of giving her something that got her sick."

"Sara thought Cooper gave Jana the fentanyl?" Tessa processed this. Cooper gave out pills at his party. Maybe he'd been distributing before then.

"You gotta understand about Sara—she gets insane when it comes to drugs. She lost a brother to them years ago. His name was Max. She adored him, but he became an addict. They tried everything to get him straight, but he ended up taking his own life, and she never, ever got over it."

Tessa winced. "That's awful. Really awful."

"He was a really cool brother when we were younger." Ariel smiled. "When we were eight, Sara and I played on the same softball team. The bluebirds."

"Bluebirds?" Something about that made Tessa laugh.

"Damn right. We weren't that good. Got stuck mostly in the outfield. Sara's parents rarely came to our games, but Max? He was at almost every one of them. Honestly, I don't think she cared if her mom and dad showed up. But she loved it when he was there."

"Sounds like a great big brother."

"He was. Until he wasn't. Drugs really, really messed with his head. She lost her brother long before he died. That's why she's so extreme when it comes to getting high."

"Joel told me that when they were dating, he offered her CBD, and she flipped out. I see why."

Ariel resumed eating. "I do grass. Drink some. She hates it, and if she's nearby, she watches me like a worried mother. So maybe the night of the party, she saw everybody getting high and blamed Cooper for it. With good reason, it turns out. And maybe she went looking for his stash."

Tessa pondered it. Maybe this was the reason Sara went into the pool house. The reason she and Cooper got into an argument.

The bell rang, startling both of them. "I hate school," Ariel said.

"There are worse things," Tessa answered.

Forty-One

LILY GRACE'S SITUATION GREW STRANGER BY THE MINUTE. CASE IN POINT: whoever Detective Michaels had allowed in next door. The guy played awful rap music so loud that the building practically vibrated. Did he ever sleep? And the smells—smoky, sometimes sweet. They scared her—if he caught something on fire in there, how would she escape?

What if she died in this awful room? She'd never get to tell her parents goodbye. And what about Joel? Would he rot in jail for a crime he didn't commit because Lily Grace never got the chance to speak the truth?

And what if—this thought terrified her—Lou Michaels wasn't really the police? What if she'd been duped? And if he was some random kidnapper, who was he? And why did he keep her locked up? What did he plan to do to her?

Lily Grace circled the room again, checking the narrow window—no way she'd fit through it—and the door locked up tight. Overhead, an air vent might be a way to escape, but she had no way to reach it. Even standing on the table wouldn't get her high enough to push through the vent cover.

She tapped the cover of the Harry Potter book, which she finished yesterday. At least, she thought it was yesterday—time had lost all meaning to her. Here she was, stuck in this hellish room, held prisoner by someone who might be good, but might be evil. And why?

All because she'd been stupid enough to go to Cooper Hawthorne's party. She'd been so excited to get the invite, picturing an evening with

180

the other kids. Making friends. Being accepted. Only to have it all turn to shit.

Shit. She'd never used that word, but somehow it fit. Her parents would be ashamed of her for even thinking it, but maybe if they'd heard about her predicament, they'd understand. Because she was definitely, totally, completely in deep shit.

The door rattled open, and Detective Michaels—or whoever he was—entered, carrying a pizza box and a six-pack of sodas.

"Hope you like pepperoni."

She'd never smelled anything so tempting. Her last meal had been a few hours earlier—another peanut butter sandwich—but she felt the heat of the warm pizza as he handed her the box and felt her stomach rumble.

"I have plates, too."

The "detective" placed two Chinets on the table as Lily Grace opened the container. Yes, she did like pepperoni, or any pizza at all that didn't include anchovies.

"Should we save some for the man next door?" She slid a slice onto her plate.

Lou Michaels froze. "Why do you say that?"

"He must be hungry, given how long he works." She bit into the pizza, closing her eyes to savor it.

"You've heard him, then."

"Heard him? Yeah. He's very loud. Especially his music. I can smell him, too."

"Smell him?" He glared over his slice.

"I don't know what he's doing over there. And I get that it's none of my business. But I smelled smoke a little while ago. And sometimes, I smell something sweet like candy."

He frowned. "Smoke? Really?"

"Not bad. At first, I thought maybe he'd started a fire, but I think maybe he was cooking something." Gooey cheese dripped onto her chin. She grabbed a paper towel to wipe it. "I've been quiet, like you told me. I don't think he knows I'm here."

"Good. But I don't like that he's disturbing you. I'll make sure it doesn't happen again."

She eyed him as she finished the piece, wondering how to approach him. How could she determine if he was really a detective? Better yet, what would he do to her?

"So, besides the noise and odor from next door, how are you doing?" he asked.

She shrugged. "Okay. I'm glad I have heat. I finished the books you got me."

"I'll bring you more."

Lily Grace helped herself to another slice. Pizza wasn't something she had at home often. Her mother wouldn't allow delivery. Sometimes, Daddy brought a frozen one from the store, but it didn't taste as good as this one did. School pizza was hardly edible.

She took a bite, steeled herself, and said, "I need to talk to my parents."

"We've been over that. It's not safe."

"Why not? If you're the police, you can find a way. I need to talk to them, to tell them I'm okay. You don't know how much they worry."

He tossed down his slice. "What do you mean, *if* I'm the police?"

She flinched at his tone, which held an aggressive edge. Still, she needed to know. "Sometimes . . . I wonder if maybe you aren't telling me the truth. That you really aren't a detective."

His dark eyes narrowed. She looked at his scar, that slash that journeyed down his face, and felt a niggle of fear. "And if I'm not, then who am I?"

She swallowed. "I don't know. Maybe you're . . . a kidnapper."

He glared, his face carved in stone, and then his mouth pulled into a weird smile. "A kidnapper? What would I be after? Your parents' money? I've met them. I've seen your home, remember? I don't think they can afford much of a ransom."

"But . . ." She hadn't thought this through very well. He had a good point.

He laughed. "If I was a kidnapper, I wouldn't target a family that drove a 2006 Corolla. No offense."

He didn't need to be insulting. Her dad did the best he could. He provided them with a safe home. Nothing fancy, but they didn't need fancy.

Detective Michaels popped open a soda and drank a good bit of it. "I'll tell you what. You want to talk to your parents? I can't really arrange that, but you can write them a letter. I'll deliver it to them personally, I promise."

"You really mean it?"

His hard features softened. "Of course I mean it. I'm not a monster. Or a kidnapper, by the way. I'll bring you a notebook and a pen. I'll make sure they get your message and bring you any response from them. You're right; it will help keep them from worrying. And it will probably help you feel better, too."

She nodded, starting to believe this really was Detective Lou Michaels and that he would keep her safe.

A rumbling noise erupted from the room next door, then the pounding bass thrum of the stranger's terrible music.

Lou Michaels closed the pizza box. "I see what you mean about the racket. Guess I need to go pay him a visit. You stay here. Stay quiet. I'll be back soon."

Forty-Two

"GEORGIA? CLANCY ASKED YOU TO MEET HER AT BAY FIVE IN THE ED."

The call came from the nursing station. I could tell by the chaos of background noise even before I checked the number.

"I'll be right there." I saved the progress notes I'd been typing—documentation was something I loved as much as a colonoscopy—and exited my broom-closet-sized office.

On the elevator, I imagined the reason for my summoning. Another fentanyl OD? I prayed not. We'd had far too many of those. And that was something Clancy would handle without me—we'd both gotten good at it. No, this had to be something unusual.

The emergency department was its usual bustle—but not as bad as it could be. I passed four bays before reaching the closed door to bay five, where I found Clancy giving hell to two med techs.

"We didn't mean anything!" one said.

"It was . . . a joke. Just a joke," said the other.

Clancy practically had them pinned against the wall. "It was cruel. And grossly inappropriate. Have you ever heard of thin privilege? I suggest you google it. I can have you written up."

"Please don't. We said we're sorry."

Clancy eyed me like I should have an answer for her.

"Hey, I just got here," I mumbled.

She turned back to them. "You will apologize to her before the end of the day, or I'll make sure your supervisor knows exactly what you did. Got it?"

Looking chastised—and maybe a little terrified—both nodded and scurried away.

"What happened?" I asked.

Clancy whispered, "They were making fun of her. Called her 'Shamu.' It was so cruel." She pointed through the narrow slit between the curtains to the bay. A woman lay on the gurney—a very, very large woman overflowing the mattress. A woman I knew.

"Oh no. That's Lily Grace's mom. What happened?" I asked.

"Chest pains. Shortness of breath. Could be anxiety, but they're doing a cardiac workup. Come on in."

I followed her into the tiny room. Mrs. Duffy had the sheet gathered close to her neck. The tube from an oxygen cannula pressed into her pillowy cheeks. She looked pale, her deep-set dark eyes crusty, her lips scaly from the dry air.

Clancy sat beside her, leaning close. "I'm so sorry for what they said. We don't allow that kind of talk here at Columbia General."

God, I wished that was true.

"I've heard worse. That's why I don't go out much anymore. When you look like me . . ."

Clancy lifted a hand. "You have nothing to be ashamed of." I knew this was a sensitive issue for my friend. Her recent weight loss had been triggered by a pre-diabetes diagnosis. Every pound was a difficult struggle.

Mrs. Duffy turned to me. "Have you heard anything about my Lily Grace?" She sounded so childlike, so tragically sad, that I wished with all my heart I had good news to tell her.

"I'm sorry, no. But the police are doing all they can."

"Where's my husband?" she asked.

"He'll be right back. The doctor wanted to talk with him." Clancy spoke softly, gently.

Mrs. Duffy reached for a tissue. "I feel better. Maybe I can go home soon."

Clancy glanced at me, then said, "We don't want to rush anything. It will take some time to run tests."

"You may be fine, Mrs. Duffy. But let's be sure," I added.

185

She shook her head. "Not fine. I'll never be fine." She looked down at her own body.

Clancy winced in sympathy. I tried to imagine what life was like for Mrs. Duffy. Things that should be easy, like going to the bathroom, tying one's shoes, or walking to the car, had to be hard. And worse, the shame she clearly felt. I'd learned long ago that shame was evil. The shame I felt because of my mental illness had weighed me down like a leaden blanket. It took years of therapy to crawl out from under it.

Could Mrs. Duffy shed hers?

A tap on the door drew our attention. Dr. Romano motioned us out into the hall, where he stood with Mr. Duffy. The small man looked unduly burdened: his sparse hair in disarray, his green eyes shadowed. I offered a sympathetic smile, which he didn't return.

"I was explaining to Mr. Duffy that we need to do a heart cath to check for blockages."

"That's not so bad," I said. "We do them all the time, Mr. Duffy."

"True, but there's an extra risk, given her comorbidities."

"Given her weight issues. And her poor overall health." Mr. Duffy sounded utterly defeated.

"We'll do the best we can. I'll get it scheduled for tomorrow. Try not to worry, Mr. Duffy. Your wife is in good hands." Dr. Romano hurried off.

Clancy and I remained. Clancy asked gently, "Has she always had a weight problem?"

He shrugged. "She's always been a large woman. I never cared about that. I cared about what I saw inside her—she's the kindest, most intelligent woman I know. But everything changed over the years. She kept gaining weight. She pulled away from our friends. Got to where she wouldn't leave the house, even for church."

"Did something happen that caused the change?" I asked.

"Her mother passed away a few years ago. Paulette had a troubled relationship with her. I didn't realize how bad it was until . . . well, she started getting nightmares. Paulette finally started opening up, and I learned how very toxic her mother had been. Berating. Mean. And Paulette felt defenseless against her vitriol, even after her death. I think food became her comfort."

"I'm so sorry," Clancy said.

"Thank you. It's why she's so protective of Lily Grace. After everything she went through, she couldn't bear the thought of any harm coming to her child, and now—"

"Now, there's no reason to assume the worst," I said lamely.

He looked me dead in the eye. "Oh, I think there is. And you know it, too."

Clancy interjected, "We need to tell your wife about the procedure. But I'd like a few more minutes with you, Mr. Duffy."

"I'll tell her," I said, curious about what Clancy needed to discuss with the husband, but grateful that I was leaving him in good hands.

When I returned to the room, I relayed the news from Dr. Romano. She took it stoically, as though expecting it. "We do heart caths all the time. It's no big deal," I said. "And it will help us make sure your heart is healthy."

"The only thing that will mend my heart is my daughter safe, right here beside me."

"I wish I could give that to you," I answered.

"I just wanted her to be safe. Maybe I was too strict. We let her have a computer and cell phone, but monitored her texts and emails. But apparently not closely enough." Hurt reverberated in this statement. A sense of betrayal. And fear.

"Hey, kids keep secrets. It's part of the job. Tessa hid the score on her math quiz from me for a month."

"My Lily Grace isn't like that. She's never been one to keep secrets. Until now," she said. "I keep wondering what else she hid from us. What didn't I know that if I did, she'd be safe right now?"

"You're giving yourself a lot of power here. I haven't been in the mom role for very long, but one thing I've learned is that when a kid is sixteen, they're independent. They're going to make decisions without us—it's part of growing up."

She watched me closely, as if trying to believe. I wanted to absolve her of whatever guilt she felt. She didn't deserve it. Whatever happened to Lily Grace was the fault of some evil asshole, not her parents.

"Do you think I'll ever see her again?" Her vulnerability coming through broke my heart.

How to answer that one? I wished I could promise her she would, but God only knew where her child was. If her child was still breathing.

"I certainly hope so. All you can do is stay strong so you can be home when she returns." I prayed one day that it might happen.

But as time went on, I had my doubts.

Forty-Three

IT WAS UNUSUAL FOR MARCUS TO SUMMON FLETCHER TO A PUBLIC PLACE. They usually met in the shadows, which Fletcher preferred. Of course, the restaurant where he'd been led wasn't exactly in the middle of town. It was a small Mexican place in the county, with bright orange walls adorned with paintings on velvet. The hostess who greeted Fletcher didn't ask for his name, simply said, "Follow me," and led him to a private room in the back. This space had a different feel: a single oak table, unlike the cheap ones out front. The paintings on the walls looked like oil originals: landscapes of farms and mountains. Marcus sat at the table, sipping some dark liquid in a crystal tumbler. He wore a crisp white shirt, a gold chain gleaming beneath his Adam's apple. His thin black hair meticulously styled back. Sometimes Fletcher forgot how small Marcus was because his presence could be so immense. But the man himself stood barely five foot seven, with a thin waistline and delicate hands.

"Sit," Marcus said.

Fletcher complied. The hostess reappeared with a glass of what looked like bourbon. She placed it in front of him without saying a word, then left.

"Strange place for us to meet." Fletcher sipped the bourbon. His brand. Nice that Marcus remembered.

"I had business here." Marcus wore a new expression. His brow furrowed. Mouth taut. He had never looked tense like this before.

"And I'm part of it?"

"You are now." His phone rang. He lifted a finger to silence Fletcher as he answered with a curt, "Marcus."

189

Fletcher tried to discern what the call was about. Marcus made a few odd comments: "I said it was handled," and "We don't know if that will happen," before closing with, "I understand."

It was Marcus's tone that threw him. He sounded humbled, a little browbeaten. Fletcher had never seen that side of him before.

Fletcher sipped. Waited.

Marcus drained his glass. "Your upcoming election has raised some interest I didn't expect."

"What does that mean?"

"It means that I'm not the only powerful person who wants you in that seat." He reached into a portfolio, retrieving a fat manila envelope, which he slid across the table at Fletcher.

"What's this?"

"Open it."

The hairs on the back of his neck bristled as he reached for it. This whole exchange felt darkly strange. Inside, he found five thick packets of one-hundred-dollar bills. He sifted through a couple. The money looked real, not fake. Each stack probably held fifty.

"There's more coming," Marcus said.

"Why?"

"To help with your campaign. Our latest research had you losing to your opponent. That is . . . unacceptable. And not just to me."

Fletcher swallowed. True, he'd seen the latest poll numbers, but he had weeks of campaigning yet. Things weren't exactly in high gear. He pushed the money back. "You know I can't accept this. There are firm donation limits. The ethics committee has regulations about that. If I'm to be attorney general, I better play by them."

"I know the damn rules, Fletcher. This money didn't come from another source. It's your money. You kept it in a security box for years, if anyone asks. You were saving for . . . I don't know. A boat. A mountain home. But now you've decided to add it to your campaign account so you can accelerate your outreach. Which is perfectly legal, as you know. So hire more damn staff. Bombard the state with your stupid commercials. Digital billboards everywhere. Got it?" Marcus used his quiet, authoritarian voice that Fletcher knew to take seriously.

"Why is my winning so damn important to you? And who else gives a damn?" This was the puzzlement. Why the escalation? Why the desperate measures to ensure Fletcher's victory?

"We need to own the attorney general."

"Screw you. You do not own me." Fletcher spat out the words.

Marcus's responding smile could freeze fire. "Oh, but I do. We are all owned, Fletcher. You. Your lovely wife. Your children. Even me—sad to say."

That was news. Who owned Marcus?

Marcus continued. "And the people who issue me orders have a strong interest in your success. I would not let them down if I were you."

Fletcher lifted his glass. "That sounds oddly like a threat."

"Oh, it is, my friend. The stakes are much higher than you—or I—ever thought."

In his mind, Fletcher heard the bars clanging shut. He'd never felt so trapped. If he won the election, and he'd better, he'd owe not only Marcus, but whoever it was that pulled Marcus's strings. He might become attorney general, but he'd always be their pawn.

His dreams of escaping the tentacles that had held him for too long vanished like a mist.

Forty-Four

SOMEONE FROM THE NURSE'S STATION SUMMONED ME TO SARA Clark's room. I booked it, fearing the worst, but a nursing tech intercepted me. "She's still with us. We even took her off the vent. Talking some—but pretty out of it. Got kind of agitated, and it upset her mom. We thought you could help."

"I'll do my best." Agitation wasn't uncommon as someone slowly climbed out of an unconscious state, but it could be disturbing to the family. We'd had one patient who confessed to his wife, who'd been weeping by his bed for weeks, that he'd had a five-year affair but usually what we heard was gibberish.

I tapped quietly on the door before opening it, not wanting to startle them. Mrs. Clark motioned I should enter. I immediately saw the change in her daughter: her skin looked less gray, her face more visible now without the ventilator. She had delicate features, with small freckles like pixels across her nose. She stirred, muttering something, and Mrs. Clark reached for her hand.

"She's been upset about something," Mrs. Clark said.

"She has to be confused, given all that's happened to her. Are they giving her pain medication?"

"Oh yes. Like clockwork. I can tell it's working because she's not crying like she did earlier."

"That's good."

The girl in the bed—so small, it seemed—made a whimpering sound, then said, "Pool house. In the . . ."

Mrs. Clark stroked Sara's hand. "That's what she keeps saying. She gets distressed."

"Bad dream, maybe?" I said.

"She says something else, too. She calls out for Max."

"Max?"

"That was her brother's name. The one who died."

I sighed, knowing that simply saying his name caused her pain. "I'm sorry. It's hard to know why she's thinking about him right now."

Mrs. Clark blinked up at me. "No, it's not. She loved him so much. I just hope she's not seeing him. That he's not an angel who's come for her."

I could feel her fear. I wanted to help her, but wasn't sure how. "Sara is doing better, Mrs. Clark. Don't think the worst. She also says pool house. Do you have a pool?"

"No. We live on the lake."

But the Hawthornes had a pool—Tessa had mentioned the pool house. Had something happened there the night of the accident? Something she was remembering? Or—more likely—random neurons were firing in her very confused brain, and we shouldn't give anything she'd said much credence.

"Mrs. Clark, was that the first time Sara visited Cooper's house?"

"Lord, no. We're friends with the Hawthornes. Or we used to be— we used to go there all the time because Max was the same age as Holden. They were buddies until . . . well, until Max started having problems."

"Problems?"

"He got with the wrong crowd. Ran away more times than I can count. We had to bail him out of jail twice." She shook her head. "I failed him. I know that. I mean, we never gave up on him, but he gave up on us. And that has to be my fault. I was his mother!" She practically spat out the last sentence.

I didn't like her train of thought. I focused on the bags that drooped below her eyes, the sunken cheeks. The air of utter exhaustion. "When was the last time you slept?" I asked her.

"She's calmer now." Mrs. Clark continued to grip Sara's hand. "I can't leave her. I want to be here if she gets upset again."

"Maybe another family member can sit with her for a while? So you can get some rest?"

"My husband will be here soon."

"Good."

She turned to look at me, her hooded eyes softening. "This is hard for him, being here. The pain is too hard."

Why did wives make excuses?

"It's hard for you, too, Mrs. Clark. I hope he'll be able to share the burden."

Forty-Five

SAUL KNOCKED ON THE DOOR TO THE WAREHOUSE BUT, AS EXPECTED, could not be heard over the booming music inside. As he let himself in, he froze at what he saw. Boris wore a hazmat suit as he stood beside a large machine made of gray metal. A large funnel fed into the machine, and as Boris scooped white powder from a bucket into it, wheels similar to a projector reel whirred and clanked before it spat out a dozen small tablets.

The blaring music was Korean hip-hop. Boris used a gloved hand to scoop the pills onto a plastic plate. He slid one pill into a beaker of water and inserted a test strip into the solution, his movements fast and efficient. Then he spun around, returned to the metal machine, and swept the pills into a large ziplock bag. He sang along to the music. Loud. Off-key. Then twirled around and swung his fists in the air in rhythm with the song beat.

The dude looked manic. Saul donned an N-95 mask, marched to the small boombox, and switched it off. The Asian spun around, his patience wore thin.

"Marcus said I needed to come see you," Saul muttered.

"Good. That's good." The small man slipped off his rubber gloves and lifted the respirator from his face. "We have errands to run."

"Errands?"

Did this idiot think Saul was his assistant?

"I need lubricating oil for the pill press. And we are to make a delivery. I have the address here somewhere." He scrambled over to the metal table and uncovered a scrap of paper, which he handed to Saul.

"This is downtown. Got a contact name?"

"Don't know his name, but I know his face. We text him before we're coming." He tapped the slip where a phone number had been written.

Saul pocketed the info. "Let's go then. I need to get back before dark."

After Boris removed his hazmat suit, they locked up the lab and climbed into Saul's jeep.

Boris directed him to an auto shop and ran inside, returning a few minutes later with a large can of machine oil. "One extra stop, please." Boris pointed at a 7-Eleven. When Saul parked there, he dashed into the building, returning with a case of some caffeine-laden beverage. Boris strung out on caffeine seemed a horrible idea.

"Want one?" he asked as he popped open a can.

"That shit's bad for you."

Boris's laugh bellowed inside the jeep. "This is bad? I handle toxic chemicals all day long. You only live once, my friend."

And yours might be a short one, Saul almost said. Of course, his own life expectancy wasn't long, not in the business he was in. He'd done bad things for bad people. Karma would catch up, and that would be that. But he wouldn't die strung out on caffeine or that shit Boris was pressing in his lab. That was no way to live. And no way to die.

Boris typed something on his phone. A response dinged in. "Okay. We go to that big mall west of town. Meet our first connection in the parking lot of a restaurant there."

"First connection?"

"Another text came from Marcus. He wants a small package delivered near campus. Fortunately, I always pack extras!" Boris spoke fast, as though his caffeine drink had already kicked in.

When he cranked up Saul's radio, Saul swatted his hand away and switched the channel to smooth jazz. His car, his rules, and Boris needed to remember who was in charge. Five minutes later, they were snarled in I-26 traffic. A car in the lane beside his held a teenage girl—long blonde hair, pink nails clicking against the open window. She made Saul think about Lily Grace, his captive. What was he going to do with her? He couldn't keep her locked up forever. Fletcher Hawthorne's election was three months away. He couldn't imprison her for that long. He was lucky Boris hadn't discovered her yet. Saul should have killed her, like Marcus had ordered. He'd been weak. He'd let sentimentality and memories of his sister take control. And now—now, what was he going to do?

"There. That Mexican place." Boris pointed to La Fiesta Mexicana, a small establishment with a bright yellow sombrero over the door and outlines of margarita glasses in neon lights. A few cars dotted the parking lot, and Boris guided him behind the building.

"Who are we meeting?" Saul asked.

Boris looked out the window and grinned. "Her. My sunshine!"

Saul spotted the very thin young woman leaning against a cement wall. She wore a skirt no bigger than a Band-Aid and midriff top. Her dark hair, with asymmetrical streaks of blue, hung to her narrow shoulders. She spotted Boris and waved.

Boris practically leaped from the car and ran to her. Saul remained in his seat, windows open, and watched the exchange.

"My sunshine!" Boris exclaimed.

"You got our stuff?" The frowning girl had a Spanish accent. She held out a hand.

"I'd never let you down." He pulled a brown package from his pocket, which she unwrapped. Soon, a test tube appeared from her pocket, and she uncapped the solution and dropped in a pill. A moment later, she smiled.

"Here's your money." She handed him a wad of bills.

Boris glanced back at Saul, then guided her around the side of the building, out of Saul's view.

"What's he up to?" Saul growled. He waited. After five minutes, his patience evaporated into mist. Another five, and he'd had enough. He slung open the jeep door and stomped over to where Boris had led the girl.

She was pressed against the brick, her skirt pulled up, Boris writhing against her.

"Jesus. F. Christ!" Saul grabbed Boris's shoulder and jerked him away. "What the hell do you think you're doing?"

"Enjoying a bit of Sunshine," Boris said with an awkward laugh.

The girl straightened her clothes, scowling. "Don't care if you didn't finish. You pay me." She held out a hand.

Boris slipped a small plastic bag of pills into her palm. "Here. Enjoy."

Saul studied the girl. How old was she? Hardly older than a teen. So thin he could see her collarbones through her top.

"You need to be careful," he cautioned her. "That's very dangerous stuff."

"And maybe you should mind your own damn business." She stuffed the plastic bag into her bra.

"What's your name?" Saul asked. "Need to tell the boss who accepted delivery."

She shot him a skeptical glare. "Dulce. Tell him Dulce will deliver the package as asked. Tell him Dulce does a great job for him. He can count on Dulce."

She pronounced her name with more pride than the situation warranted.

"We'll tell him, Sunshine," Boris said with a grin. "I'll see you next week."

"Only if you're lucky," she retorted, sashaying away from them.

The second stop was at a small bungalow south of campus. Five cars were parked haphazardly in the grass-bare yard. On the narrow front porch, a young man in a baseball cap rocked in a chair and tapped on his laptop. Old-school rock music blared inside—Led Zeppelin, Saul thought. Boris climbed the brick steps and said something to the kid at the computer, who yelled out a name. The boy who emerged from the house had pale skin and black, untrimmed hair. Under a spindly pine tree, the transaction began. Boris handed him the package and extended a hand for the money.

This kid was young. College-aged, probably. Where else had Marcus's tentacles extended? What came after college? High school? An even younger clientele?

Saul swallowed a wave of nausea as he waited in the car. They were silent during the drive back to the warehouse, except for Boris's manic tapping of his hand against the car seat. Saul checked his rearview mirror, noting a motorcycle riding his rear bumper. When he took a turn, the Harley did, too. Was he being followed?

He made a quick right, then a left, his gaze checking the mirror. The biker didn't follow on the last turn.

Was it his imagination, or did that bike look like the one on the camera outside the burned lab?

Forty-Six

RUS HADN'T HELD OR READ A NEWSPAPER IN YEARS, BUT WHEN HE SAW the Hawthorne family on the front page of the Columbia News, he dropped fifty cents on the counter and exited the convenience store, paper tucked under his arm. He drove Tanner's motorcycle to a small park and found a picnic table. A tiny playground made up much of the park. Kids played on swings and jetted down slides. Four little girls had a wicked game of double-dutch jump rope going, chanting in rhythm with their steps.

Rus spread out the newspaper and read. Fletcher Hawthorne's campaign for attorney general was in full swing, and it made Rus's stomach curl. That man should no more be in office than Hannibal Lecter. He read that Hawthorne's wife was involved in several charities, and his boys were still in school—Cooper at Dreher High School and Holden at the University of South Carolina School of Law.

Of course, Holden was following in dear old Dad's footsteps. That was where the money was.

Rus struggled to look at Fletcher's face because it conjured up so much inside. Anger. Sadness. Fear. Loss. That man had ruined everything, had started Rus down that dark path that might have destroyed him.

Would Holden follow his father that way, too? When they were younger, he'd been the fun friend. Always joking. Always getting Rus in trouble for laughing in class. Full of mischief, but Teflon when it came to consequences. They'd been good friends, the two of them, until things began to change. Rus missed Holden, but that sentiment flowed only one way. Holden cared about one person only: himself.

And now the prick was dealing drugs. Getting product from Boris and selling it—where? The campus? Be good to know for sure, Rus decided, so he tucked the newspaper in his pocket and returned to Tanner's bike.

When he rode through the University of South Carolina campus, he scarcely recognized it. It had grown to the size of a city, with towering buildings and throngs of students who seemed more interested in their phones than in paying attention to traffic. He stopped a sweatshirted coed to ask for directions to the law school, then found himself searching the parking lots and garages close by for Holden's car.

He found it on his third try. The day was drawing to a close, so he figured he'd wait, hoping Holden would show up. Twenty minutes later, Holden trotted up the concrete steps, unlocked the Tesla, and slid into the driver's seat, as smooth as any entitled heir-apparent would be.

Rus followed the Tesla out of the garage and down Gervais Street. Holden turned on Kilbourne, heading south, and pulled into a small apartment complex: brick duplexes with small porches and well-landscaped walkways. The place was far too humble for Holden to live there. He hurried around the car and pulled something from the trunk. A guy emerged from one of the apartments and met him on the walkway—he looked to be the same age as Holden. Probably another law student? They chatted for a moment. Holden handed over a small envelope, and the guy slapped some cash into Holden's hand.

Brazen, out here in the open. Holden returned to the sports car and sped off, Rus keeping a safe distance behind. He made two more stops, then turned down Bryson Road. Rus knew where he was going.

And dreaded it.

When the house came into view, Rus swallowed. He'd been here before—dozens of times—in the before-life. He'd never noticed how ugly it was—massive, overdone, with its columned front porch and curved brick drive. Holden parked behind it, and Rus continued on a half-block before parking and jogging through some trees to the rear of the mansion-like home. Holden entered through the back gate, circled the pool, and entered the pool house. Rus froze.

The memories bombarded him. Swimming with Holden. Sitting on the edge, his feet swirling the water. That afternoon, when Holden's mother was sunbathing. So beautiful—long, tan legs, discreet bikini. She talked to Holden—really talked to him—about how he felt about school. How his essay for English was coming along. And Rus had watched, mesmerized. His parents never showed him that kind of interest.

Rus grew to love it when Holden invited him over. He loved the delicious snacks the maid, Marta, prepared. The heated pool. The beer that Holden would sneak out of the bar in the pool house.

Everything changed, though. Fletcher Hawthorne started hanging around the pool, talking to Rus. Complimenting him. Paying more attention than Rus's father ever had, and Rus had absorbed every drop of it. He started to feel special.

But then Fletcher's intense attention made him uncomfortable. Fletcher must have sensed it because he had the answer: get Rus relaxed. First bourbon. Then pills. Sometimes coke. And getting high changed everything.

Stop it! He threw up a mental stop sign because this was a deadly track of thinking. The past was gone. Finished. No reason to wallow. *Shove the memories down, down. Don't let them haunt you.*

A few minutes later, Holden emerged from the pool house, carrying two small boxes. He was careful exiting through the gate, taking care to close it so there'd be no click. He hurried to his car and drove away, never going into the house, never telling his parents he'd been by.

Rus stared at the pool house. He suspected this was where Holden kept his stash, but he needed to know for sure. Still, passing through that door, entering that space, felt impossible. So much had happened there.

The beginning of his end.

He could do it. He wouldn't think about the past. He pushed air into his lungs and forced himself to slide through the gate, scanning the doors and windows of the large house to make sure he hadn't been noticed. He hurried inside, freezing at the familiarity of it, the chlorine and beer smell, the parrot pillows on the chaise.

He got to work, rummaging, imagining where Holden would hide his product. It didn't take long. A small cooler had been tucked behind folded-up patio umbrellas and a case of sodas, and inside, Rus found two gallon-size ziplock plastic bags full of bright blue pills.

Bingo.

He held them, marveling at the sheer volume of opioids. Should he take them? Toss them in the river? No, he didn't trust himself to carry them away. Better to leave them for now. Maybe call the cops on old Holden.

Maybe do something worse.

He tossed the bags back in the cooler and replaced the umbrellas and box. He hurried out through the gate, hopped on Tanner's cycle, and sped off, relieved to be leaving. Proud that he hadn't succumbed.

And determined to put an end to all this.

Forty-Seven

LILY GRACE PRAYED. ON HER KNEES, HANDS CLASPED TOGETHER, SHE whispered the Lord's Prayer before launching into her own special requests.

"Please look after Mama and Dad, and don't let them be too worried about me. Please keep Detective Lou Michaels safe and help him solve whatever it is he's trying to solve so that I can go home! And please, please let Sara be okay."

This last request made something clench inside. She had no idea if Sara was even alive. Or if Joel was in jail for a crime he didn't commit.

Not having answers had begun to wear on her. That, and the boredom. The relentless sameness of every hour, every day. What she'd do for a walk outside, being able to feel the sun on her face. To breathe fresh air.

To talk with someone.

"God, give me patience and understanding. Remind me to trust you always. Amen." She stood, brushed her knees, and moved over to the tiny window. Dusk streaked the sky with pumpkin orange and gray. Where was this place? How far was she from home?

It felt like another planet. Like she was on Star Trek and had been beamed down somewhere unexplored, only she didn't get to do any of the exploring. She just hoped she wasn't wearing a red shirt.

She wandered over to the locked door. At least the music had stopped. If you could call it music. The lyrics sounded Korean, but it wasn't like the beautiful melodies from BTS, her favorite K-pop group. No, the sounds that boomed from that room screeched and pounded, and the man that would sing along—if you could call it singing—was so off-key her ears nearly bled.

But silence now. Blessed silence. Or at least, blessed until the fear got to her, and she started pacing, and obsessing, and worrying about Mama and Dad and Sara and Tessa and . . .

No. She'd prayed. Her job now was to leave things in God's hands. If only it were that easy. She stretched out on the mattress and closed her eyes, hoping to drift off. Days and nights were all jumbled now. She slept more than she ever had, but there simply wasn't anything else to do. Maybe when Lou Michaels returned, she'd ask him for more books. Or even a small TV to watch—if he was in a good mood. If he was grumpy, she dared not ask for anything.

She must have slept for a long while because when she heard the door to the outside unlocking, it startled her. Light bloomed outside. Morning already?

Untangling herself from the sheets, she pulled herself off the bed. And coughed. Hacking had plagued her most of the night, and she worried she was getting a cold. The air in that small room had grown stale, and now and then, a strange odor emanated from somewhere—next door, maybe? Maybe that was what had made her sick. If only she could go outside, breathe some fresh air, surely that would clear her lungs.

When Lou Michaels entered, he tossed a McDonald's bag on the small table. "I brought you a biscuit."

"Thanks." She stood, grabbing the blanket and wrapping it around her.

"You cold? You can always turn the heat up." He moved to the space heater and adjusted the temperature.

"Thanks." Another coughing fit took hold of her.

Lou Michaels hurried to the bathroom, returning with a wad of toilet paper, which he handed to her. "That doesn't sound good."

"The air in here—it's not fresh. And there are some strange smells—I'm not complaining. I mean, I know you're doing your best." She didn't want him to be angry with her. She just wanted a few moments outside. To breathe and feel the sun on her face. To remember there was a world outside of these four walls.

Lou opened the door. She hurried to it, not to escape, but to imagine. She inhaled. She could hear a breeze stirring up leaves. Traffic sounds in the distance. A siren fading far away.

"That better?" he asked her.

"Yes, thanks."

"I'll bring you some cough medicine next time I come. Any other requests?"

She turned to face him, wondering what his reaction would be if she dared to ask. She swallowed and whispered, "Could you bring me a Bible?"

Forty-Eight

WE GOT THE REPORT THAT MRS. DUFFY'S HEART CATH PROCEDURE HAD gone well, but they were worried about her blood pressure and would keep her in the hospital overnight. I needed to arrange aftercare for her, so I made my way to her room to start that process.

I found her standing by the window, her hands gripping a walker as she looked out on a very sunny day. "Mrs. Duffy? It's me, Georgia Thayer."

She turned slowly, positioning the walker to support the movement. Her color was better. A little flush on her round cheeks. The dark circles under her eyes less pronounced.

"Hi, Georgia. They want me up and moving. So I'm doing my best."

"That's great!"

She nodded, taking a few slow, difficult steps toward me. "Yes. I'll do whatever it takes to get out of here."

"Nobody loves being in a hospital."

"Want to take a little walk with me? I'm working on my stamina. The PT—she's a tyrant, by the way—said five short walks every day."

I laughed at the tyrant comment and held the door as she navigated the walker through it. I kept her close to the wall as we lumbered up the hallway. If she stumbled or got too weak, she'd need the rail. I'd do my best to catch her, but I wasn't sure how well I could support her weight.

"I'm not doing this for the PT Nazi," she huffed out as she pushed the walker forward.

"You're not?"

"I'm . . . doing . . . this for my baby girl." She wore an expression of fierce determination, the walker clacking as she trudged up the hall.

"For Lily Grace?"

She nodded. "She's alive. I know she is. I feel it in my heart." Sweat dripped from her reddening face.

I stayed close in case she faltered.

"I know some don't think she's alive. I don't care. If she wasn't—" Mrs. Duffy stopped, turning to look at me. "I would know it."

I nodded. I hoped she was right. I hoped it deep in my soul, but the longer Lily Grace was missing, the less optimistic I felt.

She resumed her walk. "And I'm getting strong for her. I'm going to lose weight for her. She deserves a mama who can move and be there for her."

"You sound very determined." I worried about her rapid breathing. Was she pushing herself too hard?

"She's . . . my . . . kid," Mrs. Duffy huffed. "I'd do anything for her. Don't you feel the same way about Tessa?"

"Absolutely." The word came out without a thought, but I wasn't Tessa's mom. I was barely her foster mother. Social services could change that in a blink, a thought that absolutely haunted me.

"I've been overprotective. I've just wanted to keep her safe."

"I haven't been in the 'mom' role for long, but I'm pretty sure that's what it's all about."

We passed a window. Gray clouds hung swollen and low, promising rain. She said softly, "I worried so much that something bad would happen to her. Something that would take away her glorious innocence. And now something has. Not many people know this, but I'm an abuse survivor. My mother. Pretty much all of my life."

I froze. "I'm so sorry."

She stared down at the floor. "I was in therapy for a while. It helped. But for the past year or so, I've had nightmares. And I don't like leaving home. And keeping my girl safe—that's been everything to me."

I nodded, pieces clicking into place. The weight gain. The hoarding. The anxiety about leaving home—all trauma symptoms.

"Lily Grace has been my caretaker. I lean on her in ways that aren't fair. I didn't even realize I was doing it until she was gone. What kind of mother expects her child to fix breakfast? To take care of the housework? To cook dinner? And Lily Grace never complained. She just did what I needed her to. And it wasn't fair to her. I know that now. It won't be like that when she comes home." She halted, reaching over to grip the handrail. I moved closer, concerned by her rapid breathing.

"Mrs. Duffy? I think we've gone far enough. Shall I get a wheelchair to get you back to your room?"

She shook her head. "Give me a minute."

I admired her determination, and I prayed she would be rewarded with the safe return of Lily Grace. But the longer she was gone . . .

"Okay. Let's go," she whispered. "I'm getting strong for my baby."

Forty-Nine

ON SATURDAY, TESSA RETURNED HOME AFTER A CRAZY BUSY LUNCH shift at the bistro. Elias had shooed her out the door when the crowd finally dwindled. Tessa pulled her bike behind the house and parked it in the cluttered garage in the backyard.

When she opened the door to the kitchen, she froze. Everything looked—wrong. The counters gleamed. No stacks of paperwork waited on the table. The stove, refrigerator, and microwave looked as though they'd been polished. And the smell—the aroma of baking cookies wafted up from the oven. Tessa wanted to go back outside to make sure she'd entered the correct house.

"There you are! How was work today?" Georgia bustled into the kitchen, and Tessa stared, because her foster mom was actually wearing an apron.

"Uh, fine?"

"Good." She hurried over to the oven and pulled out a metal sheet. About a dozen chocolate chip cookies had been slightly overcooked but smelled wonderful.

"Georgia? What's going on here?" A tinge of worry entered her voice. She knew Georgia had psychiatric problems. That she sometimes heard voices. Did she have mania, too? The condition of the kitchen was alarming enough. Should Tessa call her therapist?

"Damn. Overdone. Of course." She dropped an oven mitt on the counter, then picked it up again and shoved it in a drawer.

"Are you okay?" Tessa's worry swelled.

"Oh, I'm fine. Just . . . nervous. I got a call from your caseworker, Lana. Apparently, she's working this weekend and wants to come by. So, I thought I'd clean up a bit. Make cookies. They don't smell burnt, do they?"

"They smell great, but I don't understand. Aren't you going a bit overboard?"

Georgia leaned against the table and closed her eyes. "Yeah. Probably. It's just the last time Lana visited, the house was a mess. And she kept asking me questions. It . . . didn't go well."

"What do you mean?"

Georgia motioned that Tessa should sit at the table, taking a chair for herself. "Okay, I'm coming clean here. She asked a lot of questions about my treatment. About my mental illness. It felt like she wasn't sure I should be a foster parent."

"Crap."

"Tessa—" Georgia used the cautionary voice that came out when Tessa cursed. Of course, Georgia could mouth off like a pirate, but apparently, rules were different for adults. "I just thought I'd clean up a bit more. Make a better impression this time."

"I prefer it when we shove everything in closets." Tessa smiled. There had been some ridiculous times together, frantically straightening the house and laughing like lunatics.

"I owe it to you to do a better job. I'm going to show Lana Montgomery that you are exactly where you should be. With me." Georgia grabbed a sponge and wiped the countertop that didn't need wiping.

Tessa didn't like Lana Montgomery. She asked probing questions and never looked satisfied with any of Tessa's answers. The idea that Lana wasn't convinced Georgia should be Tessa's foster mother frightened her. What would happen if Lana made her leave? Where would she go? A sucky foster home, like the ones in Pennsylvania? A group home? No. Tessa could not imagine leaving Georgia. That would hurt. Really hurt.

Car tires crunched outside the door—Lana pulling into the drive. She climbed out of a black Lexus, which meant she must have had a rich husband or something. According to Georgia, caseworkers didn't make beans. Lana had on a pencil skirt and black heels. Her lipstick matched the cherry red of her blouse. She knocked on the back door.

"Okay," Georgia whispered. "No reason to be nervous. Just be yourself."

That was going to be hard, given that Georgia was pretending to be some domestic goddess. Tessa could feel the anxiety radiating from her foster mom, and it made her anxious, too.

"Hi, Lana. Come on in!" Georgia's voice sounded unnaturally cheery. "Can I get you anything? Coffee? Iced tea?"

"No, thank you." Lana glanced around the room, her gaze fixing on the cookies.

"I thought we could do with a snack," Georgia said.

Tessa took that as permission to help herself and snagged one. Lana shook her head. Probably one of those too-thin women who were perpetually dieting.

"I think I'll start with a one-on-one with Tessa, if you don't mind, Georgia."

Georgia blinked as though surprised, then said, "Of course. Y'all stay here. I'll be in my bedroom when you need me." She shot Tessa a sympathetic smile as she exited the room.

Lana remained, sitting across from Tessa and pulling a notepad out of her leather briefcase. "So, Tessa. Tell me how you're doing."

She took another bite of cookie. "Okay, I guess."

"School?"

A half-shrug. "Kind of boring. But my grades are okay."

"Are you making friends?"

God, she was tired of this question. Her therapist asked it every week. Georgia used to until Tessa buried her head and begged her to stop.

"Yes."

"Tell me. Who's your best friend?"

"Joel McCants." She said it without thinking.

"The guy who ran over the girl? I read about him in the news."

"We don't know for sure that he did it." Tessa regretted bringing his name into their conversation, but there was no turning back now.

"I'm sorry, but that's what I read in the newspaper. And he was on drugs when the accident happened, right?"

Tessa pushed the cookies away. "First off, they should never have put his name in the paper. He's only sixteen. They wouldn't have done that if he was white, would they? Second, I don't think he was driving. I think he's being scapegoated."

Lana regarded her with curiosity. Or maybe, suspicion. "Is he your boyfriend, Tessa?"

"No. He's just a friend."

"Were you at the party at Fletcher Hawthorne's house that night?"

Part of her wanted to lie, but it felt like the truth would come out if she did. "Yes. For a while."

"Did you get high?"

Shit. Tessa steeled her expression and lied, "No."

"Good." She didn't sound convinced.

"You can drug test me if you want. Need me to pee in a cup?" Tessa didn't mean to sound sarcastic, but Lana brought out the worst in her.

"I don't think that's necessary right now." She jotted down a note on her pad. Tessa wished she could read it. "Tell me what it's like living here. With Ms. Thayer."

"It's great."

"Is it? She has her issues, doesn't she?" Lana leaned forward, probing.

"Doesn't everybody?"

"Yes, of course. But we both know Ms. Thayer's problems run pretty deep. She's mentally ill. I need you to be honest with me, Tessa. Do you ever notice her looking paranoid? Or acting strange in other ways?"

Tessa did not like Lana's tone, which was a little gossipy, a little entitled. And what did "strange" mean? Georgia certainly had her quirks. She worked too much. Obsessively watched the Red Sox on TV only to curse at the players. She had trouble sleeping—Tessa could hear her up late at night, pacing around the house. Despite all that, she was one of the sanest people Tessa knew. "She's fine."

"I know she hears voices, Tessa. It's in our report."

Tessa stared at the caseworker, at her perfect haircut. Her lined cherry-red lips. Then she glanced at the counter behind her—thinking of how hard Georgia had worked to clean the house for this visit, when it seemed Lana had already made up her mind about Georgia's competency as a foster parent.

"Tell me what else is in that report. Does it mention how I was held prisoner by sadistic pricks who sold my body? Does it say that Georgia Thayer risked her life to save me? That she's braver than you'll ever be?" Tessa didn't mean for her voice to rise or for her face to flush with anger. Lana held the keys to her future. She could remove Tessa from Georgia's home.

"Yes. I know all about what she did. She's quite the risk-taker, isn't she?"

The rage bubbling up swelled into a tidal wave. "Why do you have to see her as a problem? What do you have against her? Why are you even here?"

"Keep your voice down, Tessa. There's no reason for you to be so defensive."

She lowered her voice. "And there's no reason for you to go after Georgia, Ms. Montgomery. I've lived in five foster homes. Five! Not one has been as good as this one. None."

Lana smoothed a hand over her notepad. Her nails were perfect, too. "Tessa. I don't mean to upset you. I know Georgia is doing the best she can. And she's very fond of you. But given what you've been through, it may be that a traditional foster placement isn't the best option for you."

"What does that mean?" Alarm rang in her voice.

"I mean, there's a special group home that's opened up in Rock Hill. The focus is helping survivors of human trafficking. They have counselors on staff and a school on-site. The state has funding to send you there. It might be just what you need, Tessa."

Tessa could almost hear the door slamming shut. Or was it a jail cell? Lana would remove her from Georgia's home. Take her away from Columbia. Force her into a group home where she'd be treated like damaged goods. No. Not acceptable.

"I want you to give it some thought," Lana went on. "It might be the best thing for you, and for Georgia. You know she has a great deal on her plate—and maybe taking care of a teenager is too much for her. She would never say it because she loves you, but maybe this arrangement isn't the best for her mental health."

What if that was true? What if Tessa had become a burden to Georgia? She'd hate to do anything that would cause Georgia stress or, worse, make her mental illness relapse. But no way she was going to a group home. If they forced her out of this wonderful home, what would she do?

I watched Lana drive away in her shiny Lexus and wondered why her visit had turned into a complete, unmitigated disaster. I'd been in my room, patiently waiting my turn with the annoying caseworker and fully prepared to force feed her cookies if it might lighten her mood, when I heard Tessa stomp through the house and into her room. The slamming door was new. What had happened?

When I asked Lana, she offered a small, chilly smile and said, "Teen-age angst."

"No," I replied. "That's not Tessa's style."

"We talked about some hard things. She's been through a lot, and she has more she needs to process." With that, she gathered her belongings and left the house.

I wasn't sure if I should leave Tessa alone. The closed door felt like a wall between us. I weighed it, then knocked lightly on the frame. "Tessa? You okay?

"I'm fine."

"Can I come in?"

No answer. I hesitated, unsure how far I should pry, then opened the door. "Just wanted to see if you were alright," I said to the bulge in the bed.

"I'm fine," a muffled voice answered. "Just give me . . . some time."

"Okay. But I'm here if you need to talk." A flash of anger gripped me—at Lana. What had she said or done to get Tessa upset?

She wants to take Tessa from you, the Advisor growled out.

We don't know that, the Counselor replied.

Over my dead body, I whispered inside.

I left Tessa in peace. A strange, nervous energy made me want to clean or something, but my house was already spotless. I sat in my rocking chair, soon joined by Fenway, who kneaded my legs before curling up into a black vibrating ball of fur.

Not exactly a therapy creature, but he had a way of calming me. I've fallen asleep in this chair countless times, thanks to his rumbling purr. I was about to doze when the doorbell rang: two short blasts, signaling it was my best friend, Elias Jasper. He stood taller than me, dressed in his leather jacket, and smelled like the bistro kitchen that was his second home. God, I loved that smell.

When I let him in, he froze, staring at the state of my living room. "What happened here?"

"I cleaned."

"Forget your medication again?" Elias got away with comments like that because he understood me deep in my core. We both have mental illness, only his is more complicated by addiction. He's six years clean and does great on his current medication regimen.

"No. Social services came for a visit. I wanted to make an impression."

"How'd that go?"

"A disaster." I told him the rest—gesturing to the closed door to Tessa's bedroom. "She hasn't come out since. I don't know what Lana said to her, and I'm terrified that she plans to move her from my home."

"Why would she do that?"

"She has a bias about my mental illness. That's why I wanted to make a good impression today, but she hardly even talked to me. Just pissed off Tessa and left." I shook my head. "Well then. Someone has to eat the cookies I made." I hurried into the kitchen, returning with the plate of not badly-burnt-at-all chocolate chip cookies.

Elias helped himself to two. "Did Tessa say what upset her?"

"No, but I'm sure Lana said something that triggered this. Lana hardly even spoke to me. She never even saw how clean the living room is."

"Well, that is a shame. How's Lou doing?"

I filled him in, wishing I had better news. Not that it was bad; I just wanted my friend to wake up and be Lou again.

"Did you go to a meeting today?" I asked, ready to change the subject. I knew Elias usually attended the NA closed group downtown that met on Saturdays.

He nodded. "Full house."

"That's good, I guess."

"One of our members works in a drug treatment center. He had the latest statistics on the fentanyl crisis. Quite sobering."

"How so?"

"Did you know that South Carolina is averaging two hundred and fifty overdose incidents every week? Not all are fatalities, but plenty are. And the number keeps climbing. We're seeing it among our folks, too. We've lost two in the past month—relapses that turned lethal."

"It's flooding our ER," I said.

"We lost a teen. Looks like the dealers are targeting the young folks. And get this: one of our members works at the statehouse. There's a bill to make Narcan available for free. Even putting dispensers in high-risk areas, like that area by the river where the addicts hang out. Only it won't pass because too many of them idiots don't think the lives of addicts matter. 'Why should we pay to save them?' That's the message they're sending us. We don't matter, George. We don't."

I hated the pain I heard in his voice. I grabbed his hand, gripping it hard. "You do matter. And here's the thing. It will affect one of those idiots at the statehouse: It might be their son. Their daughter. Their wife. When they are face-to-face with an overdose, maybe they'll realize that when you don't save a life that can be saved, it is the same thing as ending it. I pray they'll do some soul-searching then."

"Don't hold your breath."

I squeezed his hand. "I have an idea. Why don't you talk to Ben Reeder? Tell him the stats you just shared with me. He's wanting to do a story on this problem and you could give him a fresh perspective."

Elias pondered. "Not a bad idea."

Fifty-One

TESSA LAY IN HER BED AND STARED AT THE CEILING, WHERE TWO fluorescent stars glowed pale green. She couldn't stop thinking about the visit with Lana Montgomery. Of course Lana wanted her to move. Wanted her to leave this home, this town, this life with Georgia. Tessa finally had found a place that brought her peace and a feeling of belonging . . . and now it would be taken from her.

There had been times when she and Brandon lived with their mom and things would be okay. Mom would stop using drugs and go to meetings, and there'd be an air of promise that the family would survive. Tessa would let her guard down, let herself feel happy, even—until it all crashed and burned. Mom would start using again and bring home some loser man, and before long, social services would pull Brandon and Tessa away.

Tessa didn't get to have a good life. Not with Mom. Not with Georgia. And it made her feel a rage from deep in her belly.

Outside the bedroom door, Georgia was talking with Elias, who'd arrived a little while ago. Tessa should leave her room and be social, but anger and sadness itched inside her as she mulled a future that felt like absolute shit.

She wanted—needed—relief.

And it waited for her in her backpack. She leaped up from the bed, grabbed the pack, and pawed through all her books and notes until she found the tiny tin. Just a half of a pill. More would be dangerous.

She used a barrette prong to slice through the tablet and slid half under her tongue, having heard that the effects came faster that way. Outside her door, Georgia took a call on her cell phone. From her tone, Tessa figured it was the hospital. She rarely got called in after hours, but it happened sometimes. Georgia and Elias conferred about something, then the back door squeaked open and shut. Georgia's Civic rumbled out of the driveway.

Tessa wondered why Elias hadn't left, but maybe Georgia had asked him to stay and "babysit," which annoyed Tessa. At sixteen, she could take care of herself.

She lay back down on the bed and stared up at the fluorescent stars. Georgia had put them there before Tessa. Her little niece, Lindsay, sometimes spent the night, which explained the yellow walls, flowered curtains, and large array of stuffed critters that had covered the bed when Tessa arrived. Lindsay was on a Disney cruise with her dad, but she'd be home soon. Maybe when Tessa had to leave, Lindsay would visit more often so Georgia wouldn't get lonely.

It didn't take long before the stars began to twinkle and dance, and Tessa found it so funny she couldn't suppress a laugh. She twirled her hand over her head, trying to catch the shimmying stars, and thought of Tinker Bell from Peter Pan.

She could be a "lost boy" and never grow up. She'd wear green tights and learn to fly and . . . more laughter erupted. Oh, it felt so, so good. How many more little blue pills did she have? Not enough.

There might never be enough.

A gentle rap on the door startled her. "Huh?"

Shit. She shouldn't have said anything. She should have pretended to be asleep because now the door was opening, and Elias stepped inside.

"I heard you laughing." He approached the bed and sat on the end. "You must be feeling better then. I know you were upset earlier."

"Yeah. Better." The stars overhead moved again, circling around the room and twirling over Elias's head. She giggled.

"Tessa?" he shot her a perplexed look. "What's so funny?"

"Funny?" Oh, hell, everything was. She couldn't turn it off, the laughter bubbling out like lava from a volcano.

"Shit." Elias stood, coming closer. "You're high."

"No, I'm not." She coughed, sitting up straighter. She could fake being sober. She'd always been a good actress.

"What did you take?" His voice echoed. His dark eyes sparked. "What was it?"

"I didn't. I—"

"Do. Not. Bullshit me. What did you take?"

She glared at him. How dare he barge in here, act like he could tell her what to do? She was fine. Better than fine.

"I'd like you to leave my room."

"Get up. I need to see you standing."

She could do that. She could stand and push him out the door. She shifted her feet to the floor and stood, immediately losing her balance and nearly toppling to the rug.

Elias grabbed her arm to steady her. "Yeah, that's what I thought. Show me what you took. I need to know how worried I should be."

"I just took a little. Less than half."

"Half of what?" He used a tone she'd never heard before. A little scary.

"Half a blue." She fumbled with the nightstand drawer and pulled out the tin.

Elias opened it. "Shit. I've heard about this stuff. It's fentanyl, Tess. Fentanyl."

Yeah, she knew that. "I've been careful. Just took a little."

"Thank God for that. Come with me." He guided her into the living room and made her sit. He hurried to the kitchen, returning with a tall glass of water, and commanded that she drink it. His hand clutched her wrist to take her pulse.

"Why are you doing that?"

"Because I'm trying to decide if I need to get you to the ER. That blue fent can be deadly. Your pulse is strong. Breathing seems okay. Finish the water."

Elias was a serious buzz kill. She wanted to return to her room, to the dancing stars and thoughts of flying, but now she had a jailer who wasn't letting her out of his sight.

She leaned back in the chair and closed her eyes, wishing she could fly. She'd blow through the window and head for the stars, away from Columbia and high school and Lana Montgomery.

Away from the crippling loss she'd feel when they took her from Georgia.

It wasn't long before she drifted off to sleep.

Fifty-Two

WHEN TESSA AWOKE, HER HEAD HAD BEEN POSITIONED ON A PILLOW with a blanket draped across her. She blinked, trying to get her bearings. Her mouth felt like cotton balls had been stuffed under her tongue, and a snare drum pounded behind her eyes.

Elias snored in the chair across from her.

She tossed back the cover and stood. Not wobbly. Not high. She found an empty glass beside the chair and carried it into the kitchen, filling it from the sink and draining it. Her thirst felt unending.

Out the window, traces of dawn peeked between the leaves of a live oak tree that dominated Georgia's backyard. Shit. She had school in a few hours and wished she could crawl under her bed and stay there for the next three days.

"Hey." Elias surprised her. "How are you feeling?"

"How do you think?" She tried to remember last night. He'd caught her, hadn't he? He knew about the pill she took.

"Hungover, I'll bet. More water's a good idea."

She refilled the glass, sipping this time.

"Georgia's coming home soon. She got called into the hospital last night. Texted a while ago, and I said I was fine with staying the night. Thought I'd spare her seeing you like—" He lifted a hand, dropped it.

She drew a deep breath, bracing herself. "Are you going to tell her I got stoned?"

He cocked his head, studying her. "I don't think I will."

"Good." She exhaled.

"Because you're going to. It's much better coming from you."

223

"Seriously?" She hated it when adults pulled this kind of bullshit. Telling Georgia would feel like sticking a knife in her chest. Georgia had done everything for Tessa, and this would be a betrayal. Shit. If Lana Montgomery found out, she'd be jerked out of this home faster than she could blink.

"Why did you take that pill?"

"Half a pill."

"Okay, half. Where'd you get it?"

"A girl at school. She had some and was in trouble with her parents, so she gave it to me."

"How many times have you done it?" he asked, grilling her like a *Law & Order* cop.

"Just twice."

"And last night? What made you take it?"

She sipped more water, not liking his tone, but he'd stayed all night to make sure she was okay. "After that stupid child services worker came here, I knew what was going to happen. I'm gonna have to leave Georgia and go to a facility. That's how it always is. If I get something good, it gets snatched away. And I got mad. And depressed. And . . . I just wanted relief."

He nodded soberly, his eyes full of understanding. "You don't know that you have to leave. Georgia will fight that like a warrior. She can be a force."

"But I know how things work, Elias. I'm gonna get screwed over."

He frowned at her. "Did the pill help?"

"Half a pill. And yes."

"You get high, you feel great. Forget all your problems. And they go away. No, wait—they don't. They're still there."

She tossed out the water and smacked the glass down.

Elias leaned against the counter and asked, "Who else do you know who thought like that? Just get a little high, have a nice escape . . . Your mom, maybe?"

"Shut up." Anger burned in her belly.

"Who else thought her problems disappeared?"

"Shut. Up!" Tessa bellowed.

Elias reached for her hand. "Okay. I think I've made my point."

She wanted to pull away, but he held fast.

"This may be an issue for you, Tess. We know there's a genetic component to drugs. I was an addict. My dad was an alcoholic. Both grandparents. So you have to be careful. People like you and me—experimenting can have deadly consequences."

She hadn't thought about that before. She never imagined she was like her mom in any way (except for their mutual love of chocolate), but last night, she'd done just what Mom had done—turned to a pill for relief.

She pulled away and stomped out of the kitchen, returning with the tin of blue tablets. She turned on the faucet, opened the tin, and dropped all the blue pills into the drain.

Elias placed a hand on her shoulder. "Thatagirl."

Fifty-Three

RUS SHIVERED AS HE DROVE THE MOTORCYCLE FROM HIS TRAILER INTO town. The fall night had a moist chill to it that sliced through his hoodie. He needed a warmer jacket. Or, better yet, once he'd finished what he'd started, he could leave South Carolina. Maybe head further south. Start over once again. Maybe he wouldn't have to die this time. Not enough people knew him to miss him. He'd vanish like a mist once he'd taken down Marcus Landry.

Destroying the first lab had been oddly therapeutic. Watching product go up in smoke, picturing Boris's face when he learned he'd lost a few hundred thou in profits. But so quickly, they were back in business. He prayed he'd live to see them meet the end they deserved.

He pulled into the parking area of JD's Roost. A dozen cars, pickups, and motorcycles filled the small gravel lot. He could hear the country music thumping inside, the clomping of heels pounding the floor in line dancing, and smiled. Something always comforted him about that sound.

But not the sound that followed. Sirens howled through the night. Instinct told Rus to hide, in case it was the police coming to raid the place, so he ducked around the corner and waited. But it wasn't the police. It was a county emergency vehicle, followed by an ambulance. What was going on?

They screeched into the parking lot. Men came from behind the building, waving and shouting at the emergency crew. Rus hurried after them to a patch of woods where several others had gathered, one bent over someone stretched out in the leaves. Small—like a kid, maybe—a girl, dressed in a short red skirt.

226

The EMTs shouted for them to stand back as they started to work on her. Rus inched closer. A small hand rested on the leaves. Chipped black polish gleamed on ragged fingernails. And the hair—black strands with blue streaks splayed across the ground.

The Hispanic girl, Dulce.

Oh shit.

The EMTs took vitals, contacted the hospital. One shot Narcan up her nose.

"It's not working," she said to the others.

They tried a second dose. Oxygen came next. They attached electrodes to her chest before loading her onto the gurney. Rus wanted to go to her. Thoughts of Tanner and what happened to him flashed through Rus's mind. He should have moved quicker. Should have destroyed the second lab as soon as he'd found it, but no. He got arrogant. Wanted to be the one to cut off the dragon's head without thinking about who'd get hurt in the meantime. And now Dulce might be dead.

The emergency crew moved fast, muttering in their radios, and Rus fixed his stare on the bluish-gray tint of Dulce's face.

It was too late. She was gone.

Just like Tanner.

He'd failed them both.

Nausea wormed up his throat. He turned, running to the motorcycle, wishing he could run from the guilt that would dog him forever. Another boulder on the load he carried.

There was only one thing he could do. And it would be done soon.

Fifty-Four

I SAT BESIDE A GURNEY AND WANTED TO SCREAM. ANOTHER DAMN overdose. Another close call—and this one was someone I knew and cared about. I clutched Dulce's hand, trying to decide when I would tell Tessa and the women at the shelter. No, that wasn't my decision to make. That was up to Dulce.

If she survived to make it.

The third administration of Narcan restarted her breathing. The ED doc had ordered a CAT scan to assess for brain damage. Those results hadn't arrived yet.

This overdose had to be the new fentanyl analog, the doc had told me. "Traditional antidotes aren't working," he had said. She remained unconscious, and he wasn't sure she'd ever wake up.

She looked so small in the bed, nearly skeletal. And so young.

Had we failed her? We gave her a good place to stay. Treatment. Support. But none of that worked for Dulce—she kept choosing the streets. Why?

Because that was where she was comfortable. We'd tried to tame her. To make her into something she wasn't.

The street kept pulling her back. Odd that she couldn't resist the siren call. That she'd choose to go to the same sort of people who'd hurt her. Who'd abused her body when she lived in Jefe's stable. And from what the ED said, she'd been selling herself for sex again. They were screening for STDs. Treating her for malnourishment. She'd survive, I decided. At least her body would.

228

But how do we save Dulce's soul? How do we stop this downward spiral that might keep pulling at her until she succumbed? What would it take for her to decide she wanted a future? She wanted to stay alive?

She stirred, mumbled something.

"Shhh," I whispered. "You're safe right now."

No, she's not. She'll never be safe, the Advisor said.

I prayed he was wrong. I knew the statistics. From my late sister Peyton's research, I'd learned that the average sex trafficking survivor would return to "the life" seven times—that was how strong the pull was. This number—seven—scared the bejesus out of me. What if Tessa felt the same compulsion to go back? It was dangerous. Possibly fatal. But it was familiar. A false sense of safety could be found in the familiar.

No, Tessa had changed. She'd learned to feel safe in our home. She'd accepted that she now had a family, albeit an odd one. Tessa wouldn't return to that life, not if I had any say about it.

A nursing assistant stopped in to check on our patient. She switched saline bags and recorded vitals that looked less than encouraging.

"Maggie? Do you know where her clothes are? The ones she was wearing when she came in?"

Maggie pointed to a small bureau. I opened the drawer and pulled out a plastic bag containing a skirt, a top, and some glittery high-top sneakers. I searched the pockets of the skirt and found a tiny wad of shiny paper, the kind that held chewing gum. It looked like trash, but to be sure, I opened it. Inside, I found a small blue pill. Eureka.

"That what she took?" Maggie asked.

"Makes sense. Can you get this downstairs to be analyzed?"

She nodded, donning a latex glove before handling it. If we could determine what the substance was, we would have a chance at helping Dulce.

And she needed all the help she could get.

When I left Dulce, I went to check on Lou again. He looked better. He had more color to his face, eyes twitching from REM sleep. But the bullet wound remained. The damage uncalculated. That I might never talk to him again, tell him what he meant to me—filled me with a bleak sadness. He deserved a better friend than I had been.

An hour later, I sat in my office and practiced slow, even breathing. It was all too much.

Lou. The bodies piling up in the ER. Dulce.

Sometimes, all the pain pouring over me sank in. Most social workers are empaths, I'd come to believe. We connect with the pain of others. But absorbing it was never a good idea, and I'd reached critical mass. I needed to breathe, to think. Odd that this hellhole of an office could be my sanctuary.

You need to get your shit together, the Advisor said.

She's doing the best she can, the Counselor retorted.

Is she? Then why is she sitting here panting like a labrador?

She cares too much, the Counselor said. *Sometimes she needs to let go.*

"Shut up!" I said. "Just . . . let me think."

"Uhmmm. Georgia? Who are you talking to?" The voice from my doorway was an outside one—a real person. I turned my chair around to find Lana Montgomery standing there, staring wide-eyed at me.

Uh oh, the Advisor said.

Oh crap. "Nobody. I mean, I talk to myself sometimes."

The staring continued. She didn't believe me because she'd seen me talking to the damn voices like a crazy person, which I sort of was.

"I wasn't expecting you. Is there something you wanted?" I asked.

She stepped inside, standing over me like a looming high school teacher. "I brought you some information on a treatment center in Rock Hill." She reached into her mammoth, expensive-looking leather purse and pulled out a thick brochure. "It's a special facility designed for girls like Tessa. Please look at this. Feel free to give them a call. There are actual trafficking survivors on staff. They'll tell you how the center can help Tessa."

I wanted to hurl the booklet in the trash. I wanted to hurl her out of my office.

She folded her arms. "I know you don't like the idea. I know you like having Tessa live with you. After losing your sister—it's nice to have someone to care about, isn't it?"

I didn't like her tone. Worse, I didn't like the truth that echoed in her words.

She went on. "But is it what's best for Tessa? It's important not to be selfish here, Georgia. Especially if you really want her to recover in the best environment possible."

Oh, no. She's going to take Tessa, the Counselor whispered.

Don't. Let. Her, the Advisor growled in my head.

I clenched my teeth. Kept my face as neutral as I could.

"Look at the information, Georgia. I'll find funding for her. Then give me a call." Lana flashed a tight smile, turned, and exited.

I looked down at the pamphlet in my hand. A beautiful, two-story cabin against a backdrop of leafy trees. Three women sitting on the steps. Survivors.

Would this be a better option for my kid? Was keeping her with me selfish?

I had a lot to figure out.

Fifty-Five

FLETCHER'S PHONE DINGED WITH A TEXT FROM VIVIAN: *PRESS THERE?*

Cameras ready to roll, Fletcher answered. He didn't add, and *I feel like a complete idiot*. Marcus had insisted on upping the campaign's TV presence. Fletcher had no say in the matter.

You'll be brilliant, Vivian replied. *We'll celebrate when you get home.*

Fletcher resumed his position behind his desk, pen in hand, a taut smile on his face, trying to ignore the lights surrounding him, the TV camera pointed at him, and the petite director darting about the room like a manic butterfly adjusting things.

"Let's move the family photos to the windowsill behind you. We want them in every shot," the director said.

Another woman, the director's assistant, Fletcher decided, hurried over to make the adjustment.

"Now, Mr. Hawthorne. Try to look as natural as you can. Think personable. Trustworthy. Every citizen's favorite uncle. That's the expression we want." The director adjusted her heavy-rimmed glasses as she circled the desk.

Natural? Trustworthy? Should he don a cardigan like Mr. Frickin' Rogers?

"Loosen your tie. You want to look hard at work," she ordered.

He did as she asked, feeling utterly, completely ridiculous.

"Now, bend over the document, or whatever it is you lawyers write on. You've been slaving away trying to help people, and someone you loved just walked in to interrupt you. Look up and smile."

Fletcher made several attempts at this "natural," "trustworthy," and "personable" expression, then recited the script he'd been given. After seven takes, his cell chimed. The name "Marcus" flashed.

"We need to take a break," he said to the frowning director. He took the call outside, glad to be away from the lights and the unwanted attention.

232

"Marcus?" he said into the phone.

"Need to meet with you ASAP."

"I'm filming a commercial right now." It felt absurd to say that. He dropped onto a lounge chair and stared out at the glistening pool water. Unbidden memories emerged: the boy. His lean body doing laps like a smooth silver dolphin. The afternoon he had the house to himself, and he and the boy sat side by side, sipping drinks and holding hands. The boy.

Always the boy.

"I don't give a shit about that." Marcus's tone reeled him in. "Come to the restaurant. One hour."

Before he could reply, Marcus ended the call.

"Crap." Fletcher didn't need any more pressure from Marcus about the election. He'd spent thirty thousand on the media blitz Marcus had requested. He'd done appearances on local TV morning shows, even when it required that he be dressed and camera-ready by 6 freakin' a.m. What more could he do?

Fletcher returned to his study, where the film crew waited. "I have to get to an appointment. You have thirty minutes to wrap this up. Got it?"

The director looked a little stunned, but nodded. A woman hurried over and patted his face with a makeup sponge. They spent the next half hour filming and refilming the same bloody two-page script. Fletcher could feel the screws holding his smile together corrode and loosen.

He really wanted to punch someone.

"That's it," he finally said. "Let me see the finished product as soon as it's done. And make that soon."

With that, he grabbed his coat and left them.

When he reached the restaurant, a dozen cars greeted him in the parking lot. He didn't relish the idea of being seen with Marcus.

As soon as he climbed out of his car, the woman from before, the hostess, greeted him with a "We go this way." He followed her to a side entrance that led straight into Marcus's private room. Marcus wasn't alone. Two men stood behind him: six feet tall, dressed in black tactical gear, one a mirror of the other. Fletcher had seen them before, silent specters out of a Jack Reacher movie. Marcus called them "The Shadows." Assassins, Fletcher suspected, a shiver climbing up his spinal column. Did Marcus plan to take him out? No, not with the election looming. But the threat remained.

"Sit," Marcus said. The Shadows remained standing.

Fletcher felt a little petulant as he complied. He hated how Marcus thought he could order him around. "I'm looking at the numbers. You're still tied with Warren Chapel."

"Tied? That's better than a few weeks ago."

"But not good enough. I need you to up your game."

"Up my game? I'm doing every damn thing I can think of. I've done TV and radio shows. Campaign appearances everywhere. I don't know what else there is." He didn't mean to raise his voice.

"Do I need to bring in hackers? Target the voting machines?"

"No." Fletcher was emphatic. "That kind of thing lands me in jail."

"Only if we get caught."

Fletcher eyed the two silent men. "What's the deal, Marcus? Why do you need me to win this seat so badly?"

Marcus leaned back. "There's a case coming up in a year. An important case, involving some very important people. People I do business with. I have to protect them. Warren Chapel's approach in this kind of case is scorched earth. He cannot remain in office."

"Shit." Fletcher wanted to know what kind of case it was. Drugs? No, something worse. Murder? There was that major human trafficking trial pending—Colby Ribault's human trafficking operation had stretched across multiple countries. Fletcher dared not ask, though. Not knowing might be the only thing that kept him from being a part of the conspiracy.

"I've given you plenty of money. Now, I'm bringing in a crew for grassroots, door-to-door campaigning in minority neighborhoods. That should give you a boost. The rest is up to you."

Fletcher hadn't heard about this crew. He doubted anyone in his campaign office knew. "When will they be here?"

"They arrive tomorrow. A small army. They will serve us well," Marcus said. "Now. One more matter we need to discuss, related to your family."

Fletcher stiffened.

"They must be beyond reproach. Vivian's issues—I worry they will surface. Perhaps it's time she took a vacation? There are drug rehabilitation programs all over the country. It would do her good, no?"

Fletcher stared at him. How dare he pry into Vivian's very private battles?

"Which brings me to your sons. Cooper needs to return to normal life. School and the like. We've handled the issue of his accident, but you must assure us he will not divulge the truth to anyone."

"I can handle my son."

"Can you? Then let's discuss our other problem. Holden."

"What about Holden?" Alarm bells rang inside Fletcher.

Marcus's smile unnerved him. "Your son wanted to make some money. I lost my campus connection, so he was the logical choice. He's been working for me for the past year. That must stop."

"Holden's been dealing for you for a year?" Fletcher struggled to take it in, but it suddenly made sense. Holden's fancy car. His expensive haircuts. This was where he got the money—right under Fletcher's nose. How did he not know? What had he missed? "How could you not tell me?"

"Seems to me that's a question for your son. But no matter. We're cutting him off. It's a shame, though. He's done stellar work. You should be proud, Fletcher."

"How dare you!" Something burst in Fletcher. He could picture his hands around Marcus's throat, squeezing the final breath from the loathsome man. The two Shadows moved as one, flanking Marcus, glaring at Fletcher with deadly intensity.

"It was a profitable deal for me. Holden made us money. I paid him well. And you—it gave me another edge when it comes to our relationship. You come after me, you're coming after your own flesh and blood."

One of The Shadows moved closer to Marcus and handed him a slip of paper. Marcus read the note, his self-satisfied expression paling. He whispered something to the silent man, who nodded. "Crap."

"Something wrong? Something that involves me?" Fletcher asked.

"Maybe. That will be all. Show him out."

Fletcher didn't like being manhandled. Didn't like being shoved out the door like a drunk in a bar.

Didn't like Marcus thinking that he owned him.

And most of all, didn't like it that his son had become a damn drug dealer.

Fifty-Six

I WAITED IN THE HOSPITAL LOBBY FOR MY KID, UNSURE IF THIS WAS A good plan. When I had told Tessa about Dulce's admission to the hospital, she shut down. She didn't cry. Didn't get angry. Her face became a blank mask. It was a risk, but I decided it should be her choice.

I'd asked, "Do you want to go see Dulce?"

"Do you think it would help her if I went?"

"Honestly, I don't know. I tend to think having people around who care about you is always a good thing. My concern is, would it be good for you?"

Tessa had given me a long, strange look, then said, "I want to see her."

When she arrived, she had on jeans, my old Rage Against the Machine sweatshirt, and a backpack bulging with textbooks.

"How was school?" I asked.

Her response was a deep-throated growl. "New list of banned books came out."

"Guess we're hitting the bookstore then," I answered.

She laughed. "Exactly."

We walked to the elevator and stepped inside when it dinged open. The smell of whatever the hell they served for lunch lingered. Maybe fish. Maybe rotten eggs. Tessa held her nose until we arrived on the fifth floor.

"Like I told you, she's still unconscious. Her vitals are good, though." I'd called the nurse's station for a report, wanting no surprises

236

when we arrived. The drug Dulce had taken was the same compound the kids at the party had taken: fentanyl mixed with xylazine.

We entered the room, and Tessa froze. Dulce looked small, nearly childlike, under the contours of the sheets. IVs protruded from both arms. An oxygen cannula fed O_2 into her nose with a gentle hiss. A monitor registered her heart rate and respiration, and I knew enough to read steady, though weak, numbers.

"She can maybe hear us?" Tessa asked.

"Like I said, we don't really know. But I tend to think the patient senses someone is here."

"Okay." Tessa moved closer, pausing at the end of the bed. "Hey, Dulce. It's me. Kitten."

I hated hearing that name come from Tessa's mouth. It had been what the traffickers called her. What the "buyers" called her. She needed no reminders of that other awful life.

"Dulce," I said. "I'm here, too. Georgia. Tessa and I both want you to know that we care about you."

No response.

"Hey," Tessa said. "Remember back in the trailer? When I tried to catch that skink?"

"What?" I asked.

Tessa moved to a chair and leaned close to Dulce. "I told you I had a new pet. That I wanted a box to put him in. When you heard what it was, you went into a lecture about how inferior the American lizards were! We have iguanas in Mexico. Bigger than your leg! America has tiny pretend lizards!" Tessa's faked Spanish accent was comical.

"You never told me about the skink." I laughed.

"I decided not to catch it. That one of us deserved to be free."

Those words sliced me in two. What both of these girls had lived through never ceased to affect me.

My cell phone buzzed—a message from Clancy needing something.

"You have to go?" Tessa asked.

I nodded.

"Okay if I stay here a few minutes?"

"Stay as long as you like."

"Would it be okay if I saw Sara while I'm here?"

"Sure. Her mom gave you permission. She's in room 312."

As I exited, I heard Tessa whispering to Dulce. "Your nails look like shit, you know. Seriously, Dulce. We can't have that. If you don't wake up soon, I'm going to polish them myself. And you know how they'll look when I'm done with them."

When I took a final look at the girl in the bed, I thought I saw the tiniest movement of her lips, a ghost of a smile.

Fifty-Seven

SOMETHING AWAKENED SAUL FROM A TURBULENT SLEEP. HE SHOT UP in bed, on high alert, because the life he led required that kind of vigilance. Something was wrong. He blinked, trying to clear his vision, and the realization hit him like a battering ram.

Smoke.

A quick inhalation verified what he saw, and he coughed as he untangled himself from the sheets. The apartment was on fire? He touched the door to his bedroom, finding it warm but not hot. Good. At least no inferno waited for him on the other side. He grabbed a jacket and shoes and hurried into the main living area. The smoke billowed denser there, and he doubled over, hacking. The floor felt warm under his feet. He had to get out of there. And he had to figure out where, exactly, the fire was.

He fumbled with the jacket, felt the cell phone in the pocket, then grabbed the fire extinguisher mounted to the wall before hurrying to the hallway leading to the metal stairs. A wall of smoke prevented any chance of seeing where he was going. He felt for the railing—hot, but not scalding—and stepped down, the metal under his feet radiating heat. Smoke turned everything a milky gray. Even with his jacket pressed over his nose and mouth, he could feel soot entering his lungs. The lack of oxygen made him dizzy. He bent low, feeling for each step, and began his descent. Every breath a desperate fight for air.

Finally, his foot hit cement. The bottom. He hurled himself against the metal door, collapsing on the ground outside. He retched, vomiting up the dark mucus that had filled his lungs, and gulped in air. Delicious, smoke-free air.

The earth beneath him felt hot. He opened his eyes to fire: tongues of yellow flame lapping out the window of the lab beneath his apartment.

The lab! Was Boris inside? He clambered up on wobbly legs and yelled, "Boris!"

No answer.

Saul staggered to the lab's front door, and grabbed at the knob which scorched his hand. He stepped back, looking through the window. Everything inside had been engulfed in a yellow and gray inferno. If Boris was there, he couldn't survive.

Another face filled his mind: Lily Grace.

"Shit!"

Saul hurried to the storage room adjoining the lab where he kept her. He saw no fire through the tiny window, but smoke lay dense as steel wool. He used the keys from his pocket to unlock the door.

Stepping into the wall of smoke was like stepping into hot, gray nothingness.

"Lily Grace!" he coughed out.

No response. He couldn't see anything. The flashlight on his cell phone offered scant illumination against the thick haze. His hands became his eyes as he groped through the utility room. Table. Chair. Heater. Lily Grace's bed on the floor rested beside that, so he bent over and felt for it.

The heat, the smoke—it consumed him. He hungered for oxygen and felt he might succumb, just let the smoke and fire carry him home.

But Lily Grace.

There. He felt a foot, so still, even with his hand gripping it. He hurried to the rest of her, not bothering to assess her, merely scooping her up and doing his very best not to crash to the floor. His brain felt muddled. His lungs burned. He needed to get them out, but each step felt more impossible than the last.

Finally, the door. He tumbled through it, pivoting before he hit the ground so that Lily Grace didn't catch the brunt of the fall. More hacking. Desperate gulps of air. Then he slid out from under her so he could see if she was alive.

Not breathing. Her heart was still as a stone. He turned her over, pounded on her back, then flipped her again and felt her lips for air. None.

He knew CPR. Had taken classes after his little sister was born. He checked Lily Grace's mouth, positioned her head, and blew. After a few minutes of chest compressions and rescue breaths, Lily Grace jerked.

Saul stared down, scared he'd hallucinated, but she drew in air and coughed. He rolled her to her side, and she ejected black bile like something from a horror movie. But she didn't wake up.

Alive though. She was alive.

What now? If he took her to the hospital, the word would get out. Lily Grace, risen from the dead, meant Saul had crossed Marcus. Lily Grace would tell the truth about that prick kid, Cooper Hawthorne. No hope for Saul surviving that.

He'd been an idiot to put himself in this situation. To take Lily Grace instead of offing her as he'd been hired to do. But that had seemed a step too far. Kill a child. There was no going back.

Think. Think! He had no choice. He had to get Lily Grace to a hospital. To hell with Cooper Hawthorne and Marcus. To hell with all of them.

Fifty-Eight

WHEN I GOT HOME THAT EVENING, NO LIGHTS SHINED IN THE LIVING room. The kitchen—dark, too. I started to get worried until I saw a yellow glow under the door to Tessa's room. I knocked.

"Tessa?"

"Yeah. Come on in."

I found her sitting cross-legged on her bed, laptop open, earbuds inserted, our massive black cat stretched out beside her. Her blonde hair had been mostly gathered in a barrette, but that self-induced haircut left a few strands hanging free.

"Homework?" I asked.

"English essay. Wish I could concentrate."

I sat at the foot of the bed. "Something bothering you?"

A shrug in response. She was such a teen sometimes.

"You're worried about Lou, aren't you?"

She nodded. "So are you."

"Hey, he's doing great. Acing every test. Just needs more rest." The relief of this had been a much-needed balm for me. I hoped it would be for her, too.

She removed the earbuds. "I got a call earlier from that Lana Montgomery woman."

No wonder she couldn't focus. "What did Lana say?"

"She wants to take me to check out that center for trafficking survivors in Rock Hill next week."

How dare Lana do this without clearing it with me?

"What did you say?"

242

"I said I wasn't interested. I don't care how nice it is. I don't care if it has classes and job training and all that. I don't want to go there." She looked up at me. "I want to stay here."

"That's what I want, too."

If it was the right thing for her. What I'd read about the program in Rock Hill was pretty damn impressive. But taking her there—saying goodbye—would hurt like losing a limb.

She stroked Fenway. His purr rumbled.

"I need to tell you something, and you're not going to like it."

"Okay . . ." I stiffened.

"At Cooper's party . . . I wasn't having a good time. And I did something stupid. I took half a pill. One of those blues."

"You took fentanyl?" My voice boomed.

She nodded.

Awful images of what might have happened careened through my brain. An overdose. Drowning in the pool. Walking away to be hit by a car. All the things that I'd seen in the ER, only it would have been my kid.

"Not a whole pill. I got high, but nothing dangerous happened."

"Which is a freaking miracle." I closed my eyes, slowing my breathing as I mentally counted to ten. Tessa was smarter than this. At least, so I thought. And how had I not noticed? What kind of guardian was I? "Tell me more about the party. About taking the pill."

She shrugged. "Everybody was having fun. But getting blitzed. They were dancing. Laughing. Talking about stuff I couldn't give a shit about. I just . . . I felt so foreign there. I didn't belong. Sometimes it feels like I don't belong anywhere." She sounded so lost, so empty, it broke my heart.

"You belong here, Tessa." I kept my voice firm. "I hope you know that."

She nodded. "But it's hard with the idiots at my school. Except Joel."

"Was that the only time you took it?"

She didn't answer, her gaze fixed on her laptop screen.

Her non-answer was my answer. Crap. I pushed harder.

"Tessa? Tell me the truth."

"One other time."

I wanted to choke her, only not really. It wasn't anger I felt; it was fear. Absolute terror. The anger I directed at myself.

"I'm sorry! I just . . . it was a bad time. An awful time, and I needed something to help."

"So you have fentanyl here in my house."

"A friend from school gave it to me, but I don't have it anymore. I dumped it down the drain. And if you don't believe me, Elias watched me do it."

"Elias?" I practically screamed. "You took it the night I had to go to work? And Elias knew?" I would strangle him.

"Don't be mad at him. He took care of me." Tessa told me the rest. It had happened after Lana's visit when she first mentioned Tessa leaving Columbia for the restoration center. Tessa had been very upset and closed herself off in her room. When I thought she was sleeping, she was getting high.

I should have paid closer attention. I shouldn't have gone to work. What else had I missed that happened right under my nose?

"Elias made sure I was safe. And when I was straight again, we had an intense conversation about my parents and how I could become an addict if I wasn't careful. So, I got rid of the pills. And I don't plan to ever take them again, I promise. Elias didn't tell you because he said I had to. Please, please don't be mad at him." She looked at me, her eyes beseeching.

"I'm not mad at either of you. But I'm scared for you. It's important that you told me the truth, Tessa. But we need to work on what you do when you're upset. Because pills can't be an option. Maybe that's something you can work on with Morgan."

I still couldn't get over the fact that this happened here in my house and I hadn't noticed. Jesus. Maybe Lana was right. Maybe Rock Hill would be a better—safer—option for Tessa.

We both had a lot to think about.

Fifty-Nine

I ENTERED LOU'S ROOM QUIETLY, HOLDING THE DOOR AS IT CLOSED SO there'd be no annoying click. He was asleep, the nurse had told me. Asleep was so much better than "in a medically induced coma," which had been his state for the past few days. The intracranial swelling had reduced, Dr. Romano told me in last night's update. Vitals were strong. When they brought him out of unconsciousness, he'd been fully oriented and passed every neurological test. Complained of a "mother of a head-ache," according to Romano, and I'd literally wept with relief.

The new bandage on his head was smaller than the last, and he'd be horrified that his hair had been shaved. His face had lost its pallor, and a low, rumbling snore huffed out of his mouth. He'd be horrified about that, too.

I pulled up a chair to watch him. To let it sink in that he would be okay. Memories of finding him that afternoon, of how he lay slumped over the steering wheel, the blood, the silence, tumbled through my mind.

I reached for his hand, mindful of the tubes attached to the top of his wrist. I had so much I wanted to say. That I was sorry I'd disappointed him. That seeing him so close to death had made me question everything and made me realize how strong my feelings were for him.

Was I wrong to push him away?

Yeah, I was a certifiable, batshit-crazy mess, but he knew that. And he knew Ben, my ex, and had probably been told lots of stories of how we ended (thank you, perky young journalism intern). He knew me and still wanted more from our relationship.

245

One thing I knew for sure—he deserved to know how I felt about him. The thought that he could have died not knowing that punched me in the gut. He deserved the truth.

I had to be brave enough to tell it.

A light rap on the door startled me. I let go of Lou's hand as a small, familiar man entered: Lou's companion at Elias's restaurant. I couldn't remember his name.

I stood. "Can I help you?"

"Hope I'm not disturbing you. I was here for work and thought I'd check on Lou. I'm Detective Jackson Purdy. We met at the bistro."

"I remember. And I'm Georgia Thayer. Hospital social worker."

"Lou mentions you. A lot."

"He does?"

"I know you had dinner with him last week. I dropped some files off at his house, and he had me sample the tomato sauce six times, wanting it to be just right. Ignored me about the smoked paprika, though. We're working together on a few cases."

"Like the fentanyl problem? Or Lily Grace Duffy's disappearance?"

"We're staying busy these days." Evasive. Typical cop. He rounded the bed. "He looks a whole lot better."

"Yeah, thank God." The lovely truth of this still hadn't quite sunk in.

"Tough dude. No stupid bullet's gonna keep him down." He tapped the sheet. "Scared the shit out of me, though. All of us."

"He'll do anything for attention."

Detective Jackson Purdy laughed. Loud. It seemed to bounce off the walls.

But Lou didn't stir. "Shhh. We want him to sleep," I whispered.

"Sorry."

"Do you have any leads on who shot him?"

A dismissive smile. "Nothing I can talk about."

I studied him for a moment. "You said you were at the hospital for work. Mind telling me what's going on?"

He dropped into a chair. "Maybe I should. Maybe you can help."

"I'll try."

"We brought in a kid. She's still in the ER. Unconscious."

"Another fentanyl overdose?" I swallowed the expletives that I wanted to scream. Detective Purdy didn't need to meet that side of me.

"No. She was in a fire. Not burned but smoke inhalation, they tell me. No ID on her. Maybe fifteen, sixteen years old."

Odd that I hadn't heard about her, but the ER had been such a zoo these days. "I'll check on her."

"How about I meet you down there in twenty minutes? I need to call the captain and update him on Lou." He waved a phone at me.

"Meet you down there."

As he left, I pulled a chair closer and took his hand. "You're gonna be fine, Lou," I whispered.

I felt a pressure on my fingers. He was squeezing my hand.

"Lou?"

"Hey." His eyes blinked open, did a slow scan of the room, then fixed on my face.

"How do you feel?"

He smacked his lips and took in a breath, as though assessing. "Like a mule kicked me in the head. A . . . a really, really angry mule."

"You remember what happened?"

"They told me some asshole shot me."

I lifted our joined hands and pressed them against my lips. "You scared me."

"Scared myself. Tessa okay? I missed our tutoring session."

I smiled. "Yeah, you did. That's why I went looking for you. You'll be making it up, by the way. Seriously. You're her only hope of passing trig."

He smiled. "Happy to oblige."

I looked down at our hands, still joined. And, of course, I had a flash of panic. The issue of what Lou wanted us to be—and what I was too terrified to allow—hadn't gone away.

He snaked his fingers between mine. "This feels good. Just relax."

"I wish I was normal." Those were the most honest, raw words I'd ever spoken to him.

He flashed another dopey smile. "Normal is overrated. And frankly, boring."

I didn't respond. There was so much to say, but he needed his rest. The fingers tugged. "What's going on?" he asked.

"I shouldn't . . . you know I hear voices. They were absent for a while, but they're back."

"I'm sorry," he said.

I shrugged. "I can manage them. Really, I can. But . . ."

"But what?"

I looked into his blue eyes. The color of the sky. "But they're a problem for Tessa."

"Has she complained?" He sounded perplexed.

"No. I mean, I doubt she even knows. But her social services caseworker keeps asking about my mental illness. She doesn't think I should have Tessa. I think she's going to take her from me." Another raw truth. Saying it out loud made the walls crumble.

He released my hand and reached for my face. He wiped the tears that had emerged, unexpected, his touch as gentle as a leaf.

"There's a treatment place in Rock Hill," I went on. "I looked it up. They do great work with kids who are trafficking survivors. I guess the state has special funding for it. She wants Tessa to go there."

"I don't care how great it is. She should be with you."

"That's what I thought at first. But . . ."

"No buts. Georgia, quit torturing yourself. That girl is yours. Hell, she's ours. Yours, Elias's, mine. She belongs here." His voice was firm, yet his touch remained feather-soft.

I looked at Lou, saw the fatigue in his eyes.

"You need to get more rest."

"Okay. But you need to have more faith in yourself. You're what's best for Tessa."

I nodded, wanting so badly to believe.

One thing I knew—whatever was best for Tessa was what had to happen. Even if that meant losing her.

***

I found Jackson standing outside one of the ER bays. When I entered, I froze at the foot of the bed. The girl reeked of smoke, but not regular smoke. It had a sweet, yet vinegary odor. Her skin and clothes were covered with so much ash she looked like wet cement. Or maybe that was her complexion from lack of oxygen—God, I hoped not.

Dr. Romano was issuing orders to the nurse for respiratory therapy to consult "immediately."

The detective asked, "Does she look familiar?"

I moved closer to her. Brown hair, unclean. Large nose, close-set eyes. Young. Probably Tessa's age. I thought about a picture I'd seen in a very cluttered house. Holy shit.

"Is this Lily Grace?"

"I think so. But we need to check something. Can you check out her ear?"

"Huh?"

"Lily Grace has a small scar behind her left ear." He pulled up a photo on his phone—a sketch of what the mark looked like.

I looked at Romano, who nodded. I bent over her to look. There. A small, almost heart-shaped mark.

"It's her. How bad is she?"

Romano said, "Smoke inhalation. Not loving her O_2 levels."

"Any signs of assault?" I whispered.

"No."

"Thank God." I turned to Detective Purdy. "Do you know anything about the fire? Were chemicals involved?"

"It's a bit confusing. She was found on a park bench outside a Starbucks. Some male called it in, wouldn't leave his name. No fire nearby. But about four miles from there, in the warehouse district, there was a case of arson. Yes, chemicals were involved—what we found were the remnants of a drug lab."

Just like what Lou had told me had happened before.

Romano said, "We're doing bloodwork and radiography on her lungs. That should tell us more."

He dismissed us, so the detective and I moved to a small meeting room reserved for hospital staff.

"She's alive," I whispered. "Lily Grace is alive. I had given up hope."

I'd tell her mother as soon as we were done. Mrs. Duffy's prayers might have been answered—if her daughter's lungs weren't too badly damaged.

"Any idea what she was doing in that drug lab? From what we've heard, she's not exactly the type."

"Not at all. Maybe she was there against her will. That would explain her being gone for so long. But why?"

"Tessa—my foster kid—believes Lily Grace witnessed someone running over Sara Clark, and it wasn't Joel McCants. Maybe that's why she had to disappear."

"The only other person in that car was Cooper Hawthorne."

"Yep."

"How would that have anything to do with a fentanyl lab?" Detective Purdy scratched his face. "If it did, then our two cases are connected. When can we question her?"

"Not until she's medically stable. But I'll let you know when she's able to talk."

The detective approached the door. "If she was held hostage, some-one might try to keep her from talking. I'll talk with hospital security. See if we can supplement with our officers."

"This kid has been through so much. I want her safe."

CLANCY MET ME OUTSIDE MY OFFICE DOOR WHEN I ARRIVED AT WORK
the next morning. She handed me a latte, sipping one herself.

"Off the wagon?" I asked, pointing to her drink.

"Skinny latte, no sugar. Two shots of espresso because it's gonna be
that kind of day. Yours is high-test, too."

I unlocked my office, dropped into my chair, and slurped. Delicious.
I think all the fat she'd rejected in hers had been added to mine.

"So what's going on?"

She took the other chair. "Richard Lockhart just stopped by."

"And what did The Dick want?"

"He's been contacted by some reporter wanting data on fentanyl admissions. I'm thinking it's your Ben Reeder."

"That does sound like Ben, but he ain't mine."

"I told Richard to give him what he wants because he's tenacious as
a terrier. I hope it makes the front page." She slurped. White froth dotted
her upper lip. "Have some good news. They've weaned Lily Grace off
the tranquilizer, and she's awake. Damage to her lungs is minor, and the
tracheal swelling has gone down."

I smiled. "That's wonderful news."

"Wanna know what's weird? She keeps asking for Detective
Michaels."

"Lou? She never met him." While Tessa had suggested she find him,
she disappeared before making contact.

"She's very insistent about it."

"Think I'd better go say hello."

Five minutes later, I entered Lily Grace's room to find her sitting up in her bed, eating Jell-O. Her face had more color. Her brown hair could use a wash, but her green eyes had a much-welcomed brightness to them. Her mom, sitting beside her, looked up at me and beamed.

"Lily Grace, this is Georgia Thayer. She's your friend Tessa's foster mom."

"Ms. Thayer! Tessa talks about you like all the time." She spoke with the enthusiasm of someone much younger.

"Call me Georgia. It's great to see you looking so much better." I rounded the bed to get closer. "How are you feeling?"

She scooped another spoonful of Jell-O into her mouth. "This is delicious. I've been eating mostly junk food for . . . how long was I gone, Mom?"

"Eight days. Five hours." She sounded like every minute of it had wounded her.

"I'm sorry if you were worried, but I was in good hands. I promise."

A nurse entered the room. "Mrs. Duffy? You're due down in cardio. They called asking for you."

"Oh, I'm sorry. I completely forgot!" She bent over and kissed her daughter's forehead. "I'll be back in a jiffy, love. Promise."

I watched her leave the room, moving faster, with more energy than I'd seen before. She'd said seeing Lily Grace was the only medicine she'd need. I suspected she was right.

Someone rapped on the door and entered. Detective Jackson Purdy. He walked in, smiling apologetically before taking a chair. "The doctor said it was okay if I asked you a few questions, Lily Grace."

She pushed the Jell-O away. "I want to talk to Detective Michaels."

Jackson shot me a perplexed look.

"He can't visit right now, Lily Grace," I said.

"Why not? He didn't get burned, did he?"

My turn to look puzzled. "Burned?"

"When he carried me out of the fire! I mean, I think it was him."

"He was at the fire?" I asked.

She turned to Detective Purdy. "Is it okay if I tell her? About the protective custody and stuff?"

His eyes bulged. "Uhmm. Sure. Tell both of us."

"Detective Michaels hid me in a room because I'm an important witness to a crime. He said there were people who wanted to hurt me. He kept me safe."

"The whole time you were gone—you were in 'protective custody?'" Jackson asked.

She nodded with great vehemence. "The detective brought me food every day. And a heater. And books, but don't tell Mama I read Harry Potter."

"Where did he keep you?" Jackson asked.

She shrugged. "It was a room. Not fancy. Not a hotel. Just like a janitor's room, but I fixed it up. And it had a bathroom."

"But you don't know where it was?"

She shook her head.

"Do you know anything about a lab?" he asked.

"A lab?"

"Where drugs are made. That's where the fire started."

Her face twisted in confusion. "Detective Michaels said I had to be quiet. That there were some bad men working next door. And sometimes, I smelled something gross. And it made me cough."

Jackson shot me a questioning look, but I was stumped. "When did you last see Detective Michaels?" I asked her.

"If he wasn't the one who saved me, then it was the day before the fire. But it had to be him. Who else knew I was there?"

I mentally calculated the time. Lou got shot long before the fire, so he hadn't rescued her. But had he been keeping her hidden all this time? Without telling her parents? Without telling me?

Jackson asked, "You said he hid you because you witnessed a crime?"

She nodded, glancing at me. "Is it okay if I talk about it here? In front of her?"

"Sure," Jackson said in a "why the hell not" kind of tone.

"I went to Cooper Hawthorne's party. Only, before I got there, I saw Sara Clark get hit by a car."

Jackson started taking notes.

"Cooper's father, Mr. Hawthorne, showed up right after. I mean, Cooper didn't even check on Sara. He just called his dad instead. Mr. Hawthorne told Cooper to blame the accident on Joel. But Joel was NOT driving. Cooper was."

"You're sure about that?"

She nodded. "Detective Michaels questioned me, then said that Mr. Hawthorne was a dangerous man and he'd do anything to protect Cooper. To keep the truth from coming out. So he hid me." She started on the Jell-O again, scraping the sides with the plastic spoon.

"I may have more questions for you soon," Jackson said, starting to leave.

"Okay. But remember. Don't tell Mama about Harry Potter!"

I followed Jackson out of her room and stopped him in the hall. He leaned against the wall, looking up at the lights. "Do you think—I mean Lou—he wouldn't hide her without telling anyone, would he?"

"No. That's just not Lou's style." It made no sense. Why would Lou be looking for Lily Grace if he had her in hiding? An idea came to me. "Wait. Before you go, let's try something."

I led him back to Lily Grace's room.

She'd finished the Jell-O but found a packet of saltines to punish. Crumbs dotted the pale sheet across her. "Hello again," she said in that childlike, sing-song voice she had.

I pulled out my phone and flipped through some photos. When I found the one I wanted, I held it up for her. "Do you recognize this man?"

She peered closely at it. "Nope. Should I?"

I flashed the picture of Lou at Jackson. "Lily Grace, can you describe Detective Michaels for us?"

"Well, sure. He's big. Like, taller than you and wider. Muscular. Shaved head. Bad scar across his face from when he tried to save someone in New York."

Shit. A fake Lou Michaels had held her prisoner. Probably someone affiliated with the drug lab. Had he been the one to rescue her from the fire?

I turned to Jackson. "You want to tell her, or shall I?"

He took a seat and told her about the fake Lou Michaels, met immediately with her denial. She insisted that her Detective Michaels was a good man, a hero, and wouldn't have had anything to do with drugs.

"We're glad he kept you safe," I told her. "But he's not a real detective. We don't know who he is."

She frowned. "It's . . . confusing."

No kidding.

Jackson gave her a subtle smile. "It's okay, Lily Grace. You ARE under police protection now. I promise we'll keep you safe. Now. Can you tell me more about the shaved-head version of Lou Michaels?"

She leaned back, eyes narrowed as though deep in thought. "Sometimes, he'd get phone calls. He didn't like whoever called him, I could tell. He'd frown, but he'd always agree with whatever they said to him. And he'd be in a bad mood after. I mean, he was almost always in a bad mood, but those calls made him worse."

Jackson pulled out his own phone and showed her a photo of goateed man—handsome, and very serious looking. "Did you ever see this man there?"

She shook her head.

Jackson jotted down some notes, then motioned for me to step out of her room. "How long are you going to keep her in the hospital? Can we keep her admission here under wraps?"

"I don't know. Probably a few more days. But despite HIPAA and all that, this hospital is gossip-central. The whole town's been worried about this kid. The fact that she's alive is going to be hard to contain. Who was that picture you showed her?"

"Not something I can discuss." He glanced at the closed door. "I'm concerned about her comment about Fletcher Hawthorne. Sounds like he'd do anything to cover up what his son did, especially with the election looming."

"So what? He was going to have the bald dude keep her prisoner until November 12? And then what? The truth would come out, eventually."

"I don't know. It's all really confusing. I'm going to send a sketch artist to talk to Lily Grace. Maybe if we get a good rendering of her captor, we can figure out what's going on."

Sixty-One

FLETCHER SAT ACROSS FROM HIS OLDER SON AND TRIED TO PULL IT TO-gether. Holden leaned forward in the winged-back chair, his hands locked together, his gaze fixed on them. How did Fletcher not know what was happening in his own family? How was it that Marcus penetrated inside his home, targeting his son? And how could Holden be such an idiot?

"How long has this been going on?" Fletcher demanded.

Holden rubbed his thumbs together. He'd do the same thing when he was a little boy, being fussed at about his grades.

"How long?" Fletcher repeated, hardly containing the rage roiling inside him. Rage at Holden. And at himself.

"Not quite a year."

"A year?!" he bellowed. "You've been dealing drugs for Marcus for a year? How could you be that stupid?"

"I'm not stupid," Holden whispered.

"What was that? I couldn't hear you."

"I'm not stupid. I just . . . It was easy, Dad. So easy. I pick up product here. I take it to a few drop-offs. Done. I'm not pushing on the streets. I don't push to non-users. I'm just the go-between."

Fletcher closed his eyes. He needed to understand. What led Holden to this terrible decision? Had he lost his son to Marcus and that bleak, ugly life?

"How did it start?"

Holden cleared his throat, looking oddly embarrassed. "It started back when Mom's painkiller prescription ran out. You were out of town—Florida, I think—and she was really hurting. I knew your friend

Marcus had supplied her before, so I tried to find him. I searched your office and found a phone. A burner, I guess. I punched the only number in the directory . . . Marcus."

Shit. Shit shit shit shit. His fault. This was all Fletcher's fault. His failure as a father punched him in the gut. One of so many failures.

Holden looked up at him. "Mom was hurting, Dad. She tried to be strong, but I could hear her crying through your bedroom door. And you weren't here. I didn't know what else to do. I mean, I could take her to her doctor, but he won't prescribe anything that works, you know that. She needed something strong."

If Fletcher hadn't been away, he could have made the call to Marcus. But no, Fletcher was at the resort. The special resort where he hid his sins.

"Okay," Fletcher said. "I get why you called Marcus, and I'm sorry I wasn't here. But that doesn't explain how you got into dealing."

Holden stood, towering over his father. "Marcus asked me for a favor. You know, in exchange for payment for Mom's pills. I took an envelope of pills to some guy by the river. It was so easy. And Marcus paid me two hundred bucks. When he asked if I'd like to do it again, I said yes."

Damn Marcus. He was a snake slithering through Fletcher's family.

"Do you know how much it pays? Do you have any idea? I bought a Tesla, Dad. I paid cash. I've got tuition for the next two years sitting in the bank, and I may buy a house to live in. That's why I did it."

"What the hell, Holden? We have money. I was going to cover your tuition. If you needed more, all you had to do was ask—"

"No." Holden spun around. "That's not how it works. You and Mom give me a small allowance, but there's no real wiggle room. I maxed out the credit card you gave me my first semester, and you lost your shit about that, remember?"

Fletcher stood and approached him. His face felt hot as embers. "You entitled little boy! I did not raise you to be so damn lazy. To take ridiculous risks that could absolutely tank your future. I'm ashamed of you, Holden. For the first time in your life, I'm ashamed."

That hit its mark. Holden blinked, tears welling. Fletcher felt it in his chest—he'd gone too far, but he had to make his point.

"It's over," Fletcher told him. "Marcus will not be using you to distribute his 'product' anymore. It's too big a risk. You're damn lucky you haven't been caught. We can't afford the risk now with the election coming up. You're done."

Holden nodded, looking appropriately humbled.

Fletcher sighed, stepping closer. "Okay then. You put your energy into school. Into being the best lawyer you can be. That's where your future lies, son. Not in messing with people like Marcus."

"But you do," he whispered.

"What?"

"When will you be cut loose from Marcus, Dad? If he's bad news for me, he's worse news for you."

"I'm trying," Fletcher replied. "God knows, I'm trying."

But trying wasn't good enough, was it?

***

Fletcher reviewed the polling numbers for the tenth time. Finally, the large financial investment was paying off—he'd risen two points and was now neck and neck with the incumbent. If he could keep up the media push, the election might be his.

Footsteps sounded outside the library where he worked. Vivian stumbled in, looking bleary-eyed and unsteady. "Fletch, honey. I've been lookin' for ya."

"I'm right here, just like always." He stood and guided her to a seat. "How are you feeling?"

"I was feeling awful. Now I'm feeling no pain." Her smile rested off-center on her face. Her hand gripped his.

"You need to be careful, honey. You promised me you'd cut back."

"I slept ten minutes last night, Fletcher. Cut me some slack."

He flinched at her tone. The pain must have been bad, really bad, to elicit that venom. "I'm sorry, hon. I didn't realize."

258

"Some days I have hope. Just a glimmer. That maybe . . . maybe . . . there will be an end to all this." She blinked her beautiful green eyes where tears welled. "Then I have nights like last night. It's damn humbling."

He hated it when she cursed. Such ugly words had no place in her lovely mouth.

"Has Holden been by?" she asked him.

"No. You're expecting him?"

She nodded. "He's doing a favor for me."

"What favor?" He dreaded her answer.

"Nothing for you to worry about." She lifted herself from the chair, wincing as she stood. "God knows, you have enough on your mind."

He lifted a hand to stop her. "Viv, I know Holden has been supplying you with painkillers. We can't let him do that anymore, can we? It's too risky."

She stared, wide-eyed—a deer in crossbeams.

"Don't worry. I'll make sure you have what you need. But maybe we should talk about getting off the hard stuff again. There's that treatment facility in Atlanta—they can teach you to manage your pain. That's what your doctor told me."

"Did he now? You and my orthopedist chatted about what's right for me? Isn't that nice?" Sarcasm oozed.

"We both want what's best for you."

She took slow steps toward the door, then turned. "What's best for me? Life without pain. That's what's best for me, Fletcher. Figure out how to get me that, and I'm all in."

He didn't want to continue this familiar argument. Thankfully, they were interrupted by a ringing phone. THE phone, which meant Marcus.

Vivian closed the door as she left him. Fletcher answered, "What?"

"There's a problem. A big one."

Fletcher collapsed in his chair. A headache began pounding behind his eyes. "Tell me."

"The witness to Cooper's accident. She has reemerged."

Fletcher hadn't wanted to know what Marcus did to that witness, but he'd assumed it was something permanent. "What do you mean?"

"One of my men screwed up. Decided he'd handle *your* problem in his own way. He'll regret that decision, but more to the point—you have to do some damage control. And I mean immediately."

"She knows Cooper was the one who hit Sara Clark? Has she told anyone?"

"It's just a matter of time."

"Dammit." It felt like his house of cards had collapsed into a heap. A steaming heap of dog shit. "Dammit," he repeated.

Marcus continued. "I'm sending a team to take care of her, but just in case, you have to act soon. Like this afternoon. You have no choice about this, Fletcher. You are to do exactly as I say."

What strategy would possibly fix this mess? Cooper had hit a girl. Nearly killed her when he was stoned on drugs. Then they covered up the whole mess, blaming an innocent Black kid. There'd be no coming back from this. Cooper could face charges. And Fletcher could end up in jail for the cover-up.

It felt like Thor was hammering a nail into his skull.

"Are you listening, Fletcher? I've consulted with a political fixer in DC. The best. If there's a way to save your campaign—and it's a big IF—you will do as I say."

Fletcher grabbed a notepad. He wrote down exactly what Marcus told him.

Ten minutes later, he sat across from his younger son and laid out the plan. Cooper had to be on board—that was the only way Marcus's plan would work.

"Coop, we don't have a choice here." Fletcher finished. Cooper did not look good. His reddish hair lay in a tangled, greasy mess. Was that the same polo shirt he had on yesterday? And when had he showered last? Reporters would arrive soon for Fletcher's press conference, and Cooper had to play his part. "I'd hoped to protect you. That they'd never learn you were the one driving when Sara got hit. But the truth is out now, and you have to face it."

Cooper glanced at the door. Vivian stood there, dressed in a lavender dress that accentuated her collarbones and too-thin arms. Fletcher had asked her to wear a sweater when the press arrived.

"Give us a minute, Viv."

"A reporter's already here."

"They can wait." Damn vultures.

She nodded and left them.

"Do you understand what I'm saying, Cooper? I'll talk to the media. I'll explain that you didn't mean to hit Sara or to cover it up. You're young. You make mistakes. And you're facing the consequences."

He looked up at Fletcher, tears glistening in his eyes.

"I'll do everything I can to keep you out of jail, Coop. I have connections. But for now, we need everything to look above board, you know? Until the election is over. Tell me you understand that."

Full-on crying now. The kid was scared. He'd be a mess on camera. Fletcher glanced at the clock; they still had a half hour for Cooper to get it together.

Fletcher moved closer and laid a hand on his shoulder. "You didn't mean to hurt anyone. That's what matters. It was an accident."

Cooper sniffled. "But . . . but what if it wasn't?" he whispered.

"What did you say?" Fletcher tightened his hand on Cooper's shoulder so he'd look up.

"I . . . What if . . . what if I hit her on purpose?"

Fletcher felt those words like a blow. "What are you saying?"

Cooper jerked away, swiping at his eyes with the back of his hand. "Sara! That night . . . she said things. Terrible things. About you, Dad."

"What did she say?" Fletcher felt the world was tilting on its axis. Had his son mowed down a girl with his car on purpose?

More tears flowed. "At my party, someone said she'd been in my room. She was looking for something. Pissed me off. So I went to find her. She was in the pool house. She just stood there, staring at that chaise longue you like. She had the weirdest expression on her face." Another swipe of his face. Snot dribbled down.

"What happened next?"

"I said her name, and she turned, and . . . she started screaming. Saying horrible things about you. She said she'd been there before when she was little. And you were there. You were on that chaise with a boy, she said. And you were . . ."

Oh no. That afternoon, so many years ago. Sitting with the boy. Bourbon warming his blood. The feel of his skin against his hand. The door cracked open, and he saw a face—just a glimpse—but then nobody was there. He'd imagined it, he was sure. His guilt simply conjured up a ghost. But if Sara had been there . . . If she'd seen them . . .

"She said you were, uh, you were touching him, Dad." He looked at Fletcher, his face twisted in grief and fear. "She wouldn't shut up!"

"Oh God, Coop—"

"Then she took off down the road. I don't think I planned to hit her. But I saw her, and I thought about what she'd said, and what would happen if . . . and I don't know! Maybe I hit her to shut her up!" Cooper collapsed into sobs.

Everything crumbled inside. Everything. Cooper knew his awful secret and nearly killed a girl to protect it. What had Fletcher done?

He pulled his arm tighter around Cooper and pulled him in. "Shhhh. It's gonna be okay, son. Take a deep breath and try to settle down."

Cooper curved into him, like he'd do as a little boy, and Fletcher stroked his hair. "I'm gonna take care of everything, I promise."

He would. He had to. The problem was—how?

The door opened, and Vivian peeked in. "Media's here."

Damn. He'd forgotten. No way he could put Cooper on camera as planned. No, he'd have to finesse this catastrophe.

"Is Cooper okay?" Vivian hurried in.

"He needs a minute. Let's leave him alone while we talk to the reporters. That okay with you, Coop?"

His son nodded, pulling away and wiping his face one last time. "Don't make me talk to them."

"I won't. You sit here and pull yourself together. Leave the rest to me."

Sixty-Two

RUS SHOULD HAVE BEEN MORE CAREFUL. HE SHOULD HAVE FIGURED out that the fire would spread that fast, especially after the flame touched the alcohol. The sudden whoosh of flame had knocked him over, and when his sleeve caught fire, he barely got his jacket off and hurled himself through the window before the lab was completely engulfed.

He didn't realize how bad the burn was at first—adrenaline had him running as far and as fast as he could go. But later, the pain flared. And now, his hand and wrist looked elephantine, with blisters blooming on blisters, his flesh the color of Twizzlers. He kept it wrapped. Lathered on antibiotic crap he'd bought at the dollar store, but nothing helped. The fire never left his arm, and twice, he'd had to stop himself from securing the one thing that would stop the pain. But he couldn't. He'd come too far to go back to that life.

Which left one option. He couldn't drive the motorcycle, so he walked the three-ish miles from his trailer to the hospital. It should have been an easy trek. It sure shouldn't have winded him, but he found himself panting and nearly dizzy with exhaustion when he finally pushed through the emergency department doors.

The pain didn't prevent the same surge of anxiety he felt whenever he stumbled into a public place. He couldn't afford to be recognized or for someone from his "before" life to see him now. Fletcher Hawthorne almost spotted him once, and that would have been disastrous. Worse, if . . . if . . .

No. That wouldn't happen. Rus looked nothing like he had as a kid. He'd lost so much weight. Grown the beard. His hair, teeth, even his complexion were different. Still. He pulled the hoodie over his head and took tentative steps toward the reception area.

"Can I help you?" the clerk asked.

"Need to see a doctor." He lifted his arm. The wound wept through the bandage. Maybe they'd give him some extra gauze so he could change it more often.

"Ouch," the clerk said. "Can you fill out a form for me, or do you need help?"

"I can manage." He took the clipboard and found a seat in the corner. The form took just a few minutes—he had little to say. No insurance. No last name. A made-up address. Just another indigent loser, like many others who filled the waiting room.

When he returned the information to the clerk, she studied it, then promised someone would be with him "shortly."

"Shortly" meant an hour later, but finally, a nurse and a petite, dark-skinned resident guided him back to the exam area. She introduced herself as "Dr. Rawls," and he wondered about her age because of her pudgy face and the small hoop in her left nostril.

"Can you tell me what happened?" she asked him.

"We lit a campfire behind our trailer last night. You know, for roasting marshmallows. A big wind blew up, and, well, I guess I was a little too close." He swallowed the truth. The warehouse/lab. Busting a window, crawling inside. The can of gasoline, the large bottle of alcohol he'd found on the table. How the flame swelled so fast, how close he'd come to getting trapped. Running through the blaze, fire lapping at his feet.

"A bit breezy for a fire," the resident commented. "You could have really hurt yourself. Or started a wildfire that took out half the county."

"I thought we were being careful. Guess we weren't careful enough."

The nurse brought over a tray that held bandages and bottles of what looked like saline and other stuff.

The resident said, "This burn is infected. I'm gonna need to debride to clear the dead skin. We'll get you started on IV antibiotics and fluids. And something for the pain."

Rus shook his head. "No opioids. Can't have those."

The resident tilted her head, studying him. "Because?"

"Because I'm a recovering addict. And I plan to stay that way."

She nodded. "I'll use a local anesthetic. Give you some NSAIDs. Hopefully, they'll do the trick."

The next sixty minutes were absolute hell. He'd felt pain before, but every nerve in his hand and wrist screamed as Dr. Rawls did her work. He consoled himself that the agony was worth it. He'd put Marcus Landry out of commission—for a while, at least. Of course, greedy bastards like him wouldn't stay down for long. He'd open another lab, and Rus would have to find it. They'd play that cat-and-mouse game until Rus could put an end to the whole operation once and for all.

The curtain pulled back, and someone else entered the examination area: Georgia Thayer, the social worker.

"Rus? The clerk told me you were here."

"Hey, Georgia." He winced as the nurse inserted a needle into his arm.

"What did you do to yourself?"

Rus shrugged. "Just being stupid again."

She turned to the resident. "How bad is it?"

"Second-degree burns, mostly. Gonna hurt for a while, and he's refusing narcotics. Mostly, we need to watch for infection. After we get the burn cleaned, it's got to stay that way, or he could lose the arm."

"I'll do whatever you say."

"Good. Georgia, can I speak to you outside for a moment?"

"Sure. I'll be right back, Rus."

Sixty-Three

I ALWAYS LIKED DR. RAWLS. ALL OF FIVE FOOT, THREE INCHES, A HUN-dred pounds at the most, she was never one to be trifled with. I'd seen her stare down a gang member who refused to leave a gun outside the exam room. Two minutes later, Rawls removed the clip and handed the firearm to security. Like I said, you didn't mess with Dr. Rawls.

"Something isn't adding up," Dr. Rawls said.

"What do you mean?"

"Rus claims he burned himself at a campfire. But I did a rotation in a burn center. There are certain burn patterns we see when an accelerant has been used. Rus has those patterns—alligator skin, a serpentine-like pattern up his arm. I don't think this was a simple campfire. Also, take a whiff of his clothes. That's not the smell of burning wood."

"What then?" I thought about it, my mind flashing to Lily Grace and her smoke inhalation. The fire at the warehouse that had been turned into a fentanyl factory. Had Rus been there? Trying to score drugs?

Or had he started that fire?

"He seems to trust you. See what you can find out."

"I'll do my best."

I returned to Rus. The nurse had wrapped his wrist in gauze and fash-ioned a sling for him to wear. His face looked flushed with fever.

"Can you give us a minute?" I asked the nurse.

He nodded and exited. I pulled a chair closer to the bed. Rus's jacket lay across the foot of his bed. I lifted it and smelled it. It had the same odor as Lily Grace's clothes.

"Rus, tell me what really happened to your arm."

266

"I told you. The campfire was a stupid idea. I've learned my lesson."

I fixed him with my glare. "That's not a campfire burn. It's something much more serious. And I'd like for you to tell me the truth."

He narrowed his eyes at me like a petulant child.

"Here's an interesting coincidence. A drug lab was burned the other night. Around the same time you got burned, I suspect."

He flinched but said nothing.

"The drug lab fire was started with accelerants. According to your doctor, accelerants cause a particular kind of burn. The kind that you have."

He avoided my stare.

"I think you were there. Did you go there to score opioids? Should I do a drug screen on you?"

"No!" he practically screamed, followed by a quieter, "No. I'm clean. Even when it's so damn hard—" He lifted his injured arm. "I'm clean."

"Okay then. You didn't steal drugs. But you were there, weren't you? Did you start that fire?"

Silence.

I hated being stonewalled. Seriously. I had no time for bullshit from anyone. I motioned for a nursing tech and requested a wheelchair. "You and I are taking a little ride."

We got him loaded in the chair and I wheeled him out of the ER, heading to the elevators. I pushed the button to the fifth floor—pediatrics. Where Sara and Lily Grace were recovering.

He hunched down in full sulky mode. Note: what I was doing wasn't exactly HIPAA-compliant, but I didn't care. Lives were at stake, and we couldn't afford any more of his stupidity.

"Where are you taking me?" he muttered.

"To see someone."

I wheeled him out the doors and down the hall, stopping just outside of Lily Grace's door. She lay in bed, her head tilted to the side, sleeping. Her mom sat beside her, gripping her hand.

"Who's that?" he asked.

"That is the girl who was being kept in a room beside the lab you burned down. Don't deny it. Your clothes smell exactly like hers."

His mouth dropped open, then quickly closed. "I . . . I didn't know anyone was there."

"She's sixteen, Rus. Sixteen! She's never done a drug in her life. Didn't know she was right beside a fentanyl lab. She almost died!"

He leaned back, closing his eyes. I could feel the guilt radiating from him.

I stooped down. "Look. I know you didn't want to hurt anybody, but you could have. And I know there was another fentanyl lab that burned a week or so ago. That was you, too, wasn't it?"

He pointed to Lily Grace. "Will she be okay?"

"She's being treated for smoke inhalation, but we think she'll be okay."

"Thank God."

"Now. Tell me the truth."

He glanced down at his arm. "If I do, will you go to the police?"

I shook my head. "That's not my place. But I think you should."

"I just wanted it to stop," he whispered. "First Tanner. Then Dulce. How many others? How many have to die, Georgia?"

"I get it. I feel the same way—but starting fires is not the way to end this. You know they just start up again somewhere else."

Elevator doors dinged open, and two people arrived on the floor: Sara's parents. I glanced up at them and nodded. Rus grabbed my arm, his grip vise-like, nearly bruising me.

"Get me out of here." His voice was an urgent whisper.

"Okay, sure." I detached my arm from his death grip and moved behind the wheelchair. I started to head toward the elevator.

"Not that way! Take me down the hall."

"Rus? Calm down." I did as he asked, taking him down the hall and around the nurse's station. When I pushed him into a small waiting area, I heard him exhale.

"Thanks."

"What's wrong? What panicked you?" I stooped down again, noting moisture in his eyes.

"It's nothing."

"I don't believe you. You totally flipped out. Why?" I kept my gaze on him, trying to figure out what upset him about the Clarks' arrival. "Did you know that couple?"

"No. At first, I thought I recognized them, but I was wrong." He bent over, good arm clutching his stomach. "I really don't feel too good, Georgia."

I felt his head. "Jeez. You're burning up. Let's get you back to the ER."

Sixty-Four

TESSA WASN'T ON THE LIST FOR APPROVED VISITORS, THE ANNOYING officer outside of Lily Grace's hospital room explained.

"My mom—my sorta mom—works here. She'll vouch for me," Tessa argued, but that got her nowhere. She thought about trying to sneak by the woman, but she had a gun and seemed to take her job very seriously. Tessa almost gave up. Then the door opened, and Mrs. Duffy emerged.

"Tessa! How great to see you!" Mrs. Duffy used a walker to shuffle into the hall. She wore a blue sweat suit and sneakers, her hair pulled back in a ponytail. Her face had more color than the last time Tessa saw her, that awful evening when Lily Grace was still missing.

"I came to see Lily Grace, but they won't let me in."

Mrs. Duffy turned to the officer. "She's okay. Let Tessa come anytime. I think Lily Grace will be happy to see her. I'm just heading down to cardiac rehab for my session. So you have a half hour at least."

Tessa smiled at the annoying officer as she slipped by.

Lily Grace lay in bed staring at something on the television. Her hair looked damp, as if she'd just been in the shower, her skin pink. An oxygen cannula rested under her nose. When she saw Tessa, she smiled. "How are you?"

"Me? I'm fine. You're the one who's in the hospital. How ya feeling?"

"Bored. A little sore." She sounded hoarse. She pointed to the tube pressed into her nose. "I have to keep wearing this thing. It's helping my lungs heal."

"Very cool." Tessa pulled up a chair and sat. "I saw your mom. She looks good."

"She's like a new person! She's exercising and on some fancy diet. She's crazy about your foster mom, by the way. Says 'Ms. Georgia is a very smart woman.'"

"She is. Much smarter than me."

"I don't know about that. You're one of the smartest kids in the school."

Tessa shook her head. "If I was so smart, I would have figured out that you needed me when you came to the restaurant that day. I shouldn't have blown you off. I'm sorry I did that."

"You were very busy. I shouldn't have come to your work, anyway. And you told me to find Detective Michaels, which is what I tried to do." She looked down at her hands resting on the sheets.

"And some stranger pretended to be him. And practically kidnapped you." Tessa couldn't believe it when Georgia told her what had happened. Lily Grace could have been murdered. She could have burned to death.

"He was mostly nice to me. I mean, he could be gruff, and sometimes he was in a bad mood, but he brought me books and a heater. I thought he was keeping me safe."

"Maybe he was."

Why else was he hiding her? The whole thing confused Tessa, but at least Lily Grace was alive and protected.

Someone rapped on the door, and it opened. The lanky man introduced himself as Detective Jackson Purdy. "I just have a few more questions for Lily Grace. Can you give us a few minutes?"

Lily Grace lifted a hand. "No, let her stay. Please. I haven't seen any friends in so long. I don't care if she hears what we discuss."

Tessa looked at the detective, eyebrows quirked.

"Okay. This shouldn't take long." He held a folder. When he approached the bed, he removed a photograph. "We took these pictures in a room beside a drug lab that exploded. Is this where the fake detective kept you?"

Lily Grace studied the photo, running a finger across what looked like a charred mattress. "I slept here. And the table was here." She pointed to a burnt hunk of wood. "Yes. This is where I was. You say there was a drug lab?"

"Yes. They were manufacturing fentanyl to distribute in the Midlands."

"Fentanyl. That's really bad stuff," Lily Grace said.

"Yes, it is," Tessa answered. "It's what Sara took at the party. By accident."

"And Joel?" Lily Grace asked.

Tessa nodded. "And Ariel."

Lily Grace sat back, taking it in. "I heard a man in there. He would play really loud music. K-pop, I think. But not BTS. Nothing good. The detective didn't like him much. Was he killed in the fire?"

Detective Purdy shook his head. "No victims inside. Except you."

"Was the fire an accident?" Lily Grace asked.

"No. We think it was set on purpose." He pulled out another picture—this one was a drawing. "Thanks for meeting with our sketch artist. This was the man who kept you, correct?"

She took the picture. "Yes. I wonder what his real name is."

Tessa leaned over to look more closely. The man had a shaved head and a thick nose. A scar tracked down his right cheek, as though he'd been slashed by a machete. He looked tough. Brutal, even. The kind of man that if she encountered him on the street, she'd want to cross over.

"There's something else. Fletcher Hawthorne brought Cooper to the police station this morning. Cooper has confessed to hitting Sara. He'll be charged today. Cooper says he hid the truth from everyone, including his family, but came forward out of guilt. Interesting timing, given that the one witness—you, Lily Grace—has finally come to light."

"Hiding what really happened wasn't Cooper's idea. It was his dad's. I was there. I'm sure of it." Lily Grace looked at Tessa, confused.

The detective said, "One more thing. When you went to the police station and asked for Lou Michaels—did you remember the name of the officer who took your statement?"

"No. I don't think he said it."

"Did you tell him about Mr. Hawthorne arriving at the scene?" Lou asked.

"No. I just told him about Cooper. I'm pretty sure, anyway," Lily Grace answered.

"Can you describe that officer?"

"He was nice. Bald, but his head was pinker than the other Lou Michaels. Not big, maybe a few inches taller than me. And his front tooth was chipped." She pointed to the right front tooth.

"That's good detail. And this was at the Shandon substation?"

"Yeah."

Tessa started to put two and two together. "Did that officer arrange for the fake Lou Michaels to take Lily Grace? Why would he do that? Was he working for Mr. Hawthorne?"

Detective Purdy's smile was evasive. "We're still trying to figure all that out. I have one more picture for you." He pulled out what looked like a mugshot: an Asian-looking man with a sparse mustache and short, bristly black hair. "Have you ever seen him?"

"No. Who is he?"

"Minjun Kim. Only he has a bunch of aliases. He's been tied up in fentanyl manufacturing and distribution throughout the Southeast. We pulled his fingerprints at the burnt lab."

"The guy who played the music so loud!" Lily Grace exclaimed.

"We're looking for him. And for the fake detective. And for the man we think is their boss. Until we find them, you stick to the script, okay? The important thing, Lily Grace, is keeping you safe."

She shot him a pensive look. "Funny thing. That's pretty much what the fake Lou Michaels said."

***

Tessa finished the text with Joel, arranging to meet for lunch the following day. He'd mostly recovered from, well, everything. His arm was better. The twisted look of fear and dread had left his face, now that his future had been restored, when Cooper took the blame for hitting Sara.

"Tessa? Can I come in?"

"Yeah."

Georgia entered and took a seat at the foot of her bed. "Texting with Joel?"

"Yep."

"He's okay?"

"Getting there." The betrayal Joel felt, though, would stay with him for a long time. Cooper had almost let him go to prison over something Cooper had done.

"He's a good kid." She wasn't making eye contact. Something was up.

"What's going on?" Tessa asked.

Her hand smoothed the expanse of bedspread between them. "You know I've loved having you here, right?"

Tessa nodded. Swallowed.

"You're the best thing that could have happened to me after I lost Peyton. I care so much about you."

"Same." She swallowed again.

"I try to be honest with you. But I haven't been lately. I've . . . the voices have come back. They're not bad. And I'm managing them. But they are there."

"I'm sorry." Tessa couldn't imagine what it must have been like to live with that noise in her head. Yet Georgia managed them. Managed them and a really brutal job and lots of other chaos.

"Lana has asked me a lot of questions about my mental health issues. She doesn't think I'm the right placement for you."

"She's wrong." Tessa spoke with as much emphasis as she could.

Georgia offered a small, sad smile. "That's what I thought. But I've been looking into the place at Rock Hill that she suggested for you. It looks incredible. Beautiful setting. Highly skilled therapists. State-of-the-art treatment modalities."

Tessa fought to hold back her tears.

Georgia reached for her hand. "If you go there, I will come to visit you as often as they will let me. More often, really, because I don't follow the rules if they keep me away from my family."

The tears dribbled down Tessa's face. Georgia handed her a tissue.

"I don't want this, either," Georgia said. "Not for me. But if it's what's best for you, and Lana thinks it is, then maybe it's what needs to happen."

Tessa blew her nose into the tissue. "Are you sure?"

"Am I sure what?"

"That it's not what you want or need? That I'm not the reason that your voices came back?"

Georgia huffed out a little laugh. "No. You are absolutely not what brought them back. It's just how my mental illness works, according to Lenore. I'll likely have them off and on for the rest of my life. But mostly, they are much better than before. They don't have control over me. You have no reason to feel guilty, Tessa."

"Then I have no reason to leave here. To leave you."

Georgia squeezed her hand. "That's exactly what I thought at first. But the place in Rock Hill was designed for people like you. It may be just what you need to fully recover and get on with your life."

Tessa pulled away. She swiped the tissue across her eyes and cleared her throat. She knew two things for certain. One: Georgia wanted what was best for her, even if it meant losing something she loved—their life together. Two: Georgia was wrong.

"Tessa? You okay?"

"Yeah. Except here's the thing. I don't care if Rock Hill has a hundred therapists and gold-plated toilets. I don't care if Ryan Gosling is the cook there. There is no way that going there will be better for me than staying here with you. You will never convince me that it is. And if Lana Montgomery tries to move me against my will, she's gonna regret it."

"What does that mean?"

"It means . . . it means I'm staying here, Georgia. If you'll have me."

Georgia studied her for a long moment. Tessa met her gaze with all the stubborn resolve she could muster.

"Okay then," Georgia finally said. "You and me, we're gonna fight Lana."

"And we'll win."

"We will."

But Georgia didn't sound convinced.

It didn't matter.

Tessa had a plan.

Sixty-Five

SAUL SAT ACROSS FROM MARCUS IN A SMALL, UNOCCUPIED COURTYARD behind Marcus's favorite cafe. Saul was ready to face the music. Marcus surely knew about Lily Grace. He probably had a hit out on him. That Marcus wanted to meet had been a surprise.

Marcus pulled out an e-cigarette and puffed. The vapors smelled of mint and weed. Ballsy for here in South Carolina, but that was Marcus for you.

"We have a new site for our operation. Boris is getting it set up. The pill press is going to be a problem. DEA is monitoring sales of the commercial ones."

"That's never stopped you before."

Marcus smiled his shark smile. "True. We can't buy, we take. Easy enough."

Saul wondered if he could get away. Flee. But where could he go that was out of Marcus's reach? He had connections all over the country. Marcus would put a hefty bounty on Saul's head and that would be that. His only hope was to leave the US, but to do that, he'd need a passport and visa, both of which burned in the fire.

Marcus puffed again, sending the vapor into a cool autumn breeze. The sky above was a milky gray, hinting that rain would come. Saul used to love the rain. Thought it was cleansing. He was beyond cleansing now.

Why wasn't Marcus confronting him about not killing Lily Grace? Was he playing Saul? A cat toying with the mouse before digging his teeth in?

"I've been reading about some new laws they're passing about fentanyl. Dealers can get charged with murder now, boss," Saul said.

Another puff. "It is nice that you worry about me. But no need."

Saul tried to understand Marcus's tone. It sounded off. Drier than usual.

Marcus dismantled the e-cigarette, placing it carefully in a leather case. "Do you get why I haven't included you in the plans for the new lab? Because I can't trust you."

Here it comes. Saul stiffened.

"You cling to some ridiculous moral code. It's absurd, really, given what you do for me."

"Boss—"

"No, you don't want kids to get hurt. This is why you saved that girl who witnessed the Hawthorne accident. Why you didn't kill her, like I'd instructed you to." He spoke quietly, a deadly timbre in his voice.

Saul felt the noose tightening. He wondered if the hit had already been ordered. If he was in someone's rifle sights right now.

"Where did you keep the girl? Where did you have her stashed?" Marcus demanded. "Your apartment? Have a cozy little one-on-one with the kid?"

"No. Jesus." Saul could barely breathe. "She was in a room beside the lab."

Marcus stood and stepped closer. "What does she know? Did she see me come to the lab? Boris? What does she know about my operation?"

"Nothing! I swear, boss, she doesn't know anything."

"If only I could believe you. No matter. She'll be taken care of." Marcus stood, bumping the table. The noise must have been some kind of signal, because suddenly, two men appeared through the bistro's service door. One stood six-five, broad-chested, dressed in tactical gear as though engaged in war games. The other was dressed in solid black, like Saul always did, with a luger strapped in a shoulder holster. The Shadows. Marcus's assassins.

Saul scanned the iron fence surrounding the courtyard. No way he could scale it before they got their hands on him. They probably wouldn't shoot him right here—not so close to Main Street. Marcus nodded at the two men and made his exit.

Marcus wasn't one to get his hands dirty.

Saul strategized. The men flanked him. A hand gripped his right arm, tight. They shuffled him toward the gate that was always locked, only now it wasn't. Saul could see an alley, a dumpster, and beyond, a black van.

They would not get him in that van.

Small steps. Fingers like pliers digging into his flesh, shoving him forward. Shadow One pulled out a revolver and pressed it into Saul's ribs.

"Not a sound," the man growled.

Saul had always been a man of few words. Shadow Two, the one in sleek black, stepped ahead and pulled a set of keys from his pocket. Getting closer. Time to act.

A sweep with his right leg caught Shadow One by surprise. An elbow smacked against his chin sent him tumbling to the ground. Shadow Two spun around, gun at the ready. Saul grabbed the barrel, directing it down and twisting. He could almost hear the man's fingers breaking. Shadow One had his weapon out as he scrambled up, but a swift Muay Thai push-kick to his chest cracked a few ribs and had him rethinking the whole "I should get up" thing. Shadow Two barreled against Saul, pain enraging him, the gun held awkwardly in his other hand. An arm pressed against Saul's neck, and cold metal slammed into his chest.

Saul did a swing kick and smashed an elbow against the man's jaw. Both Shadows lay on the ground, but regrouping. Saul grabbed the weapons he could see and took off running. He'd had no time to frisk them. Chances were, other guns hid in ankle holsters.

So he ran. Zig-zag pattern. Fast. His ultra-fit body doing its job. Praying he'd outrun the bullets pelting all around him.

Sixty-Six

RUS HAD A LOT TO THINK ABOUT. HE NEVER EXPECTED TO CONFRONT his old life. He'd had good reason to leave it behind. It was best for everyone involved, especially his family.

But Sara. She was almost grown now. Almost dead, thanks to Cooper Hawthorne. His baby sister.

He had to get a closer look. Did she still have that pale blonde hair? Those wide, inquisitive eyes? Did she love mac and cheese more than any other food and refuse to even look at broccoli or brussels sprouts?

But seeing her would mean revealing himself. Exposing the big lie that he wasn't dead. Rus couldn't afford that. Still, he found himself riding the elevator again, gripping the IV pole that fed antibiotics and fluid into his arm, dressed in a hospital gown that hung on his bony physique. He wondered if he'd even be recognizable now. He looked nothing like Max. He wasn't well-muscled anymore. His brown hair, once styled short, hung limp to his shoulders, and the beard he wore hid much of his face. His brown eyes were more sunken than before. He was eight years older, yet so much more.

He kept his head down as he approached Sara's room. No voices sounded inside. Maybe she was sleeping. Maybe she was having good dreams as her body healed from all its trauma.

One of the hardest things about disappearing had been leaving her. She didn't need to witness his decline as the drugs took greater hold. He stopped letting himself care about his family. There was no room for them as his love affair with drugs claimed him.

She was a possessive lover. Even knowing his use would kill him didn't stop him. Nothing could. His parents' pathetic attempts at forcing him into rehab certainly hadn't: the first place had a dealer on staff. The second place, the religious one, had been so easy to escape he wanted to write a letter of complaint. The third and fourth—well, he'd become highly skilled at recovery language bullshit. Earn a little trust, they grant you privileges, and then you flee.

Dad spent a fortune trying to help him, not accepting that he wanted no help. Mom wept with each admission, and when he wasn't high, it stabbed him in the heart.

Pretending to die became the best option. It hadn't been hard. A goodbye note. A pair of shoes left on a bridge. A few joints to a user who claimed to have witnessed the jump. Death had been miraculously freeing. No worries that another investigator would snatch him from the streets and plop him into a hospital. No, he lived like he'd wanted. Sleeping under a pier. Odd jobs to pay for drugs. Sometimes selling himself when desperate. He was so numb he didn't even care.

Until that one morning when he woke up on the beach. His vomit stank in a sandy mess beside him. A seagull pecked at his jacket as though he was carrion. Every bit of him hurt. When he tried to stand, he fell over and realized he'd been beaten during the night. He wondered who. And why.

He stumbled down to the water and washed his face in the briny cold surf. A wave of dizziness made him drop down in the wet sand. The seagull approached again, but didn't peck, just studied him like he was a meal that hadn't yet been cooked. That was the moment. His bottom. It hit him like a lightning bolt: he could change, or he would die. Which would it be?

He found a public bathroom and washed up as best he could. He drank from the sink—big gulps that did little to sate his thirst. He ran a hand through his dirty hair, drew a deep breath, and took his first step into the brutal, hard road of recovery.

The dinging of the elevator startled him—he'd been so lost in those complicated memories he'd almost forgotten where he was. He stepped into a small waiting area as a man stepped off the elevator.

Not just a man, but THE man. Him. Fletcher Hawthorne. Rus flattened himself against a wall as Fletcher pounded up the hall like a bull. A ringing cell phone halted his steps; Fletcher stood outside of Sara's room to take the call.

The sound of his voice hit him like ice. Early on, it had been a soothing sound. Comforting. Fletcher was Santa Claus, granting his every wish. But then came the touch. The need. "Take this. It will relax you," Fletcher had said, and Rus swallowed. The peace that spread over him made nothing unforgivable, and Fletcher took advantage.

"There's my beautiful boy," he'd whisper.

But the voice he used on his cell had a different tone: insistent. Commanding.

"I need this bill to pass. And once I'm elected, you're going to need my support. Make it happen."

Right. Fletcher Hawthorne was running for office—attorney general or something like that. Just what South Carolina needed: a predator in the highest legal office.

Fletcher hung up the phone, smoothed down his hair, and entered Sara's room.

Rus wanted to stop him. Wanted to hurl his body in front of the door, then knee Fletcher in his favorite body part, but instead found himself frozen. What did Fletcher want with Sara?

He could feel his heart pounding like a jackhammer. He eyed the nurse's station where Georgia Thayer had just arrived. Good. He could have Georgia go check on his sister.

But then a scream erupted from her room. Shit. He grabbed the pole and started to move but terror and physical pain staggered his steps. Suddenly, Georgia blew past him and pushed through the door to Sara's room. A moment later, Fletcher came blustering out, red-faced and sweaty. He hurried to the elevator to make his exit.

Had he laid a hand on Sara? Had he touched Rus's sister while Rus stood outside the room, too petrified to move? He'd never felt so impotent.

Sara's door opened, and Georgia summoned a nurse. When she spotted Rus, she pointed a finger, mouthing, "Wait here." No problem. Rus wasn't budging until he knew Sara was okay. Time passed slowly, though. He watched a hall clock tick the minutes by.

Finally, Georgia emerged and approached him. "Rus? What are you doing back here?"

"Did he hurt her?"

"No. She's just upset. She couldn't tell us why—they gave her a sedative." She stepped closer, assessing him. "You okay? You look pale. Should I get a nurse? What are you doing up here?"

Her questions bombarded him. He wanted her to go away.

"Rus? What the hell is going on?" More insistent now.

He owed her no answers. He needed to see his sister. He gathered his strength and began his approach to her room.

"Stop right there," she demanded. "I swear, if you don't talk to me, I'm calling security."

He froze. Two aides at the nurse's station came around a counter, watching. He felt trapped.

"Come with me."

She led him to a small, locked waiting area, which she opened with her name badge. It held a loveseat, two chairs, and a table. A coffee machine hadn't been turned on. Georgia switched on the light and motioned him to a chair, then sat across from him, all business. She could be formidable.

"Okay. I find you on the fifth floor pediatric unit, where you aren't supposed to be. You won't tell me why you're here. You're acting weird, like you were when I brought you up earlier. Tell me what is going on, and I mean it."

He stared at her, trapped. The rickety scaffolding holding up his wretched life trembled beneath him. But more than anything, he needed answers.

He cleared his throat. Forced the words to come. "How is she? How's Sara?"

"Sara?" She shook her head. "I can't disclose her status. Only to family."

"She screamed. Is she okay? Please?"

"Rus—"

"You said only to family." The scaffolding crumbled. He could feel himself falling. "What if . . . what if I'm family?"

"What do you mean, you're family?"

Could he trust her? The past few years had made it difficult to rely on anyone, but Georgia had always been straight with him. And she might be able to help. He was so desperate for answers.

"What I tell you . . . you have to keep confidential, right? I mean, you're a social worker."

"That's mostly right."

"Mostly?"

"If I sense that you're in danger or others are in danger, then I'm obligated to tell someone. But other than that, we can keep what you say between us."

Rus breathed in the cold hospital air. The Serenity Prayer filled his mind . . . *accept the things you cannot change, change the things you can, wisdom to know the difference.* He sucked at the "wisdom" part.

"Rus?"

"When we were up here before—a couple came out of the elevator. I know them. The Clarks." Memories emerged: baseball games with parents cheering, boring Sunday dinners with the "good china" and sterling that the maids had meticulously polished the Friday before. The day they brought home the little girl with the giant eyes who melted his heart.

"How do you know the Clarks?" Georgia asked.

Rus braced himself before uttering the brutal truth. "They're my parents." He gave her a moment, letting that sink in. She kept glaring at him, something strange moving behind her eyes.

Finally, she spoke. "Rus, are you Max?"

He dropped his head. "How did you know my name?"

"Your mother told me about the son she'd lost. Almost losing Sara brought it all back."

"Sara? Please, I have to know how she is."

"She's had a tough time. She was hit by a car coming from the Hawthornes' house. She's had two surgeries, but miraculously, she survived them both. And she's getting stronger."

"Cooper Hawthorne hit her with his car," Rus clarified.

"Yes, he did. An accident. But I'm cautiously optimistic." She tilted her head, studying him.

"But just now—she screamed."

"Something—someone—upset her. But they gave her something to settle her down. She's fine." She crossed her arms. "I'm still wrapping my head around this. Your mom's talked about you, Max. A lot. She—everybody—thinks you're dead. She's grieving. Your whole family is."

"It was the only answer."

"What was?"

"I had to disappear."

She crossed her arms and said, "I think I need more detail."

"My name is Rus. Short for Lazarus, because I rose from the grave." He paused. Saying it aloud felt so strange. He told her all of it, the words pouring out. A geyser of his truths. She said nothing, just listened.

She seemed very good at listening.

When he finished, when his life lay sprawled out between them, she let out a guttural, "Wow. Where have you been all this time?"

"The beach mostly. Then I met Tanner, and he wanted to connect with family. So we came back to Columbia. I worried at first someone would notice me, but I'm so different now."

Georgia nodded slowly, taking it all in. "What now, Rus? I mean, Max? Your family—God, it would be so wonderful for them to know you're alive."

He shook his head. "No. I can't. Too much has happened. I'm not Max anymore. I'm not who they lost."

"Maybe not. But I'll tell you this—the man you are? The man who clawed his way into recovery? He's someone they can be very proud of."

Tears pricked his eyes.

If only that were true.

Sixty-Seven

I STOPPED BY THE HOSPITAL, SOMETHING I TRIED NOT TO DO ON SATUR-days. I wanted to check on Rus—Max. After what he'd disclosed to me, I hoped he'd consider telling his family. And I needed to see Tessa. She'd been at the hospital much of the day, dividing her time between Sara and Lily Grace. I was proud of her for that. I loved that she was beginning to develop some friendships with kids her own age. Both girls, Sara and Lily Grace, needed a friend like Tessa.

My plan was to snag my kid and take her to the bistro for an early dinner, but a nurse at the elevator halted me. She had bad news.

"That girl—Dulce? She pulled an AMA," she told me.

"What? When?"

"Disappeared sometime last night. Stole some scrubs and a bag lunch from one of the techs before vanishing. I had security look for her, but no luck. Sorry, Georgia."

I closed my eyes. Stupid Dulce. No, that wasn't fair. She was doing what her instinct told her to do: returning to the streets. But would she survive there? Would she be the next body rolled in?

Sometimes, it felt impossible to win the war.

I took the elevator to check Lily Grace's room first. Lily Grace would likely be discharged tomorrow—she had been weaned off the oxygen and was doing great. Another thing to discuss with Detective Purdy: continued police protection for her home.

I pushed into a crowded elevator full of Saturday visitors holding flowers and stuffed animals. Someone was wearing way too much cologne, and I hoped they weren't visiting anyone with respiratory issues.

285

A little girl asked me what floor, and I said, "five," smiling as she proudly pushed the correct button. It made me think of my little niece, Lindsay, always had to be the button-pusher. I couldn't wait for her to return from her trip with her father. She was all I had left of Peyton, besides the comforting presence of her voice in my head.

The door dinged open, and I exited, stopping to assess the floor, something I did automatically. Nobody staffed the nurse's station, but that wasn't unusual. They were probably on rounds. I could see the door to Lily Grace's room. An empty chair outside of it. The chair where a police officer should be sitting.

A tingle of anxiety rose in me. I hurried to the door, which hung partly open, and I spotted a shoe. Black. Attached to a dark blue leg.

The police officer lay sprawled on the floor.

Male voices whispered inside Lily Grace's room. Crap. Was Tessa in there? Lily Grace? Were they okay? I wanted to storm in, but I needed help. I rushed to the nurse's station, pounded a Code Orange alarm (intruder alert) into the computer, and prayed security would arrive faster than they usually did.

Waiting wasn't an option, so I crept toward Lily Grace's room.

The elevator opened again. Two girls emerged, laughing: Lily Grace and my Tessa. Thank God.

I hurried to them, my arms scooping around them and herding them back toward the elevator. Just as the doors closed us out.

"Crap."

"Georgia? What's wrong?" Tessa asked.

"I'm not sure. But you aren't safe." I directed this to Lily Grace.

Where should we go? I eyed the door to the stairs, but Lily Grace would not be strong enough for five flights.

A man came hurrying down the corridor: tall, wide, with a shaved head and strange scars across a grizzled face. Scary-looking. I half-expected him to join whoever was in Lily Grace's room, but he hesitated in the doorway, frowning at whoever was inside, then glanced up the hall. His gaze fixed on us.

On Lily Grace.

His long stride brought him to us in a few seconds. I pushed the girls behind me, alert, but Lily Grace came around and said, "It's okay. He's Detective Michaels. My version."

"We've gotta get you out of here." He shoved all three of us toward the door leading to the stairs.

I froze. This guy was a fraud. He'd held Lily Grace hostage. And judging from the bulge under his leather jacket, he was armed.

"Who the hell are you? Really?" I demanded.

"I'm the guy trying to save your life." He looked us over, then placed a hand on Lily Grace's forehead. "You okay?" he asked her, his tone gentler.

She nodded.

"She's weak," I said.

"That's no problem." He swept her up in his arms and commanded us to follow him down the stairs.

You can trust him, Peyton whispered.

Unsure of what our options were, I complied. We'd descended three flights when we heard a door above us squeak open. Fake Lou Michaels shushed us, positioning himself to look up the stairs. He held up three fingers.

Three men.

"Hurry!" he whispered.

We pounded down the metal steps, Tessa's hand gripped in mine. I wasn't sure where we were going. I thought about bursting through the doors to the first floor, thinking a crowded lobby would dissuade the assailants, but then I realized the men might shoot up the place. We couldn't afford more innocent victims.

Fake Lou kept us moving until we reached the basement. He led us through the metal door, down a short hallway, and out into the underground parking garage. I didn't like it—this place was dark and somewhat isolated. How would security know where to find us? He lowered Lily Grace and scanned the structure with vigilant eyes. I wanted to grab both girls and run like hell, but I could hear footsteps pounding behind us.

We both checked the cars around us. An elderly couple emerged from an SUV.

"Get back in that car!" I screamed.

They looked confused, but complied.

Fake Lou guided us past a dozen cars, then opened the door to a black jeep. He tossed me the keys. "Get them away from here."

"What about you?"

He pointed to the three men bursting into the garage. Guns. Handguns with what I imagined were silencers.

I pictured Lou Michaels crumpled over his steering wheel. Were these the men who shot him? I couldn't afford to let my terror keep me from doing my one singular job: get these girls to safety. I pressed my hand against Tessa's neck and guided her to the back of the jeep. Lily Grace looked terrified, but didn't struggle when I shoved her in after Tessa. I scurried around to the driver's seat and started the jeep.

"Down!" I yelled to them. "Stay on the floor!"

Gunfire echoed through the garage structure like a firework display gone amok. The sheer volume made me jump. I headed toward the entrance, spotting Fake Lou, gun drawn, blasting at the men whose guns fired at our jeep. Shit.

"Stay down, girls!"

I tried maneuvering toward the exit as a bullet hit the windshield. It was almost impossible to see through the webbed glass. Then the car pulled hard to the right. I tried to straighten it, but it moved of its own volition. We clipped a Camry and spun around, colliding with a pickup. Tire blowout, I realized. They'd shot the tire.

Stay calm, Peyton's voice insisted. *You can do this.*

Nothing to do but try to keep the girls safe. I clambered over the seat and pressed my body over them. "Shhh," I whispered. "Be still."

I could hear a quiet whimpering—from Lily Grace. Tessa lay still as a stone, but I could feel her breathing.

Don't move, Peyton cautioned.

More bursts from a gun, then . . .

"Sirens," Tessa whispered.

"Yes. But stay still till we know it's safe."

I craned my neck to check out the window. I counted three men sprawled like marionettes with cut strings. All in black. Was Fake Lou one of them?

No. Fake Lou loomed over them, kicking weapons out of the way. Okay. We were probably safe. He turned toward the jeep, took three faltering steps, then slid to the concrete floor.

I grabbed my phone and called for a gurney and a medical team. They wouldn't enter till the garage was deemed safe, but I wanted them nearby. I commanded the girls to stay put, opened the car door, and made my way to him.

He'd been hit in the side. I had no way of knowing how severe it was, but I've seen plenty of gunshots in my work, and any torso wound bled like crazy. I pressed a hand against it.

A metal door scraped open. Another assailant? Shit. We were sitting ducks.

But the figure that made its way to us wore scrubs and slippers. He held a gun with surprising steadiness. "Lou?"

He hurried to me, looking me up and down. "You okay, George?"

I nodded.

"Girls?" he asked.

"They're in the jeep. You shouldn't be here."

The bleeding man stared up at him. I asked him, "Who are you? Really?"

"Call me Saul."

"Another fake name?"

"The only one I use now," he answered.

Three police cars swerved into the garage, the sirens deafening. I stood as officers approached, guns drawn. Note: it's scary as hell to have five weapons aimed at you, knowing each of the officers was probably hyped up on adrenaline, but when Lou ordered them to "Stand down," they complied.

"Those three men are who you want!" I pointed at the three downed assailants.

An officer spoke into her radio as others tended to their suspects. I motioned for the medical team, who burst through the door.

"Girls! It's okay!" I yelled. "But stay on the other side of the car until I tell you otherwise."

They obeyed. I didn't want them to see the bodies. Or the blood. Or the doctors assessing Saul's wounds. Once they loaded him on a gurney, I hurried over to them.

Tessa grabbed me, hugging me tight. "Hey, hey. It's okay. We're okay," I whispered. Lou approached, and Tessa released me to attach herself to him. "Easy there. He's still on the mend," I reminded her.

"Is my Detective Michaels okay?" Lily Grace frowned at the gurney being wheeled away.

"His name is Saul, Lily Grace. And our doctors are working with him now. He was conscious and alert."

"That's good, right?" She looked at me with wide, expectant eyes.

"I think so." I didn't say that shock could make people act strangely, that he might be dying and I wouldn't know. I hoped not. He mattered to Lily Grace, and he had the answers we all needed.

Lou Michaels barked out orders to the other officers and used a radio from one of the cars to request additional support. I remained with the girls, taking it all in. Finally, he approached.

"We'll need to question all of you, but we can do that inside."

I nodded.

He stepped closer, peering into my eyes. "Are you okay, George? I mean, really?"

I placed an arm around each kid. "I am now. You, however, are still a gunshot patient. How did you get here?"

"I heard the intruder alert. Went to check on Lily Grace and found the downed officer. Grabbed his gun, then I followed the noise."

I studied his too-pale face. The red streaks on his arm from where he'd removed an IV. "I want a doctor to check you out."

He smiled, reached over, and touched my cheek. I leaned into his hand. "You did good. You saved the girls."

"It wasn't me. It was him." I pointed to the gurney passing through the elevator doors. Saul. Our savior.

Who was also Lily Grace's kidnapper.

Sixty-Eight

RUS WISHED HE COULD TAKE STRONGER PAINKILLERS. NOT JUST FOR his arm, but for his heart. A wound had opened there that he'd worked so hard to keep closed. But now, the past had slammed into the present. His baby sister recovered five floors above him. His parents—who thought he was dead—waited anxiously for her to get well.

Part of him wanted to run. To untether himself from the tubes and needles, find his nasty clothes, and flee. To ride Tanner's motorcycle back to the life he'd created. To be Rus again.

But what Georgia had said stayed with him. His parents grieved him. Sara needed him. He'd caused them more pain than he'd ever imagined.

It had never occurred to him before that his escape had been selfish.

A gentle rap on the door sounded before it opened, and Georgia returned. She came to his bed and sat beside him.

"Rus? Max? Which shall I call you?"

Leave it to Georgia to distill his situation into a simple sentence. He cleared his throat. "I guess I'd better be Max. For now."

She smiled. "That's a big step."

"No promises for after today."

"I wouldn't expect any." She gave him a soft smile. "Sara is awake. I think seeing you would be the best medicine she could get."

He nodded. "My parents?"

"They're meeting with the hospital CEO. That could take a while." She patted the mattress. "Wanna go see your sister?"

The journey to the fifth floor took forever. Yet also happened far too fast. His thoughts and feelings all in a jumble. Georgia pushed the IV

291

pole beside him as they traversed the hall. Was this a mistake? He froze at her door.

"Max? You okay?"

He could see Sara sitting up in the bed, her hair a darker brown than when she was younger. Her skin was the same porcelain white. How tall was she? Did she still love swimming and softball? He had a zillion questions.

Georgia opened the door. Sara's gaze shot to them, her familiar brown eyes registering confusion. Max took two hesitant steps forward and froze again. He couldn't speak.

"How about I do the talking?" Georgia asked him. He nodded.

Georgia spoke softly, gently, to his sister. Sara's eyes never left his face. So expressive, those eyes. Disbelief. Denial. Then, absolute wonder. When Georgia had finished, Sara extended a hand.

Max hurried to her, took that delicate hand, remembered a smaller one he held to walk her to the park. She'd been a light in his childhood from the moment his parents brought her home.

"I'm sorry," was all he could think to say.

"Don't apologize. You're alive." She squeezed his hand.

Georgia excused herself, leaving them alone. There was so much to say, but no words to say it. So he held her hand, answered questions when they arose, and felt love resurface from some long-neglected place inside him. Sara was a miracle. A beautiful, brilliant miracle.

His baby sister.

A half hour later, Georgia returned. "Your parents are on their way."

He stiffened, the urge to flee grabbing hold.

"Don't go," Sara whispered. "Everything's different now. You don't need to run away anymore."

He looked at Georgia, who asked, "Well?"

"Guess I need to see them."

"You're very brave, Max," she said. "They're lucky you're their son."

Sixty-Nine

TESSA TOOK THE BUS DOWNTOWN, EXITED ON BULL STREET, AND followed the Google map on her phone to the building that housed the Department of Social Services. It wasn't attractive. Off-white. Dated. Sad attempts at wilting landscaping surrounding it. Cracked sidewalks leading to the glass front door.

A security guard stopped her. He sat behind a glass enclosure, a metal detector between her and the hallway leading to an elevator. "Can I help you?" he asked.

"I need to meet with the director."

The guard looked bored. "Which director?"

Tessa cleared her throat. "The . . . the main one. The guy who runs this agency."

"Dr. Marshall runs this agency. Do you have an appointment?"

"No. But I just need a minute. And I can wait."

He scratched his chin where gray stubble grew. "You'll be waiting a while. Dr. Marshall is out of town."

Damn. She'd finally worked up the courage to come here, to demand that social services do the right thing. She'd practiced what to say and how to say it. This had to work.

"Okay. Can I meet with whoever is over foster care placements?"

He scrutinized her again. "Do you have an appointment?"

"You know I don't. Look—I'm in the system. And my caseworker is about to screw up my life if I don't stop her. Please. Let me talk to her boss."

"Who's your caseworker?" he asked.

"Lana Montgomery."

He lifted what looked like a directory and flipped through the pages. "She's on the fourth floor. I'll see if she wants to see you. Miss—"

"Tessa Dougherty. But don't bother. It's not her I want to see. It's her boss or supervisor or . . . whatever."

He ran a tongue over crooked teeth. "Wish I had a dime for every kid that came here demanding to see the boss. I'll ring Ms. Montgomery's office."

Tessa shook her head, feeling utterly defeated. She looked at the metal detector. The badge on the guard's chest. She couldn't get past him. She couldn't get to the person who might keep Lana Montgomery from ruining her life.

The guard kept glaring at her, so she turned to leave. But a large framed photo on the wall stopped her. It was of a group of important-looking people—all in suits—surrounding a gleaming conference table.

"Who are these people?" she asked the guard.

"You asked for the boss? They're the boss's boss. The Social Services Commission."

Tessa smiled.

Maybe there was someone who could help her after all.

Seventy

SAUL UNDERSTOOD SILENCE. IT BROUGHT HIM COMFORT. BEING QUIET came naturally to him. Say nothing. Assess the situation. Vigilance, always vigilance. Marcus always counted on Saul's silence, and it had kept him alive until now.

The doctor asked him questions, but he kept his responses to one or two words. "Yes," that hurt. "No," he didn't feel nauseous. "Yes" to pain medicine, which had started to kick in. He felt himself floating a little, the pain sliding away like the tide.

His arm pinched where the IV antibiotics dripped into the needle. The doctor commented on the extent of his injury. "I'm thinking this was a ricochet bullet. It had lost velocity before it hit you, so the damage isn't bad. We'll clean it up, stitch it, and keep an eye out for infection. You're pretty lucky, you know."

Lucky? If Saul were lucky, he'd have never met Marcus Landry.

Detective Lou Michaels pushed through the curtains. Saul had worn that name. The detective wore a bandage on the back of his head—a remnant of when The Shadows struck. Damn fool was lucky to be alive.

"So. I have some questions for you," the detective began.

Silence. Saul sank into his silence.

"We know you kidnapped Lily Grace. And held her captive. But then you saved her from the fire. And I suspect you called EMS to help her. Why did you kidnap her? Some kind of odd fetish for teens or something?"

Saul jerked up, ready to punch the man, but a handcuff secured him to the rail of the bed. "Shit," he uttered.

"Ah. You can speak." The detective's smile held ice. Cops, they were all alike. "But then you saved her from three assassins. Funny thing—one of them used a Tokarev pistol, just like one that fired a bullet into my head. Not thinking that was a coincidence."

The Shadows had an array of weapons, but preferred Russian ones. He didn't know who the third killer was. Saul hoped they'd all be locked up for an eternity.

"They won't give us names, by the way. The men who tried to kill me and Lily Grace. Do you know who they are?"

He shook his head. He knew no real names in Marcus's world.

"Still looking for a motive, though. Why try to kill me? Because I visited your boss, Marcus Landry? He's behind all of this, isn't he? Behind the fentanyl trade that's killing so many people?"

"There's nothing I can tell you," Saul answered.

"I find that hard to believe." A woman's voice.

Saul turned to see the woman from the parking garage come through the curtains. She'd changed tops, now wearing scrubs, her hospital badge dangling over it. She had helped him after he'd been shot. She'd pressed a hand against his wound and called for a medical team. And before, when Marcus's men were chasing them, she'd kept her cool, focusing every cell in her body on keeping the girls safe.

He was grateful for that.

"How are you feeling?" she asked him.

He shrugged. "Okay, considering."

"I'm glad to hear it. The doctor told me you were doing pretty well. The bullet passed right through. Didn't nick anything vital."

The detective asked, "Back to my original question. Why did you take Lily Grace?"

He'd already said too much. He looked up at the IV drip. Could he jerk the needles from his arm and make his escape? No, not yet. He'd let the doctor give him the happy drugs. He needed to have his senses about him when he left. And there was the small matter of the handcuff attaching him to the bed.

Saul scanned the walls, the ceiling. He wished there was a window. He'd like to see the outside.

"The room where you kept her was beside a lab that produced fentanyl," Detective Michaels said. "We've had a number of deaths that I think are tied to that operation. Some were kids wanting a high, ending up in the morgue. What do you think about that?"

Saul tamped down the rage that wanted to erupt. At the detective. At Marcus. At the greed that drove that whole brutal industry. Instead, he let his eyes flutter closed.

"Looks like he needs to rest," Georgia said.

"I need answers, George. And I know he's got them."

"Come back in an hour. Maybe he'll be more receptive."

The detective made a noise, a low rumble from the back of his throat, but then his footsteps pounded as he left. But the woman remained.

"Okay, Saul. I know you aren't asleep. And I'm not leaving this room until you talk to me." Her voice had changed—insistent. Pissed.

He opened his eyes to study this strange, assertive woman. She didn't act like someone who'd just been shot at. She seemed strong. Determined. She'd been that way when they were being chased. She never showed fear, just . . . strategized.

"Lily Grace wouldn't tell us much about you. Even when she met the real Detective Michaels. She stayed loyal to you."

Why? He'd done nothing to warrant that kind of loyalty.

"You wouldn't answer Lou's questions. He's a cop, I get it. But you're not talking to a cop now." She came closer, bending over him. "You're talking to a woman who watched her kid almost get killed." Her anger sparked a memory: Saul and his mom picking up Fatima at school. Mom finding out some kids had made fun of Fatima. Mom storming into the classroom and screaming at the teacher about how her job was to protect the vulnerable ones, like their Fatima. Mama bear, Fatima called her.

The woman went on. "Sure, you helped save us, but I'm pretty sure Tessa and Lily Grace wouldn't have been nearly killed if it wasn't for you or whatever business you're involved in. So I want answers. Now."

The way she said "now" chilled him. "I'm glad they weren't hurt," he said.

"Why did those men come after Lily Grace?" Her gaze on him felt like rifle sights.

"Because of something she witnessed," he whispered.

"Did Fletcher Hawthorne hire them? Or you?"

"No. Not directly. He knows my boss. Guess my boss owed him a favor."

"And who is your boss?" she demanded.

He looked into her eyes. Saw a sadness there, behind the strength. Thought about Marcus. About Marcus's men, The Shadows, trying to kill him, then coming to the hospital after Lily Grace. All because Marcus thought Lily Grace knew about his operation. Never mind that Lily Grace was just a kid. That she was innocent. Marcus would snuff out her life before she had a chance to taste it.

"The fentanyl lab—that's your boss's operation, isn't it? He's used to killing people, isn't he? As long as he makes a profit."

Jesus. She didn't know a thing about Marcus, but she'd described him to a tee. As long as Marcus made a profit, nothing else mattered.

And Saul was DONE.

"I want to think you're not a bad guy. I mean, you saved us in the garage. Risked your own life to keep us safe. But what about tomorrow? Or the next day? The only way to make sure nobody hurts Lily Grace is to catch the people after her. You're in a position to help, but you're lying here with your mouth shut like you're scared or just don't give a shit." She stepped even closer, her breath warm on his face. "But I do give a shit. And I'm not leaving this room till you grow the balls to do the right thing."

Damn. She was a force. Again, Fatima's face filled his mind. Her quirky smile. Her dark, innocent eyes, always trusting him.

Trusting him to do the right thing.

He held up a hand. "Call Detective Michaels. I'm ready to talk to him."

Seventy-One

FLETCHER SAT WITH VIVIAN IN THEIR LIVING ROOM—A FORMAL SPACE filled with antiques they'd inherited from various grandparents, only used when they had company. Today, it would be the set for a very important interview. Ben Reeder, a reporter with the *Tribune*, had been selected to talk with them, though two TV stations had set up cameras to record.

No doubt, this would be the most important twenty minutes of Fletcher's career. If he had any hope of saving his campaign for attorney general, every word out of his mouth had to be perfect. He'd practiced for hours. He knew how to field questions about Cooper and the accident: *"my son feels deep regret and is ready to accept any consequences coming to him."* Fletcher knew how to appear humble, yet confident. To exude Southern charm. To demonstrate his legal prowess. To remind the people of South Carolina that, like his father and grandfather, he was their favorite son and would not let them down.

He worried about the Clark girl, though. When he visited her, she had become hysterical. "I know what you did to him!" she'd yelled—and it terrified him what that might mean. Hell, he might have to have Marcus take care of her before that became a bigger problem.

Vivian squeezed his hand.

Ben Reeder entered in a rush, took the seat across from them, and squinted at the TV cameras. "I was hoping they'd change their minds."

"Camera shy?"

Reeder flashed a sheepish smile. "Shoulda worn a tie. Are you ready to get this show on the road?"

Fletcher looked at Vivian, who nodded. Lines of fatigue and pain had been carefully concealed with makeup, but he could see them there. And in the flicker behind her eyes. He knew she was hurting.

Someone from a TV station switched on the lights. Vivian winced. Reeder cleared his throat. "Quick and painless is the goal," he said to them. "Focus will be on policy."

"Excellent." Fletcher forced a smile. Everything depended on this interview. It had to be perfect. "Let's get this over with."

Reeder began with the usual questions, and Fletcher spat out canned answers. When Reeder asked about the fentanyl crisis, spouting off some disturbing statistics of deaths in the Midlands caused by that drug, Fletcher steeled his gaze away from his wife as he promised to "pound the hammer of justice" on anyone caught distributing "instruments of death like that drug."

"Solicitor Hawthorne, I want to change focus for a minute. We have an important trial coming up next year that may affect a number of important men in our town. I'm talking about Colby Ribault's charges of human trafficking."

"A terrible, terrible thing."

"Right. For many of us, the violation of young girls under eighteen is most egregious. How do you feel about the sexual victimization of children?"

What a strange direction this interview had taken. Fletcher sat up straight and stared into the camera. "It's horrific. And will not be tolerated. Predators like that—they need to be locked up to never see the light of day."

Ben Reeder's eyes widened. "That's a strong stance."

"I'm a father."

Reeder straightened in his chair. "Yes. Which brings up another subject. One of your son's friends, Max Clark, used to visit this home, didn't he?"

Fletcher felt the blood drain from his face. Max.

The boy.

He glared at Reeder and couldn't speak.

"You remember young Max? You knew him well. Your son's friend. The boy you plied with drugs so that you could take advantage of him. How old was he when that started? Fifteen?"

Fletcher couldn't breathe. The TV lights bore down on him. Vivian's hand slid away from his. "This isn't—we need to discuss—"

Reeder leaned forward. "And the molestation continued for several years. Because of you, Max developed a dependency on drugs—oxy, cocaine. Fentanyl. It got so bad he ran away. Lived on the streets. Died by suicide, right?"

How did Reeder know all this? Fletcher tugged at the necktie that felt like a noose. Around him, the cameras pointed like guns. "I don't know where you got your information, but—"

Movement behind them. Who was that? The detective, Lou Michaels, stepped forward. He wasn't alone.

Reeder went on. "Only Max didn't die. As a matter of fact, he's right here."

More movement. Someone stepped forward from the shadows. He was thinner, older, rougher-looking—but it was Max, accompanied by his parents. As he inched closer, Reeder backed away.

"Max?" Fletcher whispered. "They said you . . . died. They—"

"You probably want me dead," Max said. "But I'm not. And everybody knows what you are. What you did to me."

Something crumbled within Fletcher. Vivian scuttled back as though he was a flame about to burn her. Sara Clark's mother approached, her eyes wide with fury. She said not a word as she grew closer. The sound of her hand slapping his face echoed.

"I never meant . . ." Fletcher whispered. What had he done? And now everything—all of it—was destroyed.

Max moved beside his mom. Up close, he looked so different. A little ragged, but less of a boy. An unfamiliar strength shone in his hooded, dark eyes. "You knew exactly what you were doing. You killed me, Fletcher. And you almost killed my sister, Sara. But we're both alive. And we get to watch you face what you deserve. The police know everything. About what you did to me. About your ties to Marcus Landry.

About your son, Holden, dealing drugs for him. Your life is over." Max flinched. His mother took his hand.

Lou Michaels sidled up, accompanied by two uniformed officers. "Fletcher Hawthorne, I'm arresting you on charges of child sexual abuse, drug trafficking, aiding and abetting after the fact, and . . . and I'm sure we'll have more coming."

The officers used old-fashioned handcuffs. Cold metal pinching his flesh. It didn't matter. Nothing did.

His life had just imploded in front of the state's largest newspaper and two TV channels.

Once again, his gaze fell on the boy. That beautiful boy.

What had he done to him?

Seventy-Two

SAUL FOUND THE NEW T-SHIRT TO FEEL STRANGE AGAINST HIS SKIN. A minuscule microphone had been embedded in the neckline—wireless, so that the police could listen to his activities. Now, he found himself in the dusty parking lot of the familiar building, scanning the cluster of cars parked beside Marcus's SUV. They weren't familiar. New men? New assassins, since The Shadows were locked away?

Saul held no illusions about how this would play out. He had one goal: get Marcus to incriminate himself on tape. One way or the other, the man had to be stopped.

"Testing . . . testing," Saul said into the mic. His cell phone dinged with a thumbs-up sign. He'd take the phone with him, but Marcus would confiscate it upon arrival. No matter. He wouldn't need it to carry out his mission.

The "Closed" sign on the front door was a bad sign. Marcus had free rein. No witnesses. Saul understood that the chances of him surviving today were slim to nil, and he'd reached a level of peace about it. After all he'd done for Marcus—bad things, fatal things—it was what he deserved. This end had been written for him since he first fell into Marcus's web. Growing old had never been an option.

The police had let him reach out to his family. He'd even talked to his little sister, Fatima. His mother had received the money he'd sent, enough for them to move to Costa Rica, enough to take care of Fatima for however long she lived. And Fatima had squealed to learn she'd get a new bicycle, as promised. The sound of her voice had made him smile and weep a little. She was safe, though. That was all that mattered.

The cell phone buzzed: Lou Michaels.

"All set?" he asked Saul.

"Ready."

"Just get the info we need, then get the hell out of there. As soon as you say the code word 'luck,' we'll come in. You hit the floor. We don't need you to be a martyr," Michaels said.

"*Too late*," Saul wanted to reply.

He climbed out of the Rover and approached the door, each step heavier than the last. His entrance was interrupted by the sound of an SUV, which pulled up beside him and parked.

"What the hell?" Boris climbed out to gawk at Saul. "What are you doing here?"

"I have business with Marcus."

"Are you suicidal? He's put a hit out on you. You have to know that."

"Thanks, man. But this is important."

Boris shrugged and opened the back of the jeep, pulling out a box—probably his latest stash of product. Excellent.

Saul pushed past Boris and entered the dim restaurant. All the tables stood empty. No sounds emanated from the kitchen. The Hispanic woman who owned the place stood by the closed door to Marcus's private meeting room. As Saul approached, Boris close behind, she opened it.

Marcus sat at the table. Two men sat across from him, two others standing behind him, all glaring with the cold distance of trained assassins.

When Marcus spotted Saul, he cocked a thumb at him. "Search him."

The men's hands were rough, and Saul grimaced as they pressed against his chest. They didn't find the minuscule mic.

"He's clear," one said to Marcus.

Marcus continued his glare. "You have too many lives. But I can remedy that."

"I know I'm the last person you want to see," Saul began, "but I'm here to strike a deal."

"A deal?" Laughter bubbled through his words. "You have balls, Saul. I have to give you that."

Saul blinked. Steadied himself. "You want to know who destroyed your fentanyl labs. I'll give you a name if you promise to leave Lily Grace Duffy alone."

"Who's Lily Grace Duffy?" Marcus asked.

"The kid you told me to kill. The one you sent The Shadows to take out at the hospital."

"She's as hard to kill as you. Guess my men have been sloppy." He looked at the three surrounding him. Saul didn't like his odds against them.

Saul stepped closer. "Losing the first lab cost you, what—a hundred thou in product?"

"More like one-fifty," Boris offered.

"And the second fire? I remember a wall of boxes lined up, ready for distribution." Saul glanced at the box at Boris's feet. How much fentanyl was inside? Hopefully, enough to send Marcus away forever.

"Around twenty thousand pills," Marcus spat out.

"Twenty thousand fentanyl. At nine-fifty a pop, we're talking close to $200,000 in lost revenue. How? Because the guy's been following your men. I'll give you the guy's name. But only if you agree to leave the Duffy girl alone."

"Give me the name and location. My men will handle it from there."

Saul did as Detective Michaels instructed, giving Marcus a bogus name and address, knowing that the police would be waiting.

Saul eyed the box in Boris's hand. "New supply?"

"Only the finest. My new formula. A thousand pills ready to go."

Bingo. "I wish you luck, then," Saul muttered.

Seconds later, the door exploded open, but Saul didn't hit the floor. He ran. He pushed through the officers and Marcus's men. Ignored shouts to stop and warning shots. He fled to his Rover. Foolish, he knew. But following the detective's instructions meant prison. He was never one for confined spaces.

As he screeched out of the drive, he heard cars starting. Shit. Marcus had other men waiting for him.

On the seat beside him, the cell phone buzzed. Lou Michaels's name flashed. No point in answering. He squealed out of the parking lot, three cars speeding behind him.

Saul was a good driver. He'd learned how to shake a tail back in Nicaragua and could handle curves at high speeds, thanks to lessons from one of Marcus's men. But this was different. There were three cars after him. Killers who had him in their sights.

Police cars blared, too, but he had to outrun them.

He swerved onto a county road, away from the other cars occupying the highway. He wanted no more casualties as this played out. His foot pressed harder on the accelerator. Fifty. Seventy. The cars behind him had no trouble keeping up. Eighty.

The road felt rough under his tires, and he struggled to keep steady at such a high speed. Suddenly, a pickup appeared ahead, coming toward him. "Shit!"

One of the black SUVs chasing him pulled into the oncoming lane as though prepared to crash headfirst into the small truck. Some stupid farmer was about to die.

Saul slammed on his brakes, jerking the car right, the black car beside him swerving back into his lane and letting the truck pass. But it was too late. Saul lost control, his car sliding off the road, down an embankment, and flipped.

It was all surreal—the car rolling and rolling. Saul caught glimpses of a cornfield, a blue sky, and trees in the distance. He flashed on home, on the deep forest, on his family. On Fatima's crooked smile. And a face flashed: the weird girl, Lily Grace, whom he had saved and who had saved him.

And everything went still.

Seventy-Three

THE GENTLE RAP ON THE DOOR THAT LATE AT NIGHT COULD ONLY BE one person. I hurried to open it. Lou stood there, looking so desperately lost that all I could do was put my arms around him and pull him close.

He told me all of it. Saul had succeeded in getting plenty of ammunition against Marcus Landry, his boss and the kingpin of the fentanyl trade here in South Carolina. There was enough "product" on the scene to lock everyone away for years.

But at what cost?

"Saul ran," Lou said. "I guess I should have expected it. Landry had men positioned outside, and they took off after him. The car crash—they said he didn't feel anything. I pray that's true."

I tugged him inside and sat him on the sofa, curling up beside him. "I had to tell Lily Grace," he said. "I don't think she's lost anyone she cared about that much. Poor kid."

"He saved her life. Twice. He did a lot of bad things, but there was a good guy in there."

Lou leaned over and kissed the top of my head. This felt right, us together like this.

"You okay?" I asked.

He didn't answer. I turned to look at his face. Still, that sadness running deep in his eyes. "Your job is hell, isn't it?"

"Sometimes. We have victories, but they come at a cost. And fighting this fentanyl problem—it's winning. It's always winning." He dropped his head back. "Guess I'm just tired."

"You have to take care of yourself. In your work, you see the dark side of everything. You gotta let in a little light."

He gave me an incredulous look. "Pot? Meet kettle?"

"You have a point." I snuggled in closer and felt his lips against my forehead. Something stirred inside that I hadn't felt in a very long time. It terrified me. And I wanted more.

"This okay?" he asked gently.

I nodded. "I'm gonna need us to take it slow."

"We have all the time in the world, George."

Seventy-Four

TESSA WALKED WITH LILY GRACE AWAY FROM SCHOOL. SHE'D PASSED the trig test, immediately texting Elias and Joel to brag. Elias promised her chocolate torte to celebrate. Joel sent a cheerleader meme.

"Hey Tessa, did you ever hear from your friend Dulce?" Lily Grace asked.

Tessa shook her head. Georgia mentioned her often, in that "be prepared" voice, as though Dulce might already be dead. But Tessa couldn't believe it. Dulce had survived so much. Something kept her going. She had to believe they'd be bitching at each other again one day.

Her phone buzzed with a message from Ariel: *Hey, Tess. Remember the Altoids I lent you?*

Tessa froze, glaring at the text. *Yeah. Why?*

Sore throat. Need a mint to suck on.

There it was. Ariel felt the pull. You feel the bliss of the blue pills; you want to feel it again. Tessa had felt it, too, and it scared the shit out of her.

Altoids will kill you. I got rid of them.

Ariel didn't respond.

Lily Grace picked up the pace. She'd been oddly quiet.

"Hey. You doing okay?" Tessa asked.

"Yeah."

"You thinking about your friend, Saul?"

She nodded. "He was a good man. I mean, he did bad things. But he was good to me. Kind. Mostly."

"I believe you."

"Your Detective Michaels is trying to find his real family in Nicaragua," Lily Grace said. "You know what his real name was?"

"No, what?"

"Carlos Amerido. Wish I'd known that when he was alive. There were so many lies, though."

"So many." Tessa bumped against her.

"Maybe I can write to his family. Tell them how he saved us. But I'll have to get better at Spanish first."

They walked a few more blocks, in a comfortable silence. Then Tessa asked, "How's your mom?"

"She's killing me! She's all about this Mediterranean diet. Our fridge is full of fresh veggies and fruits, and I cannot have pizza or burgers or anything worth eating."

Tessa laughed.

"She's getting healthier, though. Walks twice a day. She's trying hard. Have to give her that."

They reached Lily Grace's street. "Meet you here in the morning?" Tessa asked.

Lily Grace nodded and Tessa waved goodbye. She didn't tell her that she wasn't going home. She didn't tell her that she was headed to the hospital for the most important meeting of her life. She checked her watch. She had a half hour to get there. She heaved her knapsack onto her shoulder and booked it to the bus stop.

Seventy-Five

I MADE SURE THE COFFEE URN WAS FULL IN THE EXECUTIVE CONFERENCE room. Clancy had suggested they meet here and had gotten the necessary clearance from Richard "The Dick" Lockhart. "Lana Montgomery needs to see you in your element. She needs to see you as a powerful, respected member of the treatment team here," Clancy had said.

The invitations had been extended, and the guests started to arrive. Clancy, of course. Lou Michaels, dedicated law enforcement officer. Elias Jeffries, esteemed businessman and entrepreneur. Ben Reeder, respected journalist. Dr. Romano, MD.

Tessa had insisted on coming, too. I refused at first, thinking that if things went sour, it might be hard on her. But it was her life they were discussing. She had the right to give her input.

I sat at the table beside Tessa and regarded the friends around me. They were my community. My posse. I was so damn lucky to have them. They would help me fight Lana for custody of Tessa. And fight I would.

Lana entered the room, carrying her fancy briefcase, dressed in a teal business suit with a white collared top.

"Ah. Just in time," I said.

"Want some coffee?" Clancy asked.

"No, I'm fine." Lana looked at all the people around the table as I made introductions.

"Nice to meet you all," Lana began. "But I'm not sure why we're having this . . . gathering."

Lou spoke up. "Because when you talk about Tessa's placement, you're not just talking about Georgia. Several of us are a part of her life. She's important to us."

Clancy added, "And I'm here as a character witness for Georgia."

"So am I," Dr. Romano said.

"And me," Ben added.

"I can bring in the hospital CEO if you want to talk to him," Clancy added.

I smiled, imagining what The Dick would tell this woman.

Lana opened her case. "It's not necessary. What is necessary is that I do what's best for Tessa. And that's—"

The door opened. I wasn't expecting anyone else, but Sara Clark's mother entered the room. She walked directly over to Lana and sat beside her. "Am I late?"

"No," Tessa said. "You're right on time."

"Uhm . . . Mrs. Clark? I wasn't expecting you." This surprise guest had me rattled.

"Just here to support Tessa." She smiled. She looked so different from the way she had in the waiting room and at her daughter's bedside. Poised. Confident. Beautiful. In charge. "Georgia, you may not know this, but I'm the Chair of the Social Services Commission in South Carolina. It's a tough volunteer job, as you might imagine. But when Tessa called me and told me what was going on, I felt I had to step in."

"Tessa? What made you call Mrs. Clark?" I asked.

"I went to the main office to . . . make my case, I guess. They wouldn't let me in. But I saw the picture of all the important people, and there she was."

Margaret Clark continued. "I met with Ms. Montgomery and her supervisor. I think we've all come to an agreement about Tessa's placement. Am I right, Lana?"

Lana's face reddened. She cleared her throat. "Yes, ma'am."

"And that decision is?" Mrs. Clark persisted.

Lana turned to me. "While the facility in Rock Hill is a terrific option, we think the best place for Tessa is to remain with you. At least through the upcoming trial."

I exhaled. The relief I felt nearly knocked me to the ground. I looked at Tessa, trying not to cry.

I hated crying in front of other people.

Mrs. Clark spoke. "Tessa called me and made a compelling argument. But that's not the main reason for this decision. While treatment is important for girls in her situation, the most important thing kids in foster care need—and that's every kid in foster care—is family. And she has that with you, Georgia. Y'all are family."

"We are," Tessa said.

I looked at the people around me. My people. My friends. Lou gave me a broad smile that reached right into my heart.

Family, Peyton whispered.

I took Tessa's hand. My kid. "Yes. We are."

Notes

Here are some important resources about fentanyl use and recovery:

SAMHSA Helpline: <u>1-800-662-HELP (4357)</u> 24-hour help for those who need it.

<u>https://www.cdc.gov/overdose-prevention/about/understanding-the-opi-oid-overdose-epidemic.html</u>

<u>https://www.dea.gov/fentanylawareness</u>

<u>https://www.dea.gov/alert/dea-reports-widespread-threat-fentanyl-mixed-xylazine</u>

<u>https://americanaddictioncenters.org/opioids/fentanyl</u>

And here's some information about naloxone, AKA Narcan, which has saved many lives:

<u>https://nida.nih.gov/publications/drugfacts/naloxone</u>

About the Author

Carla Damron believes fiction can make a difference. A social worker, advocate, and author of suspense, women's fiction, and mysteries, Damron uses her writing to examine social issues like drug abuse, mental illness, and human trafficking. She's won multiple literary awards, including the Women's Fiction Writers Association Star Award for Best Novel and the NIEA award for best suspense.

Damron holds an MSW and an MFA in Creative Writing and teaches with Writers.com. Currently the VP for the Southeast Chapter of Mystery Writers of America, she lives in South Carolina with her husband and their family of entitled rescue animals.

You can read more about her at https://carladamron.com/